# THE SOPRANO'S DARING DUKE

## DOUBLE-DILEMMA ROMANCE
### BOOK TWO

## SUSANNE DUNLAP

# THE SOPRANO'S DARING DUKE

The Soprano's Daring Duke

# A MESSAGE FROM SUSANNE DUNLAP

Thank you for choosing to read *The Soprano's Daring Duke!* I hope you enjoy getting to know Olivia, Adelheid, Lewiston, and Hartland. This is the second book in my series of Double-Dilemma romances.

Sweet, swoony, and full of heart—**Double-Dilemma Romance** is a Regency romance series featuring not one, but two love stories in every book. Follow strong-willed heroines who defy society's rules and fall for the most unexpected (and unsuitable) men. With a perfect blend of scandal, wit, and emotional warmth, each story delivers a satisfying double dose of happily-ever-afters.

Although this books stands alone, I introduce Lewiston and Lady Mariana in book 1, *The Dressmaker's Secret Earl.*

Finally, reviews are important to authors. If you like *The Soprano's Daring Duke,* I would be immensely grateful if you would take the time to review it on Goodreads and Amazon.

Want to stay informed of upcoming books in the series? Enjoy exclusive content? And get behind-the-scenes peeks of what it's like to be an author?

Sign up for my newsletter!

You'll get a free novella just to start, and be the first to hear about any forthcoming books and events.

Thank you again for taking your valuable time to read my book. 🤍

*For opera lovers everywhere, especially my colleagues and friends in the Department of Music, Yale Graduate School of Arts & Sciences!*

# PROLOGUE

*P*rincess Adelheid Kinsky paced up and down the long gallery outside of her dying husband's bedchamber, her silk dressing gown sweeping little clouds of dust off the stone floor. Footmen wearing silver and black livery lined the walls, all staring straight ahead and stiff as the gargoyles that decorated the ramparts. The sound of the prince's labored breathing, rattling out of his failing lungs, carried through the closed door.

Each time the prince inhaled, Adelheid felt the air being drawn out of her, as if he was sucking away her life in his dying throes.

The door opened and surprised a gasp out of her. The priest, Father Hendrik, came out of the room, bowed slightly and said, "He asked for you, Your Highness."

She lifted her chin and followed him into the chamber, which was lit only by a single candle next to the heavily curtained bed. The prince's sunken eyes shifted toward her. He raised one finger.

"Approach, please," Father Hendrik said.

*He cannot harm me now,* she told herself. Still, lying there, physically weak, the prince had some kind of power over her. No longer the violent tyrant, he became the evil demon, trying to flay her with the force of his will. Would he go to hell? To hell, for all that he'd put her through?

"I-I..."

Reluctantly, she drew nearer so she could hear his papery voice.

"*Du* ... will ... not ... win." His eyes closed. But then, a thin smile curved his lips.

Adelheid took a step back and looked up at the priest. What did it mean?

He gave a tiny shake of his head.

The two of them kept their eyes on the prince's waxen face as his breathing continued to slow, becoming quieter and quieter until at last it ceased altogether. Father Hendrik reached over and closed his eyes.

It was Adelheid who broke the stillness, saying in a voice too loud for such a solemn moment, "Thank you, God!"

The priest crossed himself.

Adelheid smiled, turned, and swept out of the room.


THEY EXPECTED HER TO MOURN. TO WEEP AND WAIL. SHE could feel the eyes of all the footmen following her as she passed by them on her way to her bedchamber.

If she cried, it would be with relief.

She was free. He could no longer torment her in all those little ways that had started almost as soon as he wed her, acidly reminding her of her lowly status and his condescension in making her his princess. He kept her virtually imprisoned in the chateau. Although that didn't start until after Danton.

Danton. Only his too brief presence in her life had relieved those years of misery. The prince sent him away when the child of their illicit love was born. Otto, Adelheid called him, before the prince wrenched him out of her arms.

*He would be seven years old if he were still alive*, she thought. Adelheid silently marked his birthday every year, lighting a candle for him and saying a prayer to the Virgin. And what a beautiful child he would have been. She resolutely blinked the threatened tears away before entering her bedchamber and facing her maid, Frankel.

She had told Frankel not to wait up, but the woman leapt to her feet upon seeing her and said, "Is it over?"

Adelheid nodded.

Frankel made the sign of the cross on her breast. "He is with God now."

"Or the devil," Adelheid said.

Frankel cast her eyes down, but Adelheid caught a glimpse of a smile tugging at the corner of her faithful retainer's lips.

Instead of preparing for bed right away, Adelheid threw open the long doors that led to the great stone balcony and stepped out onto it, heedless of the snow that covered it on that February night. She inhaled the clean, icy air. In a week she would go to Vienna for the reading of the will. After that, she would be truly free.

Soon her life would begin again, on terms she would set. No one would own her. With the prince's vast fortune to draw upon she would travel, go to balls and the opera, set up a home anywhere in the world. She would close up the chateau, the scene of so much misery. Perhaps she would find friendship at least. Not love, no. She had trusted in love when she met the handsome Prince Alexander Kinsky. It took less than a year for her to understand that she was no more to him than a face, a body, and a voice. All she could do to punish him was refuse to sing.

The prince had told her Otto died while her body was

still aching from the pain of childbirth, his cold blue eyes glittering as if it gave him pleasure to wound her to her heart.

He could torment her no more. She would carry the memory of her infant always, but it was time to look to the future.

A WEEK LATER, ADELHEID SAT IN THE ATTORNEY'S OFFICE IN Vienna for the reading of the will, waiting for Niklaus—the prince's steward—to arrive. His presence at the reading had been stipulated. She thought it a bit odd, but Alexander was given to such strange starts, and Niklaus had attended him since long before he married Adelheid.

It must be a formality, she thought, because the bulk of the estate would pass to her. The late prince had told her that, using it as a weapon if she ever displeased him—which was often. His illness came on so suddenly, though, that even if he'd changed his mind, he had not had time to draw up a new will.

When Attorney Mitterling entered, trailed by a clerk with a slim portfolio under his arm, Adelheid smiled at him.

He responded with a frown that turned the corners of his mouth down and knotted his brow above his bushy eyebrows. After bowing to her, Mitterling took his seat behind the massive desk, pulled his spectacles out of his vest pocket and settled them on his bulbous nose. Then he nodded to the clerk, who opened the portfolio and slipped one sheet of vellum out of it, which he laid on the desk in front of his employer.

Without a pause, the attorney read. "To the Princess Adelheid Kinsky, I bequeath all my estates, the lands in Hungary and Austria, the plantations in Jamaica, the liquid assets in the funds."

It was as she expected. Letting out a long breath, she turned her gaze away from the attorney to a heavily mullioned window that gave a broken view of a steel-gray sky, a fixture in the Viennese winter, and let her mind wander as the legal jargon droned on and on.

Her attention returned to the room in a snap, though, when the attorney said, "A codicil. This bequest is made under certain conditions, which, if not met, will render it null and void. The estate will then pass to the foundling hospital, and the title will be extinct."

*Conditions?* What conditions? Adelheid shivered. He couldn't. Could he? Could the prince reach out his icy claw of a hand from beyond the grave, shackling her just as he did when he felt she'd misbehaved, not performed her duties as she should? He could. And it seemed he had. She braced herself.

"The princess must marry a man of noble birth within one month of this day. Further, said noble must adopt her child, the shameful issue of an otherwise barren woman, and recognize that child as heir to all he possesses."

Her child? She had no child! Otto was dead! Wasn't he? Her heart started to race, jumping and fluttering as if trying to break free from her rib cage.

"Finally, the nobleman must not know the conditions of her inheritance before he agrees to marry the princess. To ensure compliance with this last requirement, an agent of the late prince, the steward Niklaus, will attend the princess and see that every part of this codicil is strictly observed."

Adelheid only half heard the remainder of what the attorney said. What did it mean? Her child not dead! But how? Why? And what did that have to do with her inheritance?

The air in the office seemed to have thickened to the consistency of water and she felt herself drowning with every breath. Buzzing that grew louder and louder filled her ears, and the dark paneled walls of the room began to shimmer and dissolve around her. Her surroundings faded into blackness, and Adelheid surrendered to unconsciousness with the words *God damn the man!* chasing her into oblivion.

# CHAPTER 1

*H*e had avoided the conversation with Agnew, his man of business, for as long as he could. It would only bring bad news. More bad news. That was all he'd had since his father, the seventh Duke of Hartland, had died unexpectedly nearly a year before of a virulent fever. The duke was gone before his son could get to Hartmoor to say his goodbyes—if he were allowed to given the fear of infection.

Now it seemed that Philip Algernon, eighth Duke of Hartland, Earl of Malmsby, holder of several other subsidiary titles, and a bachelor of twenty-nine ill-spent years, faced financial ruin. As an only son, he was indulged beyond sense, and his father—a kind, well-respected man with no head for business at all—cheerfully paid all his debts and did whatever it took to ensure young Philip could sow his wildest oats. Thus the then-Lord Malmsby engaged in every vice available to a charming young man of noble lineage with a handsome, craggy face and the physique of a natural athlete.

"Your Grace," Agnew said, shuffling the papers in front of

him on the table in the library at Hartland House, giving him an excuse to look down at the surface of the desk instead of into the duke's eyes, "I fear there is only one course of action open to you."

"How can that be? Our holdings are immense. Tens of thousands of acres under cultivation, so I am told. And several manors and estates everywhere from Yorkshire to Northamptonshire—I've spent time in all of them. Surely one of the less important properties would answer the need?" Philip let his eyes wander idly over the hundreds of tooled-leather spines on the floor to ceiling shelves, wondering if any of them were worth a great deal of money.

Agnew cleared his throat. "As I have already told you, they are all mortgaged. Selling them would only clear the debts attached to them specifically."

"This house?" It was an inconvenient monstrosity in Grosvenor Square that cost a small fortune to maintain.

"That too."

"The funds?"

"Your father had been dipping into capital for years. I'm afraid there isn't much left."

If only his father had said something to him. But would he have listened? Probably not. Money existed to be spent, not conserved or invested. It would always be there. When it came to indebtedness, Hartland took no half measures. He'd lost twenty-thousand one evening at Faro. And he kept a series of high flyers in jewels and carriages, never grudged them so much as a bonnet and frequently bestowed horses and houses and expensive servants upon them.

That would come to an end, of necessity. Phoebe would not be happy, and there would no doubt be an ugly scene, but it couldn't be helped. Perhaps he could soften the blow with a diamond bracelet, if news of the parlous state of his finances hadn't yet reached the jeweler's ears.

"How much time do I have?" Hartland asked, pitying Agnew for his role.

"I fear, sir, that the mortgages will come due by the end of the season. It would be as well to plan for it and begin the process of selling the properties as soon as possible."

"No!" Hartland said, startling Agnew. "Not yet. Wind up the smaller assets first so the debt is less massive."

"Would you like to dispose of your racing stables?"

Hartland sighed. He had two promising bits of blood cattle in line for Newmarket that season. Perhaps their promise would enhance the appeal for a buyer. "Yes. Better do so before Ascot if you can, I think. And Agnew..."

"Yes, Your Grace?"

"How much will I have once it's all done?"

The man of business paused and pursed his lips. "I think what will remain might be described as an easy competence rather than a fortune."

Philip let his head sink into his hands. Widows of small means lived on easy competences. He could not imagine what such a life would be like. There had to be a way! This could not be his fate.

As if he'd heard the duke's thoughts, Agnew said, "Of course, Sir, there is something you could do."

Hartland looked up, a spark of hope kindling in his mind. "Yes? Out with it man!"

"Marry."

"Marry?"

"Marry. An heiress. You might have to lower your sights a little and forgo a title or some beauty. Perhaps even consider the daughter of a cit. But marrying an heiress would secure your future—provided you did not continue your...ways... once wed."

The idea filled him with revulsion. Place himself on the marriage market, after resisting it these ten years? Be pursued by matchmaking mamas eager to win a duchess's coronet for their daughters? He shivered, stood, and strode over to one of the long windows that looked out over the square.

"Do you have a voucher for Almack's, Your Grace?"

A sardonic smile curled Philip's lip as he looked over his shoulder at Agnew. "Not since my first season. I'm considered dangerous."

"I act for Jersey in some matters of business. I could suggest to him that his lady wife be persuaded to admit you, since you are determined to mend your ways, so to speak."

There was no hiding the gleam of amusement in Agnew's eyes. He was a good sort, Hartland thought. He didn't lecture or prose, just got to the business at hand, no matter how distasteful. And perhaps there would be some lady of the *ton* he could bear to marry, now that he was older and wiser. "Why not?" he said.

"The assemblies begin on the first Wednesday in March," Agnew said. "News of the exact extent of your financial straits might not have time to circulate before then."

So soon, Hartland thought. "I'm still in mourning for a few weeks yet."

"You needn't dance, and you can wear a black armband."

Making inane conversation with schoolroom misses and dowagers did not appeal to Hartland at all. But he owed it to his family—to the title, at any rate—to take some measure to avoid having to sell Hartmoor, the ducal seat. He would give it a season.

After that, if necessary, Agnew could bring the hammer down on the estate that had been in the family since the conquest.

# CHAPTER 2

*T*he honorable Olivia Fontenoy found her voice at the age of eighteen. Or perhaps it is more accurate to say, her voice found her.

It happened at the end of a long and frustrating day. She was dragged unwillingly to Madame Pauline's, the newest and most fashionable modiste in London, to be measured and prodded and looked at until she wanted to scream. Her mother, the Viscountess Ambrose, talked things over with Madame Pauline as if her daughter weren't standing a few feet away on a six-inch platform in her shift, shivering despite the fire in the grate nearby. They had come to London in advance of the season—her first—to order her gowns for the onslaught of *ton* parties that would begin in March and continue through June, before the weather became oppressive and drove the quality out to the fashionable watering places.

But just now, at the end of February, an icy mist lay over the grimy buildings of London and coated them in fine, deceptively sparkling crystals. If the sun would only come out they would melt away. But the sun refused to cooperate.

That celestial orb was just as uncooperative as Olivia herself. She tried hard not to look in a mirror, but no matter which way she turned her head, she found her sullen countenance staring back at her. Her pale oval face with its overly generous mouth turned down at the corners. The mousy-brown curls that made her mother lament that the days of powdered hair were past. Her bony shoulders from which hung lanky arms—arms that lacked the becoming plumpness so in fashion at the time. Her only asset, according to Lady Ambrose, was a well-formed bosom that needed little enhancement to set off a high-waisted gown. And, her mother had to admit that when a trick of light turned her large hazel eyes toward a misty green, they became more than passable.

Of course, no one expected her to be received as a diamond of the first water. Least of all Olivia herself.

Olivia tried every possible argument she could think of to postpone her come-out until the next year, when she was grown a little taller, perhaps, or gained more confidence instead of feeling a bit tongue-tied in company. But she was the only daughter of a viscount—and a considerable heiress —and her mother champed at the bit to display her to the judgment of her peers and snag the most eligible bachelor of the season for her.

Because, as Lady Ambrose frequently reminded her, Philip Algernon, Duke of Hartland, was rumored to have fixed on that season as the one in which he intended to become betrothed. Whether his decision was based on general inclination or because the fortune he inherited at his father's recent death was anything but—thanks to Hartland's profligacy at the gaming tables and in other fashionable vices —polite society refused to conjecture. At least, not out loud.

That meant that the only fate that lay ahead of her, Olivia

feared, would be embarrassment, disappointment, and tedium. No notoriously handsome duke would offer for her, she was certain. In fact, it was the last thing she wanted. She'd rather be left alone to live out her days as she wished.

That meant only one thing: she wanted to sing. Not that drawing-room-insipid stuff, but real singing, on a stage. Her tutor Signore Tetrazzini spoke so eloquently of the magnificent opera productions he had witnessed in London and on the Continent and brought her beautiful arias to learn. As she practiced them, she would imagine herself in the midst of the drama, an orchestra playing, the audience applauding thunderously at the end.

However, the dream was just that. Ladies of gentle birth displayed their accomplishments only in a private drawing room for the exclusive enjoyment of polite society. And again, the thought made her want to scream.

It was this urge—the desire to give vent to her feelings about the absurdity of the entire meaningless institution of the season—that led to Olivia's remarkable discovery. Despite her mother's protestations that it was too cold to go out to the park when they returned to Mount Street in the early dusk, Olivia descended from the carriage in her warmest pelisse armed with an ermine muff of vast proportions and, instead of climbing the stairs to the imposing front door of the double-fronted mansion, resolutely marched toward the park. A moment later, her long-suffering abigail, Hetty, scurried up behind her still buttoning her pelisse against the cold.

"Miss! Miss!" Hetty said. "You'll catch your death!"

Olivia whirled around to face her, forcing her to come to a sudden and ungainly halt. "That would be a blessing."

"Oh you can't say so, Miss. Not when it's your first season! All those gowns and balls and beaux…"

"Would you like to take my place?" The absurdity of such an eventuality dampened Olivia's fury a bit. "I'm sorry, Hetty, that was rude of me. It's not your fault."

"I know Miss Olivia, and you don't mean it. Not really." Hetty only gave voice to what everyone thought: that any girl would be thrilled when faced with such a future. "Please, Miss Olivia! You're going too fast!"

Olivia paused and waited for Hetty to catch up to her, then once again strode off at her customary brisk pace to the middle of the park, her object to get as far away from another human being as possible. At least, as far away as a marriageable young lady of the *ton* was permitted to go.

Once she found herself in the shelter of a stand of chestnuts as yet bare of leaves, Olivia stopped, opened her mouth wide, and screamed.

Or actually, she didn't scream. She let loose a full-throated high C, taking a breath deep into her lower torso and using it to support a note that few opera singers could achieve. It felt so remarkably good that after she ran out of breath, she took in another and indulged in a flourish of arpeggios and scales. She let her voice open and expand from an alto register to something that set a dog to howling in the distance.

When she paused to catch her breath, she turned to see Hetty standing open-mouthed and wide-eyed. "What?" Olivia said. "I've been taking lessons."

Of course, the lessons with Signore Tetrazzini at first had consisted of learning sweet, gentle Italian airs that would be suitable to sing in a drawing room. He soon realized she was a rarity, though, a pupil not only with a real voice, but one for whom music was much more than a pleasing accomplishment. He encouraged her to explore her natural timbre, giving her exercises most of the *ton* debutantes found wearying, and she embraced them, perfected them, and gloried in the accomplishment. *Ah, that such a bellissima voce could not be heard in an opera house!* he lamented more than once.

Sadly, the one time she allowed herself to open her voice to its full power in the schoolroom at Ambrose Priory, her mother had come running up the stairs with her hands clapped over her ears, begging Olivia to cease making that ungodly noise.

So Signore Tetrazzini focused her training instead on breath control and tone, on phrasing and range. Olivia had long understood that her voice had remarkable flexibility and a sweet quality, but until that frigid February day in Hyde Park, she had not been fully aware of the power it continued to attain, even without being pushed to its limit.

And no sooner did she gain that knowledge than she comprehended its danger—and the impossibility of ever being able to use it.

*So be it*, she thought. If I can't sing as I wish to, I shall never sing again. At least, not in anyone's hearing. I shall only consent to do so when I am able to bring to life one of the great operatic roles. Iphigénie, perhaps. Or Susanna. Or Isabella in that opera Signore Tetrazzini had told her about by the young Rossini.

The realization that this would never happen soon blanketed her spirits with gloom. Only lightskirts and trollops appeared on stage. Even the splendid voices of the great Italian sopranos did not absolve their owners of a certain unsavory taint.

No, she could never do it. No gently born, well nurtured lady of the *ton* could survive being seen on stage in public with her reputation intact.

"Hetty, you are never, ever to tell anyone what you heard just now. Do you understand?"

Hetty, who had never been to the opera and whose exposure to singing had been limited to music-hall airs and lullabies could barely comprehend the enormity of Olivia's voice, and would have been at a loss to explain it to anyone. Therefore, it was easy for her to nod and whisper a hasty, nervous *yes.*

# CHAPTER 3

*H*arold Ambleton, Marquess of Lewiston, was an indifferent horseman, a terrible shot, and he simply didn't have the patience to stand in an icy stream casting for reluctant trout for hours on end. He had long since given up—despite his concerted efforts the previous season hoping to impress a particular lady—trying to handle the ribbons well enough to be invited to join the Four Horse Club. As to being part of the dandy set, he couldn't see the point of spending hours tying a neck cloth in the latest complicated knot.

His looks did him no favors either. Being neither dark and dashing nor a golden blond giant, he was one of those pleasant-looking young men welcomed by all and remembered by none. Only a select few who were perceptive enough would notice that this rather comfortable-looking fellow—of middling height, soft brown hair, and a build on the delicate side—possessed quizzical brown eyes always ready to light up with laughter and crinkle at the corners, and a mouth so accustomed to smiling that it seemed to be its natural state.

These subtle charms escaped most members of the *ton* who were more susceptible to being dazzled. To his knowledge, in his six previous seasons, no ladies sighed over him or had their hearts broken.

The trouble was, the very real qualities that distinguished Lewiston could not be perceived at first glance. One might almost think he acquired his talents for no other purpose than to keep them to himself.

For instance, he was a superb dancer. He knew and could execute perfectly all the steps of the quadrille, the cotillion, the waltz, and every country dance. He had an elegant foot and faultless balance. At least he did when he practiced on his own. Put him opposite a partner, however, and he became so nervous that his limbs refused to obey the commands of his mind. As a result, instead of being eager to partner him, ladies often mysteriously vanished when he approached them to claim a spot on their dance cards.

Lewiston's other talent was so far removed from what the *ton* considered essential in a polished young gentleman that not even his mother had the faintest knowledge of its existence—or, if she did, she never mentioned it. Although of little social value, the sad fact was that it gave him more pleasure than almost anything.

He could play the violin.

It happened that he was quite an accomplished musician. He picked it up when he was a child, having been taught the rudiments by a stable hand who was also a fiddler. After that, he persuaded his sisters' music tutor to spend an hour with him every now and again and teach him whatever he could.

Thus music was on Harry's mind on that frigid February day. Gglad to move back to his lodgings in London early, before the press of endless parties and scrutiny by matchmaking mamas began in earnest, he took his serviceable twelve-year-old town hack Jasper out for a solitary ride in the park. He let his mind stray to the activities he did look forward to: plays and operas at both the Covent Garden theatre and the King's Theatre, Haymarket, and the eight chamber music concerts of the newly formed Philharmonic Society, which would take place in the elegant Argyll Rooms in Regent Street.

Lost in these pleasant thoughts with snatches of melodies flitting through his mind, he cantered down Rotten Row to give Jasper a bit of exercise before he turned onto a winding bridle path, leaving his reins slack and letting the horse pick his way around at will. Sadly, concerts and plays and operas could not occupy his entire time that season. It was high time for him to do his duty and focus on finding a wife. This thought did not fill him with dismay, however. Unlike many gentlemen of his acquaintance, he actually wanted to marry. For one thing, it would obviate the necessity of awkward, unsuccessful courtship.

The difficulty was finding the lady who would suit him. The ones he liked seldom liked him. This thought brought the captivating Lady Mariana Thorne, née Lanyon, to mind. She was beautiful, intelligent, and rich. He'd known her and her brother, Lord Bridlington, all his life. And his suit was hopeless from the beginning. To her, he was little more than another brother. He soon became deeply engrossed in reliving in painful detail Lady Mariana's torturous wedding during the little season last autumn.

Just as he recalled the most exquisitely painful moment of all, when Lady Mariana turned her radiant gaze upon her tall, handsome new husband after the vows, a magnificent, bell-like soprano voice split the air a short distance away from him. It hit what his sensitive ear determined was a high C.

Harry shivered. Had he really heard it? A moment later, the same startling voice traversed a series of scales and arpeggios in an astonishingly wide range, hitting each note squarely in the middle. The hairs rose on the back of Harry's neck. Jasper lifted his lazy head higher, too, giving a soft nicker. "Let's go see," Lewiston said, now fully out of his daydream, and gathered up the reins to head in the general direction of the voice.

But the singing stopped as suddenly as it had started. Nonetheless, he continued toward where he thought it came from, somewhere around a stand of chestnut trees about a quarter of a mile away, hoping to find the singer still present. When he reached the trees and took a turn through them, though, he discovered no one. Only some way in the distance he spied a tall-ish lady in a green pelisse, light brown curls peeking out from under her poke bonnet, walking toward the Stanhope Gate with an abigail close behind.

"Couldn't be someone like that," Lewiston said, not expecting Jasper to reply. "Probably one of the opera singers come to town early having a bit of fun." Perhaps the famed Catalani had decided on a whim to exercise her voice out of doors. But this seemed unlikely. The cold air might be ruinous to the vocal cords and lungs.

Be that as it may, the singer had gone, leaving Lewiston to wonder if he had, in fact, heard her, and to wish desperately to hear her again.

He decided to view this odd occurrence as a sign that the forthcoming season might not be as empty as the others had been, and turned Jasper toward home with a heart considerably lighter than it had been at the outset.

# CHAPTER 4

"My son!" Were the first words out of Adelheid's mouth when she regained the power of speech and found Niklaus looking down at her, his brow creased in concern above his soft gray eyes, and a vinaigrette in his hand.

"Your Highness," he said, "try to remain calm."

"Calm? How should I do such a thing! All this time. Did you know it was a lie?" Adelheid's voice had become strident, lashing out at the steward who was, she knew in her heart, not the perpetrator but an instrument.

Niklaus closed his eyes and ran his hand across his forehead. "No, Your Highness. I did not know."

Suddenly aware of the dark circles under the steward's eyes and his expression of bewilderment, Adelheid made an effort to slow her galloping heart and order her thoughts more sensibly. Otto was alive. She must find him. "Do you know where he is?"

"Yes. The prince left this letter for me with instructions." He produced a folded paper from his coat pocket.

"Instructions?" Adelheid said, only vaguely remembering

the details of what the attorney had read aloud. Something about her marriage. And the estate. And Otto being made the heir. "I don't think I can understand anything right now. Nothing more than that I must be reunited with my son." She'd seen him so briefly after his birth that she had only the vaguest recollection of a tiny, beautiful babe. He would be a young boy now. Seven years. "I want to bring him home this instant."

"Surely, tomorrow morning—"

"No! I will wait no longer than absolutely necessary. Now. I order you."

The sharp edge in her voice made Niklaus take a step back. He said, not unkindly, "You named him Otto?"

Of course he was Otto. It took a moment for Adelheid to realize that no one aside from herself could possibly know it, though. Danton had been sent away to his death on a ship back to Jamaica days after the infant was born. Once Otto had been yanked from her arms, his name had not passed her lips. Not until that very moment.

"I'm sorry. I did not mean to command you," she said. "But is it possible to go right away? How far is it? Are the horses sufficiently rested?"

Niklaus assured her on all counts and within the hour four spirited grays were pulling the Berlin along snowy roads to a destination some twenty-five miles away.

*My son is alive!*

All the way there, the words echoed in Adelheid's mind. And he had been so near to her these seven years. How the prince must have delighted in knowing it and planning his posthumous revenge. But was it revenge? To restore a child who was the product of a great love to his mother?

Only then did Adelheid's mind return to the codicil. "You'd better tell me everything, Niklaus," she said.

The steward kept his gaze steadfastly trained on the

passing snowy countryside, but turned to her when she spoke. He reminded her of what was written in the will, adding that his instructions were to ensure that Adelheid fulfilled the terms of the codicil, which included not revealing said conditions to whatever nobleman Adelheid found to marry her under such a peculiar stipulation.

It was nonsensical. And so little time! Yet still, Adelheid's spirits soared higher and higher with every mile that passed under the wheels of the carriage. It did not matter now. Nothing mattered. She would soon be reunited with the boy who was torn from her arms as a newborn, and whom she had mourned with such an ache in her heart these seven years.

When the coach came to a halt in front of a small, dilapidated thatched cottage, Adelheid stared in disbelief. "He can't be here," she murmured and shot a quick glance at Niklaus. His frown deepened as well.

Without waiting for one of the postilions to dismount in order to let down the step, Adelheid sprang out unaided, ran to the cottage and pounded on the small door. A ragged woman with an infant in her arms and a toddler clinging to her thigh opened it and gaped at her. Swathed in sables, she looked as out of place there as a peacock in a hen house. "Where is he?" Adelheid said and pushed past the woman.

*"Wer?"* the woman said, and then uttered a strange series of words in a dialect Adelheid didn't understand. Her tone was angry, and she followed close on Adelheid's heels. If her hands had not been burdened, Adelheid had the notion that the woman would have grabbed hold of her and tried to throw her out.

Then Niklaus entered behind her, spoke some words quietly to the woman which she seemed to understand, and she ceased her remonstrance.

Several children shivered in corners of the one-room

dwelling. Adelheid surveyed them all until her eyes rested on one she knew instantly had to be Otto. His large blue-green eyes caught the glow of the fire. They were almost all that distinguished him from the dim recesses of the room.

"Oh Otto!" she said and ran to him, wrapping him in her arms, heedless of his dirt. At first he struggled against her, but he was too weak to free himself from her determined grip. To Adelheid's horror, he was light enough for her to lift easily.

He continued to thrash about weakly and called out to the woman *"Anya! Mama!"*

*"Madame,"* Adelheid said, turning to the slatternly woman whose expression transmitted a combination of annoyance and suspicion. "I shall unburden you now. Thank you for keeping my son safe." Safe, Adelheid thought—barely. So very like Alexander to have subjected an innocent to such degradation.

The woman nodded to her, but her compressed lips and glances at Niklaus showed that she didn't well understand what Adelheid had said. Adelheid gave Niklaus an imploring look, and he stepped forward, explained the princess's sentiments in the woman's own dialect, and placed a heavy purse into her hands.

Adelheid hurried out of the hut still carrying Otto. Niklaus took the boy from her so the postilion could hand her back into the carriage, then climbed in himself and placed Otto on her lap, wrapping a heavy fur rug around him.

*"Mein lieblich Kind,"* she murmured into the coarse hair just above his ear as she held him all the way back to the chateau.

～

IT TOOK A WEEK BEFORE OTTO COULD BE PERSUADED TO CLIMB willingly into a bathtub and resign himself to being dressed as befitted the son of a princess. Niklaus took it upon himself to teach the boy the cultivated German spoken in the prince's court. Frankel willingly became Otto's nurse, relinquishing her role as Adelheid's attendant to a young housemaid, and before much longer Otto had settled in to his new life with the accepting adaptability of a child.

As soon as Otto was back in her charge, Adelheid wasted no time putting her mind to what she must do in order to fulfill the terms of the will. She had already come to the conclusion that she had little choice but to try. She discarded the idea of returning to a career in opera. Such a vagabond life would not suit Otto and she was uncertain she could earn enough to support him as he deserved. Likewise, she could hardly set herself up as a singing teacher. Apart from the unsuitability in terms of Otto's prospects should she engage in such employment, society ladies would shrink from sending their impressionable daughters to a woman with a bastard son.

Besides, neither occupation would afford her enough remuneration to house him respectably or send him to a good school. And she was determined he should have every advantage befitting his noble blood.

So marry it must be.

And quickly. To attract a nobleman of the right caliber she would have to exhibit herself in society with all the trappings of elegance, never wearing the same gown twice, going about in a stylish carriage with perfectly matched horses, having the right number of footmen and postilions to give her consequence, and living in the most lavish style imaginable.

And she very soon realized she must leave her home

country to do so. Not a single eligible nobleman existed in her native Austria and she was far too well known there..

Was this why the prince made this ridiculous condition to inheriting his estate? Did he want to torture her with a future that would prove impossible?

It took her less than an hour to realize there was only one place where she might find a suitable husband.

London.

Her history would not be known in that city and she was a good enough actress to persuade the English that she was wealthy. To also convince a man of consequence not only to fall in love with her but to be enough in love with her to adopt her seven-year-old boy would be difficult, but she hoped feasible. The sticking point was that he must put the child in the position of inheriting title and fortune.

Added to all that was one factor that might give anyone pause and that could ensure Adelheid would never be able satisfy the conditions of the prince's will. Otto was a bastard —a common enough state of affairs—but that wasn't all. Her son would not easily blend into the population of London. He would stand out no matter what.

Otto was Black.

Her little boy was the son of the only man Adelheid had ever truly loved: a servant with skin as dark as the mahogany that grew on the prince's plantations in the West Indies. When she closed her eyes and allowed herself to dream of those brief, golden moments, she could still see Danton's gleaming, sweat-drenched skin contrasting with the pale ivory sheen of her own as they twined together in passion.

She gazed down at the little boy curled up in the bed in the nursery, asleep with his fists tightly closed, forehead puckered in a frown. Just so had Danton looked when he puzzled over a problem to do with the prince's estate or struggled over a passage in Aristotle as he worked to improved his Greek. It had been his goal to leave the prince's employ and go to university in Heidelberg It was too soon to tell, but Adelheid saw enough to believe that Otto took after his father in intelligence as well as in looks.

In almost all of his looks, that is. It happened that his brown skin and black hair set off a pair of startling blue-green eyes surrounded by long black lashes.

Her eyes exactly.

She kissed her fingers and touched them to Otto's cheek then crept away, softly closing the nursery door before going to her own bedchamber. She must set up a household in London. But how would she account for Otto's existence there as she pursued her project? Who could he be?

A ward. She could not tell the world he was her son, not yet. Such a fiction would mean misleading Otto himself if he wasn't to inadvertently expose her. Would he understand?

It made her sick to think of it.

So with few expectations yet a generous helping of hope, Adelheid sent letters express to her friends in theatres and opera houses wherever she had performed. She told them that business would be taking her to England for a time, and asked did any of them know of distinguished families who might help introduce her to society there. While all of them wrote back with condolences and inquiring after her, none contained any information that was useful for her purpose.

Until, that is, her old friend Félicité Martin, a seamstress at the King's Theatre in London, responded with a longer-than-usual letter. Félicité's letters were always full of gossip, most of it to do with people Adelheid neither knew nor cared about. But the seamstress had a wicked turn of phrase and Adelheid always read her missives with pleasure.

The closely written and crossed sheet spoke first of the conflict between the theatre manager and his star singers, none of whom had been paid their promised fees for the coming season. Then she turned to social news, describing various hopeful come-outs and bucks, predicting who would end up marrying whom. Adelheid was prepared to skim the letter and look at it later when she had greater leisure, but one item caught her attention.

*Ma chère, the fellow no one ever thought would throw the handkerchief is launching himself on the marriage mart this season. He's the tout charmant duke of Hartland, a rogue and a gamester. Until soon he was only the Marquis or Comte or other of Malmsby but his papa died tout d'un coup late last year, and oh la! There is no money. Poor Hartland must marry a fortune or be foreclosed, so they say here. Eh bien, he is handsome and charming and I daresay he will have success. A shocking flirt and a member of the set called Corinthians—men who pride themselves on their prowess sportif.*

The letter continued to enumerate Hartland's qualities and included some conjecture about his ability to perform satisfactorily in bed. But Adelheid had stopped reading by that time.

It was too good to be true. Were there heiresses in London whose parents would snap him up? Or had he damaged his reputation too much for that? She hoped the latter. Could she do it? She must try. And if she were to secure him, she and Otto must go to London as soon as possible. Tomorrow or the next day.

There was one significant obstacle to her plans, however: money. Her pitiful allowance would not be enough for her to set up a suitably grand establishment in London. Once again, she cursed her late husband. He'd thought of everything. Perhaps she would have to abandon thoughts of this convenient duke.

As she prepared for bed that evening, Adelheid opened her jewel box to replace the necklace and earrings she had worn that day and stopped, her hand poised above the modest collection she kept in her bedchamber.

Of course. The jewels were hers.

All of them.

And there were a lot. The prince always insisted she be laden with precious stones—tiaras, bracelets, brooches, necklaces, and earbobs heavy with diamonds, rubies, pearls, and emeralds. He kept the most valuable ones in the small cabinet off the muniment room. She still had her key. The prince may not have meant her to take them away, but who was to stop her?

Adelheid thrust her arms into her fur-trimmed dressing gown, nudged her toes into her slippers, and stole out of her room carrying a small satchel. Chin high and a supercilious expression that would discourage anyone from stopping her, she passed footmen dousing candles and maids on their way to the servants' quarters, slipped softly down the stairs to the great hall, and strode through it to the muniment room.

This chamber always smelled of rotting documents and mildew. Ancient leather-bound tomes lay sideways on the deep shelves caked with dust. A narrow door between two of them gave onto the stronghold that housed the estate jewels. Adelheid hurried to it and fitted her key in the lock.

She entered and lifted her candle high, the flickering flame picking up the facets of gems of great value arranged in glass cases. Without pausing, she placed her candle on the floor and gathered up all the pieces that would fit into the satchel, choosing the ones she guessed to be the most precious.

Once she'd finished she turned, picked her candle up, and started toward the door, when a figure stepped into it and barred her way.

"Niklaus," she said, her voice barely above a whisper.

Would he keep her from taking the jewels? Had he been spying on her already?

At first he stood and surveyed her in silence. Then he brought a bag out from behind his back and said, "I thought you might be needing this, Your Highness."

Adelheid breathed a quiet sigh and smiled at the steward. "Thank you, Niklaus." What was his motive in abetting her theft? She would think about that later.

As they scooped up the remainder of the priceless trinkets until both bags were heavy, Niklaus said, "I did not care for the prince's actions with regard to the boy."

He said no more but Adelheid understood that he felt she was due some recompense for such ill treatment, and would not tell anyone about clearing the stronghold of its precious bounty. Notwithstanding those feelings, which did him credit, he still stood in the role of watchdog over her actions. "You know I am going to try to fulfill the terms of the will," she said. "We must travel to England to do so, however. Immediately. Otto and I. And I shall bring Frankel as well."

Niklaus nodded, but with downcast eyes. "You are a woman of great spirit. I speak for many of the prince's staff when I say you will be missed. When shall we begin our journey?"

*Yes,* Adelheid thought. He would have to be there to assure the conditions were met. When they arrived at her bedroom, Adelheid took both heavy sacks of jewelry and turned to go through the door, but stopped. There was more than one reason why Niklaus should accompany them to England. It was he who best understood and could communicate with Otto. Because of this, Otto had already become a little attached to him. Added to that, Niklaus was English by birth. "Could you make the arrangements for the four of us? You needn't remain in England once I have achieved my object if you would prefer to return to Vienna. I shall write to an old friend who owes me a favor and ask him to secure a dwelling for us."

He stared at her again for a few moments, meeting her eyes with an expression she'd never seen before. And then, his mouth curved up in a smile. Niklaus never smiled. "It would be my honor to take care of such matters. And I believe I shall remain in England. I have long wished to go home. And one thing more," he said.

Adelheid said nothing, but raised her eyebrows expectantly.

"My name is Nicholas. Nicholas Rutherford. I would prefer to be known as that when we arrive in England."

Adelheid nodded her assent. She wasn't certain she could trust him. But she would never be able to manage without him.

Thus armed with something of a plan, Adelheid and all her worldly possessions, along with Otto, Frankel, and Nicholas, stepped ashore at Dover at the beginning of March 1813.

# CHAPTER 5

*P*hilip half expected to be turned away at the door of Almack's despite being able to present a pristine voucher to the porter. That gentleman did, in fact, scrutinize the duke rather closely and Hartland wondered if it was the same fellow who had thrown him out of the assembly rooms ten years ago. In any case, the porter could find no fault with the voucher nor with Hartland's attire and bowed him into the room.

Hartland had the easy grace of a man of consequence who doesn't doubt his ability to attract women and as soon as he entered the ballroom, the air brightened with notice. Little knots of chaperones put their heads together and hopeful ladies hid their slightly flushed faces behind their fans. A set was forming for a country dance but as of yet, no one of Philip's acquaintance had joined him to make introductions. In any case, he would not dance. He was in mourning for a few weeks yet.

He scanned the company idly as if he were not looking for someone to relieve the awkwardness of that first moment when a voice from across the room said, "Malmsby! I mean,

Hartland! What the devil? I do apologize," the speaker added to a dowager scowling at him disapprovingly, then hastened on to join the duke.

"Lewiston!" Hartland said, extending a hand to shake.

"Sorry to hear about your father," Lewiston said, modulating his previously joyful voice. "Oh, I suppose I should call you Duke now, eh?"

"I'm not used to it. I still accidentally cut people who address me as Hartland or Your Grace. Sometimes I look around expecting to see my father."

"Same thing happened to me when I inherited. Confusing. So is your mama in town too? Of course, she's not going out yet."

"Yes, she keeps to her room at Hartland House." Hartland thought the ritual of strict mourning nonsensical. His father certainly would far rather have had everyone who knew and loved him continue to be gay and frivolous. But the *ton* wouldn't have it. In any case, the dowager was in a sad state.

"Of course you're not dancing. So why in blazes are you here? Where dancing is the only entertainment on offer—unless you want to play whist for chicken stakes."

Before he could answer, Lady Millington spotted the duke and made her purposeful way in his direction, her daughter in her wake. "And it begins," Hartland muttered, raising one eyebrow.

Lewiston spoke quickly and quietly to him. "Ah. Of course. She's got a decent portion. Not much else to recommend her," and then made his own hasty retreat.

ONE GOOD THING ABOUT BEING A GENTLEMAN INSTEAD OF A lady during the season was that one's mother needn't chaperone. That meant that Lady Lewiston wasn't likely to witness snubs or awkward moments at assemblies and balls—of which Lewiston experienced many. Marquess he may be, but with as-yet encumbered estates, few social graces beyond the minimum, and an undistinguished countenance, he was likely to find himself edged out of the way if he approached one of the diamonds of the season, or an heiress whose fortune made up for the lack of more obvious attractions.

Seeing Hartland—who was a genuine friend not prone to making him feel his shortcomings in those *ton*-ish masculine pursuits—was definitely a mixed pleasure. He wished he had run into him for the first time at White's, where the two of them could have sat quietly over brandy and cards and talked of pleasant nothings, rather than at Almack's where Hartland's superiority in every quality ladies of the *ton* valued cast Lewiston into deep shade.

Still, it couldn't be helped.

And here he was again, at Almack's for the seventh season in a row. The triumph of hope over experience. It was early in the season and in addition to the fact that the quality had not yet arrived in full force, those whose services were in high demand for parties and assemblies hadn't all returned from the various venues around the country where they scratched together a living during the holidays. As a result the orchestra that evening was a bit on the meager side, and at least one of its members was old enough to be hard of hearing—which would explain the sour notes that marred the dance accompaniment. He did his best to ignore the unpleasant noise and focus instead on watching the dancers' feet as they responded to the rhythm that propelled their movements—but he didn't entirely succeed.

After a bit Lewiston's mind wandered and he shifted his gaze from the center of the ballroom to the corner, a place near the retiring room where ladies who weren't dancing sometimes gathered to gossip on the pretext of either coming or going from that enclave. In keeping with the rather thin attendance generally, that evening only one lady stood there. A lady Lewiston had never seen before. Since hers was the only unfamiliar face he'd noticed so far, he wondered if she could be the single true ingenue in attendance. Doubtless there would be more as the season progressed. Many come-outs chose to wait until they'd had their debut ball before venturing to the intimidating hunting ground of Almack's—if they were fortunate enough to get a voucher.

The unfamiliar girl stood out not merely because she was on the tall side and a bit gawky: Her entire attitude radiated unease. She clutched her reticule as if fearful of its being stolen at any moment, fidgeted with her dress in irritation, and drew her straight, rather dark eyebrows together in a scowl.

Lewiston couldn't help feeling a pang of sympathy for her. Still, her scowl seemed a little out of proportion to the situation. At that moment another grating squeak came from the orchestra and the lady winced visibly. Ah, Lewiston thought. This was most unusual. The vast majority of guests at Almack's paid almost no attention to the music itself except in its ability to set their feet in motion. So, the lady had an ear. No wonder she appeared pained. He wished he could go and talk to her and discover whether she was truly musical. But he could not approach her as she stood alone. Sooner or later someone would join her, possibly someone he knew who could make the introduction, or he could find one of the patronesses and ask to be presented. Mrs. Burrell was there but she terrified him. Lady Jersey was a little less intimidating, but he couldn't immediately see where she was.

So he waited, trying not to stare at the stranger too obviously. No one else seemed to notice her. Lewiston guessed that it was because, although not an antidote, she had no particular beauty, nor did she have that starry-eyed bloom that often made up for less than ideal features. He was too far away to see the color of her eyes, but they were large and set wide apart in an oval face, her nose a little too short, and her hair an unfashionable light brown. Still, despite all that should have made her unappealing, Lewiston found her perversely attractive.

As he watched, a determined matron sailed proudly in her direction, chin lifted. Doubtless her chaperone, probably her mother. But when Lewiston saw who she had in her wake, his heart sank. It was none other than Hartland. Clearly the handsome duke had been the duenna's object. A duke—even an impoverished one—was a prize indeed.

Hartland had exquisite manners and he must have said all the right things, because the young lady curtsied a little awkwardly and then suffered herself to be led away to the buffet, her chaperone smiling after her.

Did he dare make his way into that room as if by chance and see if Hartland would introduce him?

"Ah, there you are Lewiston!" Too late. It was Sir Reginald Minty, one of his mother's close friends. A widower, and a little old for the marriage mart, still, he came to the assemblies to ogle the delights on offer for the season—and to pick up tidbits of gossip.

"Sir Reginald. Good to see you. Had you a pleasant holiday?"

"Beastly. Rheumatism. Spent most of it in bed."

How on earth to follow up that statement was beyond Lewiston's capability and so he changed the subject. Sir Reginald, a baronet with a large family and many connections, had one virtue: He knew everything there was to know about everyone in the *ton*. So Lewiston asked, "Who is new this season? Any promising girls fired off from the schoolroom?"

In no time, Sir Reginald warmed to the subject and for a full ten minutes listed the names of the season's come-outs, what their prospects were, and how he rated the chances of each of them finding an eligible match.

Lewiston did little more than murmur a polite "You don't say" every now and again until Sir Reginald paused dramatically, drew a deep breath and lowered his voice to say, "Of course, you know about Ambrose's daughter. Heiress. Worth twenty-thousand a year at least, thanks to her grandpapa. A cit. Rich as Golden Ball. Chit's not much to look at, though, and no address. Still, that's not why she'll make a good match."

"Is she here?" Lewiston asked.

"Course! Her mama's on the prowl for a duke, you can be sure. Not many of those around so she'd probably settle for Hartland, even though he's lacking in juice. Saw her not long ago." He looked around, shifting to get a glimpse through the milling crowds now reforming for another dance. "There she is! Just come in from the buffet. Hah! What did I say? There's Hartland with the chit on his arm."

Lewiston wilted. That did it. What would be the point in being introduced now? He'd vaguely hoped that Hartland wouldn't interest himself in a girl just out of the schoolroom with little beauty to recommend her. But the fact that she was an heiress put an entirely different complexion on the matter. In any case, if the possession of a large fortune was her only recommendation, Lewiston thought, perhaps Hartland wouldn't think her worth the effort anyway.

"I say, she'd be a good catch for you. Marquess is almost a duke."

Lewiston smiled weakly. "Almost."

This made Sir Reginald laugh. "Well, let's have a rubber of whist at the club one evening soon, eh?" He gave Lewiston a hearty clap on the shoulder that nearly knocked him over.

IT WAS JUST LIKE HER MOTHER TO PUSH HER INTO SOMETHING she really wasn't ready for.

"Your gowns are exquisite, you've got all the pretty manners you need, what else should we wait for?" the viscountess had said when Olivia suggested they not attend the first Almack's assembly but wait until the second, which would occur after her ball at Mount Street.

"But I don't *feel* ready," she had said, lacking any better words to explain why she was so reluctant to get her first appearance at the marriage mart over with.

"Nonsense. You're just nervous. Best to jump right in, sink or swim. And I have every confidence you'll do swimmingly!" The viscountess beamed at her own bon mot.

So here she was. She'd heard that the food was awful and the decor drab, but no one had prepared her for one of the worst ensembles she'd heard for a long time. Worse even than the rackety quartet that accompanied the village assemblies near their estate in Hampshire. More than simply falling flat, this one positively hurt her ears. It was all she could do to keep herself from clapping her hands over them.

She'd been struggling against that impulse when her mother came to her with a tall, handsome gentleman following a respectful distance behind her. Much too handsome to be interested in her, she believed. He moved with catlike suppleness and his features arranged themselves in a pleasantly ironic expression. But if her limited past experience were anything to go by, after the introduction he would utter a few polite phrases and excuse himself to go talk to one of the girls who was actually pretty. There were several. A dazzling blond with round blue eyes and a simpering manner, for one. She'd also spied a black-haired beauty with skin like snow who had a figure that filled out her dress to perfection.

Olivia's gown, despite having been fitted to her exactly,

was embarrassingly tight across her breasts, making them mound uncomfortably in a décolletage she was afraid she'd never become used to. The rest of it hung limply down her somewhat shapeless torso. Worse were her gloves which, instead of encasing her arms and hands in a second skin, drooped in folds here and there and despite the tight ribbons holding them above her elbows, threatened to creep down and bunch at her wrists.

By the time the vision of manly perfection was being introduced to her, she knew she must have turned an unbecoming shade of crimson—her olive complexion not being prone to blushing a more delicate pink. But the gentleman, a duke was all she could remember, looked down at her with his dark blue eyes not unkindly and kissed her hand.

"This is my daughter's first season, Your Grace," her mother said, keeping a smile pasted to her face. "May I present Miss Olivia Fontenoy. She's very accomplished."

Ugh. That catch-everything word. So meaningless. And Olivia knew that she would never reveal her biggest accomplishment to someone like the duke, if at all.

"Accomplished and lovely," the duke said, with a slight bow of his head.

*Now he's roasting me,* Olivia thought, and drew herself up.

He looked at her earnestly. "I'm afraid I'm not dancing at present. I am still in mourning for my father for a few weeks yet," he said, and pointed to the black armband he wore. "But I would be delighted to take you for a glass of lemonade, if you would wish it?"

Olivia wanted to say *no thank you,* since she didn't much care for lemonade, but one look at her mother's fierce expression changed her mind. "Thank you, My Lord Duke."

He put out his arm, and she laid her hand upon it, mortified to see that it was trembling.

After a few minutes in his company, she felt sorry for the

duke—whose name resolutely escaped her memory—valiantly keeping up a one-sided conversation. She gave him credit for his continued courtesy, but she found she simply had nothing to say to him. What did all those other girls talk about as they smiled and looked up invitingly? Gowns? Gossip? The duke spoke of the hunt, his carriage horses, the forthcoming races at Ascot. All things she cared little about, although she did like to ride. If were a braver person she would have quizzed him for his thoughts on the new Philharmonic Society, ask if he was looking forward to the upcoming performance of *The Marriage of Figaro* at the King's Theatre, and inquired which of the Italian sopranos was his favorite. When he completely failed to notice a particularly jarring mistake in the orchestra—one wayward musician started playing in the wrong key—she sighed.

"Do you have your horses here in town?" the duke asked after he had spent a polite fifteen minutes talking to her.

"Yes. Mostly the carriage horses, but I have my own hack."

"Then would you join me for a ride in the park tomorrow if the weather is fine?" he asked.

This surprised her. Surely he'd had enough of her awkwardness. More, it was truly the last thing she wanted to do—but again her mother's expression warned her against refusing. At least seated on a horse it wouldn't be necessary to maintain continuous conversation. "Of course."

"Mount Street, isn't it? Shall we ride in the morning? Say, eleven?"

He'd done his research. Naturally. He knew precisely where they lived and doubtless a great deal more about her and her family. She thought if she looked hard enough, she might see gold guineas glittering in his eyes. She had known she must be prepared for the fact that the eligible gentlemen would care about nothing beyond her wealth. But the duke's pleasant conversation and kind ways had raised her hopes just a little. At least he hadn't invited her for the hour of the strut. Perhaps he wasn't lost to all feeling. He might have perceived that her reticence would render her unenthusiastic about parading herself in front of all the fashionable members of the *ton*, who were ready to judge a lady from the feathers in her bonnet to the shine on her half boots.

He walked off, attracting sidelong glances from all the ladies in the ballroom. Olivia sighed. Even from the back he looked handsome. "May we leave now?" she whispered to her mother.

"You haven't even danced!" the viscountess said in a quiet hiss.

Olivia wanted to point out to her that in order to dance she had to be asked, but thought better of it and looked for an unoccupied chair somewhere that would not make it obvious that no one had approached her.

Except a gentleman was coming in her direction after all, accompanied by Lady Jersey. She and her mother both remained standing as the two drew near.

Lady Jersey said, "I have here a young gentleman who wishes to make your acquaintance, Miss Fontenoy. May I present the Marquess of Lewiston."

As soon as the word *marquess* was out of Lady Jersey's mouth, the viscountess smiled. A quick look at the smile told Olivia that her mother's assessment of this prospect was tepid at best, despite his grand title.

His greeting, unlike the duke's, was nearly unintelligible, and he did not meet her eyes. A flush of red crept up under his neck cloth to his chin and Olivia found herself feeling sorry for him. Could it be that he was as nervous as she was? She couldn't imagine why.

"Another set is forming," Lady Jersey said when the conversation stopped completely, clearly hinting that Lewiston should ask Olivia to stand up with him.

"Oh, yes, I see," he said, and then, "Miss Fontenoy, if you are not engaged for this dance, I would, that is, it would be my pleasure …"

At last he lifted his eyes up to meet hers with such a look of panicked entreaty that Olivia could only guess that the marquess had no desire to dance. "Actually, I'm rather hungry. Shall we go to the supper room instead?" She couldn't imagine what had made her bold enough to suggest such a thing. Her mother surreptitiously pinched the back of her arm, and not gently.

But the expression of relief that instantly relaxed Lewiston's shoulders and brightened his face with a charming, crooked smile assured Olivia that she had done the right thing. He put out his arm, and she rested her steady hand on it as they walked into the supper room together, leaving the viscountess and Lady Jersey to enjoy a quiet gossip.

Once they were out of her mother's hearing, Olivia said, "Truthfully, I'm not the least bit hungry."

"Nor am I," Lewiston said, his eyes lighting up with a mischievous glint.

Olivia cocked her head on the side. "Why did you come over to me? And why do you prefer not to dance?"

Lewiston looked taken aback, and Olivia realized such directness was not at all seemly and started to say something else when he said, "I wanted to meet you. I think you might be the only other person in the room who noticed how dreadful the music is."

Olivia laughed, much more loudly than the delicate, lady-like titter she'd been schooled to use in polite society.

This only made Lewiston grin more broadly and say, "Tell me, what else don't you like about Almack's?"

# CHAPTER 6

*B*efore they'd set out on the journey with every
possession she thought she would need, Adelheid
had sent a letter to an old friend who owed her a favor. She
had performed a delicate service for him when he got into a
scrape in Paris. Lord Brattle wrote that he was at her
disposal and engaged an agent for her in London to manage
the necessary arrangements. She said she'd like to live in
Grosvenor Square—Nicholas knew it to be where Hartland
House was located. The agent managed to hire a house in
that exclusive location, and Brattle agreed to help her dispose
of her jewels to raise the money she would need to survive.
He would know how best to sell them and have copies made
of some of them so that she could appear in society suitably
adorned.

Adelheid had already depleted her meager funds considerably to supply Otto with clothes that would ensure he was
seen not as a servant but as a valued member of her family.
Although many brown- and black-skinned people made
their homes in Europe and England, they were almost always
servants or tradesmen.

*What am I doing?* Adelheid asked herself as she, Otto, and Frankel rolled along in the elegant carriage drawn by four matched bays that Lord Brattle arranged for her, the coachman handling the ribbons, the liveried postilion seated on the near side leader, and a footman standing up behind to blow the yard of tin at the tollgates. They had spent a few days at a posting house outside of London, and in many ways Adelheid wished they could have remained there longer. She was only beginning to get to know Otto and he was in no way prepared for the scrutiny of curious Londoners. He could only say a few words in English although he had natural grace and bowed very handsomely. Teaching him manners was her first priority. The rest would take time.

For now, she and Nicholas were his teachers—he was bright, and learned quickly—and they soon moved from spoken to very basic written language. But before long Otto would need a regular tutor.

One thing she had learned quickly about him was that somehow in his past life he must have developed an affinity for animals of all kinds—the dog at the inn where they spent a few days, the kitchen cat, even a tame starling that one of the stable hands fed on crumbs. Most of all, though, he loved horses. This became apparent when he stole out to the stable and helped the lads with the feeding and grooming. Noticing this, Nicholas persuaded the landlord to allow him to give the boy a riding lesson on a placid pony kept to pull a cart.

That same day, she wrote to Brattle and asked him to procure a mount suitable for Otto to ride.

The carriage slowed and came to a halt. Here already? she thought. Although the journey had been long, she felt she needed more time to become accustomed to her new life. She gazed out the window as the footman dashed around from his perch to open the carriage door. Before she had a chance to take his hand and step down, Otto leapt over her and sprang onto the flagway, a broad grin and a cheeky expression—evidence of just how far he'd come since she'd taken him from the mean hovel that was his home for the first seven years of his life. After a quick look around, he ran up the stone steps and into the hall, and before Adelheid could open her mouth to call him back, he'd vanished from her sight, no doubt bent on some mischief or other. What would the servants think?

"*Steh*, Otto!" Frankel called and clambered out quickly with an apologetic glance at Adelheid.

"Princess Adelheid?"

It was Nicholas, who stood by the open door of the carriage holding his hand out to her. "Yes, yes. It's time to look forward."

"You don't have to do this, if you will pardon my impertinence. Another way might be found," he said in German, Adelheid assumed so that the English servants would not understand him.

What was he saying? Was he not the prince's instrument? And what did it matter to him what became of them? "Of course I do. For Otto's sake. But Nicholas, I shall count on you to give me the truth with all its thorns. Whatever your intentions while you're with me, I shall need counsel from someone who knows all, someone familiar with the late prince and his ways, and who also knows London." She took his hand and he steadied her as she stepped down, but said no more.

She had no time for second thoughts or regrets.

Adelheid drew herself up to greet her staff who stood in a line in the hall as the footmen traipsed through with trunks, portmanteaux, and bandboxes. But before she could put a foot on the bottom step a lady's voice behind her said, "Ah! I'm glad Beaumain's house will once more be occupied."

She turned to see a tall young woman with dark auburn

hair curling out from under the rim of a very stylish poke bonnet striding toward her, a friendly smile on her face.

"Forgive me!" the lady said. "I've often been accused of being unpardonably rude, but I couldn't help stopping. I've been shopping and decided to walk home the long way on this pleasant evening. When I saw a lone female who appeared travel-weary about to ascend into one of the grandest houses in London, my curiosity got the better of me. Lady Mariana Thorne," she said with a polite bow of her head.

What could she say? Adelheid had never been in the position of having to introduce herself to a stranger, at least not since her marriage. It felt pretentious to use her title, which was not hers by birth after all.

Seeing her consternation, Nicholas approached, said to her softly in German, "I'll manage this," before bowing to the lady and saying in English, "Lady Mariana, allow me to make you known to the Princess Adelheid Kinsky."

"*Ich freue mich, sie kennenzulernen,*" Adelheid said, although she was perfectly capable of expressing her pleasure at meeting Lady Mariana in English. Thank heavens for Nicholas she thought. The supposed language barrier would serve her well as she found her footing in London.

"Ah! You are German!" Lady Mariana said. "*Entschuldigen-sie!*"

"Austrian, My Lady," Nicholas said. "The princess has only just arrived in England."

Exaggerating her accent slightly, Adelheid said, "I am sorry. You took me by surprise."

"Thank heavens you speak English. My German is deplorable. And it is I who should apologize! But as I said, I'm hopeless. My whole family believes so. My husband only lets me accompany him to political events because I can be very amusing when I choose to be."

The appearance of the unexpectedly lively stranger dispelled Adelheid's melancholy mood and she smiled. "*Bitte,* I would invite you to take some refreshment, but I do not know if there is any to be had."

Mariana's gleeful laugh brought a smile to Adelheid's face. "Of course. Here is my card. Might I call on you in a day or two? If you've just come from abroad, you will need some introductions. And if you plan to order any gowns, I must escort you to my sister-in-law's modiste, Madame Pauline."

"Not yours?" Adelheid asked.

"Oh, she makes all my dresses as well. I meant that my sister-in-law, Lady Bridlington, is the designer. It's her establishment."

How very odd. A noblewoman engaged in trade. "I would be delighted if you would honor me with a visit," she said.

"You outrank me, so I believe the honor would be mine." Mariana's eyes lit up with amusement. "I look forward to seeing you again!"

On those words, Lady Mariana turned and strode off. Only then did Adelheid see a footman hovering, his arms laden with parcels, his face impassive. No doubt the servant was accustomed to his mistress's ways.

Adelheid was too tired to think more about Lady Mariana just then. Nicholas held out his arm for her to lean on and escorted her up the stairs.

Tomorrow Lord Brattle would come and she would give him some of her jewels to sell, she thought, as the butler—Grandison was his name—introduced the rest of the staff.

"I should like to freshen up," she said to her housekeeper, Mrs. Hawkins. "And then a cold dinner would be most appreciated."

Mrs. Hawkins said, "Very good, Your Highness," and led her up the grand stairs to her bedchamber on the second floor.

# CHAPTER 7

*H*artland tried to banish from his mind the image of the distasteful errand he'd just completed. He'd driven his curricle to the elegant residence in Chelsea where he had set Phoebe up in style. He knew it would be difficult, and she made sure it was as full of torment as it could be.

He could still hear her sharp voice. "You promised! What shall I do? I need new gowns and my cook just left and I shall need to hire another one. And what about Ascot? I suppose this means no new phaeton nor that pair of grays you mentioned."

So it went on for an hour. He hoped to be invited into her bed one last time before they ended their association. Phoebe's pouty lips had a way of suggesting the most indecent acts just by existing, and if those two succulent objects left him in any doubt, her smoldering dark eyes usually extended an even more definite invitation.

Not that day, though. She pressed her lips into a determined thin line and hardened her eyes to coals. She was too shrewd by half to give away what had cost him so dear for six months. She also knew better than to allow herself to be fobbed off with goodbye diamonds. Although she kept the diamonds, she still gave vent to her spleen. He couldn't blame her. Doubtless she thought he was just throwing her over because he'd grown tired of her, but that wasn't the case. Theirs was a mutually enjoyable relationship. Hartland thought he got more than he gave, in fact. But he simply couldn't afford to continue.

Unpleasant scene or no, Hartland had no doubt that Phoebe's particular combination of attributes would win her another champion easily enough. It was that which made it possible for him to leave her with if not a clean conscience, at least one that wasn't oppressed. He listened sympathetically to all her protestations that she would be destitute, knowing that the fact of her having been his paramour would soon have aspirants to become her protector queuing up at her door.

Still, it was the end of something. No more champagne-filled, debauched nights. No more thrilling, high-stakes gambling for a while either. The sale of his racing stable had raised a little cash to fund the season, but he would have to be circumspect—a prospect that filled him with dread.

If all went according to plan, this would be a temporary state of affairs. He just needed to make the heiress fall in love with him, which he believed would be easy enough.

The heiress. Miss Fontenoy. So much the opposite of the delectable Phoebe. She wasn't exactly unattractive. It wasn't that. A smile could probably brighten her serious eyes and bring out the hint of green in them, and her figure was surprisingly appealing—she was one of those rare females whose embonpoint overbalanced her otherwise delicate build. Hartland had a momentary image of those firm, round breasts and he smiled. If only they belonged to a different lady.

What would it be like to be buckled to her? Marriage wasn't supposed to provide all of a man's entertainment. That wasn't its purpose. It was the getting of an heir that mattered. Marriage in the *ton* generally didn't have to do with love and fidelity. Everyone knew that. Even his good-humored, kind father who sincerely cared for his duchess had kept mistresses.

The trouble was he would first need to secure Miss Fontenoy's fortune before he could even think of indulging in another amorous adventure—at least one that was more than a passing flirtation. He was reasonably confident he would succeed. Except in the realm of fortune, Hartland had no serious rival.

So it came as a bit of a shock to him that their first ride in the park together the day before hadn't advanced his cause very much. Conversation had been nonexistent, again. Every subject he raised earned at best monosyllabic responses. He couldn't tell whether it was a sign of reticence or disinclination. She appeared even to distance herself from him so that no one in the park would know they were together other than by chance. And when they returned to Mount Street she gave him a brief curtsy on the flagway and did not invite him to step inside for tea, or at that time of day an entirely appropriate glass of sherry.

Another opportunity was ahead, though. Her debut ball would be on Tuesday, just four days away. A dance or two— he could do so at a private ball—and maybe a stroll in the conservatory, if they had one. A few declarations of exaggerated affection. Amid friends and family she might be less nervous.

That, he thought, would do it. And he might well end by enjoying it. He had had time to notice during the hour of their ride that Miss Fontenoy was one of those girls whose looks improved on acquaintance. Although no one would call her pretty, she had an arresting profile, especially when she didn't know anyone was watching her. Perhaps, once she warmed to him a bit more, the pursuit might turn out to be a pleasure. He pictured a stolen kiss in the garden, an "accidental" brush against a silk-clad breast.

On second thought, maybe he shouldn't wait for the ball before finding an opportunity to see her again. Time enough to go to Ascot the day after the ball. She mentioned that she planned to go to the first opera of the season at The King's Theatre the following evening. Something by Mozart. Hartland had little taste for the entertainment, normally enjoying the balletic interludes and their revelation of expanses of calves and ankles more than the singing. But one went to be seen. Or to court a saucy opera dancer after the performance. He sighed. Best to put that out of his mind for now.

He would return home to change, then call on Lewiston, who had a box at the King's Theatre. And so he urged Challenger to a canter and headed in the general direction of the Stanhope Gate.

He hadn't gone far when a woman's panic-stricken voice, coming from some way down the carriage drive around a bend, caught his attention.

"*Ruhe! Steh!*"

German? Hartland thought. Odd.

He slowed to a trot and continued in the direction of the voice. As soon as he rounded the bend, he was met by the sight of a strikingly beautiful woman, a stranger, on the seat of a high-perch phaeton with a little dark-skinned boy in spotless nankeens sitting next to her, his eyes fearful. She was struggling to regain control of the horses—a fine pair of bays—who pranced and danced, one of them attempting to rear up and shaking his head as if being chased by a demon.

Hartland swung himself gracefully off his mount, threw

the reins over a nearby stump, and ran to the horses' heads. "Steady, steady boys. What's got you all in a pucker?"

"Take care, M'lord," the lady said, her voice tense. "Something has made him wild!"

Hartland didn't respond to the lady, only focusing on the horses. He soothed and murmured and took hold of their reins until their fretting nearly ceased. But one of them still showed a tendency to shake his head wildly and continued to nicker and snort and strike at the ground. That was when Hartland noticed a slight swelling below the eye and all at once knew what had happened.

"I believe this fellow was stung by a bee, Ma'am." He accompanied this with a nod in her direction, not daring to attempt the gesture of removing his hat or bowing low for fear of agitating the horses again. "Are your stables near? If the lad would run back and fetch a groom and some salve, I believe the matter can be safely dealt with. If not, send him to mine, behind number sixteen Grosvenor Square."

A slight gasp escaped the lady before she said, "It seems we are neighbors. I have only a day or two ago taken up residence at number twelve." Her voice, no longer tight with fear, was husky and slightly accented, although her face still showed evidence of her recent fright in its pallor. Not waiting for Hartland's reply, she turned to the boy. "Otto, you know the way, don't you? *Mach schnell zu Hause!* Bring Barber."

The lad jumped down gracefully and loped off with an easy gait.

She watched him go for a few moments then turned back to Hartland and said, "Forgive me, *Seigneur*, to whom do I owe my salvation?"

"Hartland, your most humble servant, Ma'am."

She turned her head slightly and raised her chin, a gesture that presented her perfect three-quarters profile and set off her stylish helmet cap beneath which her almost white-blond curls peeked out becomingly. "And I am Princess Adelheid Kinsky. Honored to make your acquaintance, Duke. I would curtsy, but this phaeton is a little difficult to descend from without making a *Spektakel*." She smiled, and her long, languid eyes came alight with amusement.

A princess? Yes, he'd heard that a lady of consequence had moved into Beaumain's house for the season. What were the odds? Not just a princess, but a creature of transcendent beauty. He could not remember ever seeing her equal in all his seasons in London and for a long moment his eyes rested on her appreciatively. Remembering himself he said, "Surely a princess needn't bow to a duke!"

Her shapely lips opened in a smile that revealed perfect white teeth. "The title is through my marriage, Duke. I am not nobly born, and now that I am widowed, it feels a bit … *szemtelen* … you do not know Hungarian, of course, and I do not know the English for this. In German, it is *vermessen*."

Hartland had to comb his recollection for what little German he had stored in his mind since his Oxford days and made an educated guess. "I gather you mean 'presumptuous.'"

She laughed. A golden trill of such unalloyed merriment that it made Hartland smile.

They remained frozen in their enforced positions, a sudden silence descending as each of them surveyed the other. Hartland tore his gaze away from hers first and looked toward the nearest gate into the park where he saw, with relief, the boy sitting in front of a grizzled groom riding toward them on a sturdy cob.

"I'll take their 'eads," said the groom to the princess when he reached them, and nodded deferentially to Hartland. "Yer Grace."

"Shall I hold them while you tend to the sting?" Hartland said.

"Otto 'ere can do it, if the princess allows, now it ain't 'im on his ownsome."

He dismounted and the boy slid down from his perch, made a courtly bow to Hartland and then took hold of the reins just below the affected horse's head, grasping them confidently with his small hands.

"'E's a dab hand with horses, this one!" the groom said with unmistakable pride.

"I suppose he'll come home looking as though he's been rolling in the mud, Barber! After Frankel cleaned him up so nicely for our drive," the princess said with an indulgent smile at the boy—Otto, apparently. *Is he a servant?* Hartland wondered. She didn't treat him thus.

"I believe it will be some time before your horses are ready to pull your phaeton again," Hartland said. "May I help you down, Ma'am?"

"*Bitte*," the princess said, standing and putting her hand out to reach his as he walked up to the vehicle.

But instead of simply steadying her while she put her foot on the high step, Hartland reached up, grasped her slender waist, and lifted her down to the ground. This was a gesture that should have brought a raging blush to her cheeks, but the lady seemed not the least discomposed by it, only slightly amused.

More and more intriguing, Hartland thought.

"I must thank you again for coming so quickly to my aid," the princess said, making good on her promise to curtsy.

"Perhaps you will allow me to escort you to your home since it is so near to mine and your horses appear to be in capable hands now." He put his arm out to her. "Challenger will not mind walking behind us if you will allow me to take hold of his reins." He nodded toward his patient horse, which he realized with a guilty pang had been left standing a little too long.

"I shall do the same with the good, docile Dusty. Otto is not yet able to ride alone, and Barber will have to drive the phaeton. I suppose it is not, perhaps, proper for me to go with only you. But the horses can be our chaperones," the princess said, suppressing a smile.

"I think there can be no impropriety in our strolling together at this hour," Hartland said. There was nothing demure and retiring about this princess. At the same time, she didn't cast out lures to him or simper. The combination was remarkably refreshing.

Before they walked off, Princess Adelheid looked back at the groom and his eager helper and said, "Do as Barber says, Otto, and don't hinder him."

Hartland wasn't sure whether Otto's grin indicated compliance or its opposite, but this didn't seem to trouble the princess.

It turned out that Princess Adelheid had many questions about London society and the *ton* that Hartland was happy to answer for her, and they conversed easily.

"You met Lady Mariana! How fortunate. She is very well connected and can procure many invitations for you. Perhaps we will attend some of the same parties."

"That would please me. Then I would know at least one other person in the room." She cast him a mischievous smile.

"Trust me, you will not find yourself without introductions or dance partners for long." He could only imagine the stir she would make on entering a room full of people who thought they knew all the diamonds of the season.

All too soon, they reached her house. The dour butler opened the door and a footman rushed out to lead the horse around to the stables.

"I have been rattling away, hardly giving you a chance to ask questions of your own," the princess said as they stood at the bottom of the stone steps to the door. "No doubt you have many. Perhaps you wonder about my ward, Otto."

Hartland was glad she introduced the subject. It would have been rude for him to bring it up. "Ah," he said. "Your ward."

"Yes. He is not a servant, unlike so many of his kind in this city. Otto is the son of a distant relation who died, and he is in my care."

It was hardly appropriate to ask more standing out in the street, so Hartland simply said, "A fortunate boy," and bowed over her hand, raising it with the intention of dropping a light kiss on her knuckles. Before he could do so, she drew it away and said, *"Auf wiedersehen,* Duke," then tripped lightly up the stairs and vanished into her house.

# CHAPTER 8

*M*ozart! And Catalani would sing! That was all Olivia thought about on her tedious ride in the park with Hartland the day before. Occasionally she noticed that other ladies' eyes lingered on the duke as they rode by or paused to greet him, extending dainty gloved hands for him to grasp and bow over slightly. He presented her to several of them but their names made no impression on her. She was too full of the music. Her throat opened and her ears tingled with the notes in her mind of *'Dove sono i bei momenti,'*—'Where have the beautiful moments gone' —truly a masterpiece. But would Catalani leave it alone? She was notorious for adding flourishes and embellishments to show off her voice at the expense of the music. At least, that was what Olivia had read in the *Chronicle*.

They had engaged a box for the season for her sake only, since her parents had little taste for opera. She'd fallen so in love with the music Signore Tetrazzini brought her that she'd cajoled them into letting her attend once last season, before she was really out. Her governess brought her just for the opera, which was second on the programme after a ballet. She was told to sit at the back of the box and leave before the bows. To be seen before she was out might brand her as fast and ruin her chances of getting a voucher to Almack's.

That small taste had been enough for her to fall passionately in love. She would have leapt down onto the stage from their first-tier box and sat amongst the singers—as indeed audience members used to do until a few seasons ago—if she could have. But failing that, it had suited her to lurk in the shadows, to be able to react without anyone seeing her, to let the tears flow when the music became too painful to bear, when Orfeo poured out his hopeless love for his Eurydice. If she could have her way this season, she would continue to stay out of sight in the shadows at the back of the box. But the viscountess squashed that hope in the carriage on the way to the theatre.

"Now that you're out, you must sit in the front where everyone can see you. And none of that over-enthusiastic applauding that is so vulgar. Do not let your emotions get the better of you. It's only music. Lightly tap your hands together and smile."

Only music! It was *The Marriage of Figaro!* "But the performers won't hear it!"

Her mother opened her eyes wide at her and shook her head. "What could that possibly have to do with you? What matters is that you are seen, not heard."

There was no point in explaining it. Olivia wondered how she could have been born to parents who, if they didn't have tin ears, had absolutely no appreciation for music.

Still, at least Olivia had managed to overcome her mother's protestations that it wasn't fashionable to arrive before the overture at the early hour of five-thirty. After the footman led them to their box, she shed her fur-trimmed velvet opera cloak, draping it over her chair to reveal the silver satin lining. Although gowns and finery were not Olivia's obsession, she had to admit that her claret twilled silk theatre dress, trimmed with silver lace at the corsage and belted with silver braid just below her breasts, made her feel positively regal. Hetty, young though she was, had a knack for arranging hair, and had coaxed Olivia's nearly straight locks into fashionable curls, with a knot on top of her head that revealed the nape of her long neck. Her only ornament was a simple strand of pearls. And the gloves she wore that evening fit her better than the ones she wore at Almack's so she didn't feel nearly as clumsy. She almost looked pretty, she thought, which soothed her nerves about sitting where everyone would be able to gawk at her.

Olivia listened idly to the cacophony of the orchestra tuning and let her gaze wander over the mostly empty boxes as the pit beneath them and the gallery above the four tiers of boxes filled. To her surprise, even by the time the programme was to start, over half of the boxes were still empty. How could that be? Surely Catalani's legions of partisans would be eager to hear her and applaud wildly and call for encores whenever she sang. And there were apparently no more tickets in the entire theatre to be had for that evening's performance.

Before she could question her mother about the empty boxes, the stage hands lit the candelabras on the sides of the stage while the lackeys scampered to set tapers to the oil lamps at its foot. A momentary hush followed and then the orchestra started to play. Olivia closed her eyes and let the music wash over her. Here were true musicians. Here were—

"I say Lady Ambrose, lovely to see you here! When did you arrive in London?"

What on earth? Olivia opened her eyes to see Lady Twickenham leaning over the barrier between her box and theirs talking to her mother in a loud voice. But that was only the beginning of the disruptions. In the well-lit theatre, Olivia spotted people entering the other boxes all around them, not minding that they were making noise, talking to each other as if they'd met in a drawing room as they settled themselves. "Mother!" she said, scorn in her voice.

"What?" Lady Ambrose said, breaking off her conversation with Lady Twickenham. "Is something the matter?"

"The music! How can you talk so during it?"

"It's only the overture," she said with a laugh and turned back to her friend.

When at last the singers walked to their places in front of the cleverly painted backdrop, a hush descended. The baritone was another popular singer, known for his comic roles, and the audience laughed as he measured out the room for his wedding night while becoming utterly distracted by his fiancée Susanna. But as soon as his set piece ended and the recitative began, the low buzz of whispered conversations resumed.

Thus went the entire first act. Olivia hadn't remembered that from last season, but she saw how it was now. All anyone cared about was listening to the famous singers perform their showy arias and duets so they could say they heard them. And so that everyone else there could observe them doing so.

It took concerted effort but Olivia kept her eyes steadfastly on the stage, listening as hard as she could, following the rapid Italian, most of which she knew from memorizing the score and libretto Signore Tetrazzini had brought her.

But the opera didn't really start, even for her, until the beginning of the second act when Catalani made her entrance to sing *"Porgi amor."* As her powerful voice cleaved the air, people shushed each other, and by the time the great soprano had reached the middle of the aria, the entire audience had stilled.

It was a simple cavatina, so Catalani performed it with few embellishments—only flying into trills and arpeggios on the repeat of the melody, mostly relying on her crystalline tone to give it power. Olivia leaned forward. She couldn't help it. Tears filled her eyes and she blinked rapidly in a vain attempt to stop them falling.

She had not paid any attention to the people who had filled the other box next to theirs. So it startled her when a gentleman's gloved hand reached quietly over from her left and held out a snowy white handkerchief. Not wanting to see who had witnessed this absurd display of emotion, she took the handkerchief without turning her head and surreptitiously dabbed at her eyes, hoping her mother hadn't noticed anything. She was torn between wishing to hide her face and wanting to express her gratitude to whoever had been so kind, wondering whether it was appropriate to give the now sodden handkerchief back to its owner.

As the music claimed her attention, she soon forgot about the bit of cambric balled up in her hand. It was well into Cherubino's 'Voi che sapete' before Olivia had entirely regained her composure. She had forced her thoughts so far away from the hubbub around her that she only remembered the handkerchief when the music stopped and the buzz of conversation once again rose in the interval. She looked to her left, embarrassed.

To her amazement, who should be occupying the box but the Duke of Hartland. He nodded to her, but when she held out the handkerchief to return it to him he looked puzzled, so she turned her gesture into a ladylike wave. Now she would have to talk to him. It raised him somewhat in her estimation to know that he enjoyed opera, and at least the performance would give them something to talk about.

.  .  .

IT HAD VEXED LEWISTON WHEN HARTLAND TURNED UP AND invited himself to his box at the opera. He'd been looking forward to an evening of solitary enjoyment—barring, of course, the necessary socializing during the intervals—and he knew Hartland had no real interest in music.

"You won't like it," Lewiston had said as he poured the duke a glass of sherry in the handsome parlor in his rooms at the Albany.

"Harry! Do you think I'm completely bottle-headed! That I don't know my Mozart from my Handel?"

That was exactly what Lewiston thought, but he judged it wiser not to say. "Might I ask what has inspired this sudden enthusiasm for music?"

Hartland flashed his notoriously disarming smile. "I'm in pursuit."

*Of course.* "Dare I hazard a guess as to your object?" Unfortunately, Lewiston had a pretty shrewd idea of what that was as well.

"You'll find out soon enough. I could hire my own box but the first tier is sold out, and I'm fairly certain no other would do."

So it had been agreed, and Hartland had gone to the trouble of discovering which box was the Ambroses' and made Lewiston change his to the one next to it for that performance—a possibility only because the renters of that box were not yet in town. And now they sat listening to Mozart's hilarious opera and the wonderful singers who performed it. Or at least, he did. Hartland, aside from arriving late, spent all his time peering through his opera glass at the occupants of the other boxes. After making such an effort to sit close to her, Lewiston couldn't help wondering why the duke trained his eyes on everyone except Miss Fontenoy.

This was especially mystifying since he found himself

disturbingly aware of her proximity to them. He'd felt a strange kinship with her in their brief conversation at Almack's, but it hadn't been based on anything physical, or so he thought. He had the sense that they'd simply been comfortable in each other's company in that very uncongenial setting, not as if they were strangers meeting for the first time but as if they'd known each other for years.

So why was the fact of her presence next to him so unsettling that evening? Lewiston did not turn to look at her when they first took their seats after the music had started. He only managed to steal a quick glance at her when he bent to pick up the libretto he'd purposely let fall to his feet. She was no more beautiful than she had been at Almack's. The same profile. The same intelligent eyes. Not beautiful, Lewiston thought, but somehow striking. At Almack's, she'd been a lost soul. Here, she belonged. She did not fidget or glance around nervously. If anything, Miss Fontenoy was remarkable for her stillness. She was the only lady in any of the fashionable boxes whose full attention remained steadfastly on the stage from the moment the music began. Catching another look, Lewiston saw her lean slightly forward, part her lips and—had he imagined it?—silently form the words of Catalani's aria.

Miss Fontenoy did not listen to music. She was the music. When tears started to her eyes and trickled down her cheeks during the plaintive exhortation to love, *"Porgi, amor,"* Lewiston felt an answering prick in his own eyes and wanted to reach over and take her in his arms, to let those tears soak into his evening coat. Instead, he quietly reached into his pocket and pulled out his handkerchief, handing it over to her in a way he hoped would be surreptitious. Their fingers touched briefly when she took it from him, and a shiver went from them up his arm to the back of his neck.

He planned to simply let her keep the handkerchief. He

did not want to put her in an awkward position by claiming it back. In fact, he hoped she hadn't even noticed who had provided her with it. Something told him she wouldn't want anyone to witness her overflow of emotion. Members of the *ton* did not cry at the opera. Watching her listen to the music felt very much like eavesdropping on someone's intimate, private dream.

But these fantasies came to an abrupt end when the interval began.

"Didn't you say you wanted champagne, Lewiston?" Hartland said to him in a low voice, nudging him to stand. As soon as Lewiston vacated his seat, the duke took it, clearly with the intention of talking to Miss Fontenoy. But before he could attract her attention, Miss Fontenoy—perhaps guilt stricken for having kept a stranger's handkerchief in custody for so long—turned to their box and held out a limp scrap of white cloth.

Hartland hadn't seen Lewiston give her the handkerchief, therefore the momentary blank look the duke cast at Miss Fontenoy when she held it out to him sent a knife into Harry's stomach. How would Hartland respond? Was there any way to rescue the lady from such an awkward situation? He took a step toward the Ambrose box, but the duke was too polished a flirt to be at a loss.

"Why, Miss Fontenoy! I am delighted to see you here. I assure you, there is no need for you to drop your handkerchief in order to secure my admiration. It is yours already." At that, Hartland rose. "Might I join you in your box for the next act?"

Lewiston saw Miss Fontenoy's momentary look of horror. Whether it was because of Hartland's offer or because she realized she'd inadvertently behaved like a shameless flirt, he couldn't say. Whichever was the cause, her face first drained of color and then two spots of crimson leapt into her cheeks. Hartland took her lack of response as assent and was already making his way to them.

Lewiston took his original seat. "Miss Fontenoy!" he said in a harsh whisper. "It was…" He started to put his hand out to take the handkerchief from her, but Hartland had entered her box and was exchanging greetings with the viscountess, who begged him to take the seat next to her daughter.

Harry drew back. Somehow he knew that the duke would try to carry on a whispered conversation with Miss Fontenoy all through the third act, likely spoiling her enjoyment of the music. He knew, because Hartland had done exactly that to him through the second act. They'd only just arrived before it began, much to his annoyance.

Out of the corner of his eye, Lewiston watched Hartland's gaze surreptitiously take in Miss Fontenoy's entire body, lingering for the slightest moment on the back of her neck just below a soft curl and moving on to her breasts before he took his seat and leaned toward her to say something in her ear.

The lackeys left the stage having reset it for the next act and lit the footlights and chandeliers. Lewiston tried to focus on the music, but his ears strained to hear Hartland's whispers and his occasional glances revealed Miss Fontenoy's alternately vexed and amused expressions. What could he be saying to her that would atone for such egregious interruptions?

With a sigh, Lewiston acknowledged that he would never know.

# CHAPTER 9

"*I* must! I absolutely must! Surely you can arrange it for me? You know Mr. Taylor. You've said so. I would be willing to pay, and you've told me that money troubles have been plaguing him lately."

Olivia strode back and forth in front of Signore Tetrazzini, who had arrived to give her a vocal lesson the morning after the opera and found himself besieged with desperate pleas to help arrange something rather outrageous, something that had exploded into Olivia's imagination as an idea she simply must bring to life. "*Ma Signorina*, it is not done," he said.

"Why? Why isn't it done? Surely I cannot be corrupted simply by standing on a stage in front of an empty pit?"

"No, no *Ma Donna*," Tetrazzini said, wringing his hands and wrinkling his brow. "The *viscontessa*. Just think! *Pensa!*"

"She need never know. I will never tell her, nor will you. And I think if we pay Taylor enough we can swear him to secrecy as well."

Tetrazzini paced around the schoolroom shaking his head, stopping now and again with his hands on his hips, then putting his index finger to his pursed lips in a pensive manner before shaking his head again and continuing his agitated walk. After a few minutes, he stopped right in front of Olivia, who had watched his peregrinations intently. He opened his mouth to say something and closed it again.

"You've thought of something! Haven't you?" Olivia grabbed hold of the singing teacher's arms.

He politely loosed himself from her grip. "If I have, you must be *molto, molto attenta,* you know, careful. No one, not even Meester Taylor, must know *vostra nome.* You must be a secret. The temptation would be too ..." he paused, searching for the right word. *"Irresistibile."*

"I don't care what we must do. Tell me and I will manage it."

"First, I must consult the ... *costumista."* He nodded thoughtfully. *"Si.* I will go. She is *mia amica.* From long time. I will need to offer her ... *comprenda? ...* " Tetrazzini gave that unmistakably Italianate open-palmed shrug that meant *need I say more?*

"How much?" Olivia said, dashing over to the desk where she had a roll of bills hidden away, saved from what she hadn't spent of her liberal allowance. She came back to him with a five-pound note in her hand.

Tetrazzini opened his watery dark eyes wide at the sum, then checked himself and said, *"Si* Signorina Fontenoy. *È munifico."*

Olivia realized she could probably have given less to Tetrazzini for whatever purpose he had in mind. But she didn't really care. "When? When will you return to tell me what I must do?"

*"Domani.* Or the day that follows. *Arrivederla, Signorina,"* Tetrazzini said with a magnificent flourish of a bow, and left Olivia in possession of the schoolroom.

Olivia stood in the middle of that familiar space without

moving for a full minute after he departed. Had she done right to involve the tutor in such an enterprise? Ever since the night before, ever since hearing Catalani, Olivia had conceived a desperate desire to sing on the stage of the King's Theatre. Not in a performance, that wouldn't be necessary. She just wanted to sing so she could know what it felt like to send her voice up to fill the entire auditorium, from behind the footlights to the benches in the back of the upper gallery. Ever since February and the afternoon in Hyde Park, she knew her voice held enough power to do that. Added to this wish was one to perform the music in all its glorious simplicity, not twisted and tortured into figures designed to show off a voice rather than the brilliance of the composition. Even in her distraction when the duke sat next to her in act three she cringed at the famous soprano's occasional excesses—all of which were loudly cheered by her partisans.

She tossed and turned all night, unable to settle for thinking about it, trying to find a way to make it possible for her to sing on that stage.

But this wish wasn't all that had kept her awake at night. There were other memories from the evening that tickled at the edge of her mind. Try as she might, she couldn't banish the sensation of the duke's finger tracing a line along her forearm while pretending to hand her his opera glass. That, and the warmth of his breath as he leaned toward her ear to say something about some detail of the stage decorations. She'd been torn between telling him to be quiet, since he always seemed to do something distracting at the most important moments of the opera, and wishing he would do it again. This surprised her. She'd been able to resist his charms at Almack's, and kept aloof from him on their ride in the park. In the first instance, they were under the glare of a judging society. In the second, her own preoccupation and the circumstance of being on horseback kept them at a distance from each other.

But last night, in the relative privacy of a theatre box, with him sitting so close to her that she could smell the pomade in his hair and the faint masculine scent of snuff, he had broken through her icy reserve.

There was something intoxicating about having a man of the town, a handsome Corinthian sought after by so many women, pay his addresses to her. She was well aware that other eyes were upon them, assessing how closely he was attending to her, wondering if he was paying her serious court.

Yet she had no illusions that it was her beauty he was drawn to. How could she, when her mother regularly pointed out her physical flaws? And the rest of the world surely saw them too. The rest of the world must, therefore, be thinking what she was forced to consider as well. Her fortune was very likely the only lure that kept so desirable a man dangling after her. True as it undoubtedly was, the knowledge did nothing to alter the response his delicate flirtations awakened in her. She had never been flirted with before. To her knowledge, no man had actually looked at her with anything other than brotherly or fatherly affection. The look in Hartland's eyes could never be called brotherly. Would he propose? Might she marry him? Become a duchess? What would that be like?

Such thoughts were silly. She wasn't ready to become anything. What did she even know about him, after all? He had a reputation. Her mother had told her that, leaving out the specific details. Olivia knew enough to understand that having a reputation meant he had been with women who would not be admitted to any society drawing room. And so? Such antics were too common to be noteworthy.

If he was a gazetted fortune hunter and she knew it, why

then did she experience an uncomfortable thrill when he gazed at her with his deep-blue eyes flecked with silver, as if he could see through her gown, down to and beneath her shift? Could she be falling in love with him? Beyond what she'd read in novels, Olivia had no clear idea what love was.

The matter of the handkerchief had thrown her into even greater confusion. How considerate, how sensitive to have given it to her in a way that would not attract notice. After her attempt to restore it to the duke, when he pressed her to keep it she'd tucked it away in her reticule. She possessed it still, secreted it in a drawer of her dressing table. Silly, really. It was no more than a plain cambric square with a little bit of embroidery in one corner that had faded enough to obscure the design.

Remembering the handkerchief for some reason brought Lewiston to mind. What was it he tried to say to her when the duke left his seat to join them in their box? The marquess was not as handsome as the duke, but his brown eyes that turned down slightly at the outer corners held warmth and sympathy.

It was all such a puzzle. Perhaps it might become clearer the next day when the duke would take her for a ride in the park in his curricle. Her mother assured her that it would be a great honor to be driven by him in full view of the *ton.*

The most important matter, though, had nothing to do with courtship or love. Olivia gave herself a mental shake. What she must focus on for the present was music. She strolled over to the pianoforte and sat down to arrangements of several arias from *The Marriage of Figaro* propped on the desk. She shuffled through them until she alighted on *"Dove sono,"* gave herself the C, and began to sing.

*a*delheid did not have to wait long for Lady Mariana to make good on her promise to call. The day after her encounter with Hartland, while she sat in her drawing room writing a note to Lord Brattle, Grandison announced, "Lady Mariana Thorne," in sepulchral tones. She stood and absently smoothed down her gown and touched her hair—as she'd been in the habit of doing whenever the prince was announced lest he find some fault with her appearance and abuse her for it.

"Princess Adelheid!" Mariana said, advancing toward her with outstretched hands. "I come with several invitations for you. The first—and I think most important one—is to accompany me immediately to Madame Pauline's so that I may introduce you to the modiste who is the toast of the *ton*. The other is for you to attend a ball for the Honorable Olivia Fontenoy's introduction to society. She is the daughter of Viscount Ambrose and the ball is at their house on Mount Street tomorrow."

A ball! So soon? All at once Adelheid perceived the true generosity of this lady's interest in her. She would act as guide and help her choose a gown that would be appropriate so that she would make a creditable first appearance in society. She little expected to receive such consideration. "I can't thank you enough, Lady Mariana," she said, sitting down and gesturing to a chair near her. "*Aber*, I don't understand why you should take such an interest in a perfect stranger."

Mariana sat and gazed searchingly at Adelheid for a while. "Yes, Lord Brattle told me about the extraordinary color of your eyes."

"Ah. The mystery is solved. Brattle has been very helpful to me in my move from Vienna."

"He's fond of you, you know. But you'll need more than his sponsorship if you intend to settle in London and be accepted into the *ton*. I think it's mad, personally. You'll find I married quite outside my class but I couldn't be happier. Still, you would find yourself utterly bored if you didn't at least have parties and the opera to attend." She stood again. "Now I shall wait here for you to ready yourself for our excursion. I'm bursting with curiosity about you, but I expect I'll have time to discover what could possibly have drawn a wealthy, widowed Austrian princess to London. So you should prepare your story. I doubt it was fear that Buonaparte would once more invade!"

Adelheid couldn't help smiling and entering into Lady Mariana's effervescent mood. It was indeed just what she needed. A shopping trip in congenial company. Brattle had assured her she needn't worry about the money, at least at first. Tradesmen were quite happy to extend credit to anyone they saw occupied a lofty place in society. Adelheid guessed that being in the company of Lady Mariana would reassure any who might be skeptical.

. . .

AN HOUR LATER, ADELHEID FOUND HERSELF THE OBJECT OF busy admiration at a very chic modiste's establishment in Conduit Street. Her measurements were taken and Madame Pauline herself promised her that the evening gown of amethyst silk with a silver gauze overdress would be delivered to her the following day—in plenty of time for Miss Fontenoy's come-out ball.

"I presume you will need a riding habit?" said a very dapper gentleman who hurried into the showroom once Adelheid had clothed herself again. Adelheid couldn't help admiring the cut of his form-fitting coat and the understated elegance of his striped waistcoat.

"Of course she will, Mr. Gordon!" Mariana said. "I think a vibrant color, don't you?"

At this, Madame Pauline, looking smart and neat with an impish smile and an upturned nose piped up in her thinly disguised London accent, "She'll look a picture in any color. I think a dark green would make the most of those eyes, if I may be so bold, Princess."

After another hour in the plush surroundings of the highly fashionable shop, Mariana declared they were ready to leave. "I expect you're quite worn out," she said to Adelheid. "You likely still haven't recovered from your journey from Vienna. If Miss Fontenoy's ball weren't so soon, I'd have given you a little more time to settle in."

Adelheid shook her head, "Lady Mariana, please don't apologize! I am deeply grateful to you. If it's not too much trouble, I would be most appreciative if you would direct me to the best milliner."

"Call me Mariana! I insist, Princess. None of this *lady* business. And let's go together. I need a new hat myself."

"Even better! And you must call me Adelheid."

They proceeded on the best of terms to Madame Carlier's in St. James's where they each acquired the necessary hats and headdresses, and then on to Harding & Howell to browse trimmings and furbelows all the while becoming better acquainted.

By the time Adelheid returned to Grosvenor Square and her footmen had unloaded the parcels from Mariana's barouche, her mind was in a whirl. It had been nearly a decade since she had felt so uninhibited, so able to enter into the spirit of frivolity of such a morning. She caught a glimpse of her face in the large hall mirror as she untied her hat and gave it to the first footman, Adam, her cheeks aglow and her eyes alight. *How foolish,* she thought. Such things mean nothing, truly. Perhaps it was little more than vanity. But in her heart she knew it meant more than that. It behooved her to put herself forward creditably for Otto's sake and to ensure the success of her scheme.

Recalling that she was supposed to be giving her son his lessons that morning, she turned to Adam and said, "Where is Otto?"

"In the schoolroom, with Mr. Rutherford," he answered, with a slight bow.

Ah, she thought. Nicholas had stepped easily into the role of Otto's instructor. And as he was a man she thought he possibly might have more influence on the boy. Otto had a propensity for mischief that had so far manifested itself in his finding obscure places around the house to hide and jumping out unexpectedly to scare the servants, but would no doubt soon become more inventive.

She climbed the stairs to the schoolroom on the third floor, a little breathless by the time she entered the room. She found Otto bent over a tablet, assuming he was learning to read simple English words. His back was to her so he didn't immediately realize she was there. Nicholas signaled to her to be silent and he continued.

"F-fetlock," he said, followed by "pommel," then "curricle." At that point he looked up proudly into Nicholas's eyes.

Adelheid walked forward and Otto jumped up from his chair and ran to her, wrapped his arms around her waist and squeezed her with glee before letter her go and regaling her in English and German with what he had learned that day.

"Master Otto!" Nicholas's commanding voice broke into Otto's flood of words. The boy stopped, let go of Adelheid, stepped back, and executed a polite bow.

"How ... do ... you ... do, Your ... Highness," he said slowly, as if having to drag each word out of his memory.

"Very well, thank you Sir," Adelheid said, barely able to suppress the laughter that threatened to bubble up and spill into the room. "It's time for nuncheon. Go down to the kitchen and Mrs. Gillum will give you something to eat."

He needed no more prompting. He tore off out the door and down the stairs.

"Would you explain what exactly you were doing please Nicholas," Adelheid said, not without a note of censure in her voice.

"It was the only way I could get him to focus on the lesson itself. Making him learn words he cared about. Right now, it seems all he wants to think about is horses."

Adelheid could well believe that her spirited son, now well-nourished and given the freedom of a large house with all its wondrous secrets, would require some coaxing to acquire the knowledge absolutely necessary to his future prosperity. "If you could just mix in some other phrases such as *peer of the realm*, and *delighted to make your acquaintance* he might well make more suitable progress." She softened her words with a smile, realizing that one of the reasons the scene she encountered took her so aback was that she felt vaguely envious of Nicholas's increasingly close relationship with Otto.

With a sigh she also recognized the necessity of reconciling herself to this, as she had little time to focus on anything other than captivating Hartland. She had impressed him favorably at their first meeting. But she had only a few more weeks to utterly ensnare him.

Ensnare. It sounded so base, so purposeful. And yet, it was her intention.

Thanks to Lady Mariana, the task ahead of her looked to be a good deal more feasible than she had initially thought. Her introduction to the duke had occurred by chance, which she could not have foreseen. Now she must ensure that she appears to her best advantage whenever they happen to meet again. The trick was not to make it look as though she were casting out lures, as though she wanted to trap him. The dashing Hartland must be accustomed to the wiles and stratagems of ambitious damsels and their matchmaking mamas. A hint of such behavior would send him running.

So she must force herself to be no more than polite and a little distant at the ball and make an effort to converse with everyone Mariana introduced to her. For the rest of the afternoon ahead, she would study the hefty copy of *Burke's Peerage* she found on the sparsely populated shelves of what must at one time have been an impressive library. It wouldn't do for her to make an error of precedence at her very first *ton* party.

# CHAPTER 11

*J*t wasn't until the day before Olivia's come-out ball that Signore Tetrazzini came back with a plan. A plan—and a mask.

When he held it out to Olivia, she stared at it blankly. "What's it for?"

He then explained that the only way he could permit her to step onto the stage at the King's Theatre without doing damage to his own conscience was if no one knew who she was. Not the management, not the orchestra musicians, not the army of stage hands, set decorators, and seamstresses. No one.

"For, Signorina, there will be *molto gente* there, the same during daytime as evening."

Olivia knew nothing about the workings of an opera company or a theatre except what was visible to an audience on the night of a performance. What the singing teacher said to her made obvious sense once she thought about it. "But will they not mind me singing while they work? What will they think?" She couldn't imagine that a masked lady arriving unexpectedly, singing an aria on the stage and then disappearing just as mysteriously wouldn't create some disturbance.

Tetrazzini shrugged. "Eh, they are, *scusa Signorina, volgare, ignorante.*"

This hardly seemed likely. Surely it took a great deal of training and education to create such spectacles. But she didn't argue with Tetrazzini. She simply took the mask from him.

It was plain white stiffened cloth made to cover the face completely, with holes for the eyes and nose and mouth. A little bit like a loo mask, only tied on with ribbons rather than held on a stick. Tetrazzini fastened the ribbons for her. Once she had it on, she discovered that the holes for the eyes were a little too close together, and the mouth hole wasn't big enough. "I'll end up singing into the mask instead of the theatre," she said, her voice muffled.

"*Si, si,*" Tetrazzini said as he stood in front of her. "Perhaps you can show ... the eyes, and ..." He pointed to his mouth. "How much you need *per cantare.*"

"I need a pencil," Olivia said.

Tetrazzini patted his pockets and after a bit produced a stubby pencil. Olivia took it and, looking in the mirror, found or guessed at the location of her eyes and size of her mouth, and drew the guidelines on the mask itself.

"Is it possible to have it modified quickly?" she said, handing the mask back to Tetrazzini.

Olivia was so engrossed in figuring out how to make the mask work better without revealing too much that she failed to hear her mother coming up the stairs to the schoolroom, and she barely had time to hide the mask under a book on the desk before the door opened to admit a rather winded Lady Ambrose.

"Olivia! Here you are."

"As you see, mother. With Signore Tetrazzini."

Lady Ambrose was a small, plump woman, a former beauty whose pleasant face bore the same wide-set eyes as her daughter, but instead of the drab brown of Olivia's locks the viscountess had a mass of barely controlled golden curly hair. "The duke is here to take you out in his curricle." She paused and took a few breaths. "He's in the long drawing room. His groom is walking the horses."

Olivia had completely forgotten. What did that say about the state of her infatuation if she could forget about an arrangement to see him? "I was just—I won't be a moment."

"I had no idea Tetrazzani was coming today," Lady Ambrose said. "Wasn't your lesson just the other day? Well, I suppose you might need to be ready to sing for the guests tomorrow evening."

*No!* She had sworn not to. Of course, her mother didn't know this. Not yet. What could she tell her? Better not to coat it in cream. "I shall not be prevailed upon to sing tomorrow, Mama."

Lady Ambrose tittered. "What can you mean? Of course you will sing. You have a lovely voice, when you don't sing too loud."

"I am afraid, Mama, that you are mistaken. I shall not sing, because my voice is not—pleasing at the moment. I have a roughness in my throat. Is that not so, Signore?" She turned to Tetrazzini for support.

After a meaningful glare from Olivia the singing master said, "*Ma donna viscontessa! È molto sfortunato, mi scusa moltissimo, la Signorina* Fontenoy, she is not ready."

"Not ready? After years of lessons! Well, I never." Lady Ambrose drew herself up, lifted her chin, and tried to look down her diminutive nose at Tetrazzini who, though not tall, towered over her. "Sir, how do you justify your exorbitant fees?"

"Mama! Signore Tetrazzini is the best. He is only trying to

protect my voice. You wouldn't want me to embarrass myself or you, would you?"

This hit a concordant note with Lady Ambrose, as Olivia knew it would. Olivia had grown up being told what an embarrassment she was to her family for not being the great beauty her mother had once been, or being so shy that she hardly spoke a word in company. She understood her mother's own fear of still being thought a mushroom. It was this that made her put disproportionate effort into making sure her daughter behaved in a manner that suited her consequence.

"Of course I would not want that," Lady Ambrose said.

Olivia pictured her mother as a distressed hen whose feathers had at last been smoothed down and barely stifled a chuckle. "I shall come to the drawing room directly. I must just have another word with Signore Tetrazzini." She took hold of her mother's arm and led her to the schoolroom door.

"You'll change your dress first!"

Olivia looked down at her sprig muslin gown with the lace sleeves and tiers of ruffled lace at the neck. She supposed she must change into a driving dress, although why exactly she couldn't say. She planted a kiss on her mother's cheek and firmly nudged her into the hallway, shut the door, and turned back to Tetrazzini. "How quickly can the mask be altered? And what happens next?"

HARTLAND WAS NOT ACCUSTOMED TO BEING KEPT WAITING BY a lady he was granting the honor of driving in his curricle at the hour of the strut. Especially not an ingenuous girl he probably wouldn't have looked at twice were it not for her fortune. But that was spiteful. He might have overlooked her at first, but having become better acquainted with her he was beginning to appreciate her subtle charms. These were just not of the sort he normally sought—or noticed—in a lady.

He liked that she didn't prattle aimlessly on subjects that held little interest to him, for instance. No gossip and meanness about other ladies, flights of enthusiasm about the latest silks and laces, or which *ton* parties would be the biggest squeezes. Her observations, though infrequent, were intelligent and surprising in their variety. And if he could coax a smile out of her, she lit up in a way that made her quite pretty. Of course, there was also her figure.

Unfortunately, that day she did not wear anything that revealed her perfect bosom. Instead she came down the stairs to the drawing room in a modest gown that covered her up to her neck, over which she wore a spencer jacket that—if anything—made her look less well-endowed than she was. Her poke bonnet framed her face becomingly, though, and its green ribbons brought out the flecks of green in her eyes.

"Lovely day," Hartland said, gaining no response from Miss Fontenoy as he handed her up into the elegant curricle drawn by two perfectly matched bays. The silence continued for several minutes as they drove down Mount Street toward the park.

"Did you have luck at Ascot?" Olivia asked without preamble once they'd entered through the corner gate.

"Do you know aught of horse racing?" he asked by way of reply, not wanting to admit that he'd not done well at all and could ill afford his losses.

"Very little. Only that gentlemen generally lose a lot of money on it."

This surprised a hearty laugh out of Hartland. "You have hit it exactly."

"Where is the pleasure in that?"

He thought about this for a moment as he turned his

horses onto the carriage drive. "It's not the winning or losing that thrills. It's the risk, the chance. It's the excitement of watching a horse that you've seen has all the right points prove his mettle and sail home in advance of the field—and then talking it all over with your friends afterward." He surprised himself with this answer. He'd never really thought about it before. One bet on horses because it was what one was expected to do. Yet he did derive enjoyment from it. Less, of course, when his horse didn't win. He wondered if any other of his activities gave him true pleasure, or if he pursued some of them because it was expected, not because he actually wanted to.

After another interval of silence Hartland turned to look at Miss Fontenoy and found she was examining him somewhat quizzically. Not with that simpering, adoring look he was so accustomed to from the naïve come-outs but as if she was trying to decipher something about him. "What amuses you, Miss Fontenoy?"

She looked away quickly and smiled. "I was just wondering what you really thought of the opera the other night. There are no winners or losers there. No opportunity to gamble on whether the soprano or the tenor will garner louder bravos." Her smile broadened and lit up her eyes.

He was momentarily disarmed by this comment. When he thought about it, everything he truly enjoyed—hunting, boxing, racing—involved winning in some way or other. "But surely there is an element of competition even in the arts," he said. "One strives to be the best musician or singer and win the best roles. Or the best painter to win accolades from the Royal Academy."

She didn't answer right away. When she did, she swiveled a little in her seat so she faced him. "Is everything in life a competition? Are you competing for me?"

Hartland caught himself before uttering a caustic reply.

What a thing to say! He was more accustomed to being the prize, and the fact that the daughter of a viscount whose viscountess was the daughter of a cit—no matter how wealthy—could presume to be the object of a duke's concerted efforts was a bit of a blow to his self-esteem. "It seems clear that you are not interested in competing for me," he said, somewhat acidly.

"I've offended you. I'm sorry." She flashed him a rueful smile. "It's just that I can't help wondering because I know I'm not a beauty, and you've never offered for anyone before. At least, not that I've been told. It seems to me that it would be better to know exactly where we stand."

"A revolutionary idea," Hartland said, a note of irony in his voice. He couldn't help being a bit intrigued by this odd young lady who appeared to have few social graces and little interest in the fact that he was a top-of-the-trees Corinthian. "And, as we're being blunt, I suspect you know that many eligible gentlemen in the *ton* would choose to pursue you for your fortune alone."

"Are you not?"

That was certainly a question. It raised an unaccustomed blush in his face. He'd started out doing so, certainly. And the money was still the most attractive thing about her. "Not that alone," he said, unable—or unwilling—to explain further. "I would be lying if I said it didn't matter to me though." Never in all his life had he ever been so honest with a lady. Hartland suspected he'd been cornered into it by knowing that if he lied she would certainly be able to tell.

At that moment, Miss Fontenoy gripped his arm and said, "Look! There's Lord Lewiston! Has he seen us?" The carriage rocked as she brazenly waved her arm above her head to catch the attention of the marquess.

Lewiston rode over on his cover hack to meet them on the carriage drive. After exchanging greetings, Lewiston said,

"So what did you think of the great Catalani, Miss Fontenoy?"

She laughed. "Oh, she has a splendid voice and I was pleased she chose to sing at least some of the notes as Mozart intended. I was amused that she thought she could improve on such magnificent music."

The two of them shared a laugh about this and several other matters completely lost on the duke to do with pitch and vibrato. *Damn*, he thought. He should have asked about the opera. Instead, it was she who had done the polite thing and asked about what interested him, the races. Well, the opportunity was lost now.

He stayed mostly silent as Lewiston and Miss Fontenoy talked about music and singing. As their conversation continued, Miss Fontenoy's countenance underwent a remarkable transformation. That detachment, the reserve that seemed so integral a part of her character melted away. She smiled and chatted easily with Lewiston, who clearly appealed to her sense of humor with his incisive observations on the personalities of the great divas and what they had to look forward to in the coming season.

"But I'm afraid Hartland finds all this a bit tedious," Lewiston said after a few minutes.

Miss Fontenoy turned her shining eyes on the duke and smiled apologetically. "Oh! I'm sorry, I was carried away. I haven't seen many operas. *Le Nozze* was only my second, so I have a great deal to say about it."

"My friend has most ungenerously exposed my ignorance," Hartland said, not without an edge of irritation. "But I would gladly be instructed by you, if you can tolerate a simpleton."

"Are you really interested? I warn you, I would take you at your word," she said.

At that, Hartland met his friend's eyes and saw in them

something that took him very much by surprise. He wasn't smiling. In fact, he detected an odd mixture of sadness and anger. Hartland had never seen Lewiston look like that. What could it mean? Surely he wasn't interested in Miss Fontenoy for himself. He'd been head over ears in love with Lady Mariana a year ago, and Miss Fontenoy was nothing like her.

In any case, it would never have occurred to Hartland to consider Lewiston a rival of any kind. Their friendship had been founded on the congenial realization that they shared none of the same interests, other than good conversation and horses, and Hartland thought that if anything, Harry was rather in awe of him.

All the same, Miss Fontenoy had come to life as she spoke to Harry, and looked at him through eyes aglow with enthusiasm. There was an ease between the two of them that bore no resemblance to the awkward pauses in conversation and strained moments that characterized his own interactions with her. But despite her reticence, the duke sensed the crackle of attraction between himself and the heiress: the parted lips when he "accidentally" leaned too close to her and other tell-tale signs that his presence affected her on a barely conscious level.

"I'm afraid I must be getting home," Lewiston said.

"Oh, you are coming to my ball tomorrow, aren't you?" Miss Fontenoy said, not without a note of anxiety in her voice.

"Of course," Lewiston said.

But he didn't ask her to reserve any dances for him, Hartland noticed. He knew of Lewiston's ineptitude in the ballroom. He also knew that he himself cut a very dashing figure when dancing, and smiled.

"Have you known the marquess for a long time?" Miss Fontenoy asked as they headed back to Mount Street.

"My whole life," Hartland answered.

"I like him," she said.

Not too much, I hope, Hartland thought as he handed her down from the curricle and waited until she was safely inside the house before heading back to Grosvenor Square.

# CHAPTER 12

The next morning, just after Adelheid settled Otto in the schoolroom for his lessons with Nicholas, someone beat a rhythmic summons with the front door knocker. She ignored it, having told Grandison to say she was not at home to visitors on the unlikely chance that any would come.

The butler opened the street door and she could just discern the dark tones of his colorless voice. But despite his quelling pronouncement, a clear female voice sailed up from the hall saying, "Nonsense, *Monsieur!* The *princesse* will see me, *j'en suis sûr.*"

Adelheid put down the Morning Post—which she'd been perusing for social gossip—sprang up and ran out of the drawing room. "Félicité!" she said, intercepting her friend halfway up the stairs to the first floor. She looked down to see Grandison staring up disapprovingly. Her friend was dressed respectably but was clearly not a member of the *ton.*

"Ah, you thought you could hide away from me when you came to London, did you not?" Félicité said, her dark eyes merry.

"How did you know I was here? I planned to write to you tomorrow." Adelheid turned to Grandison, who had made his own stately progress up the stairs, and asked him to bring ratafia to the drawing room.

"You ask how I knew of your arrival in London? Here, as everywhere, *les domestiques*. It is *inutile* to keep anything from them, as I'm sure you know," Félicité said.

The two ladies spoke on light subjects until they were alone. When the footman closed the door behind him, Félicité glanced quickly to make sure it was completely shut, leaned forward, and said with a lowered voice, "I thought you said you would never come to London, that ze English did not like your voice, so you would not waste it singing to ignorants with no taste."

Had she said that? How foolish and arrogant she must have been! "I'm not here to sing," she said as she sipped her ratafia.

"Oh?" The seamstress's eyebrows lifted and she pursed her lips slightly. "I had thought, per'aps, as a widow you might go back to the stage." She shrugged prettily. "Then say it, for what are you 'ere?"

"To find a husband."

Félicité managed somehow not to spit out her ratafia. After covering her mouth with her handkerchief and swallowing, she said, "*Mais*, you are not long widowed, yes?"

"But ten days. Yet circumstances force me to this expedient."

"Is it money? *Alors*, I heard the prince left you *tout!*"

"He did," Adelheid said, standing and strolling over to the window, giving herself a little time to decide how much to take Félicité into her confidence. "You always have been very, *discrète*, have you not my friend?"

"Yes! Yes! Please tell me all. I see you have a tale to share with me, and per'aps I may be of some assistance?"

In that moment, Adelheid decided she could not manage in London without a female confidante outside of the *ton*. So she sat next to her friend on the sofa and told her the entire story.

Once she had fully digested the tale, Félicité asked with an edge of sarcasm in her voice, "And 'ave you found this nobleman who might be willing to take so bizarre a step, and with such haste?"

"In fact, I have. I believe I know the very gentleman who might answer for me. It happens that he is a neighbor. Or I should say that there is no happenstance in the question. Perhaps you know of him? The Duke of Hartland."

Félicité sat silent, mouth open in astonishment. *"Sainte Vierge!* But how will you do this? You know it is said he pursues an heiress—she is very rich, and very young."

No, she hadn't known. *So soon,* Adelheid thought. His demeanor toward her the other day had been all courtesy and warm interest. But of course he would be too well mannered to have behaved in any other way. "How far has he gone in this suit?" If he was truly attached to someone else it would make her task more difficult but not necessarily impossible. She had confidence in her ability to unseat a young, inexperienced ingenue.

"It is not known. But he must become betrothed soon if he is to outrun his creditors."

"That will make it more of a challenge, certainly, but all is not lost. He is not yet betrothed, and I have met him—and impressed him."

"I pity this heiress if she is in love."

"Do you know her name?" Adelheid asked.

"I believe it is...Miss Font-*quelque-chose.*"

"Miss Fontenoy." And she would meet her that very evening. What were the odds?

*"Oui!* But I do not know how she looks."

Adelheid smiled and turned the conversation. They chatted away another hour until it was time for the seamstress to leave. Félicité stood in the hall with Adelheid, her bonnet placed becomingly atop her dark curls and tied in a clever bow under one ear. As she drew on her kid gloves, she searched her friend's eyes, and said, "Oh, *ma chère*, I thought you must have a life *tout charmant*, in a château with your so 'andsome prince. But I will contrive how to help you if I can. Per'aps this duke will come to the theatre looking for an opera *danseuse*."

Adelheid laughed. She remembered those lustful swains, always glad she'd managed to keep them at bay. "I will send word to you when I need you."

She embraced her friend and they parted.

After that, Adelheid was so keyed up she could hardly focus on preparations for Miss Fontenoy's ball. What a chance had fallen in her way! It was even more important now that she dazzle the duke.

"It's time, Your Highness," her abigail said after settling the delicate diamond tiara on her head so that her hair curled around it becomingly. It was one of the few pieces Adelheid hadn't given to Brattle to sell, guessing that she would need some jewels before copies could be made of them. "You are so beautiful! I 'spect your dance card'll be full before five minutes pass."

Adelheid smiled kindly at her and pressed a coin into her hand.

"Oh no, Ma'am! I mean, Your Highness."

"Why not? You have surely earned it, and more." Indeed, the girl had risen to the occasion of dressing a diamond of the first water—albeit one well past her first youth—and Adelheid thought she had seldom looked better.

Yet she was oddly nervous. She had presided over many dinners and balls with nobility and royalty in attendance, but that was at a time and in a place where her station had been well defined, her duties prescribed. She had not entered a ballroom as simply a woman, a sentient being hoping to find something, a connection at least, to another. For a brief moment, the idea that she could be hoping for love crossed her mind only to be banished as quickly as it arose. She was too old, her needs too mundane, to countenance the heady intoxication of love.

Besides, there was no time. She had but a few more weeks to ensure her son's future.

# CHAPTER 13

*H*artland tried to persuade his mother to attend Miss Fontenoy's ball, but she still did not feel equal to leaving the comfort and privacy of her own apartments. So once he was dressed in his finest evening wear—long-tailed coat perfectly fitted to his broad shoulders; satin knee breeches that, although not as form-hugging as his pantaloons, still hinted at muscular thighs beneath them; neck cloth; waistcoat; shirt of brilliant white; and the only ornament a distinctive diamond bar pin that had been his father's—he went to see the dowager duchess in her sitting room.

His mother was a delicate-boned patrician lady with a countenance that, although faded by years, had lost none of its perfect proportions. She was pale, he thought, yet when she lifted her eyes to his an appreciative sparkle soon vanquished their momentary sadness. "My handsome son!" she said, holding out her hand to him.

He strode over to where she sat on a chair by the hearth and bent down to place a kiss on her cheek, then took a seat opposite her. "Flatterer!"

This made her smile. "I daresay there's nothing I could tell you that you haven't already heard from countless beauties."

"Nonsense. In any case, none of them could hold a candle to you, Ma'am."

"Now who's the flatterer!" Her smile faded. "So, you're off to the Ambrose ball. Tell me about the girl. You're serious about this one, I collect? Not before time, my boy."

He had mentioned to her briefly that he was pursuing the heiress, but had avoided going into much detail about her. The duchess, he believed, was not aware of what terrible circumstances they were in, and had only a vague idea that her beloved husband had not left his affairs in very good order. Hartland took care that she should not be worried by the fact that they were close to utter ruin. He hoped that his alliance with Miss Fontenoy would mean that it would never be necessary for the dowager to know precisely how things stood.

"She's quite attractive, and intelligent. And on the tall side. She likes opera," he said, wracking his brain for anything he thought his mother might like to know about her.

"Philip!" she said, shaking her head. "You know that's not what I mean. Are you in love with her?"

*No, but what does it matter,* he thought. What could he say? He never lied to his mother, only avoided mention of matters she would not like. "I'm not sure I know what love is."

"That's no answer, but I will accept it for now. You haven't known her for long. Besides, I know I can't necessarily expect you to find the kind of happiness your father and I had."

Theirs had been a true love match. When Hartland thought about it at all, he realized that they'd set a standard so high that he'd given up trying to attain it before he really started. Most of the time it didn't matter to him. Perhaps that was because he always avoided the kind of relationships that might lead to marriage, and only found himself backed into that corner now.

"When the time comes," he said, "I will bring her to meet you."

"Before you offer for her?"

Probably not, Hartland thought. He couldn't face the duchess's piercing, all-perceiving gaze. She would see how things were the instant she saw them together. "I must go, or I will be unconscionably late," he said, rising.

The duchess gave a short laugh. "You already are, my dear! But kiss me. And tell me all about it in the morning."

OLIVIA HAD TO ADMIT IT: HER BALL GOWN WAS MAGNIFICENT. Madame Pauline had put her very best efforts into it, telling her that her finest designer had created it just for her. Since it was an open secret that this meant it was conceived by none other than Augusta, Lady Bridlington, Olivia felt uncharacteristically pleased with her appearance. The gown fit her as if she'd been born wearing it, yet flowed airily as she moved. The primrose silk slip was topped with a white spider gauze overdress dotted about with tiny braid bows that clustered just beneath the high waist and became increasingly sparse toward the hem. Slightly bigger bows followed the low neckline, which was embellished in the center by one large bow cunningly worked to resemble a rose. Her white satin evening gloves and slippers, a gold satin reticule, and white lace fan completed the ensemble. She wore no more than a string of impressive, perfect pearls around her neck, and clever Hetty had threaded primrose silk ribbons through her drab curls.

Standing at the top of the grand stairs at the entrance to the ballroom, Olivia was calmer and more sure of herself than she had expected to be at that moment, flanked by parents who didn't always know what to make of their daughter. Things they expected her to like she abhorred, and the oddest things took her fancy. Lady Ambrose was never quite certain how Olivia would behave when she took her out anywhere. As soon as she saw Olivia descend from her bedchamber she visibly relaxed. Olivia sighed with relief. It meant that her mother would not hover near her and nudge her to be polite or to speak to someone important.

Olivia's relative calm that evening was partly because she was much more nervous about what would occur the next morning while everyone in the house except the servants would still be asleep.

"You look almost pretty, m'dear," the viscount said when he joined them to receive their guests, interrupting her train of thought and peering through his quizzing glass at her. "Still too thin to be a beauty, but yer skin's good. Got good teeth too, if you'd only show 'em more." Ladies were required to smile. Smiles were part of their basic wardrobe. The viscount took little interest in his daughter beyond such occasional observations, having been disappointed not to have a son to inherit his title, which was entailed to a distant cousin in the north.

His disappointments kept the viscount in the country most of the year, but he had succumbed to his wife's summons for the purpose of Olivia's ball, suffering the unaccustomed evening dress pulled tight across his paunch, and Olivia knew his not-altogether-kind comments were a function of his own irritation rather than anything she had done.

In contrast, Lady Ambrose beamed.

Everyone in the *haut ton* had been invited and accepted, and Ebbings, the butler, announced guest after guest—

hundreds of them. Standing in one place was by far the most tiring thing to do and Olivia had to remind herself to keep her shoulders back, her chin high, and her smile bright. By ten o'clock she sagged ever so slightly, and not just from physical fatigue. Neither Hartland nor Lewiston had arrived yet. Guests were fully occupied with flirting and conversation. But the younger ones would soon be restless for the dancing to begin—and that couldn't happen until Olivia took the floor with Hartland.

When the butler at last announced His Grace, the Duke of Hartland, just after Lord and Lady Fitzallen, Olivia's pulse quickened. He mounted the steps with a dazzling smile and his eyes looking as bright and intense as ever. He greeted the viscountess and then Olivia, taking her gloved hand and raising it slowly to his lips. "You are a vision," he said, and Olivia felt he was sincere, not just flirting, because she knew she looked beautiful. As beautiful as she could ever look.

Guests were still trickling in, so Olivia had to remain with her parents. While she stood there she couldn't help watching the duke out of the corner of her eye as he moved through the crowd, nodding to acquaintances, stopping to talk to friends. He made no effort to hide his looks of frank appraisal at all the young ladies. It was, Olivia had come to believe, in his blood, just like his quality and his athletic abilities. His nature. She would no more expect him not to gaze at an attractive lady passing by him than give up his membership in the Four Horse Club.

The question was whether, knowing this, she could be happy married to him. Whether the flutter he caused in her when he concentrated the full force of his seductive gaze on her would be enough to sustain her through what she feared would be long stretches of wandering attention. Would he come to resent her if he was financially dependent upon her wealth?

After an hour her smile began to feel pasted on and her feet were numb. As the stream petered out, Olivia suddenly wondered why Lewiston hadn't yet arrived. Would he actually come? She would be disappointed if he didn't. Why was that? He'd said he would be there. He wouldn't stay away unless something had happened to him. Could he be ill?

She was momentarily distracted by the arrival of Lady Mariana Thorne along with a guest she had written to Lady Ambrose about. Since this guest happened to bear the title of princess, it had taken no convincing at all for the viscountess to welcome the addition to the company.

"Miss Fontenoy!" Lady Mariana said after greeting Olivia's parents. "I am so pleased to see you being launched into the world at last! We must get to know one another better this season."

Mariana had come to Olivia's rescue in the previous season when she wasn't yet out, but had accompanied her mother to a small dinner party at Bridlington house in Berkeley Square. Mariana had played the piano, and Lady Ambrose tried to push her daughter toward the instrument to play and sing. Their quiet disagreement started to attract notice when Mariana swooped over to smooth the viscountess's feathers and assure her that she was about to invite everyone to the card room for a few rubbers of whist. This elevated Mariana to the status of a heroine in Olivia's eyes.

But Olivia was unprepared for the sight of the lady who followed Mariana up the stairs. She was the most beautiful woman she had ever seen and she found it necessary to remind herself not to stare.

"I thank you for inviting me to your ball. I am a stranger in London, and have been relying on Lady Mariana's kindness to introduce me in town."

Her voice had the combination of crispness and roundness that often resulted from vocal training. *She would be a mezzo*, Olivia thought, curtseying to the princess and trying not to make it obvious that she was dazzled by the blue-green eyes that looked into hers.

The two women passed into the saloon and a few more guests came in after them, but all eyes followed the princess in her progress around the room. *Perhaps*, Olivia thought, *she will take the attention away from me.* This idea appealed to her, and, once again, Olivia mentally thanked Lady Mariana for her intervention, even if she didn't realize she was doing it.

Olivia began to prepare herself for Lord Lewiston's absence when at last Ebbings announced, "The Most Honorable The Marquess of Lewiston." He walked up the stairs alone, the final guest to arrive, a hesitant look on his face. Olivia had an impulse to hold out her hands to him and encourage him to come up but of course she couldn't do so. Instead she gave him her warmest smile and was answered by his own broad grin that crinkled the corners of his slightly downturned eyes. When he reached her and she put out her hand to him, he bowed over it but did not kiss it— and she was sorry. "I'd almost thought you weren't going to come after all," she said to him.

"So did I." A flicker of rueful sadness passed across his face.

"You'll find many of your acquaintances here already. I'm afraid I must go and open the ball." She tried to keep her tone light. His bow to her before he walked off to join the other guests heading toward the ballroom had the slightest air of defeat in it.

"Come, Olivia!" her mother said. "Your partner is waiting for you."

OLIVIA HADN'T DANCED WITH HARTLAND AT ALMACK'S because he was in mourning. Since was now six months since his father's death and this was a private ball, it was seen as less shocking for someone in his position to stand up a few times. So when the set formed and Olivia found herself facing the duke at the head of the line of ten couples, a sudden clench of nerves knotted her stomach. She was a passable dancer but no one would call her graceful. Not like Lady Bridlington or Miss Charteris, who were next to her in the line. She suspected Princess Adelheid would outshine them all on the dance floor. That lady was a short way down opposite Lord Peterham. While the couples were still settling into their places Olivia noticed Hartland and the princess exchange a quick glance, each turning away with a small smile.

"You know the princess?" Olivia asked.

"I met her by chance the other day. She's a neighbor."

Before she could ask any other questions the orchestra played the introduction. Olivia smiled. She chose the musicians herself, true professionals. It didn't matter about the guests. The music would carry the evening along. Focusing on the music sustained her through the dance, and she discovered she was able to look into Hartland's eyes when required, have light conversation, and smile with genuine pleasure.

When the first two sets ended, Olivia found herself surrounded by gentlemen eager to claim her for forthcoming dances. Her card filled up with names, most of which were unfamiliar to her: Bournville, Charlton, de Lappe, Portsmouth and more, until she had only one space left. Hartland would not be permitted to dance with her again, having had his two and in any case she spotted him across the ballroom in a knot of gentlemen talking to the princess.

In fact, Olivia didn't actually want to dance with the duke again, although he was a capable and considerate partner. What she wanted was to dance with Lewiston. She looked around for him in vain. She had kept a dance for him, but he appeared not to be in the ballroom. Three different gentlemen took her out for the next three sets and although she went through the motions, she hardly paid any attention to what she was doing. At every opportunity she surreptitiously glanced around for the marquess, but he did not appear. Would he have escaped to the card room? Surely not!

When Lord Tillmartin came to claim her for his set, she asked to be excused until the second dance so she could go to the retiring room. Instead, she hurried through the saloons and drawing rooms and peeked into the supper room and the card room looking for Lewiston. What if he'd gone home? But he wouldn't just leave. That would be terribly impolite.

She had almost abandoned hope when she looked up to the balcony where the orchestra sat. There he was, perched on an extra gilt chair quite nearby them, just listening. She sighed. Given her choice, she would be up there too. But she could not absent herself.

So Olivia simply stared at Lewiston for a short while, willing him to look down and see her. When it was almost too late, he turned his gaze away from the musicians, as if responding to the power of her will. She smiled at him, hoping it would be enough to encourage him to come and claim her for a dance.

Just then, Tillmartin returned to lead her out to the floor and she was forced to acquiesce with a good grace. When their dance ended, supper was announced. Even though by anyone's standards her ball had gone brilliantly so far, Olivia's spirits ebbed. She looked down at the floor and sighed.

"Is something troubling you, Miss Fontenoy?"

She turned at the sound of Lewiston's soft voice. "Oh! There you are. Have you come to take me in to supper?" It was rather forward of her, but she so wanted to talk to him. His sudden blush told her he hadn't expected her to say such a thing. He recovered quickly and bowed before putting his arm out to her. Olivia rested her hand lightly on it, instantly aware of how different it felt from the duke's. Lewiston's was slenderer, perhaps wiry underneath the elegant evening coat, where Hartland's arm radiated controlled power, ostentatiously muscled.

What was she thinking? It was hardly appropriate for her to be imagining parts of men's bodies. She gave her head a little shake and said, "I haven't seen you dancing. Are none of the ladies here to your liking?"

He leaned a little closer to her and said, "One of them most certainly is."

She turned her head and met his warm deep eyes and her breath caught.

"Olivia! You must sit at the head table, with the duke on your right." Lady Ambrose bustled over to where they stood.

"I shall come directly, Mama. Lord Lewiston was just telling me something about the musicians." Of course, he hadn't been, but it was all Olivia could think of to send her mother away.

"Well, don't keep the duke waiting," Lady Ambrose said with a smile and a warning glare before hastening into the large music room, converted for the evening by the addition of tables and chairs to accommodate the two-hundred guests. Only the pianoforte remained of the original furnishings.

"I must go," Olivia said to Lewiston. "But I saved you a dance."

He opened his eyes wide. "Why did you do that?"

What a question to ask! Olivia was a little offended. "Because I-I wanted to dance with you, unless you don't want to dance with me."

"Hartland—"

"He's had his two. Besides, there's no understanding between us, if that's what you think."

"I don't know what I think," Lewiston said. "But a dance—it wouldn't do."

Olivia laughed, trying hard not to feel slighted. Deciding that she may as well be blunt in turn, she said, "Why not? This is a ball, you know."

Lewiston ran his hand through his hair. "I'm sorry. I'm being rude. I can't explain. I'll put my name on your card but I'd prefer not to dance."

"I don't want to force you." By now Olivia was regretting saying anything to him about it. Did he really dread the idea of dancing with her?

Taking both her hands in his Lewiston said, "Please! I want to! I'd like nothing more, in fact. It's just…oh it's nothing. But if you wouldn't mind, perhaps we could just sit somewhere and talk during the dance instead, listen to the wonderful musicians."

Olivia saw that something truly distressed him about the idea of dancing. He hadn't stood up with anyone else, she realized, so perhaps he did not mean it to be a slight to her. She smiled reassuringly. "Sitting down would suit me. My feet are already sore, and the evening's not half over."

He wrote his name on her card. "Thank you," he said, bowed and continued into the supper room to find a seat.

IN NO MORE THAN FIVE MINUTES ADELHEID HAD TAKEN THE measure of the heiress Hartland had his eye on. What had also taken her very little time to ascertain was that the girl was not in love with the duke. She blushed when he touched her and was visibly nervous. But it wasn't a delighted blush. It was an embarrassed blush—and her nerves appeared more general than specific. The entire event made the girl anxious. Besides, she didn't simper at him or throw out lures. In fact, she seemed to always be looking around for someone else.

Adelheid couldn't help feeling a little sorry for her. She was so young, not just in years, but clearly in the ways of the world. Olivia Fontenoy was no more fit to be the wife of a rakish duke than was her abigail. Oh, Burke's revealed that she had the breeding—on her father's side, at least—and Lady Mariana had told her about the fortune. Still, Adelheid knew in her heart that the girl would be miserable if she were shackled to a man of the duke's temperament and inclinations. No one knew better than she did just how unhappy it was possible to be when you discovered that someone who had seemed ideal has feet of clay.

She didn't watch Miss Fontenoy much after that. She hardly had time. She never sat down, grateful for the convention of a dance card to remind her the next day of who she'd danced with. Perhaps among them would be another potential husband for her, if Hartland proved impossible to secure.

This thought acted like a bucket of wet sand on her spirits. As soon as she met the duke, she'd fixed him in her mind as the person who would fulfill that role. More than she wanted to admit to herself, she imagined his presence in her life, and the thought that he wouldn't be there unaccountably filled her with sadness. Why was that? She hardly knew him! He wasn't even quite as handsome as the prince had been. There was something about him though, a quality. It was more than his suave confidence and air of consequence. She saw laughter in his eyes, but also sorrow. Although his eyes were dark blue instead of deep, unfathomable brown, she met in Hartland's irreverent gaze something that reminded her of Danton.

·  ·  ·

LEWISTON BERATED HIMSELF AS HE TOOK HIS PLACE AT A TABLE in the supper room. He'd made a hash of it already. All he wanted was to reclaim some of the ease he and Miss Fontenoy had with each other at Almack's and then again when they met in the park. He had so much he wanted to say to her. Never before had he met a lady so interested in music, so fully engaged with the opera, so unafraid to talk about such things. He wondered if she played the pianoforte and sang, as most well-bred young ladies did. Perhaps she played the harp. But she didn't seem the type. Not ethereal enough. She had an essential sturdiness despite her slender build.

It did not surprise him that Lady Ambrose had engaged such fine musicians. No doubt her daughter advised her. He recognized the two violinists from the opera and the flutist was very expert. The gentleman at the keyboard also showed a high degree of skill. They chose the music well, too—the country dance arrangements had more variety than was usual. He knew it was unconscionably unsocial of him but when he had spied the spiral stairs that led up the half-floor to the balcony in the ballroom he couldn't help availing himself of the opportunity to slip away and simply listen.

"What ho, Lewiston! Didn't see you at Ascot. Too close to settling day?" A guffaw followed this teasing pronouncement from across the table by Lord Ponsonby, an aspirant to the Four Horse Club who also fancied himself a candidate for the dandy set.

Lewiston smiled. "I hear Grisham sold you his pair of bays. Bit narrow in the chest, aren't they? At least, that's what Hartland told me." It was wicked of him to bandy the duke's name about in a conversation about horses. Ponsonby's face drained of color and he turned away to converse with the lady on his left.

The other occupants of Lewiston's table made light conversation, and Lewiston did his best to join in. *The food was quite good. Had he tried the punch? Someone trod on her heel and ruined her new silk stockings.*

But all he could think about was his coming dance with Miss Fontenoy. She said she wouldn't mind sitting, but when he put his name on her card he saw that it would be a waltz. No young lady wanted to sit on the side during a waltz.

Why had she insisted on the dance? He'd seen how she was with Hartland. She smiled in a way that made her face glow and looked shyly down when he whispered something to her, just as any of the other of the duke's flirts might have done. But Hartland didn't really flirt with her. He treated her with respect and consideration, making it clear to anyone that he had her in his sights for a more serious purpose. Any day now, the announcement would come. There would be a handsome portion and the promise of a fortune. Hartland would be able to repair his finances, get an heir, and take up with a high-flying mistress while his duchess remained largely at Hartmoor with her ever-growing brood of children. A cynical laugh escaped Lewiston and the lady next to him glared at him.

At that moment, Lady Mariana approached him having finished her supper, and he stood to greet her. "Harry! How wonderful to see you. I didn't know you were in London. And you haven't called on us? For shame!"

He kissed her hand. She looked ravishing, of course. A year ago he would have found the press of her hand and the look in her sparkling eyes exquisite torture. But he'd come to realize she would never have been the right mate for him. His quiet ways would have driven her mad eventually. "I hear Thorne is making quite a name for himself in the ministry." Mariana's husband Jeremy Thorne's rapid rise from personal secretary to Whig MP had been impressive. Many said it was all because of Bridlington's influence, but Lewiston gave him credit for being a brilliant man with an incisive mind and a gift for oration. Perfect for Mariana.

As the diners laid their forks aside and some rose to seek the retiring room, a footman opened the pianoforte in the corner. Oh dear, Lewiston thought. Time for the parade of accomplished young ladies singing slightly off key and playing badly.

He was surprised, therefore, when Lady Ambrose walked over to the instrument and played a loud chord on it to command everyone's attention.

"I am so proud to present my daughter to you all this evening. Thank you for honoring us with your presence. In gratitude, she will now sing for you, probably something Italian—she's been studying with the great Tetrazzini, you know!"

Lewiston cringed. Poor Lady Ambrose. Even after twenty years of marriage to a viscount she hadn't quite shed her common ways.

"Olivia, dearest!" Lady Ambrose said, looking over to the corner of the room. All eyes followed hers, including Lewiston's.

There stood Miss Fontenoy, looking every bit the incensed fury rather than the blushing, demure maiden one might expect. Her eyes burned with rage, she clenched and unclenched her fists, and her breast heaved as she sucked in ragged breaths. She didn't make a move toward her mother.

"Excuse me, Harry," Mariana said. "I need to rescue her."

Mariana swept away to join Lady Ambrose. They nodded to each other and Mariana sat down at the pianoforte without asking her leave and played a lively movement from a Haydn sonata. Lewiston looked back to where Miss Fontenoy had been standing moments before. She was gone. He excused himself from the company and left the supper room.

This was most peculiar. Surely someone who loved music as much as Miss Fontenoy would welcome an opportunity to display her talent. Lewiston expected that she would have a lovely voice, if the great Tetrazzini had deigned to teach her. He couldn't imagine what would make her so adamant about not performing.

He wandered through the different saloons not finding her. Perhaps she had retired to her bedchamber to mend something on her dress, he thought. Would she reappear for their dance? A sudden desire to see if she was in the library sent Lewiston down to the ground floor. He paused in the center of the hall uncertain where to look, until the unmistakable sound of sniffling issued from a room whose door stood ajar. He crept to it and peeked inside.

Across the room Miss Fontenoy stood looking out one of the windows at the darkness beyond, her shoulders shaking slightly, her head bowed. Noting the table and sideboard of a family breakfast parlor, Lewiston was vaguely conscious of trespassing on a private realm. He wondered if he should just leave her to her solitary grief, whatever it was. As he stepped backward, intending to withdraw, he trod on a creaky board. Miss Fontenoy wheeled around. Her eyes were red and her bunched-up handkerchief sodden. She drew in a shuddering breath and hastily tried to erase the evidence of tears from her cheeks.

Lewiston took a few steps into the room. "I'll go away if you want me to."

She shook her head slowly.

"Perhaps you can tell me what's wrong?"

That made her shake her head again, this time vehemently, and turn back toward the window.

"You didn't want to sing," Lewiston said. "I don't blame you. I would hate being made an exhibition of if I were a girl."

She turned around to face him again and said, "It's not exactly that. I can't explain. Only I told my mother that on no account was she to ask me to sing this evening. She doesn't understand."

She looked at him with such sadness in her eyes that with his whole body he yearned to rush over to her and clasp her to him. Of course that would be impertinent, impossible, deplorable. In fact, being in a room alone with her contravened the rules of propriety. Instead, he searched in his mind for something to say that might soothe her. "Lady Mariana distracted her from that purpose, I think. I daresay others will follow her example and in a moment the orchestra will lure everyone back into the ballroom."

He walked slowly toward her holding out his handkerchief, for all the world as if he were approaching an unbroken horse with an apple and didn't want to frighten her off. "I think you need a new one."

She smiled feebly and took it from him, wiping her eyes with it. When she stopped, she smoothed it in her hands. Her vague gaze focused suddenly on it and a puzzled crease appeared on her brow. After a moment she looked back up at him in amazement. "It was yours," she said, "not Hartland's."

"Yes. Do you wish it hadn't been?" Lewiston's heart beat just a little faster, dreading her response. Of course she would rather the duke had shown her such courtesy.

S he smiled, and her eyes glowed. "No! I'm thankful it was you, really. Because I couldn't understand … it didn't seem … you—"

She couldn't finish her sentence because at that moment Lady Ambrose stormed into the room on a cloud of lavender scent.

"Olivia! What were you thinking? The duke is looking for you. We'll discuss this tomorrow." She cast an icy glance at

Lewiston before dragging Olivia by the hand toward the door.

"Lady Ambrose," Lewiston said, stopping her as politely as he could. "I believe I have this next dance with Miss Fontenoy." He put his arm out to Olivia and looked straight into her eyes.

She drew a steadying breath, unclasped her mother's hand from hers, and laid her hand atop his arm.

To Olivia, Lewiston said, "I came looking for you." Then he turned to Lady Ambrose. "I didn't want to miss my one dance with your lovely daughter."

At these words, Olivia felt her anxiety and distress drain from her body and she lightly clasped his arm and drew herself up. The viscountess wasn't happy about the situation, clearly. There was little to choose in rank between a duke and a marquess, but Lewiston was not the prize Hartland was. No one faced with that choice would deny it.

Olivia understood that rank was only part of it. Hartland was *haut ton* through and through. Lewiston stood on its fringes, but not because of his birth. It was something else. The Viscount and Viscountess Ambrose understood men like the duke. He followed the pattern of high-bred gentlemen. He did it with more finesse and aplomb than anyone else but in essence he was just the same. Lewiston, on the other hand, would be harder for them to figure out. Indeed, aside from knowing he was as passionate about music as she was, Olivia by no means felt she understood the quiet marquess. Despite having all the right credentials, he didn't show to advantage. He didn't cut a dash or make a noise.

Of course, Olivia thought with sudden comprehension—that was what she liked about him. Hartland might sweep her off her feet with his gallantry and éclat, make her thrill to the joy of being the object of his attention.

But Lewiston—Lewiston was the man with the hand-kerchief.

By the time these thoughts had spun through Olivia's mind, they reached the ballroom where a country dance had just ended. Couples sought each other out for the much-awaited waltz and made their way into the center of the room. "We could sit on the two chairs over there we could sit in," Olivia said, and started to walk in that direction.

But Lewiston held her back and said, "I've changed my mind. Let's dance."

Olivia looked questioningly at him. "Certainly. But why didn't you want to before?"

An embarrassed flush rose into his face. "You'll think it's foolish. I can't dance at a ball. I mean, I become completely awkward about it."

"Don't you know the steps?" Lewiston didn't seem like someone who couldn't dance. After all, he clearly had an ear for the music, the rhythm.

"I do. Very well in fact. I just can't persuade my body to cooperate in front of anyone."

Olivia wanted to laugh out loud, but she stopped herself at the slightly pleading look on his face. He'd confessed something to her. He didn't have to. They could easily have just sat this one out. Or they could have danced and she would have discovered for herself how good or bad a dancer he was. "So why have you changed your mind?"

He shrugged. "It's a waltz. I may never have this opportunity again."

By this time, the orchestra had struck up the introductory bars and Olivia felt the triple meter in her body and swayed just slightly. Lewiston pressed his right hand into the small of her back and met her left hand with his to arch over their heads. With the first notes of the melody, they began.

At first, his hand trembled slightly through the silk of her gown and his steps were not smooth. But as they eased into the movements, he held her more firmly and his feet moved with growing certainty. Olivia smiled into his warm, expressive eyes and soon the hesitancy in them fell away. They whirled with the music, the ensemble never missing a note and the two of them never missing a beat. It was an experience so novel that Olivia wished she could prolong it forever. His firm, sure touch. The warmth of his body so close to hers. His breathing becoming more rapid with the exertion of the dance. Was it just the exertion?

When the waltz ended, they stood still in the final position for a moment, both of them flushed.

"Thank you. That was lovely," Olivia whispered.

"Yes, it was. I don't know how. It's never happened before."

Lewiston took her hand and led her to the side of the room. Their hands remained clasped for several beats longer than absolutely necessary. When Olivia could finally make herself draw her hand out of his, she shivered. She wished they could have stayed linked like that forever, but her next partner came to claim her.

Olivia let Lord Amesbury lead her to the next set somewhat distracted. As the music started, she looked up at the guests milling about the side, chatting and laughing, and her eyes met Hartland's. He stood next to the princess who leaned toward him and whispered something in his ear. His answer made her raise one delicate eyebrow.

WHEN LADY AMBROSE MENTIONED THE NAME TETRAZZINI AT the end of supper, Adelheid stopped talking to Lord Eccleston in mid-sentence. She tried to keep her attention on the conversation the viscount was determined to have with her, but out of the corner of her eye she followed the little drama that subsequently unfolded. Miss Fontenoy would not sing. Yet Tetrazzini, Adelheid knew from years ago, would only be teaching her if she had a decent voice. In fact Miss Fontenoy's reaction to being asked to display her talents in front of the *ton* was out of all proportion. The heiress fled from the room as if from a wild beast.

Not a moment later, a young man she'd not noticed before stood and excused himself from his table and unhurriedly followed where she went. Who was he? She couldn't ask without revealing that she'd paid no attention at all to Eccleston so she decided to question Mariana later.

Her determination to do so only increased when Miss Fontenoy returned to the ballroom on the young man's arm.

"I believe I have this dance."

The voice was unmistakable. She turned to see Hartland, his eyes alight with laughter, holding his gloved hand out to lead her onto the floor for the waltz. She wanted to ask him so many impossible things! Was Miss Fontenoy the heiress he intended to catch? If so, why wasn't he waltzing with her at that moment?

The time for questions passed as the orchestra struck up a lively waltz and they whirled around the floor in perfect unity. Hartland was a wonderful dancer, and she knew she was too. No doubt many eyes fixed on them as they performed the steps and smiled into each other's faces.

But at the end of the dance, he was all politeness, a distant look coming over him as he gazed across the floor. She followed his eyes and met those of Miss Fontenoy. "Who was Miss Fontenoy's partner for the waltz?" she asked in a low voice.

"Just Lewiston," he said.

Why *just*? She wondered but had no time to ask having been claimed by another partner for the next dance.

# CHAPTER 14

$\mathcal{I}$t couldn't have been more than three hours after she fell exhausted into her bed that Olivia awoke with a start. She pulled the bell to summon Hetty.

When the maid came in her eyes were wide with surprise. "Miss Olivia! I was sure you'd be asleep until noon at least!"

"What time is it?"

"Just gone nine, Miss. You sure you don't want to sleep more? I can bring you some hot milk."

"No," Olivia said, throwing her blankets off and swinging her legs around to sit on the edge of her bed. "I shall dress. Nothing special, perhaps the Indian muslin. I have an important errand to run this morning."

"Why don't you let one of the footmen run it for you? You should rest today. There's already a deal of nosegays been delivered."

"No, I must do it myself."

Giving up on trying to persuade her unpredictable mistress to be lazy, Hetty went to the windows and began pulling the pale blue velvet drapes aside to let the sunshine in.

"Is Lady Ambrose up?"

"No Miss. Nor His Lordship."

That was good. Perhaps she could leave, meet Signore Tetrazzini, and return before they'd emerged from their bedchambers. "Quickly, Hetty. The muslin, as I said, and my York tan spencer and brown half boots."

In a very few minutes, Hetty had fastened Olivia into her clothes and tamed her wayward hair with a ribbon.

"If my mother wants me while I'm gone, tell her I'm still asleep. She won't mind if she thinks that. Whatever you do, don't tell her I've gone out. I'll be so very grateful." Olivia smiled, pressed a *douceur* into Hetty's hand, then hurried out of her room and down the stairs.


THE HACK LET OLIVIA OUT AT THE END OF AN ALLEY THAT LED to the back of the King's Theatre. Signore Tetrazzini was already waiting for her and rushed up to give her the altered mask and help her tie it on. It fitted perfectly. She could see through the eye holes, and nothing impeded the movement of her mouth.

"Come this way, Signorina," Tetrazzini said in a quiet voice, ushering her into a small side door that led to a part of the theatre only the musicians, dancers, and actors saw.

It was the smell that first struck Olivia. Burnt wax, as if hundreds of candles had just been extinguished, and an undercurrent of sweat masked by perfume. Her eyes took in everything through the holes in her mask, putting her at an odd distance from her surroundings: rough wooden walls and an unfinished floor; doors leading off a long corridor; guttering candles in wall sconces spaced as far apart as they could be and still provide enough illumination to navigate through the narrow space.

After a few twists and turns, they came to a set of wooden

stairs that led up to what Olivia could only imagine would be the stage. *Am I really doing this?* "You're sure no one is here?" she whispered to Tetrazzini.

"Only Signore Taylor, and he is in his *ufficio*." He gestured to her to precede him up the short flight.

When she reached the top, her breath caught. Such a vast open space, the ceiling so high that when it was unlit the elaborate paintings disappeared into empty blackness. Olivia had been used to a theatre filled with talking and noise and music. The silence pressed down on her.

"*Avanti*, Meess," her singing tutor said, waving his arm toward the center of the large stage.

A simple backdrop painted with a few trees was all that decorated the stage. Olivia tiptoed forward until she reached the place where Catalani had stood to sing *"Dove sono,"* and stopped. It felt odd, standing on that surface which was tilted slightly down toward the pit. Her throat was tight. She must warm up a little. A rolled chord on the harpsichord in the orchestra pit startled a little shriek out of her. She turned to Tetrazzini, a question in her eyes.

"He is friend. He will give you *accompanimento*."

Olivia didn't point out that they were certainly not alone there in that case, contrary to what he had told her. But there was little she could do about it now except decide not to sing. And who knew when—or if ever—she would have an opportunity like this again? So she said aloud to the invisible harpsichordist, "Could I have the G below middle C, please?"

He complied. Olivia began her exercises, loosening her vocal cords and her jaw, moistening her lips, pushing her range from narrow to wide, singing a pitch-perfect chromatic scale and then dazzling arpeggios in a full range of keys. As she did this her confidence grew. Her voice soared out into the empty hall. She walked around the stage, waving her arms, freeing her breath.

When she felt she was ready she found her place at the center again. "A C, please," she instructed the harpsichordist.

And then, she closed her eyes and sang.

*Dove sono i bei momenti*

*di dolcezza e di piacer ...*

The harpsichordist, when he realized what she was singing, softly filled in the gentle chords of the orchestra part.

Olivia poured every ounce of feeling she possessed into the cavatina, not embellishing, just singing the notes pure and strong. When the tempo quickened and the mood changed, her voice opened, and at the end she added one or two delicate flourishes, but resisted the temptation to soar up to the high note—as Catalani had done—instead of the lower one at the end.

The feeling. The magic of it. When she stopped singing she froze in place, her heart battering her chest. Her voice had found its home. It needed that space, that room to exist. She had the sensation that until that moment, her voice had been locked in a cage, desperate to be freed.

She remained in the center of the stage gazing out over the empty pit, the tiers of unoccupied boxes, the gallery above them, for she knew not how long.

The spell was broken by the sound of a single person clapping from somewhere out in the darkened theatre. The claps drew closer, and soon a stocky man in rumpled clothes came into view. "So, you dare to sneak into my theatre!" the man said, standing just in front of the stage where there was enough light so could see him.

Olivia cast a frightened glance at Tetrazzini who lifted his hand in a quelling gesture and walked forward. "Signore Taylor, *mi scusa*, but my pupil, she has paid for this."

Mr. Taylor, a man of late middle age with a bald patch on the top of his head—visible from the higher elevation of the stage—disappeared through a side door and then reappeared from the wings. He walked up to Tetrazzini and said, "Who is she?'

*How rude!* Olivia thought, not accustomed to being treated with anything but respect. She exchanged a furious glance with her teacher who then said, "The *madama*, she wish to remain *incognita*," and made a courtly bow to the impresario.

"Come now! Did you bring her over from Milan? What roles has she performed at La Scala?"

"The lady—she has never before ... she is for the first time on the stage."

Taylor opened his eyes wide in feigned astonishment. "So that is your game, is it? Ask her to remove her mask. I wish to talk to her. Catalani has been troublesome, demanding higher and higher fees and two benefit performances this season. Happen a little competition might make her change her tune." He looked Olivia up and down with a gleam in his eye that she didn't like at all.

Something warned Olivia not to speak a word but to trust to Tetrazzini to extricate her from this awkward situation. What was the man thinking!

Tetrazzini wrung his hands. "No, Signore, the mask, she is remaining. We will leave you now. *Mille grazie.*" He once again swept a bow to Mr. Taylor.

"Tetrazzini! Are you asking me to believe this divine soprano has not come to audition for a role in my operas? I would be willing to cast her in the next performance of the Mozart. Madama Catalani has been complaining about the noise from the audience and threatening not to appear. What would be her customary fee?"

Tetrazzini opened his mouth to say something, but couldn't get the words out quickly enough. "S-Sign-"

"If she's really so new, untried, I'll pay her five-hundred

guineas for the first performance. But she must remove the mask! Is she a fright underneath? Disfigured? That'll never do."

Olivia drew herself up and walked toward the stairs that led down from the stage. She wasn't going to stay to be insulted. In any case, she could not appear on stage in public, whatever the man offered her. She waved a dismissive hand at him and gestured to Tetrazzini to come with her.

The singing tutor had begun to perspire. He took out his large handkerchief and mopped his face with it. *"Arrivederci,"* he said to Taylor, whose brows had drawn together in a combination of anger and confusion.

"I'll have her here! Just tell me what she demands!" He started walking after them.

Olivia hastened along the corridor, anxious to get away from the man. The hack was waiting for them outside and she clambered in quickly, followed by Tetrazzini, who directed the driver to take them back to Mount Street. Olivia peered out the dirty window and saw the impresario standing open-mouthed by the backstage entrance to the theatre, his hands on his hips.

ONLY AN HOUR HAD PASSED SINCE THEY LEFT THE HOUSE. Olivia took her mask off in the hack and gave it back to Tetrazzini. "I can't thank you enough for arranging this, Signore Tetrazzini. I shall remember those moments for the rest of my life!"

"Yes, *si,*" he said, "But Signore Taylor, he want you to come back and sing. It is impossible, no?"

She looked at Tetrazzini in blank amazement. "Of course! I could never. But I wish..." The taste of singing on a real stage, being able to let her voice do all it was capable of, was indescribable. Intoxicating. All at once the thought that she would never again have that feeling sank her spirits which, despite their hasty retreat, had still carried her away on a cloud. "Well," she said, preparing to get down from the hack, "At least I have done it once." She shook Tetrazzini's hand warmly. "Will you bring me more arias when you come next week?" she asked.

Her singing teacher lifted her hand to his lips. When he lowered it, there were tears in his eyes. "*Signorina, non so come* ... I am honored. Never have I heard so a beautiful voice."

She bid him a hasty goodbye, afraid his effusion of emotion would make her cry too. There was no point. It was time to return to her real life, where the most important thing in the world was for her to marry a duke to please her parents. With slow steps, Olivia went up to her bedchamber. It was not yet noon. She would pretend to awaken then and start her day over again—as an heiress on the catch for a husband.

"THEY'VE BEEN COMING ALL MORNING, MISS!" HETTY squeaked as soon as Olivia crossed the threshold of her bedchamber. "I collect every eligible beau musta gone to the flower market before dawn just so's they could be first to send you a posy!"

Olivia cast her eyes over the mountain of small bouquets sent to her by everyone she'd danced with the night before. She couldn't even put faces to all of the names. Her mother would help her later. Of course, Hartland's was the biggest, with hothouse flowers that must have been very expensive. The ritual, Olivia knew, was to be at home to morning callers that day—even though "morning" really meant afternoon.

She looked more closely at the posies and examined each accompanying card, saying to Hetty, "Are these all of them?"

"Why, Miss! You think there should be more? I never!"

Yes, Olivia thought. I do sound vain. "What should I do with them all? Put them in vases? They'll die if I just leave them." The more she thought about it the more wasteful it all seemed. She wasn't going to marry anyone but the duke—not if her parents had anything to say to it—so all these other gentlemen might just as well have saved themselves the trouble.

"I'll have Thomas see to it, Miss," Hetty said, arranging a final curl to tease at the corner of Olivia's eye.

In fact, Olivia didn't want more flowers. But after looking through the tributes three times she found no card from Lewiston, which affected her more than she cared to admit to herself. What had he been trying to tell her the night before when he found her in the breakfast room? Well, whatever it was, he clearly did not number himself among her suitors. And yet, there had been something in the way he looked at her, how she felt in his arms, his expression at the end of their waltz. Surprise and gratitude? Was that all it was?

By the end of the afternoon Olivia's face hurt from smiling and she'd used up every polite topic of conversation at her command. Several of her partners from the night before asked to call on her again, said they'd claim the first or second or third dance at the next ball, wanted to take her out driving in the park or join her for a morning ride.

She thought the visits had ended when a knock on the door announced one more. Olivia, who had stood with the intention of going to her bedchamber to dress for dinner, smoothed her skirt down and prepared to have her hand kissed by yet another supplicant. If she thought any of them had been interested in her for more than her fortune, it would be different. But despite many compliments, she thought too little of herself to believe it.

"His Grace the Duke of Hartland," Ebbings said in his haughty drawl as he bowed Hartland into the room.

Olivia put out her hand. Her mind was so full of other thoughts that day, starting with her extraordinary experience at the King's Theatre, that she forgot just how handsome the duke was, just how much the brilliance of his dark blue eyes could unsettle her. The effect bypassed her mind and went straight into her body. She couldn't help the vivid blush that rose up her neck and into her cheeks.

"Forgive my tardiness in paying my respects, Miss Fontenoy. I had an urgent matter of business to attend to this morning."

Olivia invited him to sit on one of the silk-covered settees and resumed her place on the sofa next to her mother.

"Not at all, Duke!" Lady Ambrose said. "It's a pleasure to welcome you at any time."

*You'd think he was courting her!* Olivia thought, and a giggle escaped her.

"You may well be amused at the idea of my business, Miss Fontenoy, but I assure you it is no laughing matter." Hartland's barely suppressed smile gave the lie to his serious comment.

"I'm afraid I am not qualified to comment about business since my only experience of such things is gleaned from the novels I read," Olivia said, falling back on a suitably self-deprecating line.

"Oh, I suspect you are alive to many more rigs and rows than you let on, Miss Fontenoy," Hartland said, accepting the glass of Madeira Ebbings presented to him.

Noticing that no other of her gentleman callers had been offered refreshment, Olivia said, "I'm sure I don't know what you mean, Duke."

He just smiled and sipped his drink, letting an uncomfortable silence settle on the room.

Leaping in to rescue the moment, Lady Ambrose said, "I understand your estate—Hartmoor, I mean—is located in Yorkshire."

"It is," Hartland said, not offering anything to continue the conversation.

"I've never been to Yorkshire," Olivia said. "It's too far away from the sea for my taste. Not that I've seen anything beyond the channel, in Brighton." Were they really having such an insipid conversation?

"Oh dear," Lady Ambrose said, pointedly looking at the clock on the mantelpiece, "I must go and discuss a detail of the dinner menu with cook, if you'll excuse me for just a moment."

Olivia closed her eyes. Her mother didn't just manufacture an excuse to leave her alone with the duke.

Hartland stood as Lady Ambrose glided out of the room, then took the place she'd vacated on the sofa next to Olivia. She was very conscious of his solid weight on the cushions, the proximity of him, and a shiver passed from her back all the way down her legs. She was furious with herself. He clearly knew exactly what he was doing, understood how to breach the defenses of susceptible young women with his confiding smile and dangerous eyes.

He leaned slightly toward her and reached for her hand. Was he going to offer for her? Already? Surely courtship should last longer, Olivia thought, vaguely aware that there ought to be a sort of cat and mouse quality to the game.

Before he could gain possession of her hand, Ebbings entered the parlor with a silver tray on which a large folded and sealed document lay. "This was just delivered, and the gentleman requested it be given into your hands directly, Ma'am," Ebbings said with a stiff bow.

Olivia took the package, uncertain what to do with it. She

didn't want to open it in front of Hartland, but it had been presented to her so ceremoniously in his presence that it seemed rude to simply lay it aside. "I don't know..." She smiled at Hartland apologetically.

"By all means, open your post," he said, and stood. "I must in any case take my leave of you now. I have an evening engagement."

Lady Ambrose returned at that moment. "Not leaving already Duke?"

"I am afraid the hour is later than I thought," he said bowing to her.

Olivia stood and put out her hand, which he took and kissed then held for a moment longer. "A drive? Tomorrow?"

She nodded.

"I'll call for you at three."

And then he was gone, taking with him the rampant confusion his presence caused her. "I shall go up and dress," Olivia said to her mother, and left with the document in her hands. Now that the duke was gone, she burned with curiosity to see what could have been so important that it had to interrupt a tête-à-tête with the gentleman who was likely to offer for her any day.

She didn't ring for Hetty right away but broke the seal and opened the package.

It was sheet music. At first she thought perhaps an aria from Tetrazzini. But no, it was for piano only, no vocal line. A manuscript, not printed. A waltz.

*The* waltz. She scanned the melody line, hearing it in her head. It was indeed the one she and Lewiston had danced to at her ball. Where did it come from? Someone had taken the trouble to transcribe the orchestra music for pianoforte. Someone.

Of course she knew who it had to be.

He hadn't sent her a posy. That would have been too ordinary.

Instead, he sent her his soul.

# CHAPTER 15

Hartland went back to the house in Grosvenor Square unaccountably vexed. He hadn't meant to offer for the girl at that time, but he had hoped to go a little further in fixing her interest. He just needed a few more minutes. She displayed all the signs of succumbing to his notable charms. Color heightened, hand slightly trembling, breath shallow. She was in fact much prettier than she thought herself, especially when her feelings were engaged. Not, still, a diamond, but more than acceptable. He'd come to the realization that she would make the perfect duchess. She wouldn't hang on him or demand attention, and her manners in company were good.

And yet, when he really pictured a duchess at his side, it wasn't Miss Fontenoy's face that came to mind. It was a perfect oval with large, blue-green eyes, all framed by a cascade of flaxen curls.

He shook himself. He knew nothing really about the princess. The rumors that she was wealthy could be just that —rumors. Why would an Austrian princess leave her home behind and move to a city where she knew almost no one? It didn't make sense.

After handing his hat and cane to the footman, he went up to his mother's parlor, which she seldom left except to have dinner with him when he dined at home—which was rare. He found her dressed in black silk, a lacy confection of a cap covering her gray-streaked curls, and seated on the small sofa, a scattering of old letters around her like so many wilted flower petals.

"It's in here somewhere, I know it," she said.

"What is, Mama?" Hartland said, lifting her hand to his lips and then taking a seat on the comfortable armchair nearby.

"A particular letter from your father. He was away in London and I had stayed at Hartmoor because I was increasing. Not with you—that was later."

She referred to one of the several stillbirths she'd had, no doubt. "What did this letter say?"

"It spoke of his hopes for our children, the marriages they would make."

Marriage. He avoided the idea for twenty-nine years and now everywhere he looked it seemed to impose itself upon his notice. And so it should. He wondered fleetingly if, even if his finances hadn't pushed him into it, he might have found himself entering the marriage mart that season anyway. And then he marveled at himself for thinking it.

"Did he say anything I might not already have guessed?" Philip asked.

The dowager sighed before saying, "No. Except that I wonder if he would quite approve of your dangling after a young heiress whose father is only a viscount and her mother the daughter of a cit. And dangling after her *because* she's an heiress. He wanted—we both wanted—more for you than that."

"Miss Fontenoy *is* more than an heiress, Mama. She has qualities that I feel certain father would have appreciated." Her plain speaking, direct gaze, and ingenuous honesty would have appealed to the spirited duke, Philip felt sure. "Besides ..." He was about to say that no other eligible heiress was available just then so he had to take what he could get. But was that really true? Instead he said, "I like her." At least that was true. But would it be enough?

"I gather, then, that she isn't much like her mother. A well-meaning creature, but she tries too hard." She shivered.

"Yes, you have it exactly. But Olivia isn't like that at all."

"You use each other's first names already?"

"No," he said, although he'd hoped to get to that point earlier that day. "But I trust we will soon."

"Tell me honestly, Philip darling, could you be happy with Miss Fontenoy as your duchess?"

He didn't answer right away, and then somewhat surprised himself by saying, "Yes. I think I could." He didn't believe he'd ever fall in love with her but that they'd rub along well together. Falling in love was dangerous for a man in his delicate predicament. It was better this way by far. The mother was annoying, but that needn't trouble them over much. Once they were married, he could easily find amusement as he previously had. Although he would certainly have to be more discreet.

"Are you dining at home this evening?" the duchess asked.

"No," Philip said. "I'm meeting friends at White's." He stood in need of a night of camaraderie and gaming. Something to take his mind off the serious business of courtship, which he would engage in tomorrow when he took Miss Fontenoy for a drive in his curricle.

The duchess rang the bell. Philip stood to take his leave just as Sidley, her dresser, entered.

"I'll have a tray in here for dinner, I think, Sidley," she said.

~

HARTLAND ARRIVED TO TAKE MISS FONTENOY FOR THE promised drive promptly at three o'clock the next day. She wore a very handsome redingote of dark blue kerseymere with gold frogging, and her smart matching shako bonnet was trimmed with a ribbon rosette and a single turkey feather. The simplicity of her dress suited her. She was not a fainting damsel to be decked in ruffles and lace. He handed her up into the curricle then took his place, told the groom to let go of the horses' heads and jump up behind, and gave his pair the office to go.

They went into the park and the carriage drive, but, instead of circling around it, Hartland drove out again and continued west on the road.

"Where are you taking me?" Miss Fontenoy asked, not with any alarm in her voice, just simple curiosity.

"The day is fine. I thought we'd drive toward Richmond."

"Isn't it late in the afternoon to do that?"

"Not if you don't mind a brisk pace." He turned to meet her gaze, and was pleased to see a smile on her face.

"Are you going to spring 'em, as they say?"

He tipped his head back and laughed. "I wouldn't quite say that, not on the road, but we'll get a few good canters in."

He cracked the whip over his horses' flanks. They picked up their heads, ears forward, and broke into a very brisk trot. Hartland could tell by the tension on the ribbons that the pair were ripe for a gallop. He wasn't sure it would be quite the thing with a lady sitting next to him, however.

"What made you decide not to stay in Hyde Park?" Miss Fontenoy asked after a while.

What could he tell her? That he wanted to take her some-where secluded so he could propose to her? That would hardly do. "I just thought it a pity to waste such a fine day. Have you been to Richmond?"

"Yes. My governess used to take me there for picnics. I always tried to feed the deer."

Just the kind of thing she would do, Hartland thought. When he saw deer it made him want to get his Manton double-barreled flintlock out. He didn't share that with her. Instead they talked of the upcoming *ton* parties, and Miss Fontenoy said she was planning to attend the opera the next night.

"Weren't you just there? Is it a different opera?"

"No, it's the Mozart again."

Why on earth would a lady go to see the same opera twice within the space of about a week? A young man might make a habit of loitering in fops' alley night after night, perhaps try to get into the dressing rooms in search of a willing opera dancer. He had done so more than once. But a lady? "The same opera? The same singers?"

"Yes, of course. I want to hear Catalani again. She may not return next season, her fees have risen so high."

It occurred to Hartland to wonder how she came to be possessed of that knowledge, but he didn't ask. They reached the park. He slowed the horses to a decorous pace and cast his eye around for a likely spot to walk in relative seclusion. He found a path that followed a meandering stream, its banks shaded by budding willow fronds. "Shall we perhaps stroll a little?"

"But the horses," Miss Fontenoy said.

"Jacko will walk them for …" He looked at the groom, who had already leapt down to go to the horses' heads when Hartland pulled them up, "… half an hour?"

Jacko nodded his understanding and soon Hartland and

Miss Fontenoy were strolling arm-in-arm along the winding path. When the groom passed out of hearing distance, Hartland said, "Miss Fontenoy, you can't be in ignorance of why I've brought you here today."

She stopped and turned to him, that frank, open expression in her eyes. "Apparently I can," she said.

He gave her his most charming smile, turned her to face him, took both her hands in his and said, "Why, you must realize that I am in love with you and want to marry you."

"Are you? And do you? Truly?"

This was not the response Hartland thought he would get. He expected downcast eyes, a shy smile, maidenly blushes, a stammered response. Not these forthright questions. And that was another thing: she had a disconcerting habit of answering a question with a question. "Why, yes. I do not offer marriage to ladies every day, you know."

To his surprise, instead of drawing closer to him, Miss Fontenoy gently but firmly removed her gloved hands from his. "I do not know what you do every day, Sir. In point of fact, I do not know you at all."

It crossed his mind to tell her that very few affianced couples knew each other before their wedding day, not really. Marriage in their class was more like a political alliance, a commercial agreement, than a bond of affection. The fact that it resulted in the most intimate act human beings were capable of did strike him as a bit of a contradiction. But that was only sex, after all. He knew as well as anyone that sex was merely a gratification of physical desire.

Instead of saying anything of the kind he said, "What would you like to know about me? How may we come to know each other better?" He might have imagined it, but he thought he detected a slight lowering of Miss Fontenoy's shoulders.

"I think, Your Grace, we should spend more time

together, perhaps show each other the things we really enjoy. I love opera, as you know, and music of all kinds. I already told you I'm going to the opera tomorrow evening. You know we have room in our box, should you be desirous of joining us."

Philip searched his mind for a good excuse. "I am unable to have that pleasure, I am afraid. I have a previous engagement," was all he could come up with.

"Then perhaps you would enjoy the next concert of the Philharmonic Society. A Haydn symphony and a quartet by Beethoven are on the programme, I believe, among other works. The orchestra is superb—better than the bands that play in the King's Theatre and at Covent Garden." She had obviously lit upon a subject that fired her enthusiasm.

"I am so unfortunate as to have failed of purchasing a subscription to those concerts," Philip said.

"You may purchase a ticket to an individual concert. My mother—one of the founding members—could easily procure one for you. The Argyll Rooms are beautiful, too."

By now they had finished their stroll and the groom brought the curricle up to them. Hartland helped Olivia in, pressing her hand as he did so. She was a most frustrating, obstinate young lady. He could name at least four others who would leap at the chance of marrying him. They were prettier and better born as well. Of course, they were not heiresses.

She wanted to know him better, she said. Yet the idea of going to endless concerts and operas filled him with alarm. He had no real ear for music. If she expected him to become something he was not, she would be disappointed.

Still, he wasn't to be defeated. He would have to think of something.

And then suddenly, as they were once again on their way and he noted Miss Fontenoy's obvious appreciation of his superb matched pair, "You are fond of horses, I gather," he said.

"Yes, I certainly am. These are glorious creatures, your pair. I love to ride, and have long wanted to learn to drive—however, my mother doesn't consider it ladylike."

"One need not be as outrageous as Lady Lade and engage in curricle races to drive your own curricle or phaeton in the park! I would be honored to instruct you in this skill." Hartland silently cursed himself for agreeing to something he vowed he would never do.

"Would you, really?" Miss Fontenoy turned shining eyes on him.

"Of course! Shall we say tomorrow at eleven in the morning for your first lesson?"

As soon as Olivia walked through the grand front door of the Brook Street mansion, Lady Ambrose flew out of the front saloon and down the stairs to the hall. Olivia hadn't even finished removing her hat and gloves before her mother said, "Well? Did he offer for you?"

"Hello mother. I had a lovely drive. Thank you for asking." Olivia kissed her mother's cheek and blithely walked up the stairs.

Lady Ambrose scurried along behind, a little breathless. "But did he offer for you?"

Olivia paused on the half landing and said, "Yes. He did."

The viscountess hastened to catch up to her but Olivia continued to the bedroom floor always a few steps ahead of her mother. "Oh my dear! You will be a duchess!" she called after her daughter.

Olivia turned as her mother tripped toward her down the second-floor hallway and said, "That is not yet certain."

This pulled Lady Ambrose to a halt. "What can you mean?"

"I mean that I have not accepted his proposal."

"Oh, Olivia! How can you decline a duke's offer of marriage!"

She wrung her hands and showed signs of going off into a fit of hysterics, so Olivia said, "I didn't say I declined, only that I had not accepted."

The tears stopped as quickly as they had started. "So there's still hope. Of course you will accept him! I order you to accept him!" She stamped her foot and lifted her chin, a belligerent spark in her dark brown eyes.

Olivia stared her mother down. As she was considerably taller than Lady Ambrose, this was not difficult to do. She said, her voice calm but icy, "I alone will decide whom I marry. I know the duke wants my fortune, for all his charming ways. I believe he would be a kind husband and I admit I find him beguiling. But I don't think that's enough. Not for me. Now I must dress for dinner." She whirled around, but her mother caught hold of her arm, digging her fingernails into it.

"You have it in your power to raise our family up to be one of the most illustrious in the land. If you let this opportunity slip through your fingers, it will be out of pure selfishness."

Olivia's eyes flashed. "I do not think our family, as it stands, is anything to be ashamed of!"

"That's all well and good for you to say, but you haven't faced the snubs and snickers. You didn't help matters any by embarrassing me in front of the entire *ton* at your ball." Lady Ambrose's voice faltered.

Olivia put her hand over her mother's and the viscountess's grip slackened. "Let us not quarrel. I warned you that I would not sing. I am sorry you were embarrassed." She lifted her mother's hand off her arm and laid it on her cheek. "And besides, it didn't seem to matter to the duke."

This brought a reluctant half smile to the viscountess's face. "I'm counting on you. Don't disappoint me."

At this, Lady Ambrose went back down the hall to her own room to change for dinner.

Hetty was waiting for Olivia in her dressing room, having already laid out a silk evening gown. "So, Miss! His Grace offered for you!"

"You were listening," Olivia said, knowing that her abigail had visions of being a duchess's personal maid. "Then you also heard that I have not accepted him."

"Not yet, Miss," Hetty said, a knowing gleam in her eyes. "When will you see him again?"

"Tomorrow. He's going to teach me to drive a curricle."

"Does Lady Ambrose know?" Hetty's eyes opened wide in astonishment.

"No." Hetty unfastened her cambric gown and Olivia stepped out of it. "But she won't stop me. It's the duke, after all."

Olivia sat at her dressing table so Hetty could rearrange her hair. She saw the frown on her maid's face reflected in the mirror. "What is it?"

"A letter, Miss. It was delivered while you were out, given into my very hands. He told me not to let anyone else know you received it."

Olivia, who was idly looking through the jewels in her case, stopped. "A letter? Give it to me!"

Hetty reached into her pocket and handed it to Olivia who recognized the writing. It was from Tetrazzini. She didn't know who she expected it to be from, but she felt a moment of disappointment.

*Signorina Fontenoy,*

*Signore Taylor wants that you come and sing for him again*

*tomorrow. He has agreed that you will remain masked. I will attend you in a hack around the corner at eleven in the morning.*

"Damn," Olivia muttered. "I mean … I don't know what I mean."

"It's no matter, Miss. Not bad news I hope?" Hetty said.

"Who gave this to you?" Olivia asked.

"A little boy, no one I ever seen before."

Olivia chewed the side of her thumb. Her driving lesson with Hartland was supposed to be at that time. She should keep her appointment with him. Wwhy would Taylor want her to come back and sing again? Tetrazzini already told him she was not for hire. She had been trying to reconcile herself to the fact that she would never be in a position to sing with her full power. Now, she might do so again, apparently. To what end?

She didn't know how to get a message to Tetrazzini before tomorrow without her mother knowing. Lady Ambrose examined everything that went out of the house, whether or not the viscount had franked it. But she could send a note to the duke by a footman. She would tell her mother she was thanking him for her drive. Instead she'd really be putting him off, saying she forgot a longstanding commitment that could not be changed and would he be available to come for her the following day. After all, she hadn't told her mother about her appointment with him.

"Fetch me paper and the standish," Olivia said.

Hetty did as requested, and soon Olivia had penned an apologetic letter to Hartland.

# CHAPTER 16

*Not only did she not leap at my offer of marriage, but now she's put off the driving lesson!* In truth, Hartland couldn't have said which offer was the more unusual for him. He didn't know whether to be completely vexed, a little relieved, or to laugh out loud at the surprising audacity of Miss Fontenoy, who was little more than a schoolroom miss.

In some measure, his admiration for her increased as a result of her actions. Definitely not in the common way, that girl. If only the way in which she was uncommon was a little more to his taste. If only she possessed some of the ineffable attributes of a woman like Princess Adelheid, for example.

He shook his head. No sense thinking along those lines. Something told Hartland that danger lay in that quarter. He knew nothing about the princess beyond the hearsay about her fortune and what she'd told him the two times he had been in her company. At their first meeting her revelations had been somewhat startling. The existence of a ward of indeterminate parentage, for one thing. But he did not have an opportunity satisfy his curiosity about that. They could only exchange light pleasantries at the ball. All that their interactions there had achieved was to increase his futile desire. Holding her in his arms for a waltz was tantamount to torture. Even two days later he could feel the contour of her waist and smell her subtle scent of jasmine.

Since Hartland found himself with no engagements that morning, he decided instead to go and work off some of his frustration and confusion at Jackson's Boxing Academy. He hadn't been there since the death of his father for reasons he couldn't quite account for. The late duke was an enthusiast of the fancy and, although Hartland did not believe himself to be in the least sentimental, something about that particular place brought his father's face to his mind in a way that tugged uncomfortably at feelings he sought to suppress.

Foolish, he decided. The late duke would certainly have thought so. And so he resolutely handed the reins of the curricle over to Jacko to walk the horses while he went in to pass an hour sparring, thereby reminding himself of his body's exceptional capabilities—capabilities that seemed to have left no very favorable impression on Miss Fontenoy.

"My Lord!" Jackson said when Hartland entered the training room, "Or rather, Your Grace, of course. Your late father is missed. But you will step into his shoes with distinction, I'm sure."

Hartland nodded. "Thank you. Shall we?" he said, not wanting to prolong the encomium about the late duke.

For the next hour, Hartland sparred with John Jackson and others, throwing himself into intense physical activity until he was breathing hard and sweat poured off him in rivulets.

"You're still in fine fettle, Hartland," said Lord Ebbersley, who had just finished his own workout. "Getting in training for the marriage mart?"

Hartland wanted to use his left fist to wipe the sardonic

smile off his friend's face, opting instead to raise one scornful eyebrow before going to the dressing room.

Expecting to simply climb into his curricle and drive the short distance back to Grosvenor Square, Hartland dressed himself in haste and thus stepped out onto Bond street with his hair a little less neatly arranged than he liked and his neckcloth somewhat carelessly tied. He spotted his curricle at the top of Bond Street, raised his hand, and Jacko trotted back in his direction. While he waited he gave the capes of his drab driving coat a twitch and cast his eyes around to see who else was about on that fine spring day.

To his surprise, a moment later Princess Adelheid emerged from Goldsmith's Jewelers a few doors away. She had no packages with her, however, and when she looked up and met his eyes he could have sworn that a look of discomfiture passed over her face before she adjusted her expression to one of gentle amusement.

Hartland approached her. "You are unescorted, Your Highness?" he said.

She put her hand out to him and he bowed over it. "I do not yet have all the servants I need for that house. My groom has charge of the phaeton and is walking the horses. I expect him at any moment." She smiled. "Please don't feel it necessary to wait with me."

Just then, Jacko pulled the curricle up to where they both stood. "Go around one more time, Jacko. I'd like to see the princess safely into her carriage."

The smile faded from Princess Adelheid's face and she turned away from him. "As I said, it is not necessary."

That was odd. What caused her embarrassment? And then, he realized what it must be. "You did not come here in your phaeton, did you. A hired hack? I would be more than willing to convey you back to Grosvenor Square in my curricle." Hartland couldn't imagine why the princess would have lied to him about something so trivial, but clearly he had hit the mark with his guess.

She lifted her chin and met his eyes. "I did not hire a hack. I walked."

"Alone?"

"As you see. It is not so very far. And this district is quite genteel. If you will excuse me, I shall take my leave of you." She nodded to him and stepped away.

Without thinking, Hartland reached out and grabbed her wrist. "I beg your pardon, I don't mean to interfere, but I would feel much easier about you if you would consent to drive with me. Especially if you happened to make any purchases in that elegant jeweler's shop. Even in this part of town there are pickpockets."

He also wanted to tell her that it really wasn't the thing for a lady to be alone in Bond Street, where Pinks of the *ton* went to see and be seen, even if they had no business there. She would become known in a way he was certain would not be to her liking.

Her somewhat forbidding expression softened. "I made no purchases. I simply left some pieces to be repaired. But thank you. I should be grateful, I know. You are right. I'm just finding my way around. Lady Mariana has been so kind —but she is also bold and doesn't pay attention to the conventions. Besides, I wanted to get a sense of the town. My mind was otherwhere when I went out with Mariana. We had so much to talk about and in a carriage one misses much."

"Yes, one misses the slop in the streets, the urchins begging, and uneven flagstones!"

She laughed. "You are making fun out of me, I think. But when I am abroad, I listen, too. I hear people talking and the tone beneath the words, the happiness or sadness." A faraway look came into the princess's eyes.

"Well, perhaps you will forgo that pleasure and grant me the greater pleasure of escorting you to Grosvenor Square instead." Hartland put up his hand to call Jacko back.

"How can I refuse such a gallant offer?"

Her smile chased her moment of wistfulness away. *My god, she is beautiful,* Hartland thought as he helped the princess into the curricle. It wasn't who he expected would be sitting next to him that day. He had been prepared to exert himself to keep his temper and avoid grabbing the reins out of Miss Fontenoy's inexperienced hands—and also to make her fall in love with him. Instead, that telltale hint of jasmine wafted to him as light conversation flowed all the way to Grosvenor Square. He soon had the princess laughing at some of the absurd strictures placed on the movements of single women in the *ton.* "You should always have your footman with you, even if you choose just to go for a stroll. Or a maid would do as well, if you don't want to be remarked. And whoever it is should follow you a few paces behind. Be sure to load them up with all your parcels too so everyone knows you've been spending freely."

"I forget that I am not in Vienna sometimes. Although how I can do so, with all these different English accents everywhere, some so strange that I can hardly understand them. I listen, as I said, for the cadence, for understanding, to try to become more familiar. In truth, today I thought at first I would hire a hackney but when I went to the stand, I couldn't make out what the driver was trying to say to me! So I thought it the lesser of evils to walk."

Such a strange combination of worldliness and naïveté, Hartland thought. She was the opposite of Miss Fontenoy, whose ingenuous remarks hid a kind of common sense and matter-of-factness surprising in one so young. "Why didn't you take your phaeton?"

"I couldn't bear the thought of getting the horses put to for such a short time."

"Ah, but if you wish to be respected, you have to indulge such extravagant whims as making your groom spend an hour grooming and harnessing your pair and then another hour cooling them down and putting the carriage away, all for an errand that might take no more than thirty minutes."

This made her laugh again. A rich, silvery peal, her head thrown back in pure glee to reveal the white expanse of her throat. Hartland wanted so much to kiss that throat.

"I can see I need much instruction about how to become a bona fide member of the British *ton*," she said.

Hartland almost blurted out, *let me be that instructor*, but stopped himself. He had other business to attend to. He must not be seen too often in the company of this beautiful princess if he was to ultimately succeed at winning Miss Fontenoy's hand. Instead, he said, "I suspect you need less instruction than you claim. Propriety and manners are the same all over Europe, I believe."

She gave him a sidelong, impish glance. "Ah, but it is the subtle differences that matter."

All too soon they arrived at number twelve Grosvenor Square. Jacko jumped down from the back and went to the horses' heads while Hartland descended and then helped the princess out of the carriage. "It is perfectly seemly to walk alone from here to your house," he said, putting on an expression of mock seriousness.

She laughed again. "I shall remember that in future. Thank you, Duke," she said, giving him a quick curtsy, then hurrying away up the steps to the door that her butler held open.

~

IT HAD BEEN A NEAR THING, ADELHEID THOUGHT AS SHE TOOK off her hat and gloves and laid them on the table in the entry hall. It was all because Brattle had encountered some scruples on the part of Rundell & Bridge when he tried to sell the more spectacular of her jewels. Although the prestigious jewelers had not recognized the specific pieces, they were sufficiently expert to realize that they were heirlooms of great import to some family or other, and had declined to take them off his hands. They knew they weren't his, and his explanation that he'd taken on the task for a friend who did not want to be identified gave them pause.

"They're ladies' jewels, you see m'dear, and some suspicion attaches to me trying to dispose of 'em," he said the day before when he'd brought them back to her, full of apologies and promises to find another jeweler.

In that moment Adelheid realized she would have to do the deed herself. That such valuable trinkets would belong to her would hardly raise an eyebrow. She could not return to Rundell & Bridge so she went to Goldsmith's, whom Brattle had recommended to her. They were happy enough to give her a handsome sum for the pieces, and she left with her purse laden with enough money, she guessed, to last her at least for the rest of the month in London and settle all the bills she'd incurred so far.

Happening to step out onto the flagway after she completed her business just as Hartland did was a piece of bad luck. He'd been in Jackson's Boxing Academy—which she knew of from Nicholas, who explained something about the Corinthian set and what amusements someone like Hartland would indulge in. And the duke had clearly dressed himself in a hurry, leaving the unmistakable odor of masculine sweat clinging to him even through his coat. It was an honest smell, and she liked it. The last time she had been so close to someone after physical exertion was with Danton, wrapped in his strong arms.

There was no point dwelling on the past. Yet she could not help picturing Hartland shirtless, muscles tensed, perspiration streaming down his face and back. The image was a stark contrast to their actual circumstances and their bantering conversation about propriety. What would the duke think if he knew the direction her thoughts had taken? She had fallen back on the excuse of her foreignness to cover up any awkward moments. When she confessed that she had walked to Bond Street rather than taking a hack, his brightened eyes and a dimple in one of his cheeks gave him a boyish cast that instantly doubled his allure.

More than that, though, Hartland had been kind. She had the impression that he was glad to see her, more so than he might be on seeing a casual acquaintance. He didn't say or do anything that would have made her feel foolish or uncomfortable. Instead, he put her at her ease and seemed to understand right away that her European manners had not entirely prepared her for all the strictures of *ton*-ish society. Even as a widow she must observe the proprieties, he said. *Especially a young and beautiful widow*. Those were his words. Glib, certainly, except that she detected a note of sincerity in them.

Had she been too flirtatious? That was not her intention. She didn't want to make her pursuit obvious. He must come to her. The Ambrose ball had been a start. Only a fool would fail to realize that he was not in love with Miss Fontenoy. That was hardly surprising. The girl was attractive but no beauty, and very young in the ways of the world. That she did not cherish passionate feelings for Hartland was also obvious.

In fact, she suspected that the young man Miss Fontenoy had waltzed with—*just Lewiston*, the duke called him—stood a better chance with her than Hartland did.

Why couldn't he see it? Or perhaps he didn't want to. Would she herself be able to make him see it? How? It was frustrating. Here she was only a few hundred yards away from the man she'd pinned all her hopes on—and yet, a gulf stretched between them. To be too flirtatious and coming would doubtless put him off, no matter how attracted he was to her. Being too aloof might discourage him altogether.

Perhaps she should abandon her project.

But no. Too much was at stake. She reminded herself that everything she did was for Otto. At least, she could persuade herself it was if she could only banish the vision of Hartland's chiseled features and laughing eyes, his deep, cultured voice and perfect manners.

Wouldn't she also be saving him from a disastrous marriage? One that might solve his immediate financial problems, but would not suit him in the end?

She pulled the door of her bedroom closed with a slam. This would all be so much easier if he'd been a fright!

# CHAPTER 17

$\mathcal{T}$he morning she was supposed to have her first driving lesson with Hartland, Olivia very nearly missed her appointment with Tetrazzini. As she was putting on her poke bonnet with the flowers on one side, her mother emerged from the breakfast parlor still wearing her brocade dressing gown.

"Mama! You're up so early." Lady Ambrose almost never breakfasted downstairs.

"I haven't been able to sleep. All I can think about is you and the duke!"

Olivia tried to put herself in her mother's shoes but couldn't get past the fact that she, Lady Ambrose, would not be the one whose life would be altered permanently if she married the duke. "That is to no purpose. If it is meant to be, it will be."

"But it is up to you! Oh wretched girl." The viscountess fished a handkerchief out of the pocket of her dressing gown and blew her nose into it. "Where are you going? You should remain at home so you're here if Hartland calls. Yes. Go and put on one of your sprig muslins." She took hold of her daughter's arm and tugged her toward the stairs.

Olivia stood her ground. "I shall when I return."

"But where can you be going at this hour?"

"Only to Hookham's to borrow a novel Lady Mariana told me about." It was all Olivia could think of on the spur of the moment.

Since Lady Ambrose was a little in awe of Olivia's smart, confident friend, she said, "Very well. But don't dally!"

*Oh I won't!* Olivia thought as she walked as quickly as she dared toward the corner of South Audley Street where Tetrazzini would be awaiting her in a hack.

He had stopped a little way down and when he saw her he beckoned furiously. The conversation with her mother had made her late.

Once in the hack on the way to the Haymarket, Olivia asked Tetrazzini, "Why? Why does he want to hear me again? He already knows I can't perform there."

"*Ascolta, Signorina,*" a very agitated singing tutor said. "I don't know, but he say is *molto importante!*"

Clearly she would gain no enlightenment from the Italian and occupied herself with once again tying on the mask he'd had made for her.

The interior of the theatre now a little familiar, Olivia walked briskly through the backstage corridor and climbed the steps to the stage. This time, rather than being empty, the stage had been set for the second act of *Nozze* and there were one or two workmen moving bits of scenery around. It was the countess's boudoir. The incongruous figure of Mr. Taylor, in buckskins and a rumpled shirt, occupied a delicate gilt settee. He stood when Olivia arrived.

"Miss—what shall I call you?" he said, marching toward her with his hand held out.

Olivia gave him two limp fingers to shake and didn't answer.

"You find me in the greatest difficulty. Catalani awoke with a sore throat and says she cannot sing this evening. There is no one presently in the company who could take her role, save Madame Storace who must take the role of Susanna. The boxes are all sold out and the pit has been filling all day."

Olivia shrugged and glanced at Tetrazzini.

"The Signorina say she cannot perform for an audience unless she remain *in maschera*."

That wasn't what she said! She drilled a furious look toward Tetrazzini, but he avoided her eyes.

"Do you know the part? All the recitatives as well? And the ensembles?"

In point of fact, Olivia did know it all—well, she was a bit fuzzy on the recitatives. She'd dreamed of being able to sing Mozart's beautiful trios and quartets with real voices in the other parts, not just Tetrazzini picking them out at the piano. She nodded.

"I'd like to hear you sing *Porgi, amor*, here, on the set, as if you were the countess." He gave her no opportunity to decline, but shooed the workmen off the stage, and himself left to reappear in the pit. He nodded to the harpsichordist, who played the introductory bars.

Olivia stood still and listened at first. Then she took in a deep breath and prayed the few vocal exercises she'd done when she was dressing would be enough. As she began to sing she strolled to the prop dressing table and sat in the chair angled toward the audience. This aria was Countess Almaviva begging the gods to restore her faithless love to her. Although Olivia had never experienced such betrayal, her imagination, combined with the music, soon transformed her into the heartbroken countess.

The cavatina was short. Once again, silence reigned at the end. Olivia stood looking out toward Taylor who appeared absorbed in thought, his head bowed.

An instant later his head snapped up, and, all business, he strode back and climbed up to the stage. "All right," he said. "If you do this one performance for me, get me out of a terrible predicament, I'll pay you half what I was going to pay Catalani."

Tetrazzini had come out from the wings and stood listening to this. Olivia turned to him, a question in her eyes. The question was as much for herself as her tutor. Would she dare? How could she possibly manage such a thing? No question she would have to remain masked and not give her real name. But to be in a real opera! And earn money of her own! What would she do with it?

Tetrazzini and Taylor were both waiting for her answer. Without thinking, she nodded once.

Mr. Taylor ran to her and engulfed her hand in a crushing handshake. "Thank you! Now, we need to get you to the costumer right away—I don't suppose you have your own costumes?"

Olivia cast a panicked glance at Tetrazzini who said, "No, no Meester Taylor. She was not expecting to perform."

"As I thought. We'll need a rehearsal or two with the rest of the singers, but that can be before the performance at half voice."

Olivia's mind reeled. Of course doing the performance would involve more than just coming here, standing on the stage and singing. She mentally sped through her day. She could get away with being here for an hour longer at that moment and could say later that she was having dinner and then going to the theatre with—whom?

Lady Mariana, of course! She would write a quick note to

her asking her to say she was with her all the evening. How would she explain? The less she told her the better.

Before she knew it Olivia was behind a screen being undressed and put into an elaborate court dress with wide panniers and having a high, powdered wig settled on her head. The gown was enormous on her and too short, and the wig itched and smelled of powder and sweat. The seamstress, Félicité, clucked incessantly. How she did it with so many pins between her lips Olivia could not imagine.

Almost as quickly as she'd gotten into it, she stepped out of the costume and donned her own gown. Then a stage hand led her out to where Tetrazzini waited for her in Fops' Alley.

Neither of them said a word until they were in the hack. Olivia fumbled with the ties on her mask, desperate to get it off. It made her face sweat. Once she'd mopped herself with her handkerchief, she said, "How much money is half what Catalani is paid?"

"It is *molto denaro, Signorina.* Catalani receive *tre mille* guineas."

Half of that was still fifteen-hundred guineas. For herself alone. So much money! She had no banking arrangements, receiving her generous allowance from her father on quarter day and referring any extraordinary expenses to him. Olivia knew nothing about managing money. Who could she turn to? How would she explain it?

Elation and terror battled for control of her emotions. She would realize her life's dream that night. She would perform in an opera with professionals. Then terrible thoughts intruded on the heels of her high spirits. Would she be able to do it? Would the other singers be kind to her? What if someone recognized her?

Her mind was otherwhere when Ebbings let her into the

house and took her bonnet and pelisse from her. "My Lady is in the long drawing room," he said in his polished drawl.

The last thing Olivia wanted to do was face her mother. But it couldn't be helped. She drew a few deep breaths to regain calm herself, then walked sedately up the stairs to the drawing room.

"Olivia darling! You missed your nuncheon," Lady Ambrose said, pausing in her needlework to glance up at her daughter.

In fact, Olivia had had no breakfast either. "I shall ask for a tray to be brought up when I change."

"But then it will be dinner!"

"Lady Mariana has invited me to dine with her this evening, then go with her to the opera and sit in her box. So you don't have to go again. It's only *The Marriage of Figaro* and I know you don't like to see the same opera more than once."

"That is true, and I'm relieved. I'll be able to go to Lady Marimont's card party, then."

Olivia made a mental note to make sure Lady Mariana hadn't been planning to attend that event as well—although it was hardly the kind of thing she enjoyed. "I shall retire for a while and read, Mama. I'm still a little weary from the ball."

"Very well, dear."

Lady Ambrose didn't take her eyes off her tambour frame as Olivia left to do something quite other than read.

Olivia sent Hetty to South Audley Street with her message for Lady Mariana and told her to wait for a reply. When that came back assuring Olivia that she would be delighted to help her in this way, and that no, she wasn't going to a whist party, Olivia sighed with relief. Now she just had to figure out how to make sure her mother didn't suspect anything. The viscount wasn't a problem—he spent most evenings when he was in town at Watier's doing his best to lose some of the vast fortune that had come to him through his wife. Fortunately, a great deal of it was in trust for Olivia.

Every nerve in her body was on edge. She tried to relax her throat and did some quiet vocal exercises up in the schoolroom after she had dressed in a manner that would not excite Lady Ambrose's curiosity. The biggest difficulty lay in persuading her mother that she didn't want to take the barouche with its telltale crest on the side. She pointed out that her mother would need it herself, and, in any case, Lady Mariana's carriage could bring her home at the end of the evening. Olivia professed a desire to walk the short distance to South Audley Street on such a beautiful day. Her mother protested vigorously saying that no lady going out for the evening would walk alone. Olivia relented on this point and undertook to have Hetty accompany her.

This required her to take Hetty a little into her confidence. "I'm not going to Lady Mariana's," she told her maid while she was drawing on her gloves. "I promise you, I won't be doing anything foolish or dangerous. It's something I feel I must do, however, and her ladyship would most definitely not approve."

"But Miss! Surely—"

"I need you to keep this secret for me. I will be forever grateful to you if you do," Olivia said, with her most pleading look and taking hold of Hetty's hands.

It was more difficult than she thought it would be, but she eventually prevailed with her protective abigail. They started out in the direction of Lady Mariana's house, but once they were out of sight hastened to the nearest hack stand.

Safely in the smelly privacy of the much-used

conveyance, Olivia took her mask out of the large pocket in her cloak. Tetrazzini made sure she had it before they parted that morning. She would have to secure it herself since Tetrazzini wasn't with her and it was a little difficult. However, the elaborate wig she would be wearing would cover any strings.

Backstage at the theatre had been transformed since she was there that same morning. For one, a few soldiers were stationed at the entrances to prevent any unwanted ingress by audience members. One of them tried to bar her entrance, doubtless suspicious of someone wearing a face-concealing mask, but the footman inside had obviously been alerted to look for her and persuaded him to let her pass.

Once inside, she found herself in a maelstrom of carpenters and seamstresses dashing everywhere, as if everything must be done in the greatest hurry, with every spare dressing room or inch of dressing table in frantic use by someone more or less in costume. Vocal exercises and snatches from the libretto created a cacophonous soup of sound.

"This way, Mademoiselle. I am Félicité, you recollect?" The seamstress rushed over to Olivia as soon as she laid eyes on her and led her to a dressing room that had a door and no one else in it. "'Ere is your room. I help you in the costume. I altered it to fit. You will see." The Frenchwoman's accent was less pronounced than Tetrazzini's Italian one. Or perhaps she just tried harder. Working backstage she hadn't the need to remind the *ton* that she was an exotic rarity.

Félicité must have been very skilled indeed because the gown that had hung loosely on Olivia that morning now fit her perfectly. It had been lengthened by means of an added flounce, and the wig was freshened a little to rid it of the worst of its odors. "Per'aps some rouge on your mask, so you do not frighten the audience?"

Olivia wasn't certain that would make a difference, but

consented to have just a little patted on. She saw herself in a mirror for the first time in the face-covering mask and agreed that it made her look spectral. It couldn't be helped, though. She hoped the audience would soon forget it and just listen.

"Soloists and chorus to the anteroom!" came a shout that sounded like Mr. Taylor.

"Where is that?" Olivia asked.

"Come. I show you."

The seamstress led her to a large parlor where the entire cast of the opera were milling about in their costumes. When she entered, everyone stopped talking and stared. Mr. Taylor said, "This lady is the Countess for this evening."

"What's the mask for?" asked Bartolo.

"Never you mind."

"What's 'er name?"

Taylor turned to Olivia. She would have to talk at some point. She'd already spoken to Félicité of necessity. "l'Incognita," she said, and curtsied low.

They all eyed at her with varying expressions of skepticism, curiosity, or suspicion. Olivia thought it was a good thing she wore a mask or they'd see her face turning the color of beetroot.

"First, we'll skip over some of the Countess's recitatives. They aren't really necessary." He turned to Olivia. "You're prepared with the ensembles, so Tetrazzini says?"

Olivia nodded. It was a scramble, but she had a good memory, and had refreshed it that afternoon on the intricate duos, trios, quartets, and the final scene with the entire cast —all eleven of them.

"We'll go and mark Act II, no recitative, just arias and ensembles at half voice so … L'Incognita … can get her bearings. I'm counting on all of you to help her along. We'll mark the other acts during the intervals between, back here."

"Where's the Cat?" asked the man Olivia recognized as the count. Everyone sniggered at this unkind nickname for the great Catalani.

"Indisposed," Taylor said, and herded everyone out and onto the stage. The doors of the theatre hadn't been opened yet but footmen and maids were walking to and fro.

Olivia concentrated with every ounce of focus she had, committing to memory where she had to stand, who was who, and every detail of what she had to do. They had only an hour before the overture, so they sped through the libretto. She was grateful she didn't have to sing until Act II. It would give her time to go over everything in her dressing room while Susanna, Figaro, Cherubino, the Count, Basilio and the others were all on stage for the first act.

As she started for her dressing room, someone caught hold of her arm and stopped her. She looked around and saw that it was the boyish soprano Cherubino. "I don't know how I'm going to look infatuated with you in that mask."

"I'll do what I can to help you with my eyes, my gestures, and my voice." Olivia said, but the singer didn't look convinced.

"Well, it's *your* neck," she said, and went away to take her place for Act I.

Alone in her dressing room, hearing the overture and the music from the first act muffled and distant, Olivia had never felt so alone in all her life. The hostility of the rest of the cast was palpable. She'd always thought there would be a great sense of camaraderie in a company like this, all banding together to create a magnificent work, an unforgettable experience. But somehow she knew that when she stepped on the stage she would be as one cast out into the sea with only the flimsiest lifeboat. It would take all her fortitude to get through it.

Still, this was what she wanted. She didn't have to do this.

And underneath the nerves that were making it a little hard to breathe lay a fiber of exhilaration, of knowing that she was about to enact something so outrageous that if anyone knew about it she would be cast out of society.

No one would know. She would see to that. From that moment and for the next few hours, she was not The Honorable Olivia Fontenoy. She was Countess Almaviva, desperate to win back her philandering husband.

Through her door she heard many footsteps and much talking. It was the interval. She walked up and down her small dressing room, going over her music in her mind, praying that she didn't forget anything.

A tap on her door was followed without pause by its opening to reveal Mr. Taylor. "It's time."

She nodded. He unexpectedly put out his arm to lead her to the wings so she could take her place on the stage and whispered to her moments before the boys lit the footlights again, "Just sing."

LEWISTON AND HIS MOTHER SAT IN THEIR CUSTOMARY BOX AT the King's Theatre for the second performance that season of *Le nozze di Figaro*. He had realized on reflection that the first one passed rather hazily for him, distracted as he'd been by the presence of Miss Fontenoy in the box next to his. That had been engineered by Hartland, who took advantage of it for his own purposes. But the recollection of passing his handkerchief to the much-moved Miss Fontenoy and her confusion about where it came from teased at the corners of his mind. As did their waltz together at her ball, her refusal to sing for the company, and her realization that it was he, not Hartland, who had given her the means to hide her tears at the opera.

He did not expect anything more to come of it. His gesture in sending her the music he'd adapted for her was as much a farewell memento as anything else. Hartland had made it abundantly clear to him that he planned to catch Miss Fontenoy. To be fair, his friend wasn't behaving as if only her fortune attracted him. Harry expected that Philip was unaccustomed to women who did not set their caps at him and flirt outrageously. A duke—and a handsome duke at that, even if his pockets were to let—could expect to be considered a prize. It was probably good for him that Miss Fontenoy did not treat him as such.

Hartland's effect on ladies was in direct contrast to that of Lewiston himself, a rather diffident, unremarkable marquess who scraped by without a large fortune but by "holding household," as the country folk termed it. He was not destined to win a contest for any lady worth having. He would end by numbering Miss Fontenoy among his friends, accustomed to being asked for counsel and invited to make up the numbers at her table, just as had happened with Lady Mariana.

He laughed to himself. The two women were not dissimilar. Neither of them had the common sort of looks or played the *ton* game of matchmaking without protest. Bridlington had told him after Mariana and Thorne were married about the outrageous scrape she'd gotten herself into, wearing men's clothes and going into the House on the very day of Perceval's assassination. The thought brought an inappropriate smile to Lewiston's lips.

"Something amusing you, Harry?" his mother said.

"Just a pleasant memory. I wonder what's holding up the overture?" It was past six-thirty, and the almost-full pit below was starting to grow restless. Soon items might find their way onto the stage, tossed up by angry audience members. Catalani had her adherents, even though she was by no means news at this season, and they were eager to see her. The wait for her appearance in Act II was bad enough without an additional delay before the opera had even started.

Almost before the thought about Catalani had fully formed in his mind, a man in evening dress and a flourish of orders on his lapel—whom Lewiston recognized as the impresario Taylor—stepped out from the wings and raised his hand to the audience. Curiosity stilled the hubbub, at least temporarily.

"My Lords, Ladies, and Gentlemen, I beg your indulgence this evening to introduce to you a new soprano in the role of Countess Almaviva. Madame Catalani is indisposed and will return for the next performance of this opera."

By the time he got to the end of this announcement, shouts of protest flew up from the pit, down from the gallery, and even from some of the boxes. Lewiston wanted to know the name of this poor singer who would doubtless have a hard time of it with the spectators in such a rage. But, although Taylor continued speaking, his words were entirely drowned out by the noise of the audience.

The overture started right away, battling against the furor coming at the players from all directions. A large number of audience members in the pit walked out and a couple of the boxes emptied as well. The orchestra played on valiantly. Lewiston couldn't understand how they could hear each other to stay together until he spotted the harpsichordist nodding his head vigorously to give the beat.

At last the singers entered the stage. A few wadded up bits of paper landed at the Figaro's feet, but he kicked them out of the way with good humor, and the audience gradually settled down.

Since the first act retained its original cast, with the principal role of Susanna still sung by Mistress Storace, it was possible to hear the music and concentrate on it—except, of course, during the recitatives, when many people customarily took the opportunity to chat with their neighbors or take a turn in the corridors until the next popular aria. During the interval before the second act, though, a buzz of conjecture spread around. No one, it seemed, had any notion who the substitute Countess was to be, since the impresario's announcement of her name had been inaudible to all.

The stage was reset for Act II, the footlights lit, and the entire audience gasped. Comments that began as murmurs grew to a veritable roar, and the introductory bars of the Countess's cavatina could barely be heard.

The woman singing the role of Countess Almaviva wore a white mask over her entire face. Not a single one of her features could be discerned.

Lewiston leaned forward in his seat, nonplussed, intrigued to hear what would issue from behind that mask, desperate with curiosity about what could possibly inspire an opera singer—normally notoriously exhibiting creatures —to obscure her face to the audience at the most prestigious theatre in London.

*"Porgi amor*
*qualque ristoro..."*

The voice started on a tentative quaver which, by the second note, gained power and confidence. And then, before his eyes, the masked soprano became the sad Countess. The voice itself was as arresting as a nightingale's plaintive song, with only the most delicate vibrato. With seemingly little effort, it grew to fill the entire theatre. The audience quieted.

While everyone else soon settled into their enjoyment, overlooking some awkward stage business no doubt the result of the last-minute substitution, Lewiston's mind was aflame. He knew that voice. He had heard it once before, in

February, in Hyde Park. It was the same one, he felt certain. Who was she? Where did she come from?

He must find out. He would ask Taylor next time he saw him at White's.

By the third act of the opera, the audience forgot to jeer at the masked soprano.

When the opera was over, instead of rotted fruit and balled up paper, bouquets sailed from the audience onto the stage. But the lady only took one bow, did not remove her mask, and Lewiston could swear he saw her run into the wings as though someone pursued her.

Lewiston was not one of those dandies who made a habit of going backstage after a performance ostensibly to congratulate the singers, but really to see if there was a prime article among them. But he was tempted to do so today—and not because he wanted to find some lightskirt to take under his protection. He wouldn't go, however. Aside from the fact that his mother was with him, he felt sure the masked soprano would not remain in the theatre. She had clearly fled. It seemed she did not want to reveal her identity for reasons he could not guess.

"Well, Mama, what did you think?" He turned to Lady Lewiston only to see that her chin was resting on her chest, her bosom rising and falling steadily in the rhythm of sleep.

OLIVIA'S HEART POUNDED AS SHE FLEW INTO HER DRESSING room, ripped the stitches that held the back of her costume closed, stepped out of it, and tore the wig off, pulling some strands of her own hair out along with it. With trembling hands, she did her best to get her own gown over her head. By pulling it up high and reaching behind she was able just barely to tie it closed. It would be covered by her cloak in any case. Next, she had to put her hair in enough order so that she could get it neatly under her hat—all without removing her mask in case anyone came in.

She could still hear the roar of the audience as she raced out the back door of the theatre to the hack. She'd told the jarvey to wait and return her to the same corner, and having taken care to be turned away from him when she descended with her mask on. Except there was no way to avoid being seen in that face covering when she came out of the theatre, and the driver's round-eyed gape told her she'd have to invent some reason for such a bizarre trick.

"Masquerade!" she said, hoping it would suffice. She leapt into the vehicle and pounded on the ceiling and removed the mask at last. Underneath it, her face was bathed in perspiration. The heat on stage, with the oil footlights and massive wax candelabras in the wings, had nearly overcome her.

By the time they reached the corner, she'd mopped her face dry and tucked the mask in her cloak pocket. She pressed a generous gratuity into the jarvey's hand and put her finger to her lips. "Mama would be so angry!" she whispered. His answering wink assured her he'd accepted her inference that she was a young damsel who had attended a masquerade without her parents' knowledge.

She worried that when she walked up to the door without having been let down from Lady Mariana's carriage it would raise suspicion in Ebbings's mind. She would claim to have decided to walk home and press a guinea into his hand. As far as she knew, he wasn't doggedly loyal to her mother. And just this once…

Ebbings looked at her a bit strangely when he answered the door to her, but the gratuity seemed to do the trick. Olivia hastened up to her dressing room, eager to wash and undress and think over what she had done that day.

When Hetty took her cloak and hat and saw the state of

her hair and gown underneath them, she said, "Miss! What have you been doing?"

Her maid's wide eyes and raised eyebrows had Olivia thinking madly if there was some way of explaining how managed to arrive home with her gown not properly fastened at the back. Hetty would no doubt think the worst. "Don't tell Mama, but I went to a masquerade ball, and changed into my costume at Lady Mariana's. We were in such a hurry when we got back that there wasn't time to fasten everything properly." She thought she might as well use the same excuse she gave to the driver of the hack, and hope that Hetty wouldn't point out that Lady Mariana had a perfectly good abigail who should have helped her.

"Oh Miss, you shouldn't ought to, you know. It's not proper, such things." Hetty clucked over her and shook out her gown, helped her into her night shift and dressing gown and then brushed the ringlets in her light-brown hair into more natural waves before twisting the curling papers through them.

While Hetty fussed and petted and brought her up a glass of warm milk and a slice of bread and butter, Olivia stared at herself in the mirror. *I did it.* It had gone by so fast. The music just tumbled out of her, coming from some place beyond her conscious mind, as if it had been part of her body. Aside from walking the wrong direction once or twice, she made no mistakes, blending her voice with the others in the ensembles. At first the audience jeered. She expected that. She wasn't Catalani after all.

But then there was a magical moment when they all went silent. And then after she finished the cavatina: cheers. That sound flooded through her, giving her courage and determination to go on and sing her heart out. And she did.

Tetrazzini said he would be in the pit to see her. She wanted to know what he thought.

His wasn't the only opinion she wished she could get, though. She had a brief fantasy that Lewiston might have been there and that he knew he was hearing her voice, and that she could talk to him about it, describe to him the ineffable sensation of being the vehicle through which Mozart's great music flowed.

Even if he'd been there, though, he wouldn't have known. No one aside from Signore Tetrazzini must know. And she must be certain to pay that singing tutor as much as she could to make sure he remained silent. Mr. Taylor had said she would be paid fifteen-hundred guineas. She imagined a great pile of gold coins and giggled. Of course it would be a bank draft. But what would she do with it? She would have to trust Tetrazzini to put it in a bank for her, she supposed.

And then, how would she put it to use? She couldn't imagine. Her allowance covered every expense she incurred in London, since the modiste's bills went directly to her father.

It wasn't the money, though. She would have done it for no payment at all. She would be able to go forward to her destiny as a duchess knowing that, just once, she had tasted the joy of making music at the highest level. Tomorrow she would have a driving lesson with Hartland. If he asked her again, she supposed she should accept him.

Despite the tantalizing image of his smoldering eyes and charming ways, the thought lowered her spirits.

# CHAPTER 18

*O*tto was doing so well at his lessons that the day after her visit to the jeweler Adelheid decided he deserved a treat. Lord Brattle had procured a beautiful black Welsh pony for him along with a spirited bay mare, Bella, for Adelheid to ride, and they had not yet been out together. It was too early in the day for fashionable promenades, so she was tolerably certain they could ride unobserved by more than nursemaids and their charges.

Barber lifted Otto into the saddle and saw that he was seated properly with quiet hands on the reins and attached the lead line to the bridle. Their sedate train navigated the few streets to the Stanhope Gate and entered the park.

Barber found a clearing where Otto could circle around him as he kept hold of the lunge line and told Otto when to walk and when to trot—he even let him canter a little. Adelheid walked Bella a little away, staying near only long enough to see that Barber had Otto well in hand, then trotted to the carriage drive to shake the fidgets out of her mare.

She was a competent horsewoman although, having learned only as an adult following her marriage to the prince, Adelheid didn't have the bred-in-the-saddle seat that girls brought up on country estates sometimes enjoyed. But her cherry velvet riding habit—exquisitely tailored by Stultz on the advice of Mr. Gordon at Madame Pauline's, along with her jaunty matching shako—made her a vision that would distract from any close examination of her riding ability.

On her third circuit of the park, she spied a very familiar curricle being driven somewhat hesitantly by a lady seated next to Hartland—by Miss Fontenoy, in fact. The sight gave her a little pang. There was something intimate about the scene. Even from so far away, she could see that the shared endeavor and focused concentration connected the two of them even more than they appeared to have been connected in the ballroom. Adelheid turned Bella and began to ride away from the pair.

After a few moments, though, she thought better of it. She owed Miss Fontenoy polite attention after she so courteously invited her to her ball. And if they should happen to catch sight of her, not making that effort would appear rude.

Adelheid lifted her chin, adopted her most serene expression, and urged Bella to a sedate canter—the easiest gait to show her to advantage. As she approached she did not look directly at Hartland, who seemed fully occupied adjusting the reins in his student's hands, so their eyes did not meet until they were almost abreast of each other. Adelheid raised her eyebrows and smiled in mock astonishment. Hartland reached over and took the reins from Miss Fontenoy so he could pull the horses up.

He doffed his hat and nodded to her. "Princess Adelheid, how delightful to see you."

She slowed Bella and came to a stop herself, nodding politely, first to Miss Fontenoy, then to Hartland.

"I am so pleased you were able to come to my ball, Your

Highness," Miss Fontenoy said with a nod and genuine pleasure in her voice. "You have come from Austria, I'm told?"

Adelheid smiled. "Yes, very near Hungary."

Miss Fontenoy looked at her with wide, frank hazel eyes,
her lips slightly parted in a small smile. "I didn't expect to be
entertaining a princess!"

The candid youthfulness of her exclamation touched
Adelheid. She wanted to say something nice about the occasion. "I especially enjoyed your ensemble, Miss Fontenoy.
They seemed quite professional, a pleasure to both the ears
and the feet. You are musical?"

The girl's face flushed slightly pink, calling to Adelheid's
mind the scene in which she refused to sing for the company.
"I love music more than anything," she said.

*Much more*, Adelheid thought, an idea suddenly dawning:
*much more than you love the duke.*

Hartland had said nothing after the initial greeting,
pretending to be occupied with his hands, which were
quietly holding the reins and keeping the horses still.

She wasn't going to lose this opportunity to at least find
out more about what they were to each other. "I see you are
conducting a lesson, Duke! That is brave of you, especially
trusting a novice with your magnificent horses." Adelheid
turned to Miss Fontenoy. "Have you ever driven before?"

The girl's mouth twisted into a rueful, conspiratorial
smile. It was a candid, likable expression. "Never. Which of
course you must have guessed."

"She's doing splendidly," Hartland said, uttering a polite
fiction and at last lifting his eyes from his hands and looking
full into Adelheid's face.

The electric force of his gaze nearly made her gasp. Did
he ever look at Miss Fontenoy that way? If he did, she would
be under his spell in an instant. *What about me? Am I under his
spell?* It was supposed to be the other way around. She must

ensnare him. Adelheid dragged her thoughts back to the moment. "Don't let me keep you. I am just exercising my new mare. We are as yet unaccustomed to one another." She reached forward and patted Bella's neck and the horse gave an answering twitch.

"A handsome animal. Who procured her for you?" Hartland asked.

"Are you acquainted with Lord Brattle?" Yes, horses were always a safe topic. Adelheid's heart slowed as she reined in her galloping thoughts. "It was he who introduced me to Lady Mariana."

Hartland creased his brow in a considering way and then said, "I don't know him well. We belong to the same clubs."

"Ah yes, the clubs. A pity we ladies do not have our own establishments where we might get to know one another away from the judging eyes of the gentlemen!" Adelheid lifted an eyebrow.

This brought a broad smile to the heiress's face, and an appreciative sparkle to her eyes.

*Oh dear*, Adelheid thought. The girl was clearly charming and quick, although not what Hartland would account a beauty. She was almost certain she would like her, might even be tempted to make her a protégée, had circumstances been otherwise. "I must go back and find Otto, who is on his pony being given a lesson of his own by my groom," she said, touching the handle of her whip to the narrow brim of her hat.

"Delighted to see you, Ma'am," Hartland said with another nod.

Adelheid rode off and forced herself not to look back.

Miss Fontenoy had proved to be an apt pupil once she got over her nervousness. This wasn't helped by encountering the princess at the beginning of the lesson, though. In her elegant habit seated atop a blood mare, she presented a stark contrast to the ingenuous Miss Fontenoy. But Hartland saw no evidence of envy or jealousy in Miss Fontenoy, only admiration. He didn't know whether this surprised him or not. Both of the ladies were clever. Perhaps cleverer than most. And they seemed to be free of that petty meanness that so often characterized the competitive ladies of the *ton*.

"I think that's enough for your first time out," Hartland said to Miss Fontenoy on their third go around the park. They stopped on the carriage drive and he took the reins from her. "You did well. My horses are not the easiest to manage."

She flushed slightly under the effect of this compliment. "I hope you'll take me out again sometime. Perhaps teach me how to point my leaders? Or feather edge a corner?"

He laughed. "You're a ways off from that as yet, and we'd need four horses. A few more lessons and you'll be a creditable whip, though, I should think."

It was Miss Fontenoy's turn to laugh, a sparkling peal that took him by surprise. He'd never heard her laugh like that before. She wasn't given to giggling, which was a relief to one who had been giggled at more times than he could count. Was it just the driving lesson that made her so high spirited that day?

"Tell me about the princess," Miss Fontenoy said. "You said she's a neighbor. She's very beautiful. There's something sad about her, I think."

"You know as much as I do, Miss Fontenoy."

Miss Fontenoy's questions ceased and she went into a reverie.

When they were almost to the gate, Hartland realized

they hadn't spoken at all about the opera, which he had told himself he must endeavor to find more interesting, for her sake. "Did you enjoy the Mozart last night?" he asked.

Her look was at first confused, but then it transformed into an expression of such glowing delight that it seemed out of all proportion to the question. "Oh yes! So much."

Such a strange reaction to seeing the same opera in the space of a few days. What was it Lewiston had told him about the previous evening's performance? Yes, something quite intriguing. "I saw Lewiston at the club after the opera and he said something about a new singer with a mask on."

"Yes," she said, "It was extraordinary."

Hartland would have left the matter there, but after a moment Miss Fontenoy asked, "Did Lord Lewiston think the masked soprano any good? Did he like her voice?"

"I should say he did! He wouldn't stop talking about it. I don't recall exactly what he said. Something about a pure, perfect tone, if I remember correctly." It was too bad he couldn't speak a little more eloquently about such things, Hartland thought.

Miss Fontenoy smiled, her eyes fixed on the distance as if she were far away herself.

"What did you think?" he asked.

"Think? About what?" It was as if she'd gone somewhere else for a moment and had to drag herself back.

"About the singer in the mask, of course!" How very odd of her, Hartland thought, to be so absentminded when the conversation turned to opera, something she loved.

"I thought…I thought it must have been difficult for her to take the place of Catalani, who everyone in the audience was looking forward to hearing. She must have been terrified."

Hartland considered this. "I expect so. But maybe not so frightened with a mask on."

By this time they had arrived back at Mount Street. Hartland jumped down and then handed Miss Fontenoy out of the carriage. When she stepped on the flagway, the heel of her half boot caught on the edge of one of the large stone flags and she lost her balance. Hartland grabbed her arms and held her until she regained her footing. She was slender and gangly under her pelisse and she became rigid with tension, as if afraid of letting him any nearer to her than necessary.

"Thank you, Sir. I can manage now," Miss Fontenoy said, pulling away from him and smoothing down her skirts. "Silly, really."

"Not at all. The flags are uneven. Shall I walk you into the house? Jacko can look after the horses."

"No!" she said so suddenly that he widened his eyes, bringing a sudden blush to her cheeks. "I mean, oh dear, I'm sorry, I don't want to put you to any more trouble."

In the space of a moment the awkward, inarticulate ingenue reappeared. *What caused this transformation*, Hartland wondered—although he could guess. He well knew the effect the pressure of his hands could have on a susceptible female. He must take care not to frighten her off with attentions that were too ardent. "Well, we'll say goodbye here then. I would like to call on you in a day or two, if I may." The words came out sounding more formal and stiff than he intended.

"Perhaps we'll see each other at Lady Ferndale's rout party," Miss Fontenoy said.

"Ah, yes. That's next week." She clearly didn't want him to call again so soon. He took hold of her hand and drew her a little nearer to him, sensing a bit of resistance. "Miss Fontenoy, I hope you didn't find me impertinent the other day in declaring myself to you so soon. I would by no means rush you to come to such an important decision. You may count on me not to mention the matter again until you are ready."

Her color heightened and she looked right and left as if she might find someone to tell her what to do or say. "How will you know when that is?"

Hartland lifted her hand to his lips. "I'll know." Then he waited while she ran up the steps to go in through the door that the butler had been holding open.

OH, WHY WAS SHE SO CONFUSED! OLIVIA'S MIND TIED ITSELF IN knots as she made an effort to calm down before eating a distracted nuncheon and escaping to the schoolroom to practice the pianoforte—or so she claimed. All she really wanted to do was gather her thoughts. So much had happened so quickly. It was as if all the preparations of her entire life before that time were suddenly being compressed into a few days. Her years of music and voice lessons. All the dancing and drawing and other lessons. Endless stitching and curtsying and learning to behave like a lady, all the time preferring the academic subjects most other girls found vexing. Now, seemingly from one minute to the next as soon as she turned eighteen, she was deemed ready to put it all to use.

The social transformation would have been daunting in itself. With the added turmoil of her operatic debut, she hardly knew who and what she was. She'd looked forward to the driving lesson with Hartland as a welcome distraction. But she wasn't prepared for the intimacy of sitting close to him on the seat of the curricle, his hands ready to cover hers if need be, his arm pressed up against her side and his voice vibrating so close to her ear. He did not make love to her, but his instructions were somehow infused with unspoken invitations she was not at all certain she wanted to accept.

And now, she awaited Tetrazzini. He would come and pass judgment on her performance. And what about Lewiston? She both dreaded and yearned to see him, to find out what he had truly thought about the masked soprano. If what the duke told her was true, it seemed his opinion would be favorable, but if she pressed him, he might find things to criticize.

All these thoughts chased each other through her mind like the squirrels in the trees.

By the time the singing tutor at last arrived, Olivia had given up trying to concentrate on the Clementi sonata she thought might distract her. Instead ,she paced aimlessly around the room, picking up books and putting them down again, pausing from time to time to stare out of one of the round windows, and humming snatches of the Countess's arias.

She had told Ebbings to send Tetrazzini directly to the schoolroom. The starchy butler regarded the effusive Italian with a great deal of suspicion, but yielded to Miss Fontenoy's instructions despite his misgivings. So when the tutor arrived, only a scratch on the schoolroom door announced him and he entered without being bidden.

At first startled, Olivia then flew to him and grasped his forearm with both her hands. "Tell me! Tell me honestly! How was I? Did I make a fool of myself? Did the audience hate me? Were they just being polite?"

Tetrazzini smiled benevolently at his student. "*State calma, Signorina!* You were…" He shook his head then put his thumb and index finger together and kissed them. "*Magnifico!*"

"You're just saying that to please me. Tell me truly, I want to sing better. What do I need to know?" She'd hurried over to the pianoforte and lifted up the score of Mozart's opera, flipping its pages.

Instead of answering her, Tetrazzini opened the small valise he carried and drew out two newspapers, *The Morning Chronicle* and *The Times*, both folded to particular sections. He prodded *The Chronicle* excitedly, pointing to the notice in great agitation. "Eet say, Signorina, 'We wish to excite the *attenzione* of all *cognoscenti*—'"

Olivia snatched the paper out of his hands and read the notice with greedy eyes. It first said that they would not have written about the second performance of the same opera were it not for a highly unusual circumstance. Then it described her as "*a l*issome young soprano who sang with disconcerting power and passion." Her performance was proclaimed a triumph. The critic did express some disapproval of the mask, saying it interfered with the audience's right to enjoy a visual as well as an auditory spectacle, especially those in the boxes on the sides of the stage.

She let the paper fall from her fingers and turned her stunned gaze on Tetrazzini's beaming face.

She had done it. She, The Honorable Olivia Louise Albertina Fontenoy, had sung the role of Countess Almaviva at the King's Theatre, Haymarket, in front of many hundreds of people. Almost two-thousand, in fact, as the theatre was close to full.

But now it was over. She was herself again. Just a come-out of the *ton*, an heiress looking to make a brilliant match. How could she, when the man she married would never know who she really was? Would never know of her greatest gift? Who—aside from Tetrazzini—would ever know what she had done, what she had dared? She would become a society hostess—perhaps making an effort to gather great artists around her in the manner of a *saloniste*, but her role in that case would be a facilitator, an organizer, a manager. She was not particularly good at any of those things and foresaw social disasters ahead of her. She would become only slightly better than her mother, who couldn't help occasionally putting her foot wrong, not having been born and bred to this bizarre world they inhabited.

Her mood of elation fell from her like a gossamer cloak, taking with it the illusion of beauty and mystery that her mood had inspired.

"Signorina Fontenoy, *che tristezza!*" Tetrazzini came to her and lightly pinched her chin with his pudgy fingers. "I have what, *io penso, forsè*, is good news. *Momento.*" He once more reached into his valise, retrieved a bank draft, and handed it to her.

She looked at it carefully. "But it's only for seven-hundred and fifty guineas," she said.

"*Si, si, ma* the rest, she will come. But Signore Taylor, he want you to sing *ancora*, again." He stopped, waiting for some reaction from her. Olivia only stared at him, uncomprehending.

"But I thought ... it was just that Catalani was ill."

Tetrazzini shrugged and pursed his lips in that completely Italian manner but with a slightly guilty look in his eye and said, "*Chi sa?* He pays you the rest and *molto di più* if you will do this."

"When?"

"*Martedì.*"

"Tuesday!" That was only four days away. She once more paced around the room, chewing the side of her thumb and thinking. Could she do it? She couldn't do it. But maybe she could? How? No it was impossible. She was lucky to have had a single chance. It would be foolhardy to think she could get away with it a second time. Yet she would have another opportunity to appear on stage. Her low spirits began to creep upward again. If she could only do this. But how? "I can't agree to anything right now. I must consider. You see, don't you?"

Tetrazzini nodded. "Meester Taylor, he want an answer *domani*. I will take it to him."

The tutor swept her a low, courtly bow. Olivia stretched out her hand and he took it. "I never thanked you properly, Signore Tetrazzini. I would never have had this opportunity —these opportunities—without you."

His dark brown eyes sparkled with something that might have been tears, but he blinked them away, smiled, and took his leave.

Olivia had little time to ponder her momentous decision however. Hetty came up to the schoolroom to tell her that Lord Lewiston had called and was in the blue drawing room with Lady Ambrose.

"Lord Lewiston? Here?" It wasn't that she didn't believe Hetty, who would never dream of teasing her in such a way, only that she didn't quite know how to face him. Add to that the fact that her mother thought she had gone to the opera last night with Lady Mariana. If he'd been there Lewiston probably noticed she wasn't in the Thorne's box, which was one of the ones closest to the stage. Come to think of it, she didn't know for certain that Lady Mariana had gone at all. She combed through her memories, trying to piece together her fleeting impressions of the people in the boxes that were near enough for her to see.

It was no use. She reached the drawing room without discovering any way to fool her mother and Lewiston.

"Ah there you are Olivia, dear. Lord Lewiston has been kind enough to sit with me while waiting for you to come down."

The rebuke was subtle, but unmistakable. Olivia went to her mother and clasped her hand apologetically. "I'm sorry,

Mama. But you know what I'm like when I practice the pianoforte. I quite forget the time!"

Lord Lewiston had risen when she entered and now walked forward and bowed to her. She put out her hand, which he shook.

"I was so pleased to receive the music you sent, Lord Lewiston. A lovely memento of my presentation ball." She heard the icily formal tone in her voice and wished she could find a way to be more natural.

Disappointment flickered through Lewiston's eyes when they met hers. Olivia smiled, trying to dispel the awkwardness between them. This wasn't right. They'd been so easy together. It was Hartland who disturbed her peace, not this diffident, warm-hearted marquess. "Please, Sir, be seated."

He resumed his seat opposite Lady Ambrose and Olivia perched on an armchair between the two sofas.

"I wanted to tell you about the opera last night," Lewiston said, abruptly changing the subject. "So extraordinary. But your mother says you were there as well. I wonder that I didn't see you."

*So he was there. What shall I say?* "I wasn't in our box. Lady Mariana Thorne invited me to go with her." She had to look away from him and was certain he saw through her lie.

"But—"

Olivia flashed him a pleading look, trying to send a message that would stop him saying what she feared he would next—that Lady Mariana hadn't been there either, or at least, that he hadn't seen her in her box.

"But then you heard the remarkable soprano wearing the mask."

Olivia's racing heart slowed and she looked her gratitude at him. He raised a quizzical eyebrow.

Lady Ambrose said, "Lord Lewiston has been telling me about this freakish female singer who performed the entire opera with her face completely hidden. It sounds outrageous to me!"

"Yes," Olivia said, "It was most unexpected. Tell me, Lord Lewiston, what did you think of the lady? Her voice, I mean, of course."

He shook his head and sighed and at first Olivia thought he would say something terrible, that he'd been disappointed, or that her voice was too weak. But instead, he said, "I have never heard anything more exquisite. And the acting—quite unusually good. The soprano did not rewrite Mozart's melodies, either." His suppressed smile dimpled his cheeks and Olivia couldn't help a glow of joy.

"I sat quite near, so I heard every syllable of her singing. Your box is farther back, I believe. Did her voice carry enough?" Olivia said, shamelessly embroidering on her lie.

"Yes! Every bit as well as Catalani's does."

"Do you ... " Olivia said, probing more, pushing for something else from him, she didn't know what, "Do you know her identity? I did not hear what Mr. Tay— ... the theatre manager said in his announcement."

He laughed. "The pit was most indignant about the substitution. I don't think anyone heard it. But they did print it in today's Times."

Olivia's heart flipped over and the blood drained from her face. Fortunately, Lewiston had looked away. "Oh?" she said, weakly.

"Apparently she goes by the name *L'Incognita*. I expect she's Italian."

Her pulse slowed to a normal rate and she let her shoulders drop from where they were gradually inching up toward her ears.

"But, I have heard her before," Lewiston said.

Olivia wanted to laugh and tell him he couldn't have done

so—but he had moved forward to the edge of his seat, his eyes brimming with excitement. What could he mean?

"I think she must be lodging somewhere near the park," he said, "Perhaps north of it. I heard her one day in February. Just briefly. It was the same voice. I could swear it."

"How odd," Olivia said, searching for a light tone that felt just out of her reach.

Lady Ambrose, who had continued her needlework as the two of them talked, looked up at this. "I expect it's just something to stir up some interest, sell more tickets."

Trust her mother to come up with a commercial reason for something. "But if that's the only time she would appear, and it was a complete surprise, I don't see how it could have had any effect on ticket sales."

"No. In fact, I don't know if you noticed, but I think at least a third of the people seated on the pit benches left when they heard Catalani would not be singing."

This illogically stung Olivia. They would have left before she'd stepped on stage, but somehow it still felt like an insult. "You'd think they'd give a young singer on stage for the very first time a chance, not judge before she's sung a note."

Lewiston looked at her with a frown puckering his brow. "It's not at all certain that she'd never been on stage before. Certainly not in London, but I think she's probably performed in Italy, at La Scala or La Fenice."

"Of course, silly of me to assume," Olivia said, realizing she'd possibly exposed herself inadvertently. "But she's likely not going to sing again, I assume, because Catalani will surely recover."

"On the contrary," Lewiston said. "The advertisement in The Times said she would be appearing again in the Mozart Tuesday."

*What?* She hadn't given her answer yet! How dare that Mr. Taylor!

"I should like to see this mysterious singer," Lady Ambrose said. "Perhaps I'll get up a party to go to the opera on Tuesday."

Olivia said nothing, trying instead for a disinterested smile.

"If you go, I shall see you there. I intend to take every opportunity I can to hear this remarkable soprano," Lewiston said, standing. "But I have been remiss. My principal purpose in coming to you today was to find out if you will attend the Philharmonic Society concert on Monday. I believe you are a subscriber? How else would you have engaged such fine musicians for your ball."

In all her turmoil over the opera, Olivia had forgotten that the second concert in the series of eight was to be the day before the opera. She had wheedled her mother into subscribing. Lady Ambrose was not enthusiastic about sitting and listening to music without any attendant spectacle. As to whether she could persuade her to go on Monday, she had no idea. "I hadn't thought … I believe, I will try to be there, but I am not certain of our engagements."

"Of course. I'm afraid I've taken up too much of your time already. I must go."

Olivia stood and walked over to him, her hand extended. It trembled slightly as he took it and this time kissed her knuckles lightly. "Until Monday, perhaps?" he said.

She simply smiled.

# CHAPTER 19

No matter how hard he tried Harry couldn't get his cravat tied to his satisfaction. Normally he didn't care, but it was the night of the Philharmonic Society concert and he had every hope that Miss Fontenoy would be there. He thought he had convinced himself that he should cede the field to Hartland, who needed to beguile an heiress more than he did. The duke may not deserve her, and he didn't really know what it was she loved, what it was that truly made her happy. But he had that devilish charm, that way of making women fall in love with him. Lewiston thought he saw the signs in Miss Fontenoy at her ball—the blushes, the tongue-tied shyness. He couldn't compete with that effect. Then he remembered their waltz. He could still feel the warmth of her body close to his and the press of her hand, could see her soft gaze as she looked into his eyes. It had been more than a dance. They made a connection on some barely conscious level. A connection born of music.

When he saw her the other day, on her own in her house without the duke present, there was something different about her. He couldn't quite say what it was, but she addressed him with decided warmth and seemed to be looking for something from him.

There was one odd circumstance about the visit that day, though. She told him she'd gone to the opera with Mariana, but he knew she hadn't been there with the Thornes. His box was on the opposite side of the theatre to theirs and he always looked over to see if they occupied it and what guests they had with them.

Why did she so clearly signal to him that he mustn't betray the fact that she hadn't attended the opera? And how did she know so much about the soprano in the mask in that case? Some of her knowledge could have come from the reviews in the papers,yet she spoke as if she had actually heard her, seen her. Was Miss Fontenoy seated in a different box? Surely she had not been among the blades in the pit.

Whatever the answer, Lewiston was hopeful that she would attend the Philharmonic Society that evening. On the chance that she did, Harry borrowed his mother's landaulet choosing not to arrive at the Argyll rooms in a hired hack. He cared little for his own consequence. But even if Olivia didn't need to be impressed by him, Lady Ambrose did.

Dusk was drawing in when the coachman pulled up and let Lewiston out at the entrance to the elegant hall on Regent Street.

"Harry!" It was Bridlington, no doubt having been dragged there by his wife. She liked music well enough but also went with an eye to seeing how the ladies dressed so she could create her own unique designs to be sold at Madame Pauline's.

He put out his hand. "George! I haven't seen you at the club lately."

The two friends chatted and greeted other acquaintances, Lewiston keeping one eye on the entrance, looking for Miss Fontenoy and trying not to make it seem as if he wasn't perfectly content just to be passing the time of day. When he failed to answer a simple question Bridlington put to him, the earl said, "Are you quite well, Harry?"

"What? Oh! Yes, of course. I just expected to see someone here who hasn't arrived yet."

Bridlington raised an eyebrow. "Who is she?"

Lewiston colored. "Oh, it's nothing like that, just a friend."

At that moment Olivia and Lady Ambrose entered the vestibule and gave their cloaks to a footman. Lewiston straightened his shoulders and said, "Excuse me," to his friend.

Miss Fontenoy was gazing up and all around at the beautiful room that had been newly furbished for the society, with elegant classical elements and muted colors, all in the best taste. Lewiston had to clear his throat to get her attention. "I'm so glad you decided to come," he said, bowing to Lady Ambrose and then to Olivia.

"I was sorry to miss the first concert," Miss Fontenoy said. "Is there a printed programme? I know of two works to be performed but not the others."

"Take mine and I will secure two more," he said, and before she could protest hurried over to the attendant.

When he returned, Miss Fontenoy pointed to the programme and said, "It's Mr. Clementi himself at the pianoforte!" The bright candles caught the green glints in her hazel eyes, little shards of emerald. "I was just practicing one of his sonatas earlier today."

"He is one of two who act as directors in the concerts. May I escort you inside?" Harry put out his arms, one to each of the ladies. They were not sitting with him, but agreed to meet in the break between the first and second parts of the evening's programme. "After the Haydn quartet. There is a lovely saloon where refreshments are served. It's most congenial. The very finest musicians not only perform but often mix with the audience there."

"Thank you, Lord Lewiston," Miss Fontenoy said, a faint blush stealing into her cheeks.

Lewiston hardly dared hope that she was blushing because of him. Perhaps he'd just imagined what seemed more than a friendly response from the lady, but she looked at him with such kindness, such interest that evening. Whatever the case, he could hardly concentrate on the excellent music for thinking about talking to her during the interval. At least he knew their conversation would be easy because they'd have the music in common. She was knowledgeable enough to discuss small details and to debate the merits of the German composers compared to the Italians.

After an overture, a symphony, a quintet and a quartet, the performers rose and bowed while the audience clapped appreciatively. Lewiston hadn't remarked anything particular about the performance, his mind being so occupied with thoughts of Miss Fontenoy, and he hoped she wouldn't question him too closely. He stood with everyone else and politely waited for several elderly people to leave their seats so he could get by.

But he kept his eyes on Miss Fontenoy and Lady Ambrose as they made their way to the adjoining saloon, wishing they would look in his direction. They nodded to a few acquaintances, not stopping to talk to any of them. He threaded through the crowd as quickly as he could without being rude until he joined them just as they were passing into the opulent reception room.

"Shall I procure some lemonade for you both?" he said.

"Would you, Lord Lewiston? That would be so kind," Olivia said. "And then we can talk about the Beethoven when you come back. Wasn't it splendid?"

He really had no desire to leave her side, but courtesy

demanded he perform this service for them. He had almost reached them with the two glasses of lemonade in his hands when Josiah Cudmore, the first violin and leader of the orchestra, stopped him. "Lewiston! What did you think? The Boccherini felt a bit rough—we hadn't time to rehearse it properly—but I think it's going well so far."

A moment later, James Oliver, the oboist, joined them. "Quite gratifying to have such a crowd here, don't you think?" he said, encompassing both men in his jovial smile.

Harry looked up and saw that Miss Fontenoy was gazing at him in astonishment and nodded to her before saying, "I didn't notice any problems. And yes, clearly the Society fills a sad lack in the musical life of the capital. Now, I must join my friends, if you'll excuse me!" He held up the two glasses in explanation.

"No such thing!" Cudmore said. "Introduce us and then we can continue our chat. I value your opinion."

The two musicians walked beside him up to Miss Fontenoy and her mother. Lewiston made the introductions. Olivia responded warmly, congratulating the two men on the performance so far. Lady Ambrose, after a chilly nod, spotted an acquaintance across the room and went over to join her. *She doesn't approve of me,* Lewiston thought. No doubt she wants her daughter to become a duchess.

"Of course, Lewiston would have done the Beethoven every bit as much justice," Cudmore said, "perhaps more."

Harry felt his face go hot when he met Miss Fontenoy's eyes, which had grown wide with wonder.

"You? Do you play the violin, Lord Lewiston?"

"Does he! If it weren't out of the question for a marquess to perform in public, I'd drag him myself to take his place in the orchestra," said Oliver.

Harry didn't know where to look. How could he explain not having mentioned his violin playing to Miss Fontenoy, when, given her enjoyment of music, it would have been the most natural thing in the world?

Before he could make any remark, a footman announced that the interval would end in a matter of minutes,and Lewiston offered his arm to Olivia. At the same time, Cudmore and Oliver had hastened back to the anteroom for the musicians, leaving the two of them alone—at least, as alone as two people can be in a crowd.

"Why didn't you tell me?" Olivia asked, giving his arm a light squeeze and training her intense eyes upon him.

He shrugged. What could he say? That he wasn't sure enough of himself? "The subject never came up."

"Now I understand a little better, I think. About the manuscript you sent to me."

"What? Oh yes, that. I did that the night of your party."

"Just from hearing the waltz once?" she asked, amazement in her voice.

He flashed her a lopsided smile. "It's not difficult. I've always been able to do it."

"And the right key as well." This wasn't a question, but it sent Miss Fontenoy into a reverie.

Harry took a deep breath, summoning all the courage he could, and said, "I was thinking that, maybe, sometime, if you felt inclined to do it, we could—"

At that moment, Lady Ambrose bustled over and claimed her daughter. They wouldn't have another chance to speak until the end of the concert.

When it was over, the three of them were waiting for their carriages to be brought around when Olivia said, "What is it you were going to ask me at the end of the interval, My Lord?"

How he wished he could hear his name, Harry, on her lips. "I was going to suggest we play together sometime, you know, just for our own pleasure."

"Not trotted out like an amusement for company," she said, a bitter edge to her voice and a surreptitious glance at her mother.

"No, not that. But I would very much like to play a duo with you accompanying me on the pianoforte. Something simple, perhaps?" His heart pounded wildly. Had he really just dared ask her such a thing? And why simple? She was as accomplished on the pianoforte as any lady in the *ton* if she'd been practicing a Clementi sonata. He hoped he hadn't offended her.

The Ambrose barouche pulled up, its gilded crest catching the light from the gas lamp nearby. He handed Lady Ambrose and then Miss Fontenoy into it and closed the door. She lowered the window, smiled at him, and said "A duo would be lovely," and then the groom set the horses in motion.

Even though his landaulet arrived immediately after that, Harry stood watching their barouche until it turned a corner and was no longer visible, a warm glow of possibility stealing through his body.

"THANK HEAVENS THAT'S OVER. REALLY, OLIVIA, YOU DO choose the most tedious entertainments!" Lady Ambrose fanned herself vigorously as the carriage navigated the evening streets. "Nothing to look at but a group of undistinguished men sawing and blowing on their instruments. And that lady who sang—not even in a costume!"

Olivia knew it would be a futile exercise to try to persuade her mother to enjoy sitting quietly and listening to music expertly performed in a magnificent setting, so she said nothing.

"And what was Lord Lewiston thinking, asking you to

play music with him? Does he intend to cut out Hartland? Hah! Playing the violin is hardly gentlemanly."

"He's a marquess, Mama, and his fortune is not as depleted as the duke's, for all that." Her mother's dismissal of Lewiston angered Olivia. He was just as eligible as Hartland, even though his title was one degree lower than a duke's. Clearly, the prospect of having a daughter who was a duchess had blinded her mother to any other possibility.

Was he a suitor? she asked herself. She supposed that making plans to play chamber music together was as intimate as driving through the park in a curricle. In fact, more so. In a curricle, one was on display to the public. In her music room, it would just be the two of them and a chaperone. Not her mother, though. Lady Ambrose would never consent to sit with them up in the schoolroom for more than a few minutes. It would have to be Hetty. In her way, Hetty was every bit as scrupulous and careful of Olivia's reputation as Lady Ambrose was.

Yet still, was Lewiston a suitor? Lady Ambrose said things daily that conveyed to Olivia that she considered her marriage to Hartland as good as settled. It was indeed very flattering to be courted by the catch of the season. The problem was, despite his obvious charms, Olivia had troubling misgivings about marrying a man like the duke, although she couldn't have said exactly why.

He'd always been well-mannered with her, a little flirtatious, but not in a way that made her uncomfortable. At least, not *very* uncomfortable. The crux of the matter was the fact that—despite his occasional protestations to the contrary—Hartland was clearly indifferent to music. He would never share her excitement and delight at going to the opera or a concert, and likely never get over the annoying habit of trying to talk to her when she'd rather be listening. Perhaps foolishly, she'd always held out a hope that she would marry someone who might enter into that passion, and at last make her feel less alone in it.

Could Lord Lewiston be that individual?

She didn't think she'd imagined that the marquess was trying a little to fix his interest with her that evening. Without Hartland hovering nearby, Lewiston came out of the shadows and addressed her more directly, not flirting, but making an effort to be agreeable. People admired the duke, but people liked the marquess. Lewiston's eyes were so kind, and a soft, limpid expression of warmth suffused them when he looked at her. She wondered if he looked at other girls the same way and if so, why he wasn't already married.

But she was overlooking the most astonishing part of the evening. She had made the remarkable discovery that not only was Lewiston a connoisseur of music but a musician himself. It even seemed he was enough of one to earn the respect of the professionals performing in the concert.

Why had he not told her?

She wondered if he told anyone. Did Hartland know for instance? Probably not. Lewiston must be so accustomed to being outshone by the duke in all the qualities society really cared about that he wouldn't try to put his unusual talent on display.

When at last she found herself alone in her bedchamber at the end of what had been another tiring and confusing day, Olivia had no leisure to puzzle out Lewiston's feelings—or her own, for that matter. Tomorrow would put her resolve and ingenuity to an even more challenging test than her first performance. She had almost worked out the logistics of her second appearance as the Countess, but try as she might, she couldn't figure out how to accomplish the feat without the cooperation again of Lady Mariana to deflect her mother's suspicion.

Poor Lady Mariana! She would be sorry she'd taken a liking to a troublesome ingenue. This time, Olivia felt a note would not suffice. She must pay a morning call on her friend. She had come to her rescue three times now—once the previous spring, then the night of her ball just a few days ago, and on the night of her first performance. It would be presumptuous to assume her help again without offering her a better explanation.

As she snuffed the candle on her nightstand, Olivia thought how different her season had turned out so far compared to what she had expected. Only a couple of weeks into it, and she'd already dared so much more than she ever thought she could, had received an offer of marriage from a duke, and, perhaps most surprising of all, underwent her own transformation. Something else had happened, something she could barely admit to herself, but the more she thought about it, the surer she was that it was so.

It seemed that she was on her way to falling in love with a shy, unassuming, musical marquess.

He hadn't declared himself, or even made his feelings clear. If he did so soon, and she admitted her own, no end of difficulties might arise. To risk going against her mother's wishes when she had so much else to hide would be to court disaster.

Many of the hopeful come-outs of the season would have been surprised—no, shocked—to know that instead of conjuring up the image of the dashing duke's handsome countenance as she drifted off to sleep, Olivia found herself going over and over her conversations with Lewiston, reliving the moment she discovered he played the violin, recalling the look in his eyes after she said she would love to play a duo with him.

# CHAPTER 20

*O*livia dressed quickly the morning of her next performance at the King's Theatre and dragged Hetty to walk with her to Lady Mariana's house on South Audley Street. This wasn't a grand mansion in the style of the Ambrose residence but a tall, narrow brick building with only two large rooms, a smaller one on each floor, and a stairway on one side of the house. The ground floor held the dining room, book room, and a small breakfast parlor. The first floor rooms could be opened to make one sizable drawing room, and the four bedchambers on the next two floors were commodious enough to include dressing rooms. A small suite of servants' rooms in the attic housed one footman, two housemaids, and Lady Mariana's abigail. The butler and housekeeper, a married couple, occupied a bedroom and a pokey sitting room of their own in the basement next to the cook's room behind the kitchen with its modern closed stove. Notwithstanding the modest size of the dwelling, Lady Mariana had furnished it in the most elegant and comfortable fashion, and no one fortunate enough to be invited to her parties and soirées would have thought it lacking in the slightest.

While Hetty went down the stairs to the entrance that led to the kitchen, Olivia reached for the door knocker, only to have the door opened by the stern-faced butler, Walton, before she could lift it. He bowed her in and soon had announced her to Lady Mariana. She was in the drawing room seated at a desk near a window, apparently writing a letter.

Upon Olivia's entrance she put her pen in the standish and waved the paper in the air to dry the ink before tucking it beneath the blotter. "Olivia! How delightful to see you!" She rose and approached with both her hands out, taking Olivia's and kissing her on the cheek. "I was just writing a note to Princess Adelheid inviting her to join me in my box this evening at the opera. To what do I owe the pleasure of your unexpected visit?"

That might complicate things, Olivia thought. If the princess would be with her, could she still be helpful? "Lady Mariana, you were so kind as to come to my aid last week when I needed you to support my story that I'd attended the opera with you. I must now explain exactly why I needed your help then, and why I'm daring to ask you for it once again."

Mariana put her forefinger against Olivia's lips. "Do not say another word until I have had tea brought in—unless you would prefer ratafia at this hour?" She rang the bell and the footman entered to receive orders to have a tea tray sent up. "Now, let us sit here and you can tell me all about it."

She drew Olivia to a small sofa warmed by the sun that streamed in through the windows. Olivia took a deep breath and launched into her story, telling Mariana everything about her adventures at the King's Theatre, only pausing when the footman brought in the tea tray.

Mariana listened to the entire recital without uttering a word. When it ended, she remained silent for a minute. "You know," she finally said, "I always knew I liked you, ever since the time at my mother's dinner party last season when you stood up to Lady Ambrose and refused to sing for the company. And then, you did it again at your ball. I was curious as to why and I'm glad I understand now."

"Now that you do, you must think me a frightful hoyden," Olivia said.

Mariana smiled. "I have no right to think any such thing! A year ago, I was behaving in a much more hoydenish manner, I assure you!"

Olivia couldn't imagine that this remarkable beauty with her deep blue eyes and glossy mahogany hair could ever be considered anything as shameless as a hoyden.

"And," Mariana continued, "I did not possess a fraction of your talent. My dear, you have a gift beyond price!"

Contrary to making Olivia feel pleased and flattered, Mariana's words sent her heart plummeting into her stomach. What did it serve to have such a gift if it must always remain hidden from the world?

"But this does not please you?" Mariana said, too perceptive to miss the change in Olivia's demeanor. "How may I help you today? What has brought you to me?" She reached out and took Olivia's hand, pressing it between both of hers.

Summoning all her courage, Olivia explained her current scheme for making another appearance on the stage of the King's Theatre that very evening. And also why simply claiming to be Lady Mariana's guest would not entirely serve her purpose this time.

Both of Mariana's delicately arched brows rose. "But this is perfect! As I said, I am indeed planning to attend the opera again. I, too, saw the notice that *l'Incognita* would be appearing once more, and wanted to hear her." She pursed her lips in a mischievous smirk.

This brought the color rushing into Olivia's cheeks. "I hope you won't be disappointed. I'm not at all certain it will go as well a second time. I should have declined, I know that. And this time...well, I thought of a way to manage, but if the princess is going with you, I don't know...You see, everything is more complicated."

"Tell me and let's see if we can figure it out together."

Olivia took a deep breath. She had nothing to lose. "I need you to come and fetch me in your carriage and for your carriage to await me at the end and convey me home. You see, I must don and remove the mask in a place where no one can see me and I'm afraid—now that there is so much notice about me—that to do so in a common hack would risk exposure."

Lady Mariana rose and took a turn around her elegant drawing room, stopping every now and then to pick up a trinket and put it down again as if keeping her hands entirely idle was beyond her capability. After what seemed like a long time she returned to the sofa and sat down. "I see that Princess Adelheid makes it a little more complicated, but..." She paused again, looking off toward a corner of the room. "Yes. I think that would work. Adelheid needn't come with me in my carriage. I'll tell her I will be arriving late and give her the number of the box. I don't think she'll mind. The timing, though, is what will undo us if it is altered in the slightest. Which means you must leave the theatre almost immediately after you've sung your last note." A smile spread across Lady Mariana's face and her eyes shone. "You can't know how much it pleases me to be engaged in a secret scheme again! One day I will tell you of the many I participated in before I was married which I'm sure will scandalize you."

Together they hammered out the details of the plan, which, when shared with another conspirator, seemed not quite so daunting to Olivia. She would tell her mother that she was going to a play with Lady Mariana. This would avoid her having to explain to someone like Lewiston, if he again attended the opera, why she hadn't seen it. Lady Mariana would only arrive at the King's Theatre at the beginning of Act III, so she could reasonably have been supposed to go after the play finished and have sent Olivia home with the headache. It seemed unlikely that the princess would have occasion to tell Lady Ambrose that Mariana had gone to the opera after all, not to the play.

Once all was settled, Olivia rose. "I am more grateful than I can say for your help in this."

"And I am only sorry that after this evening I am unlikely to have the enormous pleasure of hearing you sing ever again." Mariana embraced Olivia warmly. She rang the bell for Walton to see her out then turned to Olivia again, her eyes serious. "Are you truly determined not to perform in drawing rooms? You know that Catalani herself sings at private parties occasionally."

"Yes, but not because she's being offered up as a sacrifice and guests simply suffer through because they are caught unawares."

Mariana laughed. "Too true. But once your voice was known, it wouldn't be like that, I'm sure."

"It's more than that," Olivia said. "On the stage, behind a mask, I can be just my voice. No one is judging me as the ungraceful heiress being sought in the marriage mart for her fortune."

Taking Olivia's hand again, Mariana said, "If only the world were a little different. If only women were allowed to be more active, to do more. But alas, if such a situation ever comes to pass it will not be in our lifetimes."

Olivia felt a tug of sadness somewhere in the middle of her chest, above where her deepest breaths started, a place perilously near her heart, and raised brimming eyes to her friend.

THE EVENING LEWISTON MET OLIVIA AT THE CONCERT, Hartland went to White's for dinner and cards—an entertainment that never failed to divert him. As the tables were being made up for whist, Minty said, "I suppose you've heard about the masked singer at the opera."

"So I've been told by Lewiston. Have you seen her?"

"Hah! A connoisseur would have asked if I had *heard* her."

"But that is understood," Hartland said, never at a loss for a quick rejoinder. "It's the mask that makes her remarkable. Singing at the opera is to be expected."

"Certainly. But the voice is extraordinary. Although I'll admit to curiosity. She moves with grace and I thought I spied a well-turned ankle at one point. And she is possessed of a very handsome bosom."

Feigning lack of interest, Hartland said, "That's all well and good, but it's still opera."

What Minty said, though, piqued his interest more surely than any of Lewiston's waxing lyrical about the quality of the mysterious soprano's voice.

Besides, his courtship of Miss Fontenoy was beginning to test his patience. He thought she would have leapt at his offer of marriage, but no such thing. A part of him respected her for her circumspection, but it wounded him more than he cared to admit to be on the receiving end of such uncertainty. He longed for the simplicity of the kind of relationship he had with Phoebe. Or did he?

To be honest, he was more likely to find himself occupied

with imagining what it would be like to enjoy the intimate company of Princess Adelheid. He was smart enough to realize that danger lay in that direction. Whatever the case, he needed a distraction. He needed something to ease the sting of Miss Fontenoy's hesitancy and to purge thoughts of that beautiful, intelligent, soulful princess from his mind. Some imp of mischief told him he might find that distraction at the King's Theatre.

In any case, he had nothing to lose except a few hours of his time. So the next night he togged himself in his evening gear having sent his valet Hinson to procure him a ticket for the pit earlier in the day. Apparently, he was lucky to get one, although he found that a little hard to believe and rather suspected that Hinson was angling for a gratuity by exaggerating the difficulty of waiting in line, in the end having to pay over the cost to persuade another gentleman to part with his seat.

However, he now possessed the coveted ticket, and would do his best to blend into the mass of oglers. He'd be more inconspicuous in the crowded pit and could leave when he wanted—or even go backstage and visit some of his former flirts among the opera dancers, just to indulge in some light amusement without being seen by everyone he knew in the *ton*.

Thus he found himself elbowing his way into the King's Theatre just before the beginning of the second act of *Le Nozze di Figaro* having fortified himself with a quantity of claret at White's before arriving. It seemed that the pit had indeed been sold to capacity, if not oversold, and he had to stare down a young buck sitting spread-legged in order to squeeze himself at the end of one of the hard benches. Apparently everyone was curious about *l'Incognita*.

Hartland wasn't sure what to expect. All the descriptions —except Minty's—were of the mysterious singer's voice—its power and purity, the emotion captured in it that spilled out into the theatre.

So when a lithe, graceful young woman wearing a face-obscuring white mask stepped onto the stage and began singing in a voice even he could discern was spectacular, he was dumbfounded. Her gestures, the way she took command of the stage without bluster, and her hands. Most of all her hands. They were very white and slender, with tapering fingers that gripped a handkerchief, or fluttered a fan nervously, or balled themselves into angry fists—all he could think of was what those hands might do to him.

That and several other fantasies chased his troubles away for a while and he entered into the spirit of the evening. He even found himself shushing his neighbors whenever *l'Incognita* sang, and discovered that he could discern the timbre of her voice in the sparkling ensembles. He would have told anyone that he had no ear for music at all, but that evening, he realized it wasn't that he lacked perception, only interest. Such a captivating enigma as this young woman had the power to rouse him to unaccustomed fascination.

At the end of the opera, he roared his approval along with everyone else and was ready to celebrate the masked soprano when she came on stage for her bows—but she wasn't there. All the other singers were smiling and bowing. A chant of *l'Incognita!* went up from the audience. But Hartland's voice wasn't among them. There was only one place the singer could possibly be, and he dashed out the side door to the corridor leading to Fops' Alley and beyond without a backward glance.

THE BEGINNING PART OF THE EVENING WENT PERFECTLY. LADY Mariana came to fetch Olivia in her barouche and deposited her discreetly masked at the back entrance to the Theatre. Félicité met her there and having costumed her once before, got her into the gown and wig remarkably quickly, so that Mr. Taylor had no time to be afraid that she'd backed out at the last minute.

Because she'd been through the performance already, this time Olivia made no awkward missteps, ensuring she was in the right place not only for her arias but for the ensembles. She positively sparkled and thought that maybe, just maybe, the audience was a little quieter when she was singing than when the others were singing their solos. She wasn't so naïve as to not realize she was a curiosity, a freak—but if this were to be her final performance on the stage of the King's Theatre, she at least hoped it would be even more memorable than her first.

At the end, of course, she couldn't stay for the bows. She had to get to Lady Mariana's carriage in time for it to take her home and return to collect her and her party without making them wait too long.

She'd almost forgotten that the princess would be among their number. For some unknown reason, something made her want to know what that lady thought of her voice.

Olivia's mind was far away as she hurried to her dressing room where Félicité waited—having told Olivia that she had no desire for the soprano to again destroy her handiwork by ripping off her own gown. She was halfway there when a gentleman who had somehow got past the guards came forward and stood directly in front of her, barring her way.

"*Scusi, Signore!*" she said, and tried to maneuver around him, but his hand closed on her upper arm in a strong grip. Olivia hadn't looked at his face at first but now, being forced to pause long enough to do so, she gazed up into a pair of intense blue eyes. Very familiar blue eyes.

The duke.

*My god! I am found out!* she thought, her heart banging against her ribs and her breathing fast and shallow.

"I mean you no harm, lovely nymph," Hartland whispered in his smoothest, most seductive voice. "I am now your slave. Having heard you and seen you, I am lost. I beg you to do me the honor of allowing me to kiss the hem of your gown—or at least to enjoy your company in private."

She lowered her eyes. At first she was confused by what he said. Was he teasing her? Cruel of him, if he was. She drew in a breath to protest, to explain. But he spoke again.

"Do not torture me! I am wholly in your power to send to the heavens or cast in mortal gloom."

It took a moment, but Olivia soon realized that the duke didn't recognize her at all. He wasn't teasing her. He was trying to seduce someone he assumed to be a complete stranger, a woman of low order who had dared to exhibit herself on a stage. When he looked down at her masked form, he didn't see the reticent debutante who became awkward in his presence and said things no one angling for a marriage proposal ought to say. He saw a challenge. A challenge that could be won and then discarded. The mysterious masked soprano. And he was doing what men did when they "fell in love" with opera singers or dancers, uttering honeyed words and trying to offer her a slip on the shoulder.

How dare he!

Adopting an exaggerated Italian accent, Olivia said, "Signore ees too kind, but I must make haste. I have another... how you say...*assegnazione?*" That this assignation was with the seamstress he needn't know.

"How can you be so cruel! Please, tell me I have a hope of engaging your affections. Agree to meet me! I know a discreet house, out of the way, in Hampstead. No one will know you there."

Olivia fought to control her growing rage. "*Ma, signore,* I cannot be unmasked. No one must see me." She simpered at him—something she had never done before in her life—fluttering her eyelashes, which brushed against the inside of the mask.

"I shall send word!" he said, "Do not fail me!" He took her hand and raised it to kiss, not just touching her knuckles with the perfunctory peck of chivalry but pressing his warm, fervent lips on her skin for longer than was proper.

She jerked herself out of his grip and made use of his surprise to run away, turning the corner to head to her dressing room, praying she had not been delayed too long for Lady Mariana's carriage.

Well. That settled one thing for certain. All doubt fled from Olivia's heart. She now knew that her misgivings were well founded. Still, her disappointment in someone she had come at least to like was profound. Was this really who he was? This stranger who said such things, things she never had any desire to hear? And why would he do it? By the time she reached the dressing room her tears were flowing hot and fast. How could she have been so stupid to think there was even a chance someone like Hartland could interest himself in her for anything beyond her fortune. It was mortifying.

On her way home in the carriage, Olivia at first thought she would reject Hartland's suit the very next day and put an end to the farce. But after a bit, she decided that to do so would not be enough of a punishment for his insult. Although unwitnessed by anyone else, he had deeply embarrassed her. Not gaining her fortune and a biddable wife would be one punishment, certainly. But she wanted more. She wanted to expose him, to make him ridiculous in the eyes of the *ton*. To embarrass him as much as he had embarrassed her. She didn't know how she would accomplish such a thing, but somehow it would be done.

She had a momentary pang that such an action might be unworthy of her. But what else could she do? Olivia derived no comfort from knowing that Hartland had acted no worse than almost every other well-born gentleman his age. She derived no comfort, and did not excuse him, but somewhere in the back of her mind she knew that she was being a little unfair. What encouragement, after all, had she given him as Olivia Fontenoy? He'd exercised all his charm to beguile her, and she hadn't responded. Why?

He didn't love her. That was clear. But more importantly, she didn't love him. That fact needn't hinder a marriage, as everyone said. Weren't such arrangements *de rigueur* in the *ton*? Once they married, he would be expected to continue to pursue such dalliances as he suggested to *l'Incognita* that evening. His affairs would be whispered about in the clubs, the subject of ribald jokes.

Still, it rankled. Even more than Hartland's behavior, the idea that the *ton*, if they ever knew she had appeared on a public stage, would cut her and disdain her, consider her damaged goods not worthy of being accepted into the first circles, yet would turn a blind eye to actions such as Hartland's, made her white hot with impotent fury.

By the time she arrived in Mount Street she was in a stew of conflicting emotions.

She wanted to make Hartland sorry, to make him feel the full force of what he had done and its effect on his prospects with her. Yet wasn't she, in her own way, a little responsible? It was she who had placed herself beyond the pale. It was solely her decision to take that dramatic leap, to ignore the dictates of polite society. So why should it surprise her that someone would not treat her with the respect she'd been accustomed to?

No. He still didn't deserve to get away with it. He did more than wound her vanity. He laid bare the sordid workings of not-so-polite society. It was a view no gently bred lady should ever have to see and it disgusted her. He would have to find another heiress to charm.

After all, her heart had not been touched by the dashing duke. She'd been flattered by his attentions, fooled herself into thinking that his regard for her might extend beyond her fortune. No, her heart remained unscathed.

Unscathed, and in a fair way to being lost to a far-less-dashing marquess.

$\mathcal{A}$delheid waited with Lady Mariana for her carriage to come and collect them at the King's Theatre after the performance of the remarkable soprano in the mask. It surprised her that they had to wait so long for it—Mariana put it down to the crush of people leaving the theatre.

Still, her friend seemed a bit agitated—more so than the experience of even such a remarkable evening might make her. "She was splendid. Quite a voice for one so young," Adelheid said once they were seated in the barouche.

"What makes you say that? How would you know whether she was young or not?"

Was there an edge of anxiety in Mariana's voice? "It was an impression. Perhaps an assumption. The way she moved." She didn't want to reveal her own past to Mariana just at that moment and tell her that such a voice would have been the talk of European opera houses had the lady been a veteran performer.

They said little after that, Mariana only asking if Adelheid had received the invitation to Lady Ferndale's rout party, which she had. "If you thought the Ambrose ball was a squeeze, wait until you see this!" Mariana said. "After that evening, everyone in the *ton* will know who you are."

"Yes, thank you for procuring the invitation for me." When Mariana had offered to suggest it to Lady Ferndale, Adelheid agreed without hesitation. She must seize every possible chance to encounter the duke again. Her allotted time was half over, and she was by no means certain she had done enough to win him away from Miss Fontenoy.

By then they'd arrived at the house in Grosvenor Square. Adelheid said her adieus to Lady Mariana and climbed the stairs to her door, Grandison standing just inside to take her cloak. "Beg pardon, Your Highness, but there is someone here to see you."

"Here? At this hour?" It wasn't late by town standards, but it was certainly late for an unexpected visit. Could it be Brattle?

"She insisted you would want to see her. She's in the green saloon."

"Thank you." Adelheid hurried up the stairs. She knew only one person who would presume to call on her unannounced so late. "Félicité!" she said, holding her hands out to greet her friend as she passed through the open door.

"Oh, *mon amie!* I had to come. You will not believe."

"Is it to do with the mysterious masked soprano?" Adelheid said, unable to think of anything else that might have brought Félicité to her in such a rush, and immediately after the opera.

"*Oui … ou non … en effet.* She is, how you say, old news now. It is the duke! I saw him."

*Hartland?* "Where?"

"This very evening. Behind the stage. He comes to see the lady in the mask!"

Such an action was hardly surprising in someone of the duke's age and character. So why did the news sting her just a little? "But I did not see him there—at least, not in any of the boxes. Are you certain it was he?"

"Yes, yes of course. It is *amusant*, no?"

Amusing? Certainly, in a way. "I wonder if Miss Fontenoy is aware that he participates in such activities."

"Precise! Have you met this lady? Is she beautiful?"

Adelheid thought for a moment before answering. "Not beautiful, no. But very engaging. She has something of the unusual about her. She's also very young."

"And per'aps too innocent in the ways of the world to ignore such a dalliance, *non?*"

"What is it you're trying to say?"

Félicité pursed her lips in a saucy moue and tossed her dusky curls. "Only that you could, if you choose, make her aware of such activity?"

Ah. It would be a logical tactic. And absolutely no surprise that it should have occurred to someone like Félicité, herself such a seasoned observer of the frailties of men. But it occurred to Adelheid that she didn't want to stoop to such a thing if she could manage some other way. She already knew that Miss Fontenoy was not in love with the duke. And, if what she had observed at the girl's debut ball was correct, very likely she had a tendre for that unassuming fellow she waltzed with after supper, the one Hartland had called *just Lewiston*. With no real affection for Hartland, only Miss Fontenoy's vanity would be piqued by knowing of his indiscretion. And what would that achieve? "I shall think about it. I have other plans that don't necessarily involve me in such unhandsome tricks. Still, I am glad I know of this." She stifled a yawn.

"Ah! It is the hour for me to go," Félicité said, standing and smoothing on her gloves. "*À tout à l'heure.* But do not let your scruples interfere with your plans. There is not another gentleman like the duke in the *ton*. And you told me you have little time."

ADELHEID LAY AWAKE FOR A LONG TIME THAT NIGHT. FÉLICITÉ hadn't told her anything out of the ordinary about Hartland. His actions were no more or less than what anyone would expect of a man like him. Yet the idea of him flirting with another woman disturbed her. His attentions to Miss Fontenoy had little to do with flirtation and even less to do with love, so she could contemplate them without any misgivings. This possible dalliance, though, very likely leapt over flirtation directly to desire. And she could not think of it without entertaining the scandalous wish that if Hartland was going to interfere with any lady's virtue, she would rather it be hers.

THE NEXT DAY ADELHEID MADE AN EFFORT TO PUT THOUGHTS of Hartland, Miss Fontenoy, and the masked soprano out of her mind and to focus her attention on Otto, who she had spent little time with lately. According to Nicholas, he was making good progress in his lessons and she could see that he was becoming more and more confident. His reading and writing of English was coming along, as though he knew somehow that he had to make up for lost time. Clearly he had a knack for languages because he also seemed to find the challenge of Latin enjoyable. Her own knowledge of that language was rudimentary, but Nicholas surprised her by having much greater facility than she presumed he would. Otto had a head for sums too, but Adelheid had had little tutelage in mathematics herself so couldn't move much beyond the rudiments. He would soon need a tutor, but not yet.

Along with his burgeoning confidence, though, came an ever more restless undercurrent of mischief. Otto kept the servants busy by playing little tricks on them—stealing tarts from the kitchen, hiding in cupboards and leaping out to surprise a housemaid causing her to drop her burden of linens or silverware all over the floor, catching mice and letting them go in unsuitable places. Adelheid knew she should discipline him but his expression at those times was so like Danton it gave her the most exquisitely painful pleasure.

In addition to his academic instruction, the groom Barber said Otto had come a long way riding his pony already—but that did not surprise her. The one thing he lacked, and that Adelheid had no idea how to supply, were friends of his own class. But unless it was known that he had expectations certainly no one in the *ton* would consent to their children associating with him, no matter how smart and engaging he was.

It was her effort to find some healthy amusement for him —beyond occasional rides in the park and helping the groom with the horses—that led to yet another unexpected encounter with Hartland that very same day. The afternoon was beautiful in the way only spring in England can be, with a soft breeze carrying the scent of early flowers, birds exercising their voices in the trees, and a brilliant blue sky patched with fluffy white clouds. Adelheid told Frankel to take Otto into the garden in the middle of Grosvenor Square at a time of the afternoon when the few other children who lived there would be unlikely to be playing, and gave her the only key she had to that private sanctuary. It was a little measure of freedom, contained in a safe enclosure.

Adelheid watched them out of one of the drawing room windows on the first floor, keeping herself just hidden by the silk curtain so she could not be seen from the street. She smiled as Otto ran and skipped about, climbing up on the iron benches, playing "least in sight" with Frankel—who had truly risen to the challenge of being Otto's caretaker and was becoming increasingly fond of him.

Adelheid lost sight of her little boy for a short while, however, and assumed he'd ducked behind a tree somewhere, behaving in his usual cheeky manner. But from where she looked, it appeared that Frankel, too, could not find him. *Imp!* she thought, glad in her heart that he had the spirit to be a little naughty at times.

Except that as she continued to watch out of the window, Frankel's increasing anxiety became more and more apparent until the nurse stopped beneath a gnarled oak tree, looked up, and shrieked.

A moment later, Otto's little head peeked out from amid the high branches. At first, he appeared to think this a funny trick. But as he started to climb down, Adelheid could see that he became afraid. It was very high up. How did he scramble so fast up those branches? He'll fall!

Before she had a moment to think and not even stopping to put on a hat, Adelheid ran out of the room, down the stairs, out to the street, and across to the gate that led into the garden.

"Frankel!" she called, then "Otto! Don't be afraid!"

The trouble was, Frankel still had the only the key and Adelheid couldn't attract her attention to come and let her in. The nurse was frantically but ineffectually trying to reach up to Otto. By now, the boy's strangled, tear-stained voice crying, *"Hilf mich!"* was beginning to tear at Adelheid's heart.

At that moment, a curricle rounded the square. Adelheid was aware of horses snorting, the driver pulling them up then springing down, and a moment later, Hartland stood next to her.

"What is it? What is the problem? Please let me help you in any way I can!"

She looked up at him, realizing that tears had started down her cheeks. "Oh! My Lord Duke, it's Otto!" She pointed to the tree. "Please, do you have a key? I must get in and help him!"

By now the little boy's sobs echoed throughout the square. Hartland shrugged off his driving coat, took hold of the iron fence, hoisted himself up to the top and jumped down on the other side, landing easily. He ran to the tree and said, "Pardon me, Ma'am" to Frankel before steering her out of the way. Then he tore his fitted coat off so fast the sleeves turned inside out, and pulled himself up on the lowest limb.

He climbed up through the budding branches, finding hand holds and completely ignoring the scratches made by the twigs on his shining Hessians. Adelheid followed his progress by the waving and dipping of the smaller branches, and when he finally said, "Easy, boy. Otto, isn't it? I'll get you, and together we'll climb down," she pressed her hand to her heart. Hartland kept up a soothing stream of nothings as he tried to coax Otto to trust him. The boy clung hard to the branch he was sitting on and didn't want to let go. "Just put your arms around my neck. I can carry you. I won't let you fall, I promise."

Adelheid held her breath and gripped the iron fence, watching amazed as the duke began his progress down the tree, Otto hanging on to him and crying into his neck cloth as he retraced his route to the ground.

By now, Frankel had recovered enough to be aware that she should return to the gate to let her mistress in. Once inside the garden, Adelheid ran to meet them. Without thinking, she reached her arms out for Otto as Hartland stood him on the ground. The sobbing boy threw himself into them and buried his face against her stomach. "You naughty boy! You're safe now. Shall we go in and have some sweets?"

She looked up at Hartland who stood staring at her, eyebrows raised, a quizzical expression in his eyes. "Do you always reward your misbehaving ward with treats?"

*I've done it now*, Adelheid thought. What must he think? How will I explain it? Thinking quickly, she said, "Otto is the son of ... a very great friend of mine. I have undertaken to care for him as if he were my own child." It was all true, in its way. "And I cannot thank you enough for your gallant help. I am afraid your waistcoat and your boots are quite ruined. And you've torn a shirtsleeve!"

At this, Hartland looked down and frowned. "My man will have a job to fix them. He'll be cross, but he'll succeed. We seem to meet in the most interesting circumstances, Princess. Might I once again have the honor of escorting you home? It's not far, but it looks as though you could do with someone to lean on."

Adelheid crouched down and took hold of Otto's hands. "Otto, say thank you to His Grace for rescuing you." She turned him around and give him a little nudge in Hartland's direction.

Otto stood straight and lifted his chin before giving Hartland a grave little bow. "Sank you," he said. And then, before Adelheid could stop him, he ran to Hartland and embraced him swiftly, then ran back to Adelheid and took hold of her hand.

After Otto had been sent off to bed in charge of Frankel, Adelheid and Hartland sat in her drawing room, an awkward silence between them as Grandison brought in a tray with a decanter and two glasses.

They both started speaking at once. "You must wonder …" "I couldn't help noticing …"

"I'm sorry, Duke, I interrupted you."

"Not at all. I was about to observe that young Otto has the most extraordinary eyes. I've noticed them before, but only from a distance. I was used to think Negroes' eyes were invariably brown."

"Yes," Adelheid said, sipping her sherry in an effort to buy some time. "Only he is the product of a union between a white woman and a dark-skinned man."

"Not the other way around?"

"Of course, I misspoke," Adelheid thought. Naturally the duke would assume some slave-owning grandee had taken an attractive black girl to bed to satisfy his lust. She longed to be able to explain that, on the contrary, Otto was the result of a very great love, but held her peace.

Hartland cast an examining gaze around the drawing room. "I haven't been in this house since the time of old Lord Beaumain. I think it used to look just like this. You haven't refurbished it? It's not at all what I would expect a home of yours to look like."

Of course he assumed she was enormously wealthy and could make such unnecessary expenditures without blinking an eye. "No, not yet. I have had so much else to occupy me. I shall turn my attention to it before I entertain—which I must do soon to repay the generous hospitality I have been shown."

He nodded. "Will you be at Lady Ferndale's rout party?"

"Yes, Lady Mariana has seen to that." She smiled.

"Then might I engage you to dance the first two sets with me?"

To her surprise, a blush stole into her cheeks. Adelheid couldn't remember the last time she'd blushed with pleasure. In her imagination she could already feel the heat of his body close to hers again, the intimacy of moving in time to the music. "Of course, Duke," she said.

After a moment of awkward silence, Hartland said, "I fear I must take my leave of you, Princess Adelheid. My valet will need all the time he can get to restore my clothing."

They both stood and without thinking, Adelheid reached out and touched his torn cuff. "I am afraid this cannot easily be mended."

Before she let go of it, Hartland grasped her hand and pressed it, looking down into her eyes. "Are you quite recovered from your ordeal?"

The kindness in his eyes, his evident genuine concern, brought a lump into her throat. It took her a moment to master her emotions. With a rather shaky smile, she said, "I cannot thank you enough for your service to Otto."

"Anyone would have done the same," he said, her hand still in his possession. After another moment, he raised it to his lips. When those lips touched her bare knuckles, a shiver of awareness shot up her arm and into her body. "Adieu, Princess," he said, and bowed out of the room.

Adelheid stood there for a long while, listening to his steps decrescendoing down the stairs, the pause as he took his hat and coat from Grandison, and then the door opening and closing behind him.

HINSON LOOKED AS THOUGH MIGHT CRY WHEN HE SAW THE state of the duke's boots. "Your Grace! Did you have an accident? Was you in a mill?"

"Not fighting, Hinson. Climbing a tree."

At this the valet wisely asked no more questions, being too well trained to display the slightest curiosity, and set about laying out Hartland's evening clothes.

As he dressed for dinner and cards at White's, Hartland puzzled over Adelheid. Was she the worldly lady, perhaps somewhat bored and a little distant, he met for the first time in the park? Or the lively, warm woman who charmed everyone at the ball, and who conversed so lightly and easily on different subjects, sharing his sense of the ridiculous? Or perhaps she was neither, but only presented a façade to protect the soft core of her heart, the side that showed that afternoon, and whenever she lovingly regarded at her ward.

Her ward. There was something about him. He shook his head. His fancy was running away with him. Minty had mentioned something about a by-blow. Was she caring for her late husband's bastard, and in deference to his memory did not name him? Hartland had some recollection that Minty had mentioned the prince's plantations in Jamaica. Such a thing was common enough. Who could say?

Whatever the case, the princess was a dangerous distraction. He'd already offered for Miss Fontenoy. He could not cry off, even if he discovered that the princess was as handsomely endowed with a fortune as the heiress. But the desires she awoke in him were becoming harder and harder to suppress. He'd thought he could scratch that particular itch by indulging in a light flirtation with the soprano in the mask, by becoming his younger self for a little while, the self that careered headlong into the life of a rake and didn't think of much beyond the gratification of his physical desires.

Perhaps the dalliance with the diva would serve. He would have to make it do so. Because Philip knew that any involvement with Princess Adelheid would all too easily lead him down a path from which it would be impossible to retreat. And then he'd be in the basket.

*e brave, Harry.* Lewiston repeated the words to himself as he penned the note to Miss Fontenoy using the excuse of visiting in order to tell her about the veritable riot in the pit the night before when *l'Incognita* did not come onto the stage to take a bow—and mention that he planned to bring his violin in case she would consent to play with him.

He made a point of saying that he hadn't seen her at the opera the previous evening—in case she'd told her mother she was attending it but had opted to go somewhere else. He hoped she would read between the lines that he had no intention of mentioning that fact to Lady Ambrose. Some kind of subterfuge to enable her to attend an entertainment of which Lady Ambrose did not approve was the only excuse he could imagine for Olivia's lying to her mother about being Lady Mariana's guest the previous week. At least, it was the only reasonable excuse.

The other one—that was outrageous to the point of folly. A suspicion had flashed through his mind the day after *l'Incognita* first performed. He had never heard Miss

Fontenoy sing, but her mother made much of her having voice lessons with Tetrazzini, the best vocal tutor in England. Could her unwillingness to sing in front of company be due not to shyness but to something else altogether? Could she have a different reason for keeping her voice a secret and could hers be the face hidden by that obscuring mask?

No, impossible. Having seen the remarkable soprano a second time, he could not reconcile the bold sureness of her command of the stage and her open-hearted vulnerability with the closed, reserved, sometimes spiky Miss Fontenoy.

As he rode over to Mount Street in a hack so he could keep a tight hold on his violin case, Harry reminded himself not to expect anything beyond a pleasant afternoon of reading through a couple of sonatas for violin and piano. He'd borrowed a small selection from the music lending library and had them in a portfolio tucked under his arm. He tempered his expectations, but still, he knew as well as anyone the power music had of breaking down barriers between people. His collaborations with the professional musicians from all qualities and backgrounds showed him that more than just birth and wealth could connect people on a deep level. Would it have that magical effect on the two of them that afternoon? Who could say.

Ebbings greeted him at the door with a suspicious look at his instrument case, but soon regained his customary froideur, took Lewiston's hat and overcoat, and announced him to Lady Ambrose and Olivia.

To Lewiston's surprise Miss Fontenoy rose and hurried to him, her hand outstretched. "Do come in and sit with us for a while before we go to the schoolroom and practice. You see, I promised Mama I would not annoy her by making her listen to us going over and over the same music and making terrible mistakes—which we most certainly will because my sight reading is not very good. My maid Hetty will sit with us as chaperone."

He spied an impish sparkle in Miss Fontenoy's eyes and marveled at her transformation. She hadn't been unfriendly before, but now her excitement swept away the awkward veneer of self-containment. Was she so starved for musical companionship? Or simply looking for an excuse to be out from under her mother's close scrutiny?

"You missed quite a stir last night at the opera," he said, after accepting a cup of tea from Olivia.

"Oh?" she said, taking a sip before saying, "I had a previous engagement with Lady Mariana to see the play at Drury Lane or I would have been there."

And yet, Lewiston thought, he had seen Lady Mariana in her box. He didn't mention that, though. "I daresay you've read about it this morning!"

Not taking up this line, Olivia said, "I had hoped to accompany her to see at least some of the opera afterwards but the gas lights in the theatre gave me a headache, and I returned home early instead." She cast a sidelong glance at her mother, who didn't look up from plying her needle on the endless and frivolous piece of embroidery.

"Well," he said, "*l'Incognita* was even better last night. At the end of the performance the theatre was wild with cheers and demands for more. People stood at the back of the pit and I heard that the galleries were overflowing. When the masked soprano did not come on stage for her bows it set the crowd to chanting for her and many tried to storm the stage. The soldiers had to come in and restore order."

A curious, distant look of bemused wonder passed across Miss Fontenoy's face before she said, "How extraordinary! Imagine a performance inspiring such a furor." She set her teacup down on the tray and said, "Let us go up to the schoolroom. Hetty will meet us. Although it's only a square pianoforte up there and inferior to the instrument in the music room, we won't have to worry about disturbing anyone with our inevitable mishaps!"

THIS TIME, OLIVIA WAS CAREFUL TO BE MORE PREPARED TO parry Lewiston's comments about not seeing her at the opera. When he recounted what had happened at the end of the performance after she'd fled from the stage, she felt a secret thrill.

The fact that the soldiers had had to leave their posts also explained how Hartland was able to slip backstage without being stopped.

As she led Lewiston up the final pair of stairs to the third floor, Olivia said, "I have no brothers and sisters so the schoolroom is entirely my own domain. It's given over to music mostly, now that my governess is gone and I'm considered to have as much education as necessary for a lady."

Hetty rose and curtsied when they entered, then resumed her seat in the corner where she was engaged in sewing a button on a mesh purse. Lewiston walked to the middle of the sunny room and stood there, his eyes roaming over everything, from the shelves full of books and music, to the globe next to the table surrounded by four wooden chairs, to the pianoforte open and ready to be played. "I can see why you like to come up here. It's a lovely room." He cast her his crooked smile. "Ah, I see you have a music stand set up. May I also use the table?"

Olivia gestured for him to do so and watched, fascinated, as he laid the instrument case down, opened it, and lifted the beautiful violin from its nest of velvet, lightly brushing his fingers over the strings on the neck then tucking it under his arm while he tightened the hairs on the bow. There was something intimate about it, this process of preparation.

"Could you give me an A?" he said, without looking at her.

She shook herself out of her daze, went to the pianoforte and struck the required key as well as an A-major chord.

"Your pianoforte is in tune," he said, somewhat surprised.

"Did you think it wouldn't be?" Olivia said with a rueful smile. Of course, if her mother had anything to say to it, the tuner would come only when absolutely necessary. But Olivia had insisted otherwise.

Once he had tuned, Lewiston said, "I thought perhaps, in keeping with the general theme, we might read through some Mozart." He opened the portfolio and selected the sheet music, placing the keyboard part on the desk and resting the separate violin part on the music stand.

Olivia sat on the bench, touched the keys lightly, then looked through the score. Not an easy piece. She could play creditably, but she was worried that she might not be equal to such a challenge. "I'm afraid you have perhaps overestimated my proficiency, Lord Lewiston. After all, you've never heard me play."

"Or sing," he said.

A blush stole into her cheeks. "Or sing," she echoed. "But as I say—"

He interrupted her. "Nonsense. In any case, don't worry about mistakes. It's just us after all." He lifted the violin to his shoulder, then lowered the instrument again. "I do have one request, however."

Having regained her composure, she lifted her eyes away from the score and up to his. He stood quite close, just beyond her right shoulder. When they were both standing, they were much of a height, so this was the first time she had to really look up to meet his gaze. His expression of acute tenderness caught her off guard. Olivia suddenly felt heat radiate from her middle up to her neck and down her arms. "Yes, My Lord?" she said, a little unsteadily.

"That's just it." His lopsided smile lit his face again. "Do you think, while we're tackling this music and are bound to make a mull of it, you might dispense with this 'Lord Lewiston' and just call me Harry?"

Olivia smiled. "And I suppose, then, that you should call me Olivia. Just while we're in this room."

He nodded. "Shall I count us in?"


MORE THAN AN HOUR PASSED AND THE TWO OF THEM LAUGHED heartily at their clashes and the moments when they came adrift from each other and had to start again. Olivia had forgotten—if she'd ever really known—how enjoyable it could be to bring a piece of music to life not on one's own, but in company with another person who was as devoted to it as she was. The afternoon passed in a delightful blur, except for one dangerous moment when Olivia was trying to tease out the fingering for a passage and made a hash of it, and sang the melody line to keep the tempo going. Not at full voice, but enough to reveal that her vocal skills far exceeded her keyboard skills.

"Your voice—" Harry said, stopping his playing abruptly.

"Yes, let's try that again." Olivia made an effort to brush past the moment, hoping he hadn't heard too much.

To her relief, after a short pause Harry said, "From the beginning of the repeat."

Olivia kept her eyes trained on the music, not daring to look up at Lewiston, and soon her anxiety abated.

They'd managed to get only the first movement tolerably executed when the door of the schoolroom burst open and Tetrazzini flew in.

"Signorina Fontenoy!" he said, "It is *molto importante!* We must talk, we must—" He suddenly caught sight of Lord Lewiston, who had stopped with his bow in mid-air above the strings of his violin. "Ah, *scusa,* Mees, Mi'lud," he said, his florid face dotted with perspiration and his eyes darting around in panic.

"Lord Lewiston, may I present Signore Tetrazzini, whom I was not expecting today," she said, glaring at the Italian.

Lewiston nodded and the tutor gave one of his flamboyant bows.

"We have come to the end of the first movement, and I see the hour is late." Lewiston smiled at Olivia reassuringly and moved to the table so he could put his violin away. "I hope I may have the pleasure of massacring the rest of this sonata with you sometime soon?"

She laughed, but couldn't help thinking what ill luck! She had never enjoyed playing the pianoforte so much in her life, mistakes and all. And the sound of the violin—so like the human voice. It made her own vocal cords tremble in sympathy. Ill-judged though it had been, she didn't regret her instant of vocal madness. "Oh, I insist! But only if we then endeavor to put it all back together in the end. I shall see you out, Harry," she said, then suddenly conscious of Tetrazzini's presence, "I mean, My Lord." She cast a shy smile at him.

Olivia led the marquess along the corridor to the stairs. He stopped her just before they started to descend. "I meant what I said. I want to do this again." His voice was barely above a whisper. "I think, I know, we are meant to." He took her hand.

She gazed into his kind brown eyes, so full of understanding. He knew her. She felt he could see deep inside her, all the way to her soul. The sensation exposed her, but not in that dangerous, physical way Hartland's scrutiny sometimes did. "Yes," she breathed, then quickly withdrew her hand and looked away in confusion. What was she doing? She couldn't fall in love with Harry, especially now. Not when things were so confused with Hartland. She needed him to believe for a while yet that she had fallen under his spell and meant to accept him. "But perhaps, we should wait a while."

The intense light in Lewiston's eyes dimmed. "Yes, if you wish it." The change in his tone of voice wrung her heart.

Olivia didn't want him to go away on such a dispirited note, and said, "Do you plan to attend the next performance of *Figaro?*"

"Alas, I cannot. I must escort my mother to a card party with an old friend. An engagement of long standing."

Olivia wasn't at this point certain she would be called upon to sing the role of the Countess again, but if she was, at least she wouldn't have to worry about making up a Banbury story to explain her absence to Harry. "I, too, am unable to go. I wonder who will sing Countess Almaviva?"

He looked at her curiously. "The masked soprano, of course. Apparently Catalani is still indisposed."

This was news to her. Had Taylor now started to assume her cooperation? "Of course, silly of me. Will I see you at Lady Ferndale's rout party?"

"I plan to attend. I would ask you to save me a waltz, but I can't guarantee we'd scrape through it as well as we did at your ball." Now his eyes sparkled with amusement.

"I don't care how we manage," Olivia said. "I will save you that dance. And we didn't just scrape through. You are an excellent dancer."

Somehow the space between them diminished, and they stood so close that Olivia could feel the heat of his body and the faintest tickle of his breath on her face. She met his eyes.

"Olivia," he whispered, and his lips parted.

At that moment, a door near them opened suddenly and a parlor maid hurried through it, her arms full of clean linens. Olivia stepped back from Harry and said, "Thank you again,

Lord Lewiston," putting her hand out to shake in a decidedly friendly manner. He bowed over it, his color heightened, and went down the stairs.

A VERY DISTRACTED OLIVIA RETURNED TO THE SCHOOLROOM, having nearly forgotten that Tetrazzini was waiting for her.

He accosted her as soon as she entered. "Signorina Fontenoy, ees *terribile!*"

Olivia held up her hand and said, "Hetty, you may go. I expect you've had enough of listening to bad performers and it's just Mr. Tetrazzini now."

"Very good Miss," Hetty said, gathering up her mending basket and dipping two quick curtsies before scampering away—although she cast a suspicious glance at the agitated Italian.

Olivia waited until Hetty's footsteps faded and she was certain the abigail had gone down the stairs before saying, her teeth clenched, "How dare you burst in here like that! Are you mad?"

Tetrazzini covered his eyes and shook his head. "I am sorry. I have failed, Signorina."

Olivia was accustomed to the singing teacher's overly dramatic utterances and assumed he was upset about nothing more than perhaps forgetting to bring her some music or missing the time of a lesson. "Please sit down, Signore." She led him to one of the chairs at the table and sat across from him. "What is this failure?"

"Eet is the money. The guineas. Signore Taylor, he cannot pay."

Olivia had all but forgotten she'd been promised fifteen-hundred guineas for each performance—meaning the impresario now owed her three thousand, minus the seven-hundred and fifty she'd already received. But something about the way this news affected Tetrazzini made her think perhaps there was more to the circumstance than that. "You'd better tell me all. Let me pour you a glass of wine." She went to the desk where she knew one of her governesses had always kept a bottle of claret and a tumbler, fetched these and poured out a generous portion for him.

Tetrazzini downed the first glass and then refilled it. "The theatre—she is *insolvente, rovinato*—in ruin."

What was he saying? Bankrupt? The King's Theatre? It took her a moment to comprehend this. "How can that be?" she asked, stunned. It was so beautiful, and the audience—as far as she could tell, the theatre had been full to bursting. And they'd only recently raised the ticket prices—which had caused quite a furor, although now everyone seemed to accept the change.

Tetrazzini did his best to explain. After a time and managing to decipher his polyglot utterances, Olivia pieced together the fact that Taylor had not been able to meet his obligations to Catalani, his star performer, as well as to many other singers, musicians, and stage personnel. Apparently it was due to his overspending the previous year on the necessary renovations to the theater—improvements in lighting, repainting, refurbishing the lobbies. Many of his assets had been seized, and although he still retained his position as manager, he had been given little time to rectify the finances before the entire operation would go into default.

This, thought Olivia, explained why Catalani hadn't sung lately, why Taylor consented to put an untried soprano in such an important role—an untried soprano who wore a mask, no less. She thought with a grimace that her worldly education had certainly been enlarged in the past couple of weeks. "I am sorry to hear it, Signore, but I don't know what this can have to do with me." She would likely never see the promised money, but that wasn't why she'd sung, after all.

"He, Taylor, say he can fix all. A grand benefit performance. A *spettacolo*. With *iscritti* who pay *molto soldi*."

She thought a benefit performance with patrons who subscribed for higher prices because it was to raise additional funds could work quite well, but he would likely have to persuade Catalani to cooperate. "Why doesn't he arrange it? It seems a good plan to me. I expect Madame Catalani would relent for that purpose."

Tetrazzini drummed his fingers on the table and stared at them, as if they were the most fascinating thing in the world. He finally said in a timid voice, "He want you. He want you to …" He made a gesture of pinching something beneath his chin and then sweeping his hand upward. *"La masquera, comprenda.* Take off your mask. Is only thing, he say, that will make *le gente pagare."*

Olivia was struck dumb. It was out of the question. How could Mr. Taylor be so bold as to ask such a thing? To unmask herself in public! Of course, Taylor didn't know who she was. He had no idea she was the daughter of a viscount. And why would people want to come and see such a thing anyway? Were they really so foolishly curious? She stood and walked away from Tetrazzini. "I cannot."

*"No, Signorina.* Is as I thought." The portly Italian's shoulders drooped. *"Soltanto,* only, for … *beneficenza.* Is possible, no?"

For charity! What charity was this? Mr. Taylor's pockets? And how could she know he would actually use the money to redeem his debts, pay his singers and musicians, and set the workings of the theatre to rights? Might he not be tempted to take the proceeds and flee to the continent? And then where would all those people who depended on him for their livelihoods be?

All those people. In fact, it seemed that unless she agreed to this unthinkable expedient, many individuals could find themselves without a feather to fly with before long. "When is Taylor proposing this benefit performance?"

Tetrazzini, who had sunk his head in his hands dejectedly, looked up with a gleam of hope in his eyes. "*Venerdì.*"

Friday. The day after Lady Ferndale's rout. If she did it, she would be ruining herself socially. No one would want to associate with her after she exposed herself in that way. As far as the *ton* was concerned, she would have been spending her time among loose women and the scaff and raff of London. She would be tainted, labeled *fast*, a hoyden. Her marriage prospects would be considerably damaged—despite her fortune. In fact, it would be enough provocation that a duke could withdraw his suit and not face censure.

A duke. Withdraw his suit.

An inkling of a plan began to form itself in Olivia's mind. Perhaps this extraordinary event could be turned to good account. If Hartland withdrew, her mother could not accuse her of willfully refusing the opportunity to become a duchess. Any effort on Lady Ambrose's part to force the union would be useless. It would all have to be very cleverly contrived, of course, and she would need some help to ensure it went off seamlessly. She didn't care if her reputation was ruined. At least, she didn't care much. And in all likelihood it would be the scandal of a season and then forgotten—and she would not have to refuse to marry the catch of the season and make everyone believe she had lost her mind.

For her plan to work, Hartland would have to be there. From the way he spoke the other night, she thought the odds were that he would be.

"Don't give Taylor an answer yet," Olivia said. "I need some time. Besides, there's another performance before then. Tomorrow, in fact. I have it on good authority—the papers, apparently—that Mr. Taylor assumes I shall perform. Indeed,

I suppose I must, being that Catalani is still refusing to do so."

"*Si*, he ask through me, he ask you, *per favore*, to sing Countess Almaviva again."

"Even though he knows he won't be able to pay me. And even though he hasn't actually asked, only assumed." If the thought of being paid for the unequalled experience of singing a great operatic role on the stage of the premier theatre in London didn't seem so absurd to her, she would have considered the impresario beyond impudent for even suggesting she expose herself to discovery by singing again. But she was too involved to step away now. With a sigh she said, "Very well. I will at least do that. But don't, whatever you do, make him think I agree to the benefit performance. I'm not sure I do, yet."

Tetrazzini reached across the table, took both her hands in his and raised them to his moist lips. "*Grazie, grazie tantissimo!*"

She freed herself from his grasp and surreptitiously wiped the backs of her hands on her skirt. "I will send word if I need your help or if I come to a final decision about the benefit."

He stood, bowed to her and turned to go, then swiveled on his heels to face her again, his face beaming with gratitude. Struggling to speak entirely in English, he said "You are great lady with the voice of an angel. It is for me a privilege to know you."

# CHAPTER 23

*T*he more Adelheid thought about the evening she had spent with Lady Mariana at the opera and Félicité's visit and revelation afterwards, the more she suspected something was going on just out of her sight—and that of most of the *ton*. That this hidden drama involved Lady Mariana and Miss Fontenoy she was almost certain. She couldn't have articulated what it was that gave her that feeling, but it sent her to call on Lady Mariana the next morning. If she needed to explain her visit, she could claim simply to want more information about some of the members of the *ton* who would attend the rout party.

It couldn't have been a coincidence that Mariana had been inexplicably late to join her at the theatre, that she seemed a bit agitated throughout, or that the Thorne's carriage arrived after almost all the others at the end of the opera—as if it had had been used for some other purpose before then.

Added to that was Mariana's strange reaction to her observation concerning the masked soprano's youth. In her years as a cypher in the prince's court, an ornament to be brought out and admired and then fade into the background again when conversations turned to other subjects, she had developed keen powers of observation. To occupy her mind during tedious dinners, she made it a game to guess which of their dinner guests was having a torrid affair with the wife of one of the others, which ones hid baser motives behind their obsequious attentions to the wealthy prince and his beautiful wife, and which ones had more dangerous secrets to conceal.

Her instincts told her that a secret lay at the heart of everything that had happened the previous evening. Just as she came to that certainty, Walton opened the door to Lady Mariana's modest but elegant town house and ushered her into the drawing room, where Mariana was just finishing her instructions to the housekeeper.

"Adelheid! I didn't expect to see you today, but I am delighted you have come." She looked over Adelheid's shoulder to where Walton still stood behind her in the open doorway and said, "Tea, I think, Walton."

Once he closed the door, Mariana bade Adelheid sit.

"You must think it odd that I am here," she said, "but I have some questions I would wish to have answered before Lady Ferndale's party. I thought of them as I sat and observed so many members of the *ton* at the theatre last night and I wanted to ask you while they were still fresh in my mind."

"I will gladly furnish you with any information you desire, if I am in possession of it," Mariana said with an impish smile. "It is well to be aware of any pertinent *on dits* before you find yourself in the lion's den."

Walton returned with the tea tray giving Adelheid a little time to arrange her thoughts. "My questions have to do with the English customs and proprieties. For instance, I noticed that although most of those in the first circle of society sat in boxes in the first two tiers, several gentlemen I recognized from Miss Fontenoy's ball sat in the pit, among the—I don't know how to express it—the—"

"Scaff and raff?" Mariana laughed and said, "Those seats in the pit are conveniently located near the doors that lead behind the stage, where gentlemen sometimes go to meet women who have been performing."

"So it is in the opera houses in Austria as well. I suppose men are men the world over. I was just surprised that your proper Englishmen would behave in such a way."

"Oh, I assure you, being of exalted station is in no way equivalent to being of exalted moral character here in London, as indeed is the case everywhere, I imagine."

Adelheid struggled to think how to turn the conversation in a more specific direction. "It does seem to me unfortunate that such a young, innocent girl as Miss Fontenoy should intend to marry someone like the Duke of Hartland. He is a man of the world, no?"

"It is often the way here. A gentleman may sport his canvas well into his thirties if he wishes, and, when he's ready, pluck a girl right out of the schoolroom to set up his nursery."

"You speak as if you find this practice distasteful. Do you find it so in the case of Miss Fontenoy?" Adelheid sipped her tea and waited for Mariana to answer.

Mariana stood and wandered to the mantelpiece where she straightened a china shepherdess that didn't need straightening. "To my knowledge she has not yet accepted the duke's proposal. I have a particular fondness for Miss Fontenoy. I don't know why exactly."

"There is something—how do you express it? ... taking ... about her. I have seen it too. Why would she not sing at her ball? And why has she still not accepted such an eligible proposal?"

Mariana took a deep breath. "Ladies of the *ton* are

expected to follow the dictates of their parents and it is quite clear Lady Ambrose desires the match. It is less clear that her daughter's wishes align with hers. And as to the singing—" She stopped at the sound of a knock on the street door. "Now who could that be?"

A few moments later, Walton showed Olivia into the room. "Lady Mariana, I had to come and make a clean breast of it. The most shocking thing. I need your help again, I—" At that moment she spotted Adelheid and stopped speaking. "Princess Adelheid, forgive me." She dipped a hasty curtsy, her face flushing hotly crimson.

Adelheid did not miss the warning glance that Mariana threw to her new guest, and rose. "Not at all. Lady Mariana and I were just finishing our visit." She turned to Mariana. "I expect I shall have more questions as time goes on. Might I be so bold as to ask if you will allow me to trouble you for additional insight and answers?"

"Of course, my dear! I was delighted to have your company at the opera last night. Perhaps next time we can go to the play together. If you can bear the gas lamps at Drury Lane, that is!"

Adelheid could have sworn that Olivia uttered a tiny gasp. *I was right*, she thought. Mariana is engaged in something to protect Miss Fontenoy, and somehow it is related to her reluctance to sing in company. So, opera. Singing.

The link, once perceived, appeared obvious.The question was what it had to do with Hartland's proposal to Miss Fontenoy.

"WHAT DOES SHE KNOW?" OLIVIA ASKED AS SOON AS SHE heard the front door close behind Princess Adelheid.

"I don't think she knows anything that would link you to the masked singer," Mariana said as she helped Olivia out of her pelisse and handed her discarded bonnet to the footman who stood at the door awaiting instructions. "Now what has got you all in a pucker? You were magnificent yesterday evening, by the way."

Olivia couldn't even respond to this praise she was so agitated about her business with Lady Mariana. "Something has come up, something I never expected, and I don't know what to do about it. I know what I want to do. But it might ruin me, and possibly one other person."

For the next hour, Olivia poured out more of the details of her entanglement with Mr. Taylor at the theatre. That she would perform again the next night surprised Mariana but did not shock her. "I can see how difficult it would be for you to bow out now. Surely one more performance—I understand it is to be the final one for this opera this season—will not place you in more danger than any of the others?"

"If that were all …" Olivia paced back and forth in front of the fireplace, her hands clutched together. If Mariana knew what she was contemplating, the step she had decided to take in order to both punish the duke and give him the excuse he needed to cry off from his proposal, would she refuse to help her? If she did, what would she do? There was no avoiding it. She told Mariana about the benefit and the unmasking in public. "So you see, things are different in this case."

Mariana let a long minute elapse before answering. "Well, I must say I am delighted that the world will have possibly two more opportunities to hear you sing at the King's Theatre." She took Olivia's hand and drew her to sit down next to her on the settee. "But are you certain you should expose yourself in that way? I strongly advise you not to."

"I haven't yet agreed to it," Olivia said, although she knew it to be a lie. "As to the coming performance, sometimes I wish I'd never said yes the first time. I've got myself into quite a corner, lies upon lies. How can I do this without letting on to my mother? I've already used you as an excuse twice!"

"Let's leave aside the benefit for now. You don't have to make that decision immediately. As to tomorrow night's performance, I think the only thing left to you is illness."

"I thought of that. But if I claim to be unwell, my mama will want to stay home with me."

"Not if it's only a headache and someone else is accompanying you both to the card party." The mischievous glint had flashed into her eyes.

"Yeeesss. I see that. But who?"

"I think that my mama is planning to go to that party. Lady Hilford is a dear friend."

"But Mama is not well acquainted with the dowager Lady Bridlington. She would very much like to be, but as of yet…"

"Precisely."

Ah, Olivia thought. If one of the most revered ladies of the *ton* condescended to associate with her mother, Lady Ambrose would be loath to decline the opportunity, even if her daughter were indisposed. "How would you bring such a thing about? Would your mother be willing?"

"If I said it was important, she would do it. I can call around to her later this morning and ask her to send a note to Mount Street saying she has heard of your come-out success, and has long wished to be better acquainted with Lady Ambrose, and hopes to have a tête-à-tête with her at the Hilford's."

Olivia smiled. Lady Mariana had such a store of mischievous ideas. If things were not in such a muddle in her mind she would enjoy sitting and chatting about Mariana's past. But time was of the essence. "I think that would work. I hope so. It will have to, for I truly can't think of anything else. The party starts early—Lord Hilford is quite elderly—which helps." Then she thought of something. "I'll have to get home before she does, which might be difficult."

"Leave it to me. My mama can be devilishly charming when she wants to be."

AN UNABASHED CORINTHIAN WHO FOUND THE OPERA A DEAD bore unless a ballet was on the programme, Hartland underwent a transformation in one evening. The phenomenon of the masked soprano—and what he thought of as a risk-free pursuit, one that would never reach the ears of Miss Fontenoy or her parents—made of him an instant opera fanatic. This interest and everything associated with it operated like a dose of salts, a distraction from his growing obsession with the princess.

If he was going to throw himself into this flirtatious pursuit and attend the opera again the next evening, Hartland decided that he should at least know the plot of *The Marriage of Figaro*. He never paid much attention to the rapid Italian, only occasionally listening to a particularly pleasing tune. Now he burned to understand exactly what the mysterious lady behind the face-obscuring mask was singing so he could compliment her on it with expert finesse. Such flattery was a vital tool in his seduction arsenal, and he well knew that pretending complete fascination with some quality of the lady herself never failed of being a successful tactic. The flirtation would end as precipitately as it began—as such things normally did—but creatures like the singer encountered these episodes all the time, and would expect nothing else.

Of course his Cicero for all cultural matters was the obliging Lewiston. He would say he was cultivating an interest that would make himself more acceptable to Miss

Fontenoy. Lewiston liked both music and the heiress, and would probably applaud his desire to enter into some of the things that mattered to her. So he suggested a morning ride with his friend. Lewiston accepted, and after about a half hour Philip successfully maneuvered the conversation to the Mozart.

"The story isn't the most important part of it although it's based on a play by Beaumarchais that caused quite a scandal when it was first mounted," Lewiston said as they walked their horses at a leisurely pace through the park the morning of the next performance of the opera.

"Why?" Philip asked. "Seems a pretty foolish bit of nonsense to me." He knew his comment would provoke Harry, who took these things so seriously, and rightly assumed it would encourage him to say more.

"Foolish? At the time, it was thought treasonous to write a play where the servants outwit the masters, and the master is shown to be a duplicitous scoundrel."

"Hah! An upside-down world."

"Is it? I'm not certain it doesn't rather accurately reflect society even today."

Hartland couldn't help but notice the acid tone in Lewiston's voice, but chose to ignore it. "Do go on. What should I know if I want to talk to Miss Fontenoy about the opera? What are the clever comments I could make that would assure her I don't hold her fancies in disdain?"

Harry was quiet for a while, appearing to examine something in his horse's mane. "I suppose you could mention Mozart's use of ensemble set pieces for comic effect."

"Very good! What else? What about the part the masked lady plays? Anything I could say about that?"

This made Lewiston jerk his head up to stare at him. "You mean Countess Almaviva? She's mostly bemoaning her faithless husband who is trying to exercise *droit du seigneur*, even though he's the one who abolished the barbarous custom."

Hartland thought about that for a moment, and then said in jest, "An entirely understandable desire."

Lewiston reined in his horse and turned to Hartland, his normally affable countenance uncharacteristically stern. "I think it's time for me to return home to change for an early dinner. I'm escorting my mother to a card party this evening."

A feeble excuse, Hartland thought. "So you're not going to the opera?" What had so annoyed Harry? It wasn't like him to be prickly.

"No. Much as I would wish to."

*All the better*, thought Hartland. No risk that Lewiston would figure out his intentions with regard to the diva.

Hartland knew he was flirting with disaster as well as a possibly pretty opera singer. If Miss Fontenoy should ever find out what he was about, she would likely turn down his suit on the spot. Could she but understand that his attempt at seducing the masked soprano was in fact an act of self-preservation, something to prevent a more dangerous dalliance, she might turn a blind eye. But was that all it was? Something drove him on, an instinct for rising to a challenge that was so deeply ingrained in him that he could not have said where it came from. He didn't even know if beauty lurked beneath that obscuring mask. It didn't matter. The mere fact of the mystery added materially to the sport of it. And such sport made him feel alive. Alive in a way that—he hoped—would never have reason to trouble Miss Fontenoy.

If only the princess had come to London sooner! His haste to solve his family's financial difficulties had perhaps led him too precipitately to his offer for Miss Fontenoy.

Hartland's head was starting to ache with trying to tease out its obscure workings. He never thought serious courtship would cause him so much agitation. Much easier to put his mind to immediate plans concerning the masked soprano. He would send flowers to her dressing room, along with a note. It was a bit early days to nest a jewel among the flowers but, if all went as he had reason to believe it would, the time would come.

HARRY GROUND HIS TEETH ALL THE WAY BACK TO HIS SET IN the Albany. He'd never felt more like planting his old friend a facer. Hartland's words rankled. So, the duke wanted to pretend interest in Miss Fontenoy's 'fancy' for opera. Philip would soon find himself bereft of conversation if that was all he thought music meant to her. And why the interest in the role of the Countess? This disturbed him perhaps more than his general disdain for his friend's courtship tactics.

That was because something that had started as an absurd notion in Harry's mind was rapidly approaching the realm of the possible. He had been a bit suspicious of the way Miss Fontenoy danced around the subject of her attendance at the opera during the run so far of *Figaro*. He thought at first that instead of going to the King's Theatre, she was indulging in some illicit form of entertainment, although how she could possibly have acquired friends who would take her some- where like Vauxhall Gardens or to a masquerade at the Covent Garden opera house or the Pantheon without her mother's knowledge was a mystery.

His vague uneasiness around her caginess sharpened into suspicion the moment she sang that one brief melody line in the sonata. Though no more than a few measures long, it was enough to reveal to him that she had an exquisite voice. A voice she had refused to display at her ball. He thought it was simply shyness at first. Then, perhaps an unwillingness to be held up like a horse being put through its paces for the highest bidder. But it wasn't that at all. He was slowly but surely beginning to understand exactly why she was so reluctant to sing in a drawing room.

She had such a voice. The pure, rich tone, the unerring pitch and nuances of phrasing, the faultless flexibility—he'd been reminded instantly of the voice he heard in the park in February. At the time, he had discounted the lady he'd seen from a distance with her maid, thinking it inconceivable that someone of that quality would ever be trained as a true opera singer. If only he had been near enough to see what she looked like.

Olivia had been singing at half voice in the schoolroom to match the volume of his playing. The tones that issued from her vocal cords were not only beautiful, but obviously supported by practiced breath control. They had a quality of suppressed power, like a team of magnificent horses being held in check by their top-of-the-trees driver. He wondered whether, if Olivia were to give her voice free rein, it would prove powerful enough to fill the King's Theatre. He suspected it might.

The tragedy of it was that she would never be permitted to set foot on that stage as an heiress of the *ton*. It would be social ruin for her. Yet, if he was right, the operatic stage was where she belonged and she'd already taken that step in the only way she could.

Then he recalled with a chuckle the dramatic interruption of Giacomo Tetrazzini, a singing tutor who knew his value and never failed to make those fortunate enough to engage his services recognize it. Yet he hadn't condescended to Olivia as if she were being blessed from on high by his tutelage. He treated her not just with civility but with a combination of familiarity based on long acquaintance and— actual reverence.

Add to that the fact that he'd arrived unannounced, apparently accustomed to being granted entree to Miss Fontenoy's schoolroom at any hour, and Lewiston was tolerably certain that he and Olivia had some secret purpose.

To his knowledge, that evening would be the final performance of *Le Nozze di Figaro*, and he had other plans. It occurred to him, though, that if the card party broke up early, he might arrive at the theatre in time for at least the last act. If it led to nothing more, and he found he was entirely mistaken, at least he would have an opportunity to hear the lady sing one last time.

# CHAPTER 24

*F*or some reason, the lies Olivia had to tell her mother on this evening of the third—and possibly final, if her courage ultimately failed her—performance made her more nervous than ever. Lady Ambrose was a solicitous parent, at least as far as her daughter's health was concerned. So when Olivia begged off attending the Hilford's party because she had a headache, her mother was ready to call in Knighton to attend her.

"Mama! Don't be ridiculous. It's just a tiny headache! I expect it's all the parties and concerts I've been to. I'm not used to such a hectic schedule. A night of solitary quiet will do me good and I'm sure that's all I need."

The viscountess touched Olivia's forehead with the back of her hand to assure herself that her daughter wasn't feverish. "Perhaps I ought to stay home with you, in case you're sickening for the influenza or, heaven forbid, the measles." Olivia hadn't had that childhood disease, and Lady Ambrose lived in fear that it would strike her in the middle of her first season.

Olivia truly felt sorry for causing her mother so much

distress. But she couldn't back out now. "I haven't been anywhere near anyone who has the measles and I don't have a sore throat or a stuffy nose. Just the headache. Quiet and calm. That is what will cure me, I'm sure."

"All the same …"

"You can't stay home with me! Remember you're to sit at whist with the Dowager Countess of Bridlington, who especially wants to talk to you." *I'll surely burn in hell for all these bouncers*, Olivia thought.

This seemed to mollify Lady Ambrose, who exhorted her to go straight to bed with a handkerchief soaked in lavender water on her forehead.

As soon as Olivia heard the carriage drive away, she went to her bedroom and snatched up her cloak, checking to ensure that the mask was still in the inner pocket, and crept out of the house by the back door. She had told Hetty just enough to secure her secrecy. Her loyalty to her mistress—and the promise of a guinea—was ample to ensure her cooperation.

Lady Mariana's chaise was waiting for her just around the corner as arranged. She arrived, masked, at the theatre well before the overture would start, taking advantage of her mother's absence to give poor Félicité a little extra time to get her into her costume and wig.

"Mademoiselle," the costumer said as Olivia untied her cloak and draped it over a chair in the dressing room. "These flowers—they are for you."

Olivia was so focused on the performance to come that she failed to notice an immense bouquet of roses on her dressing table. A card peeped out from between the blooms. She took it and read.

*Fair mystery! You have conquered me with your artistry and your grace. Please take pity on one who adores you and sup with me in private after tonight's performance. I will await you.*

*Hartland*

Although she was prepared to possibly face the duke again after the performance, Olivia could not have guessed he would be so brazen as to leave a card with his name on it. The clear message regarding his motives for doing so nauseated her, despite knowing that the flirtation meant no more to him than it would have meant to any other fashionable gentleman.

But for the moment she must put this out of her mind and prepare to step on the stage once again, to become Countess Almaviva. Because she'd hitherto been too late to do more than dress and appear at the beginning of the second act, she'd had little opportunity to witness her fellow singers, what they did, how they behaved with each other before the performance. Thinking she may never have another opportunity to do so, she made sure she was ready before the orchestra struck up the overture and wandered to the backstage area where the costumed cast members walked up and down in attitudes of concentration—some humming quietly, others stretching their jaws with wide yawns or nodding their heads to a tune locked in their own imaginations.

As the overture came to its final section, all the singers stilled and became alert. Mistress Storace as Susanna and the baritone in the role of Figaro looked down at the floor, taking slow deep breaths. Olivia took up a position where she would be able to hear the first act but not be seen by the patrons in the on-stage boxes. If this were to be her final opportunity to exist in this world, she wanted to impress every bit of it on her memory, so she could conjure it up at sad or trying moments, to recall her brief career as a diva.

When the act ended and the singers streamed off the stage to the wings, perspiring and breathing hard, she said to the ones who passed her. "You were magnificent. So funny, so beautiful," or any other appropriate compliment. Mostly they just nodded their appreciation and went to their dressing rooms or tables to repair their sweat-streaked makeup and slake their thirst with a cup of ale.

Cherubino, who had been so skeptical of her at her first performance, stopped and made an old-fashioned, courtly leg. "I must own to having misjudged you. I still think it's a showy affectation to insist on remaining masked, but you can certainly sing. In fact, it would be my honor to appear on stage with you again in the future." The boyish soprano then hastened to her own dressing table.

To her dismay, Olivia felt her throat tighten with threatened tears. That would be disastrous for her voice! But the thought that, after this unlikely period of inhabiting the world of the operatic stage she would go back to her mundane life and never step on the boards again, never be dazzled by the footlights, never have to accustom herself to the raked stage, never again experience the hush of a previously restless audience as they gave her all their attention during an aria, filled her with sadness. She lifted her hand to brush away a tear, forgetting the mask for a moment, finding it was impossible. The tear trickled down the inside of the stiffened cloth. It didn't matter. She wouldn't need it for much longer anyway. It had already considerably wilted due to her repeated perspiration.

"Countess to your spot!" the stage manager called.

Olivia could still hear the loud voices of the audience members who had taken advantage of the scene change to socialize and refresh themselves. She went to the prop dressing table and sat on the stool angled toward the foot of the stage. The lackeys once again lit the footlights and the orchestra played the sweet introductory notes of her cavatina. With real regret and longing in her heart, from that moment on, Olivia sang as if it were the last time she would ever raise her voice.

As he hoped, the dowager marchioness became fatigued at an early hour and begged Harry to see her back to the house in Curzon Street. Once the groom had headed away to the stables in the landaulet, Lewiston hurried to the nearest hackney stand.

"The King's Theatre, and be sharp about it!" he said to the driver then sat, wound up with tension, in the odiferous vehicle.

He arrived at the hour when patrons could enter for half the cost, but apparently the theatre remained full and none of them could get in. He pushed through the crowd of clerks and tradesmen and the porter, recognizing him, opened the door and then shut it behind him to prevent anyone else getting in.

Lewiston's haste was rewarded. He was in his box in time to hear the masked soprano sing her big aria in the third act, "*Dove sono i bei momenti.*" He lifted his opera glass to his eye and trained it on her as she poured her heart out in one of Mozart's most poignant moments. The mask truly covered all of her face, and the powdered and curled wig gave no clue as to the color of her hair.

He gave up trying to find some shred of Olivia's face beneath the disguise and let his eyes wander over the rest of her body. Mostly it was encased in the heavy brocade costume with its shape-obscuring panniers. The only parts of her body that remained uncovered were her décolletage and her hands. Lewiston was not a connoisseur of women's bosoms, and he knew that the disposition of a corset could change a lady's shape, so the becomingly mounded breasts did not reveal anything he could identify as Olivia.

Her hands, however, were a different matter. The day before, he had spent two hours in her company as she played the pianoforte with her long, delicate fingers. At first, the soprano's hands were clasped together in an expression of anxious hope and he couldn't get a good look at them. When the cabaletta began and the mood changed to one of confident determination, she unclenched them and spread them wide in a gesture Lewiston had seen before, and not on the stage of the King's Theatre.

His acute ear then took over, listening for the timbre that he could recognize as Miss Fontenoy's from the brief phrase she'd sung in the schoolroom. He focused all his attention on every little nuance.

Yes. It was subtle, but present nonetheless. But what if he was wrong? Were hands and a voice enough to identify her? Or did he believe it was Olivia because he wished to? And then, even if he was correct, how would it change anything? She was masked and secretive because she wanted to be, and he well understood why. No one must know that the face behind the mask belonged to the daughter of a viscount. His heart twisted to imagine the exquisite frustration of having an extraordinary ability that could bring pleasure to a faceless audience but could never be appreciated by those who knew and loved her.

The wonder of it was that even if she never confessed it to him, never sang in his hearing ever again, he would still love her. She was enough just as she was. And he knew it was up to him to make sure she believed that.

He sat in awed stillness through the rest of the opera, pondering the impossibility of Olivia's situation. At the end of the final ensemble, just as at the previous performance, the audience leapt to its feet and cheered.

Instead of keeping his eyes on the stage, Lewiston scanned the crowd below, picking out a few people he knew, who all seemed to have taken leave of their senses as they jumped and waved and yelled their *bravas*. Except for one. One gentleman, rather than applauding and cheering, was quickly weaving through everyone else and heading for the door that led backstage. The door should have been guarded to prevent his breaching it, but even from his first-tier box, Harry could see the fellow slip a gold coin into the hand that opened the door for him.

The gentleman was none other than the Duke of Hartland.

# CHAPTER 25

*J*n all his adult life, Hartland had never received a rebuff from a lady whose favors he sought. The combination of his dark good looks, his physical grace, his charm and wit, his ability to intuit the precise compliment that would most please—and, of course, his title—added up to a devastatingly irresistible package. He generally only exerted his attentions on women who were not in the marriage mart for one reason or another, not desiring to trifle with some hopeful maiden's expectations. He did have scruples, after all. That he was going against them in another way at the moment he preferred not to dwell on.

So when he made his way to the masked soprano's dressing room, aided by greasing the palms of a couple of guards and flirting with the costumer (who wasn't so bad looking herself), he had every expectation of achieving his object: a private, intimate assignation with the lady who had all of London in a state of feverish conjecture and admiration.

He desperately wanted to be the man to strip off her

mask. What a tale that would be to tell over brandy in the club!

As he lounged elegantly in the one available chair in his long-tail coat, his superb cravat, buff silk knee breeches, and striped stockings—admiring the effusive bouquet he had sent earlier while he thought through his planned approach—he indulged in imagining this passionate scene of revelation. It was clearly within reach. His card had been read—it lay on the dressing table. The flowers hadn't been tossed aside and were not fighting for attention among a bevy of similar bouquets. Perhaps he was the only aspirant to the lady's favors. Squeamish youths might be reluctant to take a chance on a face hidden by a mask. Were none of them true gamesters?

Of course, Philip had also decided how he would behave if the mask hid an antidote, if the face behind it didn't live up to his optimistic vision. He would fall back on expressing sentiments such as that his heart had been won by her voice and his interest in her was that of a true connoisseur. Yet a mask could do nothing to disguise the lady's lovely physique, the curve of her breasts above the costume, the grace of her movements. They held promise that a visage of at least tolerable good looks lay behind that intriguing covering.

Only a minute or so passed before the masked soprano ran into the dressing room followed speedily by the costumer. "*Vite, vite!*" the singer said, looking over her shoulder. She reached around behind herself with trembling hands and began picking at the fastenings in the back of the costume before she lifted her eyes.

Hartland stood and bowed deeply to her. "My lady of the mask, I prostrate myself before you."

·  ·  ·

OLIVIA STOPPED WHAT SHE WAS DOING AND STARED. She expected another onslaught from Hartland, but thought it would be in the backstage area and had been relieved when he wasn't there. How on earth did he contrive to be admitted to her dressing room?

"*Signore*," she said with a slight inclination of her head, and grasped Félicité's wrist to arrest her progress in unfastening her costume. "I do not ... *non comprendo*." She wanted to demand he tell her how he came to be there, and then to give him a slap across the face before having one of the guards take hold of him by the shirt collar and toss him onto the street.

She wanted to, but she wasn't going to. She needed to keep him wondering for a while longer.

With a lead weight in her heart, she realized that truly the only way to teach Hartland a lesson—and simultaneously free them both from a betrothal that, at heart, neither of them wanted—would be to reveal herself in public. It seemed that she was being backed into a decision about the proposed benefit concert.

"Beautiful lady—for even without seeing your face, I know you are beautiful in your heart. Such loveliness deserves to be appreciated. Perhaps you would allow me to tell you more about the many ways I could appreciate you— in private." Hartland looked beyond Olivia's shoulder.

*He's signaling Félicité away*, Olivia thought. "No, no Signore," she said and shook her head vigorously. "I cannot— *mia madre*—my mother, she is unwell. I must go to her now." Oddly close to the truth, she thought.

"But let me take you there!"

"Eet is no *possibile...*" She turned a helpless look on the costumer, whose mystified expression soon transformed to one of understanding as Olivia mouthed the words *help me!* to her.

"The message from *votre mère* was most urgent, Mademoiselle," Félicité said, rising to the occasion quite expertly.

"You see, Signore, is no *conveniente*. Another time, yes, but not *questa sera*."

Hartland grasped both her hands and squeezed them, pressing close to her with a quick glance down her décolletage. "How can I be sure you will honor me with your company at a more propitious time?"

How indeed? Then Olivia had a thought. Something so deliciously apt that she had to suppress a wicked chuckle. "Perhaps, Signore, you give me a … token—is right word? And I return it to you when we meet."

"A token? What shall it be?"

Olivia thought something with his crest or a monogram would be perfect, but she didn't know if he had any such thing on his person. And if she were to be playing the part of someone he might offer a carte blanche or a slip on the shoulder, she would likely fix on something of more value. She let her eyes linger on the diamond pin, a bar with three large brilliants set in gold filigree fastened among the folds of his perfectly tied neck cloth, and smiled coyly up into his eyes.

"Madame, I will gladly give this trinket into your keeping, to pledge our future association." He let go of her and unpinned the jewel, took her left hand and pressed it into her palm.

Olivia closed her fingers around it in triumph. "I shall return this to *Monsignore* at his command," she said, and curtsied deeply.

He pulled her up out of her curtsy and Olivia believed he would have taken her into his arms and kissed her, were it not for the forbidding mask. Instead, he lifted her other hand to his lips and said, "Soon, lady mystery!"

Félicité quickly reassumed her role and said, "*Allez*

*Monsieur!* Or I call ze guard," adding a coquettish smile to the end of her utterance.

At that, the duke swept out of the dressing room.

Olivia closed the door and leaned against it. "Oh Félicité, I cannot amply thank you for your work this evening."

She shrugged. "I am used to such things. But why do you wish to discourage an English duke, who is *de plus* so 'andsome?"

"If I told you, you would not believe me. Besides, you'll likely find out Friday evening."

"Eh?" the seamstress said, having resumed her expeditious work behind Olivia and helped her step out of her hooped skirts.

"I can't tell you more. Quickly get me dressed again. I've wasted too much time already!"

Before she left, Olivia suddenly had a thought about the duke's diamond pin. She could never hide it from Hetty, who knew every trinket and ribbon in her wardrobe. She supposed she could keep it with her in her reticule, but the idea of having such a valuable item always on her person made her nervous.

"Félicité," she said, stopping before running out the door. "Can I trust you? I need your help."

The dresser, who had been carefully laying the gown in a trunk, turned and smiled. "Ah! Mademoiselle, you want my help with a liaison?"

"No! Not that exactly. Oh, you will soon know, but until that time, would you keep this for me somewhere safe? Somewhere no one would expect to find such a thing?" She opened her fisted hand to reveal the precious pin.

Félicité stared down at it in amazement. "*Mais, c'est magnifique!* The duke, he must want you very much."

"But he will not have me, and this bauble will play its part in ensuring that." She reached for Félicité's hand and pressed the pin into it.

The seamstress closed her fingers over it. "It is well to do this. I know where this jewel will be safe."

"*Merci, merci*, Félicité," Olivia said, and quickly embraced her and ran out of the dressing room.

I MUST REMEMBER TO GIVE FÉLICITÉ A HANDSOME DOUCEUR, Olivia thought as she hurried through the corridors to the stage door.

Just before she turned the last corner, the sound of many voices reached her—men's voices.

"We want to see her!" "Let us in!" "Surely she cannot have gone already!"

Olivia pressed her back against the wall. Oh God! Her way out was blocked. Where could she go? Damn Hartland! He'd stalled her just enough for the young bucks to throng the stage exit.

Footsteps approached from down the hallway behind her.

It was Mr. Taylor. Normally someone she would not like to see but this time, she was grateful.

"Madame," he said, sweeping her a graceful bow.

"*Aiuta!*" Olivia said in a hoarse whisper, and pointed in the direction of the voices. "I must escape!"

He stroked his chin, looking her up and down in a considering way. "I could get you out through a different door that no one knows. But I need your answer, about the benefit. I collect that Tetrazzini has informed you of my plan?"

How Olivia wished she could tell him to go to the devil. But unfortunately, his need corresponded with hers in this regard. "*Bene.* I will do as you say."

A smile spread across his face and the irises of his gray

eyes glittered as though they were made up of splinters of silvered glass. "Follow me, Madame!"

He led her a short way back down the corridor to a low door she hadn't noticed before. It opened to some steps down to what was surely a cellar. Only a faint glow of light emanated from it. She cast a nervous glance at Taylor.

"I am afraid this is your only choice. Here." He pulled one of the lit candles out of a wall sconce nearby and handed it to her. "Just keep going, and you'll reach a door that leads to a yard. Don't linger there. I need you to be here at five sharp on Friday." He bowed, a bit facetiously, Olivia thought.

She walked with tentative steps down the flight of stairs. As soon as she was at the bottom, the door slammed behind her.

Completely alone, Olivia found herself in a sort of storage room, full of discarded bits of broken scenery. She raised the taper in her hand and surveyed her surroundings, catching the tail of a rat disappearing among the mess.

She shrieked.

*Don't be stupid!* she thought. A rat wasn't going to hurt her. Opposite her a dark corridor led away, a distant drip of water echoing from it. With no option but to proceed in that direction, she went forward, the candle flame flickering and casting odd shadows all around.

The corridor was narrow and hung with cobwebs. She tried to brush them away as she went and was aware of scrabbling and squeaking, of mice, rats, and probably bats as well. She shivered. Taylor wouldn't have sent her anywhere dangerous. Too much was riding on her appearance in the benefit. So she pressed on.

Her progress was slow. The light of the candle barely pierced the gloom in front of her, and here and there stones and bits of wood jutted, making it hazardous going. Most disconcerting of all were the flashes of tiny red eyes as the rats stared at her and then scuttled away. The ground was damp, too, and her delicate evening slippers soon soaked through. She began to shiver, which only made the candle flame waver and wobble more.

The corridor curved around to the right and after what seemed an eternity, she could just perceive a filament of light around what was surely a door at the end. "Thank heavens," she breathed and had a strong urge to cross herself.

She hastened to the door and felt for a handle, meeting slimy creatures whose identity she couldn't bear to imagine as her fingers traced the outline. At last she felt an iron ring lower down than she expected and pulled.

The door didn't budge.

Her heart started to do the most uncomfortable things, knocking against her ribs and flipping around in panic. *Calm yourself,* Olivia thought. Then, aloud, "He wouldn't have sent me somewhere I couldn't get out." Likely the door was just stiff.

She pulled again. No luck. Then she had another idea, and pushed instead. She thought the door gave a little. But her arms weren't strong enough. It would take the effort of her entire body.

Little as she wanted to do it, Olivia pressed her shoulder into the grimy wood of the door and pushed with all her might.

After sticking for a moment the door burst open, and Olivia cannoned out of it and found herself sprawled on the ground amid a pile of garbage.

She retched as she stood and tried to shake off the mess. It was indeed a yard, one littered with all manner of refuse, with an iron stairway up to the street.

Olivia extinguished her candle and flung it away before clambering up the rickety stairs to what she assumed must be the alley behind the theatre. Lady Mariana's carriage was to await her a short way down on Haymarket, so she ran as fast as she could to the corner untying her mask as she went, turned onto the street, and to her immense relief, the chaise was still there.

The groom looked at her askance.

"Yes, it's me, Bracket. Tell Lady Mariana I apologize for the stench. No need to get down!" She clambered in and sat on the edge of the seat, not wanting to lean her filthy cloak against the velvet-upholstered squabs. When she took a moment to examine her mask she was horrified to see that it had been smudged all over as a result of her fall.

As soon as the chaise pulled up at the back entrance to Mount Street, she jumped out before the groom could get down from his perch and lower the step. How much had he guessed, she wondered. Lady Mariana had assured her of her servants' discretion, but Olivia had no confidence that the whole affair wasn't being talked over below stairs all through the *ton.*

In any case, after Friday night there would be no more mystery.

She made it in through the servants' passages and stairs and slipped into her bedroom where Hetty awaited her. When she saw her mistress she exclaimed, "Miss Olivia! What has happened?"

Olivia shushed her and said, "Never mind that now. Just get rid of these filthy clothes and get me into my night shift before my mother comes home. She isn't here yet, I hope?"

Hetty said, "No, Miss. Although I expect her any minute."

As if her words had the power to conjure, the sounds of a carriage pulling up and the front door of the mansion opening, followed by the murmur of a female voice, made its way to Olivia's ears.

"Quickly!" She tore off her evening dress and flung it at Hetty, then scrambled into her night clothes, slipped between her sheets and blew out her bedside candle just as Hetty disappeared into the dressing room and Lady Ambrose came along the hallway and stopped at her door.

Olivia ignored the light scratch, wanting her mother to assume she was fast asleep. The door opened a crack, and the viscountess whispered, "Olivia?"

Olivia focused on breathing slowly and deeply, just audible enough for her mother to assume she was fast asleep.

A moment later the door closed with a quiet click, and then the viscountess passed on in the direction of her chamber.

It took a long time for Olivia to fall asleep, but when she did, she slept deeply and dreamlessly and didn't awaken until Hetty drew back the curtains on a brilliant, sunny day.

A day perhaps destined to be her last before her complete social ruin, and the end of all possibility that she would ever make a creditable match.

# CHAPTER 26

*A*delheid was still in her dressing gown the next morning when Félicité burst in upon her. Again. She was so surprised she dropped her bottle of scent and it spilled all over the floor. Agnes peered around the seamstress with an apologetic look on her face.

"*Princesse!*" Félicité said, not waiting for any kind of greeting. "I have something for you, something I believe you may find very useful." She reached into her reticule and drew out a handkerchief tied in a knot with something small and hard wrapped within it and handed it to her.

"That will be all, Agnes," Adelheid said. Once the maid left, she asked, "What's this?"

"Open and see, *mon amie.*"

She teased apart the knot, spread open the cambric square, and found an exquisite diamond bar pin, the kind gentlemen sometimes wore in their cravats. Its design was very distinctive. "I don't understand."

"Last night, ze duke—he once more comes back to the masked soprano's dressing room and tries to lure her to come away with him. She says no—but if he gave her a token, she would return it to him, as a *promêt*."

"This belongs to Hartland?" Adelheid was dumbfounded. "What a foolish thing for him to do! But how come you to be in possession of this trinket?"

Félicité explained what Olivia asked of her.

"I'm certain she must have meant you simply to lock it away somewhere," Adelheid said. "Why are you giving it to me?"

"Because, *chère amie*, you might use it, to frighten the duke, per'aps."

Ah. Her friend seemed determined that she should use unseemly wiles to win the duke away from the heiress. "No, *ma chère*," Adelheid said. "I will not stoop to blackmail."

"*Eh bien*." Félicité shrugged. "But I think it will be safer with you than with me at the theatre."

"That is certainly true." The merest trifles often went missing during a performance. But surely, the masked soprano would know that if she had ever sung on the stage in any of the European opera houses?

Félicité interrupted her thoughts. "I must go. I have so much mending to do at the theatre. I hear that the mysterious soprano will perform again and she tore the hem of her costume *hier soir*. You have 'eard about the benefit?"

"The benefit?"

"Monsieur Taylor must raise money so he may pay Catalani and she will sing again. So he make a benefit performance by subscription. You must come—the lady in the mask, she will sing."

"I have already heard her. And I have no desire to pay the exorbitant ticket price for such a thing when it's only to fatten Catalani's purse."

Félicité's eyes danced. "*Beh*, per'aps. But at this benefit," she said, gripping her friend's hand, "the soprano will remove her mask."

Adelheid had to admit, she would like to see what that bizarre mask hid. Would Lady Mariana be attending, she wondered? And what about the duke? "Very well. I shall find a way to come."

With that, the two friends kissed fondly, and Félicité left as precipitately as she'd arrived.


THE DAY'S SURPRISES WEREN'T QUITE AT AN END, HOWEVER. Later in the morning Adelheid received another visit, just as she was about to go up to the nursery to teach Otto his lessons.

"His Grace the Duke of Hartland," Fulton said in sepulchral tones as he ushered the duke into the drawing room. His entrance coming so soon after Félicité's revelations and with the memory of all she had seen the previous night unsettled her and it took her a moment to compose herself.

After he greeted her with an elegant bow, Hartland said, "Forgive the intrusion. I thought I might give you some hints about who you can expect to meet at the rout party this evening. You will make quite a stir, I'm certain."

"How kind of you, Duke," Adelheid said, not quite able to banish the idea of him flirting backstage with the soprano. "I am afraid I have little time, however. I must meet Otto in the schoolroom upstairs and try to teach him more of the English language so that he will be ready for a tutor."

Hartland cocked his head on the side and gave her a quizzical look. "To what purpose? Is he to be put into a profession when he is older?"

Adelheid realized her attention to Otto's education must seem odd to Hartland. It was natural that he might think of a boy like Otto as more likely to go into some respectable trade than anything more. "It is too early to make any such decisions for him. I would like him to go to school, if it will be possible. He must be well educated. Surely you can see that." It was the only way she could think of for the boy to make connections with children of his own class. Through this, she hoped he would be accepted eventually on his true merits, rather than be judged by the color of his skin. But she said none of that to Hartland.

"You care greatly for a boy who is no relation of yours. I confess, he is a taking child, and from what I've seen of him very bright—as well as full of pluck. Perhaps I may be of some help?"

"Help?"

"I know a bit about schools," he said, a glint of amusement in his eyes. "The choice is generally Eton or Harrow, although Winchester is also a fine option. I am acquainted most of all with Eton and have some influence there, should you decide on it."

"That would be beyond what I would ever ask of you. But I see that you appreciate how important it will be for someone like Otto to have every possible advantage. It is a burden, I confess, to prepare him for the future."

"Something tells me from what I know of the lad that he will prevail. Perhaps we will see him in Parliament, or on the king's bench." His eyes sparkled with amusement.

"His ambition at the moment reaches no higher than to be a groom in a stable full of blood cattle, as you call them. It's all I can do to keep him away from the horses long enough to teach him his letters and arithmetic."

"I envy him," Hartland said, coloring slightly, as though he hadn't meant the words to escape his lips. "But I have been remiss." He reached into his coat pocket and retrieved a folded paper. "I wrote down the names and styles of the most influential guests likely to attend Lady Ferndale's party this evening, with a note or two about each of them."

She took the paper he handed her and glanced down it. There were at least twenty-five names. "You have gone to so much trouble for me. How may I ever thank you?"

"You can thank me by enjoying the party this evening. I hope you will allow me the honor of presenting you to my friends and acquaintances. And don't forget to save those dances for me."

Adelheid wanted to ask if Miss Fontenoy wouldn't be more appropriate for that honor, but thought he might think it impertinent. Who was she to know where things stood with the heiress? "Of course, Duke." She stood and held out her hand. "Thank you. I'm sorry I didn't have time to offer you any refreshment, I am afraid the schoolroom calls."

Hartland took her hand in a warm, firm grip, then turned it palm upward and kissed it. The feel of his lips on her palm stirred something in her. She held her breath. He turned her hand over and gave it the more conventional kiss on her knuckles, then looked up and into her eyes. "If there is ever anything else I can do for you, you need only ask."

What was it she saw in those brilliant blue depths? She would have expected flippant flirtation. But that wasn't it at all. If anything, his eyes seemed darker than she remembered —and rather than a smile, she saw a flicker of sadness. "You are too kind, Duke." *I will ask something of you soon, but perhaps not what you expect,* Adelheid thought as she watched him go through the door and step lightly down the stairs.

At that moment, Nicholas came out of the office on the ground floor where he had been examining the household accounts. He watched Hartland leave and then looked up at Adelheid with a question in his eyes. "Have you told him?"

"Not yet," she said, then climbed the stairs to the schoolroom.

# CHAPTER 27

or Olivia, getting ready to attend her first rout party felt sadly flat after the intrigue and adventure of the past week. Dressing and worrying about possible dance partners was nothing to the excitement of sneaking out masked and donning a costume to sing on stage at the King's Theatre. Olivia tried her best to seem enthusiastic about the evening ahead, but it was a struggle. When only Hetty was in the room, she made little effort to respond to her exhortations about what fun she had to look forward to and listened with half an ear to her enthusiasms about Olivia's white round gown, with its willow green sarsenet overdress, trimmed tastefully with a few satin rosettes, and the delicate topaz and emerald necklace that reflected the complex colors in Olivia's eyes,

But when Lady Ambrose entered in her own finery to inspect her daughter's appearance, Olivia pushed herself to appear nervous and excited. She knew how important these events were to her mother and didn't want to disappoint her. In fact, she was nervous enough, but more in the sense of dreading what was to come than looking forward to it.

"Your first rout party! It will be a squeeze, I'm certain. There will be dancing, and everyone will be there, perhaps even the Prince Regent himself. You'll no doubt see the duke again. He hasn't been here for a few days to take you out driving. Has he been away? Are there races or a prize fight out of town?"

Having just seen Hartland the night before—unbeknownst to her mother—Olivia almost contradicted her. She caught herself though and changed the subject. "The Norwich silk shawl, do you think Mama? Or the spider gauze?"

"Did Madame Pauline say which would be better? I can't remember. She outdid herself. She was so right about the color of this gown with your hair and eyes!"

"You mean the Countess of Bridlington outdid herself," Olivia said. That lady was accepted in the first circles, despite being the real genius behind the *ton's* most famous modiste's establishment. She supposed it helped that the business of fashion was so integral to every aspect of life in the *ton* that it hardly seemed as if Lady Bridlington had stepped out of her realm. In fact, having started out a seamstress, it could be argued that she'd stepped out of her realm in becoming a countess.

Whatever the case, the question of which shawl to bring had Lady Ambrose debating with herself for a good quarter of an hour while Hetty arranged Olivia's hair, weaving in ribbons and tiny artificial flowers so artfully that Olivia exclaimed in admiration. "You have made me look so pretty, Hetty!"

"No one could make you look prettier than you already are, Miss Olivia," Hetty said, blushing with pride.

Lady Ambrose came and frowned into the mirror over Olivia's shoulder. "I think you need something more. I'll fetch my diamond brooch and you can wear it at your corsage." Either the viscountess didn't hear what Hetty said or chose to ignore it and hastened out of the room.

*Am I pretty?* Olivia peeked a little sideways into the mirror, trying to see what someone else might, how she would appear from the outside, and to discover if it differed from how she felt on the inside. How she might appear, for instance, through the Marquess of Lewiston's eyes. As she recalled his gentle, intelligent expression, she smiled, and her whole face softened. Her eyes brightened, her cheeks lost their sullen hollowness, and the curve of her slightly parted lips held a suggestion of coquetry.

She looked away quickly. She mustn't think of Harry. This evening she must exert herself to be charming to Hartland, to lull him into a false sense of security that she was planning to accept his offer. As she drew her satin evening gloves over her lanky arms and Hetty tied the ribbons that held them above her elbows, her confidence that it was within her power to act as she intended showed signs of wavering. After all, Olivia Fontenoy was a nobody, a cypher, compared to the duke's imposing presence. The question was, after what had happened at her previous two performances, would she still be able to look him in the eye without betraying her mortification? And how foolish she would feel. Who was she, after all, to quibble with the private actions of a duke who she knew didn't love her?

Olivia Fontenoy was nothing, but Countess Almaviva, on the other hand, was very much more than nothing. If she could but feel the same that evening at the rout party as she did when she was on the stage, the same calm confidence and sense of importance, everything would be easier. In the role of the Countess, supported by all the power of her voice, Olivia had reserves of strength. Countess Almaviva believed in herself, believed in what she deserved from her faithless husband.

But when she was on stage, Olivia also had the sparkling music to support her, the mask to hide behind, and a cast of others working toward the same end: teaching the wayward count a lesson for daring to attempt to seduce a maid.

There was one important difference between Olivia and the countess Almaviva, though. While the fictional countess loved her husband and wanted him to return to her, Olivia's ultimate aim was to achieve the opposite.

"What are you mooning about, Olivia? I've brought you the diamond brooch." Lady Ambrose bustled back into the room, her hand outstretched to reveal the gaudy brooch.

Olivia had been so lost in her thoughts that she jumped in surprise and knocked her vinaigrette over.

"Clumsy girl!" Lady Ambrose said. "Here it is. Let me see it on." She gave her the heirloom.

"Are you sure I need it? I think it will be too much, especially for a rout party. It's not full dress, you know," Olivia said, looking at the diamond-caked treasure in her mother's hand. With that pinned at her breast no one would look at any other part of her. She held it at the dip in her bodice between her breasts for her mother to see.

Lady Ambrose sighed. "Perhaps you're right. But all you're wearing are those trumpery topazes!"

"I like them. They look well with my gown. I'm only eighteen, remember Mama." She tried for a teasing note but the words came out sounding forlorn.

For one more day, she had to play her role as the naïve heiress, dazzled by the attentions of the most sought-after bachelor in the *ton*. Just one more day.

Thanks to her experience at the King's Theatre, she had a chance of being able to succeed at it. In acting like someone she wasn't, Olivia had learned an entirely new language of seduction and courtship. She had several techniques at her command, including subtle ways of leaning close to a man so her charms were unmistakable, of peeking over the top of her fan and then lowering her eyes demurely, and of always placing herself just out of reach without seeming to tease.

The Mozart was a farce, but weren't all the rituals of the season the same? Everyone acting their parts, hoping for the right happy ending, that the couples would sort themselves out and all would be well in the end.

"Don't just stand there! Put on your evening cloak. I expect Garvey has the coach ready." Lady Ambrose said, leading the way out of Olivia's bedroom in the unwavering expectation that her daughter would follow.

WHERE RIGID FORMALITY AND PAINSTAKING PROPRIETY HAD been the watchword at the Ambrose ball, the atmosphere of Lady Ferndale's rout party bore a striking similarity to that of a carnival. It wasn't so much what the guests looked like, Adelheid thought—they were all dressed in the kick of fashion, decked in costly jewels and clearly representative of the first circle—but in the heightened energy, the undercurrent of fierce enjoyment, that seemed to have infected everyone there. No one waited for the hostess to start the ball, or held themselves back from partaking of the lavish delicacies arrayed to tempt their appetites. Dozens of footmen wove their way through the crowd bearing trays of drinks like so many green and gold threads—the colors of the Ferndale livery. And knots of conversation formed and broke apart with unaccustomed informality.

Even in this maelstrom of social activity, Adelheid was aware that her entrance caused a stir. Unlike the Ambrose ball, where she arrived on Lady Mariana's status-conferring arm, she took her own carriage to this party and walked into the main saloon alone. Many eyes swiveled in her direction, examining her with frank curiosity, some dismay, and much admiration. She was used to provoking those kinds of reactions and maintained her composure, casting her eye around for a familiar face to smooth her entrance into the crowd. At first she saw no one she recognized from the only other *ton* party she'd ever been to. But before long, her eyes alighted on Miss Fontenoy herself.

Alighted, and then became riveted. Was it truly the same Miss Fontenoy she had met less than a fortnight earlier? That evening she had appeared the reticent, uncomfortable ingenue, performing her role correctly but stiffly—only unbending for those brief moments when she was dancing with the marquess. This was not that Miss Fontenoy. Nor was it the one she met briefly at Lady Mariana's house, when she showed all the signs of fretful anxiety. Here, among a crowd that should have daunted all but the most assured society belles she carried herself like a lady of consequence accustomed to moving through the world as though it existed for her pleasure only.

What could have happened to effect this transformation?

Adelheid had little time to ponder the question because Miss Fontenoy had seen her, and in a smooth and practiced manner detached herself from the group of guests she'd been talking to in order to glide over and greet her.

"Princess!" Miss Fontenoy said, reaching her two hands out in a familiar gesture—more familiar than their degree of acquaintance warranted, Adelheid thought.

"Miss Fontenoy, I'm delighted to see you here, and looking so well!" She did look well, although Adelheid couldn't mistake the hectic glow of her eyes.

Before they could embark on a conversation, the Duke of Hartland emerged from the crowd around them and made his bow. "The two most beautiful ladies here!" he said, although he, too, appeared a little nervous.

Miss Fontenoy curtsied, smiled, looked down at the floor and then up at Hartland through her lashes. "How lovely to see you again, Duke."

She's flirting with him! Adelheid didn't know what to think. Was she going to accept—or had she already accepted—the duke's proposal after all? It didn't fit with all she had seen of Miss Fontenoy so far. But these matches were seldom concerned with love, after all. And Adelheid's heart sank just a little, knowing that Hartland would be a considerate, conscientious, and discreet husband—no doubt still pursuing his opera dancers and high flyers—and doubtless the two would find a way to be happy enough.

"I hope you will honor me, Princess Adelheid."

She tore her thoughts away from Olivia when Hartland addressed her. "Honor you, Duke?"

"I had intended to lead you out for the first two dances this evening. But since the dancing has already commenced, if you are still not engaged, I would be delighted to take you to the floor when the next set starts. He reached out and took a light hold of her dance card, flicked it carelessly, and then managed to brush her wrist as he let it drop, sending an unexpected shock through her body.

Adelheid glanced into Miss Fontenoy's face and just caught a fleeting expression of displeasure in her eyes before she once more adopted the serene mask of a *ton*-ish female. What could it mean? Was she jealous? Why, when Adelheid was well aware that her affections were not engaged with the duke but in quite another direction. On her way to accepting Hartland's proffered hand to lead her into the ballroom, she scanned the company idly to see if she could spy Lord Lewiston. He was nowhere to be seen.

"We shan't abandon you, though," Hartland said to Miss Fontenoy. "Here are Lady Mariana and Thorne to keep you company. Remember, I have claimed the next waltz."

. . .

Olivia's strategy of imagining herself to be Countess Almaviva was attracting so much notice that several eager come-outs cast sidelong glances at her and whispered behind their fans. Was she behaving outrageously? She didn't care.

Soon Lady Mariana reached her with her husband in tow. "At last," Mariana said, "we can leave politics behind and talk about the real business of life! How do you do, my dear?" she said, warmly shaking Olivia's hand. "I don't believe you've met my husband, Jeremy Thorne."

Mr. Thorne bowed gallantly over Olivia's hand and she nodded politely. He was an elegant, lanky man with a square jaw, an abundance of wavy dark brown hair, and a pair of deep brown eyes that were hard to read but somehow still friendly. When he straightened, he gave Olivia an appreciative look bearing an unmistakable gleam of knowledge. Had Lady Mariana told him her secret? Olivia hoped not, but couldn't keep the heat from her face and stirred the air in front of it with her fan. "I hope no one else is going to arrive! It's far too crowded in here," she said.

Mr. Thorne signaled to a footman who brought a tray with glasses of lemonade on it. He picked one up and handed it to Olivia, who took it gratefully and sipped. "I understand you're an opera lover, Miss Fontenoy," Thorne said, the corners of his mouth pinched as though suppressing a smile.

Olivia nearly spit out her lemonade and had to cover her mouth. How wicked of him! "Yes," she answered, once she'd swallowed, her voice a little shaky. "Are you? Or do you prefer the Philharmonic Society concerts?" She hoped he would take the hint and veer to a safer topic.

"I like a spectacle, myself. The costumes, the scenery, and the voices are quite extraordinary. It reminds me of the floor of the House in its way. Why, the other night I found myself captivated by a soprano wearing a mask, of all things. Have you heard her?" Two decided dimples appeared in his cheeks as if he could no longer keep his amusement under complete control.

"No," said Olivia in all honesty and with a furious glare, "I have not had that pleasure." She looked toward Mariana who, although still holding Olivia's arm captive, had turned a little away to talk to Lady Jersey, who had ambled up to then.

Thorne leaned forward and spoke so that only Olivia could hear him. "If the rumors are true, tomorrow night she will be unmasked."

"If, as you say, they are true." *Yes,* Olivia thought, and then, *I wonder if this will be the last* ton *party I am ever invited to.*

"Darling," Mariana said, turning back to her husband, "would you excuse me if I take Miss Fontenoy away for a private conversation?"

No! The last thing Olivia wanted was to speak privately to Lady Mariana. She already knew that she would try to dissuade her from going through with the benefit. She had intimated as much yesterday. It took all her resolve to stick to her purpose and she didn't want any more doubts to assail her.

Before Mariana could pull her away, Lady Bridlington glided over to join them, wearing a gown *à la russe* of gold satin with a white spider gauze overdress. "Ah! Miss Fontenoy, the gown is perfection. Madame Pauline has a faultless eye." A knowing gleam shone in her eyes.

"Yes indeed, Lady Bridlington. I almost feel pretty." All three of them laughed. Olivia had told Mariana enough of her mother's damping criticism for her to appreciate the joke.

Conversation turned to fashion. Soon the two ladies were deep in the subject and Olivia drifted away. She had other things to think about.

At that moment, one of her partners came to claim her for the Boulanger, and she gratefully allowed herself to be led to the ballroom, obedient to the siren call of music that—if not quite as good as the music at her ball—more than passably supported a room full of enthusiastic dancers.

They took their places in the line of couples. To Olivia's discomfort, they were in the same set as Hartland and the princess who stood four couples away from them, waiting for the music to begin. At first, they both smiled and nodded to the dancers next to them. But with the introductory chords, they looked up and into each other's eyes.

Olivia stifled a gasp. Nothing could be clearer. She knew in that one instant that they—Hartland and the princess—were in love with each other. And also, that nothing could be more right, more suitable. *Surely he will be grateful when I give him an easy way out of his offer!* Although this lessened her planned sting, her intended set-down, she could be content with knowing simply that she would have fooled him, beaten him at his own game, so to speak, and likely embarrassed him in a way that he would not easily forget.

She moved through the dance steps with mechanical precision, keeping her pleasant expression, responding politely to inane conversation. But all the time Olivia was thinking *how could the duke possibly want to marry me?* She was utterly unsuited to be his duchess. It was all wrong. All he wanted from her was her fortune. And wasn't Princess Adelheid enormously wealthy? She, Olivia Fontenoy, could never be the wife for Hartland, even if there were no princess to step into her place. Married, she would disappear in his aura of magnificence. To marry him would be to doom herself to obscurity, to be cast into shade not only by his magnetic presence but by his showy mistresses.

The dance ended at last and Olivia found herself momentarily isolated in the ebullient crush.

"What has caused that frown in your eyes, Olivia?"

Relief, pleasure, confusion, and yearning flooded Olivia in equal measures as she turned to face the owner of the voice. "Harry! I mean, Lord Lewiston! I didn't see you. Have you just arrived?"

"No. I've actually been standing over there..." He nodded toward a corner of the room flanked by silk-covered settees. "...watching you for a while. And the princess. She's quite the diamond, is she not?"

Olivia sighed. "Yes, indeed. Puts us all in the shade. Not that I mind, since the shade is where I feel most comfortable."

"You should not. You have a light that outshines even the loveliest creature in the room, if you were ever willing to share it."

"What do you mean?" Olivia's heart leapt into her throat. What exactly was he saying?

"Your music. You must know how extraordinary it is for a lady of your station to have such a gift."

"I am not so talented on the pianoforte," Olivia said with a nervous laugh.

"I didn't mean that."

At that moment, strains of a dance air filtered into the saloon from the ballroom, and several of the younger guests started to move in that direction as if a huge magnet exerted a force that compelled their feet to obey its pull.

"Did you save me the waltz?" Lewiston asked.

"I have to dance the first one with Hartland," she said, and then realized she sounded as if it were a fate to be dreaded. "I mean, he's a wonderful dancer, I didn't mean—"

Lewiston smiled his enchanting crooked smile and cocked his head on the side. "You should accustom yourself to him, if the rumors are true."

Olivia's shoulders drooped. "I'm not ... I mean ..."

"He has offered for you, though. You seemed to be enjoying his attentions."

"I wasn't—you don't know—it's not..." She wanted so badly to explain to him why she was being so charming to the duke. "But yes, he has offered. I haven't given him my answer, however."

The look in Lewiston's eyes changed. A sudden light glinted in their depths. "Why not?"

She looked away in confusion. She didn't expect such a direct question.

"I'm sorry, I had no right to ask you that," Lewiston said.

"It's what my mother wants," Olivia blurted out in a feeble attempt to lighten the tone.

"And you? Do you want it?" Lewiston's voice was barely above a whisper, but it cut through all the noise in the room and lodged somewhere near her heart. She searched his eyes for some meaning, but the brief look she'd seen had disappeared. How could she explain to him why she wasn't going to cry off just then? Why she hadn't done so yet? She hardly knew herself.

"Have you heard about the benefit performance at the opera tomorrow night?" he said, drawing closer to her.

"Yes. You are the second person to mention it to me," Olivia said, an uncomfortable pressure in her chest. She still wondered how much he had guessed because no one could have told him anything. "Will you attend?"

"Of course! Apparently the mysterious soprano will reveal herself. And you?"

"I shall be there," she said, truthfully.

"You would have to be, I imagine."

Olivia let a small gasp escape her and opened her eyes wide at him. What did he know? But there was no time to say anything more, because her partner for the next country dance came to claim her hand. "The second waltz?" she said over her shoulder as Lord Peterham led her into the ballroom.

WHAT HAS COME OVER MISS FONTENOY? HARTLAND WONDERED. He was used to think of her as an awkward, somewhat prickly—albeit quick and intelligent—child. But that evening, she had the poise and address of a true lady. She was in excellent looks as well. Her dress perfectly suited her and she'd resisted the temptation to deck herself out in diamonds —or rather, he suspected she'd persuaded her mother that it wouldn't be seemly.

His mind was far away when the princess, still on his arm, spoke to him. "The last time I attended such a party I felt nothing but fear."

Hartland's attention snapped back to the moment and he turned to Adelheid abruptly. "Fear? But how could that be? You must surely be the jewel of any gathering you attend." He colored a little, realizing he'd let his true feelings slip out.

She smiled, her expression suddenly clouded. "It is unwise to judge solely on appearances, Duke. I imagine you are not always full of *esprit* and joy, even among your friends. Perhaps especially when you are on display at a party such as this one. People envy those whose looks draw attention to them wherever they go, seldom taking any trouble to look beneath the surface."

He didn't know what to say. It was as if she'd looked deep inside him to a place he kept carefully hidden from the world. "Yes," he finally said after they'd wandered a little away from the press of the crowd. "But it is not fear that troubles me in those moments." He would not tell her that sometimes despair overcame him in the midst of the gayest settings and that sometimes the only way to keep that feeling at bay was to engage in some extravagant, unwise folly. Yet somehow, he thought she guessed. But he'd said enough. "What made you fearful, Your Highness?"

She turned her glorious gaze upon him, searching his eyes, not smiling. "I cannot explain this here. I should not have spoken so. Sometimes I forget I am in London, not in some place less, how do you put it, strict with propriety. You English do not really talk."

Philip smiled at this. "Really? I hear a great deal of chatter all around us at this very moment."

"I think you know that is not what I meant. Polite conversation—it is not talking, not telling anything." As Adelheid said this, something in her eyes shut down. "But we must play our parts, no? To whom will you present me now?"

She had pulled aside a curtain and let him glimpse a secret that lay behind it, and then drew it closed again. Why? And why here? He wanted to ask her. Instead, he said as they continued strolling, "Allow me to present you to Bridlington and his wife." What was she hiding? What deep sorrow troubled her? He wanted to know the answer. But not in the midst of a party, not with all the world keeping an eye on the two of them and hoping for scandal.

Giving himself a mental shake, Hartland led the princess to the knot of guests that included the Earl and Countess of Bridlington and made the introductions. Then he went to find Olivia and claim her for the waltz.

LEWISTON NO LONGER HAD ANY DOUBT THAT OLIVIA AND THE masked soprano were one and the same person. The several circumstances of her attending and not attending the opera, the tantalizing few phrases of her glorious singing voice she'd let slip when they were playing together, her evasive and keyed-up air that very evening—all these things combined to make him certain that Olivia had a secret so remarkable that no one in the *ton* was likely to believe it without absolute proof.

The question remained: exactly what would he do with that knowledge? If she appeared on the stage of the King's Theatre tomorrow evening and removed her mask, revealed herself as The Honorable Olivia Fontenoy, she would no longer be received by polite society. It was entirely possible that Hartland would withdraw his suit from her, forgoing her fortune. Especially, Harry thought cynically, when a wealthy, widowed princess had seemingly fallen from the sky and into his arms. Only a fool wouldn't be able to see that she would make him a far better consort than the quirky Miss Fontenoy.

But what about Olivia's feelings? How would she react if Hartland withdrew his suit and she lost her reputation? Which of those two outcomes would be more devastating to her? When he watched them together on different occasions, he thought he'd seen the usual signs that she had fallen under his charismatic friend's spell. Then the impression would vanish. Even now, as she and the duke waltzed, she gazed fixedly into his eyes, smiled, and every once in a while, blushed. How could she help it? Philip was like the prince in a fairy tale—with a few more rough edges and some decidedly unsavory characteristics. But it all added up to an irresistibly charming package. Did Olivia's response to Hartland mean she was in love with him? Would she be brokenhearted when he turned his back on her as he was bound to do if she were allowed to go through with her performance at the benefit?

These were questions he couldn't answer. But what Harry did know beyond the inkling of a doubt was that the duke did not love Olivia in return.

The duke did not—but he did.

And if he decided to act, it would be for no other reason. It burst upon him in that moment that he loved Olivia enough to want to prevent her throwing her life away when it had barely begun—even if it meant that he would be forced to attend another wedding that tore his own heart to shreds. He loved her enough to sacrifice her good opinion of him. He loved her enough to be cast out of her life forever if she was furious with him for his actions.

Perhaps the saddest thing of all, though, was that in preserving Olivia's reputation, he would be depriving the world of an extraordinary talent, the kind of talent that blossomed once in a generation. Which was more important?

Unfortunately, with the world as it was, the answer was obvious. If Olivia revealed her identity on the following night, society would shun her. And for a lady of her breeding, her background, and the sheltered life she had led, that would be the most hideous fate of all.

So he must at all costs prevent her from doing it, whatever it cost him. He would call on Olivia tomorrow morning and find a way to have a private conversation with her. He felt compelled to understand why she had consented to perform in the benefit, what hold Taylor might have over her. She could not be acting out of vanity. It would be entirely against her nature. Therefore she must have another motivation.

Before then, he must partner her in the waltz and hope that holding her in his arms in that way would work its magic on his feet once again and he would not disgrace himself.

# CHAPTER 28

*I*n addition to the strain of performing a role for the duration of the rout party, Olivia had to guard her voice in the noisy, boisterous environment so she wouldn't strain it before her next performance. She nodded and smiled instead of speaking whenever she could, and escaped to the retiring room as often as possible without arousing her mother's suspicion. But hearing and being heard above the din was sometimes impossible. Dancing was the only certain way to avoid having much conversation so Olivia accepted every solicitation for her hand, even refusing any suggestions of sitting down instead of dancing.

Thus physical exhaustion joined the mental strain that should have made her collapse into bed and fall instantly asleep in the wee hours of the morning. Instead, she tossed and turned and dreamt of stepping on stage in front of a massive crowd only to discover that she was naked, or that she suddenly had no idea what she was supposed to sing, or —worst of all—that someone handed her a violin and told her to perform a concerto on it.

Surely, she thought, after three successful appearances as

Countess Almaviva she should not be so desperately nervous. A note from Tetrazzini had conveyed the information that she would be required to sing only one aria—"*Dove sono*," of course. That should be simple. Except that this performance was to occur immediately after her unmasking.

It would be the first time she'd faced an audience as who she truly was.

The idea of removing her mask raised all the doubts and uncertainties she harbored about herself and her voice quite apart from the inevitable repercussions of exposure. Who was she to presume she could sing well enough to captivate an audience? She had a suspicion that from the outset her success had mostly been due to the novelty of her masked state, and that anyone who had heard Catalani, say, would think her a poor imitation indeed if they knew who she really was.

And the very real anxieties about the social consequences of such an action weighed on her more than she cared to admit. She would not be the only one to suffer. All who knew and cared for her would be affected too.

Her mother. Her father. Lady Mariana. Hartland.

Harry.

Try as she might to imagine what her life would be like after that evening, she could not. She supposed she and her mother would join her father at Ambrose Priory in Hampshire. Perhaps they could travel abroad, although the war against the French made Paris impossible and the seas were consequently unsafe as well. But then what?

Olivia tried to shake such thoughts out of her head. What would come would come. Before then, she had no choice but to continue her deceptions. She would listen to her mother dissect the party, gossip about the people she talked to, criticize Olivia's dance partners, and ultimately calculate the social credit they gained by attending the *ton* party of the season.

*Poor Mama*, Oliva thought. *I'm about to spoil everything.*

She had made no plans the day after the rout party on the pretext of wanting to rest, deliberately putting Hartland off when he suggested a drive in the park, saying she had a long-standing commitment with a school friend. So the sound of a light carriage driving up to the front of the house late in the morning startled her. Who could it be?

"The Marquess of Lewiston," Ebbings announced as he opened the saloon door.

Olivia and her mother both set aside their needlework, stood, and curtsied. Lewiston bowed to her mother, then turned to her.

"I thought I'd try to tempt you out for a drive in the park," he said. "Fresh air is the only cure for fatigue, in my view. I've only the gig, I'm afraid, so there's just room for myself and one other. The weather has become delightful. A shame to waste such a day."

His obvious efforts to strike a light tone and not give the impression that he had any motive other than her pleasure stabbed at Olivia's heart. She forced a smile and said, "A lovely idea! You will not mind, Mama, if I go out for a short while with Lord Lewiston?" She could not object to the lack of chaperone in an open carriage.

The viscountess looked as if she very much did mind, however, but could think of no reasonable excuse to refuse her consent. "Very well, but mind you return for nuncheon."

"I'll just go and get my hat," Olivia said, and scampered out of the saloon.

VERY SOON AFTER THAT, SHE AND HARRY SAT SIDE-BY-SIDE IN the small two-wheeled carriage drawn by a single horse. This was not the usual sort of vehicle for showing off to a lady, but a serviceable choice for running errands or dashing off to visit friends. Although amply comfortable for a single person, two people had to squeeze together, so Olivia found her shoulder coming into contact with Lewiston's every time they went over a small bump. Why hadn't Harry driven his stylish—and more commodious—phaeton instead?

"I thought we'd go to The Green Park instead of Hyde Park," Harry said.

"Why?" Olivia turned to watch his profile as he drove, his straight nose and fine lips, which were not smiling, and she thought she could perceive some tension just above his eyebrows.

"I wanted especially to talk to you about something important and I'd rather not be overheard by anyone we know," he said.

Olivia caught her breath. Did this have anything to do with what he'd guessed about her? Or was he going to offer for her? He had seemed so close to some kind of declaration several times, but something always stopped him.

As to how she would answer him if he did, she hardly knew. She longed to be able to confess her feelings to him. The idea of Harry being the man she would spend the rest of her life with had come to be the one thought that filled her with joy and contentment. Even in the first blush of infatuation with Hartland she'd never felt like that. Now, she could not think of marrying the duke under any circumstances and feared that, after she exposed her identity that evening, any hope of marriage with anyone would be at an end.

*But what if Harry offers for me now?* How she wanted to accept him! She couldn't do so without confessing all to him, though. Anything less than the full story would be to accept him under false pretenses. Yet if she told him, he might not make the offer, or withdraw it after he did. She was in such a state of confusion that she went hot and cold by turns, depending on the direction of her thoughts. Fortunately, the fresh air could easily be blamed for any disturbance to her complexion.

The two of them said little beyond commonplaces as they covered the short distance through the streets and crossed Piccadilly to enter the park via the Bath Gate. Lewiston slowed the horse to a leisurely walk once they were on the narrow carriage drive in the much less populous park and kept a loose hold on the ribbons.

"It is a lovely day," Olivia said, nervously breaking the silence that had risen like an invisible barrier between them as soon as they entered the relative privacy of the park.

"Yes. No. I wanted to tell you," Harry blurted out, "that I know you are the soprano in the mask." He did not look at her, but kept his eyes focused ahead, his jaw tightening.

Even though he had intimated that he knew it last night the blood drained from Olivia's head at so bald a statement, and she thought she might faint. She took a deep breath or two and willed herself to remain sensible. So this was it. Not the other thing. After a moment to collect her wits, she said, "That's absurd. What can you mean?"

Harry shook his head. "It's no use pretending. I know. Everything adds up to that certainty. I've heard your voice, not just those few bars in the schoolroom, but in February in Hyde Park. I told you of it after your first performance. Before I knew it was you."

So he had.

"I saw you from a distance that day leaving through the Stanhope Gate. With Hetty, I believe, although I hadn't made your acquaintance then."

How long had he known for certain? And why mention it

now? "I don't see how that's any of your affair," her voice was small and pinched. She couldn't deny that her response bordered on impolite.

He pulled the horse up, looked around to make sure no one was nearby, turned in the seat and took one of her hands. "It is my affair, because I—" He shook his head as if to clear it. "No, that's not what I meant to say. There's so much. But most of all I want you to know ..." He paused. "I want you to know that I think you're the bravest person I've ever met."

That was unexpected. She certainly didn't feel brave. She was always afraid, in fact. Tears pricked behind her eyes. She pressed her lips together. Her hand trembled in his grasp. "Brave?"

"So very brave. I don't know how you dared do it, or why. But you know you cannot allow anyone else to discover that the magnificent opera singer who has all London at her feet is the lovely heiress, Miss Olivia Fontenoy."

"What are you saying?" She didn't recognize her own voice. It was all a nightmare. Perhaps her dreams were more prophetic than she thought.

"I'm begging you. Do not perform for the benefit this evening. It can do you and your family no good whatsoever, and will likely result in permanent damage to your reputation." He paused. "I can't see the Dowager Duchess of Hartland ever reconciling herself to having an opera singer as a daughter-in-law."

"The dowager?" Had she heard him correctly? Not only was he not offering for her, he appeared to be advocating for her match with Hartland. How could she have been so stupid! Was all his attention, his friendship, no more than that? She must have been mistaken. Lewiston was Hartland's friend. Perhaps he presumed she would accept the duke's proposal because—why? Because she was bowled out by

Hartland's handsome face and irresistible charm? Or did Harry think she was blinded by social ambition? "You presume a great deal, Lord Lewiston. Is that what you think of me?" she asked, unable to keep the unsteadiness out of her voice. "That my real wish is to marry a duke?"

"Perhaps not *a* duke, but possibly *a particular* duke." He had let go of her hand and once more looked straight ahead. A red flush stole up from his neck into his cheeks.

Everything Olivia thought she knew about Harry suddenly broke apart and lay in fragments around her. She wanted to jump down from the gig and run all the way home. She thought he knew her, understood her. How could he mistake her so?

"It's not too late to back out," Lewiston said. "Taylor will survive—"

"I will never marry Hartland!" Olivia blurted out. "I will not marry him whether or not I perform in this evening's benefit—which I fully intend to do for reasons I cannot, I will not share with you!"

This silenced him for a few moments. Olivia watched him take a breath, open his mouth, then close it again. Finally he said, "You don't know what you're saying. Even if it's true that you won't marry the duke, you can have no idea just how much damage you would do to your life by going through with this performance. It's a mistake so great that no one will ever receive you again. You are naïve, you don't know—"

"Yes, I do know!" Now Olivia was angry. Did all men presume to know what was best, or believe they could impose their will on all women of their acquaintance? "I will thank you not to assume I am not fully aware of the unavoidable consequences of my work this evening."

"How can you be? I won't let you do that to yourself!"

"You won't—" She couldn't believe what she was hearing.

She turned to face him. "Look at me. And listen to me. I shall sing this evening and you can't stop me. I have a very good reason for doing so, a reason I have no desire to tell you."

"I see," he said, his eyes hardening. "Is your ambition to sing so great that you would destroy your family?"

Olivia shook her head, stung by his words. "I thought you, of all people, understood. But you don't. You're just like all the others. What everyone else thinks is more important to you than how anyone feels. We have to play by the rules or suffer for it." By now, unstoppable tears streamed down Olivia's cheeks and she made no effort to wipe them away. "You needn't associate with me after tonight, if it will harm you so very much."

Lewiston reached into his pocket and withdrew a handkerchief. He raised it to her face, and Olivia tried to bat it away, but he took hold of her chin with one hand and gently dabbed the salty streaks. "How can you think it of me?" he said, his voice softened. "If you knew what I really …"

"No, I don't know," she sobbed, "Tell me! Tell me what you really feel, why you are doing this, and why anything that happens to me can possibly matter to you!" Olivia had lost all desire to curb her tongue. There was no one nearby to hear them and Harry already knew most of the worst.

His face had drawn very close to hers. She could see his eyelashes reflected in the soft brown of his irises and feel his ragged breaths on her skin. Before she knew what was happening, their lips touched, at first gently, then with more urgency. He put his arms around her and drew her to him. She could feel the rapid beating of his heart through her chest, her own reaching toward his, matching it beat for beat. Through the kiss she tasted the salt of her own tears, let herself bask in the warmth of his firm yet gentle embrace. She sank into him, wanting to abandon herself to the sensation of closeness, a kind of closeness she'd never known in her life, to let the flutterings in her body grow and tingle in a way that was both disturbing and pleasurable.

But she mustn't give in. It was all wrong. Somewhere within her she found the strength to push him a little away, to break the contact that felt so intimate. "I shouldn't have let you...You didn't have to..."

"I wanted to. So much. I've wanted to kiss you since the first day I met you," he whispered into her ear, his arms still warm against her back, resisting her half-hearted pressure to free herself.

"Oh, Harry." Olivia looked down. She couldn't bear to meet his searching gaze. "It's no good, you know. I'm still going to sing tonight. You won't feel the same about me after that."

He pulled her closer again. "Yes, I will—or would, if I had any right to. But if you do it, and Hartland does not cry off, you would have no choice but to accept him. If you do not, all the world would think he turned his back on you because of your actions and would follow suit."

"Does all the world include you?"

"That is not to the point. I would not be able to save you from censure. Don't you see? I'm nobody. No one cares what I do or takes their tone from me. My influence extends only as far as the people I know intimately and even then I sometimes think that if I disappeared, no one would notice."

*I would notice*, Olivia thought, unable to bear the idea of a world without Harry. Why didn't he simply make her an offer? And if he did, would she give in to his request and not sing, give up any thought of publicly humiliating Hartland? But he hadn't spoken the words, so it was no use wondering. "It's too late to back out now. Hartland will cry off. He has to. And I will face whatever comes after."

"But I don't think he will withdraw his suit. He has very strong motives for marrying you and I believe he holds you in affection, in his way. Olivia, sweet girl, the choice is yours, don't you see? If it's true that you don't intend to marry him in any case, you could walk away from him and the concert right now, and no one would think any the worse of you."

"If I did that, what then?" She wanted him to utter the declaration that hung in the air between them. She wanted him to, yet dreaded it.

"You'd have to make that choice to find out," he said, his kind eyes drenched in sadness. "I should take you home."

OLIVIA'S WORLD HAD TURNED UPSIDE DOWN IN THE SPACE OF half an hour. She hardly knew what to think, what to believe. Her plans suddenly became much more complicated. When she and Harry returned from their drive, Olivia in a foggy mix of despair and exhilaration, he escorted her inside and asked for a private interview with Lady Ambrose. If she were in full command of her senses, Olivia might have suspected he was soliciting her mother's permission to make his addresses to her. But she was in too much turmoil to consider it so she took her leave of him and retired to her bedchamber to think.

Olivia had already told her mother that she was going to the benefit with Lady Mariana. Since her identity would be revealed by the end of the evening, she did not feel it necessary to ensure secrecy from beginning to end. So she assumed she could simply hire a hack to take her to the theatre, perform, then return to Mount Street with Mariana or alone, whichever way she chose once she was forever transformed into a notorious hoyden.

But when she joined her mother in the drawing room some time later attired in theatre dress, Lady Ambrose informed her that Lewiston had invited them both to sit in his box at the opera for the benefit performance.

"He says that all the tickets in the pit and the gallery have been purchased for twice their usual cost and the box renters have been required to pay an additional ten guineas if they want to attend."

The familiar gleam in her eyes told Olivia that her mother had already calculated the advantages of not only going to an exclusive event (where she would be bored), but also of sitting in a box where someone else had to pay the excessive bounty.

She opened her mouth to protest but couldn't think of an argument against the plan. What was Harry doing? Had he figured out a way to make it impossible for her to sing that evening? If he thought he could keep her captive in his box at the King's Theatre, he was sadly mistaken!

Unlike the usual opera performances, the benefit would start at seven. The advertisement said that refreshments would be served in the lobbies before the programme and patrons were urged to arrive early, or they would miss the most dramatic feature of the evening.

Which, of course, meant her unmasking.

# CHAPTER 29

They met Harry outside the theatre. Olivia searched his eyes for some clue as to what he intended but he simply acted the solicitous host, guiding them to his box, where he had already procured cakes and champagne.

He offered Olivia a glass. "No, thank you," she said, glancing nervously down at the pit surging with patrons jockeying for positions near the stage.

"I have programmes for both of you," Harry said, handing Olivia hers, with a frown on his brow.

She opened it and pretended interest but the words danced in front of her eyes. She must find a way to leave the box and go down to the backstage door without being seen. Mr. Taylor was probably beside himself with worry that she had changed her mind and wouldn't show up.

"Have you seen?" Lewiston called her attention to an item in the order of numbers to be performed.

She forced herself to bring the words into focus.

Catalani.

Taylor did not tell her she would be sharing the stage with the most revered opera singer in the world. Trust the impresario to create an even more shocking situation! The diva would sing an aria from *La Clemenza di Tito* immediately before Olivia's unmasking. The audience would hear their favorite soprano first, and then hold Olivia up for comparison.

Harry leaned close to Olivia's ear on the pretext of arranging her cloak over the back of her chair and said, "You don't have to do it. It's not too late to withdraw. There will be enough interest in Catalani's return without that. I beg you. Stay here."

Olivia surveyed the boxes. Absolutely everyone in the *ton* had come that evening. Several people she knew who had declared their aversion to opera had inserted themselves into their friends' boxes just to see this spectacle. Even the royal box, which had lain empty for all three of Olivia's performances as the Countess, contained two royal dukes. Olivia's mouth was suddenly as dry as sand.

Bare of any furniture or props, the stage looked peculiarly hostile.

She could just stay there, as Harry said. She could preserve the secret of her identity. She owed Taylor nothing. He hadn't even paid her what he promised. She would feel a little sorry for Tetrazzini who, despite his initial discouragement of her project to perform on stage had clearly thrown himself into her *incognita* career.

Then she spied Hartland making his way to a position in the pit where he could exit through a small door to reach the backstage area. Olivia had almost forgotten her real reason for agreeing to the benefit performance, but the sight of him raised her indignation and renewed her determination.

"I must visit the retiring room," Olivia said, standing, whisking her cloak off the back of her chair, and draping it over her arm.

Lady Ambrose was too busy looking at all the patrons

through her opera glass to notice Harry stand and place himself between Olivia and the door out of the box. "Don't," was all he said.

"Let me pass, please," Olivia said, schooling her voice to be steady. "It really is quite urgent."

He did not take his eyes off her. Shoulders drooping, he moved aside and bowed her out.

# CHAPTER 30

$\mathcal{O}$livia ran out of the theatre, pushing past the porters and a few curious people waiting outside. She had to slip down the alley next to the building and go all the way to the back in order to reach the door that led backstage. By the time she got there and tied her mask on, she was gasping for breath. She paused and did her best to calm herself. She needed all the air her lungs could hold in order to sing even one aria. As soon as she felt she could manage it she approached the door, where the guard recognized her and nodded. "'E's beside hisself waitin', Ma'am."

Mr. Taylor was just inside the door pacing up and down, wringing his hands and glancing at a large pocket watch. When he saw her he ran forward, gripped her arm, and all but dragged her up to the backstage area.

The place had become so familiar to her just in the few times she'd had the privilege of performing there. But instead of the entire cast of *Figaro* milling around and waiting for their cues, only one person occupied the space.

That one was enough.

Olivia stopped dead and dropped into a deep, reverent

curtsy. "Madame Catalani, I am honored," she said, not daring to look up into the legendary soprano's face. She was aware of the approach of light footsteps and fleetingly wondered if the famously temperamental diva would strike her.

But a small, soft hand took hers and pulled her to her feet. Olivia stood several inches taller than the dark-haired beauty whose round, limpid eyes scanned her mask, faintly amused. "I am not royalty, *Signorina*," she said with a little chuckle. "We are the same, no?"

The same? "I am the merest novice compared to you," Olivia said in a small voice. "I hardly dare sing a note after the audience has heard you."

Her flattery had its desired effect. Madame Catalani smiled and took hold of her hand. "We shall go out together, Signore Taylor says. Do not be afraid!" She lightly squeezed Olivia's hand.

*I'm trembling*, Olivia thought. For so many reasons.

After a moment, the lackeys scampered out and lit the oil footlights, and then Taylor strode out to the brightly illuminated center of the stage to address the audience. He held up his arms to quiet the roar that greeted him, but it took a little while. Once the noise had abated enough for him to be heard, he described in effusive terms what the audience would be privileged to witness that evening. Two great sopranos on stage together. The moment of revelation of one of them. And so on. Olivia thought he sounded more like the master of ceremonies at Astley's Amphitheatre than the well-respected—if impecunious—manager of the premier opera house in London. It was fitting. After all, wasn't she no better than a spectacle? A curiosity to be ogled and wondered at? At least for that evening.

"Time to go out," the stage manager whispered.

Madame Catalani kept hold of Olivia's hand and led her

onto the stage. When the two of them appeared, a great cheer went up from the audience, along with shouts of "Take off the mask!" "Let us see who you are!" "Catalani's back!" and other things Olivia could not quite make out.

The orchestra played the introductory bars of *Deh, se piacer mi vuoi* from Mozart's *La Clemenza di Tito,* the aria Catalani was to sing. She released Olivia's hand and stepped slowly forward down the slope of the raked stage, commanding the space as if she were not a diminutive Italian lady but an imposing presence capable of exerting her will on the entire theatre. Every inch the powerful, scheming Roman woman accusing her lover of harboring doubts, Catalani performed the aria that was calculated to show her distinctive voice to full advantage. A challenging two-octave range and passages of runs that sparkled like drops of dew in the morning sun held the audience enthralled. Olivia did not even mind her embellishments, each of which provoked *bravas* from the Catalani partisans. Without any props or even a painted backdrop, Catalani became Vitellia.

The applause and cheers at the end were so loud the floor of the stage shook. Olivia herself clapped until her hands tingled. How could she ever think she had the right to stand on the same stage as this magnificent lady? It mattered not. After that evening, the issue would be moot. *This is the last time I will stand just here*, she thought.

Catalani made graceful bow after graceful bow. Patrons threw flowers up to the stage and she swept them prettily off the floor in handfuls, clutching them to her breast, kissing her fingertips to the adoring crowd. But she ignored all the cries of *"Encore!"*, shook her head, and finally turned her back on the audience to walk upstage to where Olivia stood.

As if they all suddenly remembered the spectacle they had really come to witness, the raucous noise abated until the crowd was nearly silent, only the occasional cough or throat-clearing to be heard. Mr. Taylor walked slowly back to downstage center and surveyed the scene before him. Then he, too, turned and held his hand out to Olivia.

It took every ounce of courage she had, but she walked forward, head held high.

"Your royal highnesses," Taylor said, nodding to the alarmingly close royal box, "My lords, ladies, and gentlemen, you have been waiting for this moment. It has been our privilege to introduce to the operatic stage a soprano of extraordinary gifts who has hitherto appeared only masked. Her maidenly modesty demanded this expedient, but she has graciously consented to make this evening the occasion of her unveiling, to help raise funds to ensure that the King's Theatre can continue to present the superior Italian opera you have come to expect."

*"Stop talking and take her mask off!"* someone yelled from the pit, setting off a roar of laughter.

Taylor scowled at the unruly audience and said, "Without further ado, I give you, *l'Incognita.*"

He swept his arm and bowed gallantly to Olivia as he stepped to the side.

The orchestra was silent. Taylor jerked his head at her. He wanted her to remove her mask before the music even started. Somehow that made Olivia feel more than naked. She had imagined the moment would take place under the cover of music at least.

But she nodded to him and then turned to the audience. She scanned the pit near the door that led down to Fops' Alley until she found Hartland's face. His gaze burned into her, a faint smile on his lips.

Without looking away from him, she reached up to untie the mask herself, but her fingers met others and she realized that Madame Catalani must have walked up to stand behind her. *"Permessa,"* she whispered, and set about unknotting the strings for her.

When they were almost fully loose, Olivia took hold of the somewhat wilted fabric at her chin, and then slowly, carefully, lifted the mask up until she revealed her face.

First, silence. Then a collective gasp, and a moment later a shriek from the direction of Lewiston's box. Olivia did not look toward it. Instead, she kept her eyes locked with the duke's. His mouth hung open, his eyes widened, and his face was as pale as a winding sheet.

She smiled.

And then she nodded to the leader of the orchestra, who gave the signal for the opening bars of *"Dove sono."* She closed her eyes, letting the character of Countess Almaviva inhabit her body, and sang. At first, she stood very still. But soon, as the music engulfed her, she moved around, going through the actions as if she were on the set, as if the dressing table and the chairs were there as they had always been. Olivia soon lost all sense of being watched, feeling as if she was in a bubble of fantasy, in a world where no one would touch her, where only beauty existed, and everything set to come to rights in the music and the drama. When her aria ended, she half expected Susanna and Cherubino to run onto the stage to continue the scene.

Instead, the audience erupted into shouts and cheers, and many stamped their feet. More flowers—whole bouquets—rained onto the stage. Olivia curtsied deeply, first to the royal box, then to each tier and to the gallery, one by one, blowing kisses as Madame Catalani had done. She saw Lady Mariana. Princess Adelheid was in her box, but from that distance Olivia could not read their expressions. She looked for Hartland where he had stood in the pit. He was no longer there.

At last she lifted her eyes to Lewiston's box. Her mother sat stony-still, her face drained of color. Harry leaned his elbow on the edge of the box and rested his forehead in his hand. He wasn't looking at her.

*Well,* Olivia thought, *it's no more than I expected.*

SHE WAS MAGNIFICENT. THERE WAS SIMPLY NO OTHER WORD. She was magnificent—and she was ruined.

Harry felt as if someone had reached inside him and squeezed the blood out of his heart, trying to wring the love away, but it was useless. He could hardly bear to look at her, not because he was ashamed but because he thought his soul would burst. This mere girl who hadn't even seen nineteen summers possessed the kind of power that could not be taught. Who was he to stand in the way of such a gift?

And yet, he had no doubt the *ton,* her family included if Lady Ambrose's reaction was anything to judge by, would shun her. She had done what ladies were not permitted to do. She had dared to display her extraordinary gifts not in the elite privacy of a drawing room, but in a public forum. She had given her whole self not just to the privileged few, but to everyone from royalty to clerks and shopkeepers sitting in the very highest row of the gallery.

"Excuse me, Lady Ambrose," he said.

"The carriage. I must leave. Please see if my carriage is here," the viscountess said in a hollow voice.

"I shall ask an usher to do so, but I must go." He gave her a polite bow and left before she could argue.

The rapture of the audience was unabated. The evening's entertainment would continue with a ballet and a farce, but Lewiston didn't care. Olivia was about to leave the stage and he needed to be waiting for her. He must support her.

Harry ran down the stairs two at a time and found a door that led to Fops' Alley. He had no idea if he would be the only person there or if others had grasped the opportunity to see the now-unmasked soprano. Whichever it was, he would find a way to talk to Olivia alone.

"Where is she?" he asked a man who looked to be a carpenter.

"Which one?" he answered, a smirk on his face. "The cat or the mask?"

Harry didn't dignify his insolence with an answer. He brushed past him toward what he hoped would be the back-stage area and dressing rooms. A flock of ballet dancers in their knee-length tulle skirts streamed around him toward the stage.

Ahead he saw Mr. Taylor, his arms crossed over his chest, smiling as he watched the legs of the dancers disappear toward the stage.

"Where is Miss Fontenoy?" Harry said, not bothering with civility.

Taylor drew himself up and his smile vanished. "She is at present engaged."

"I must see her! Right away!"

"You'll have to wait your turn. Until His Grace is gone."

"No! She'll see me," Harry said and tried to go around Taylor.

But the impresario put out his arm and stopped him. "Now that would be impolite, wouldn't it? There's plenty to go around."

A burning rage burst into Lewiston's body and before he could think better of it, he landed a cracking blow on Taylor's chin. It didn't knock him down as he was no Corinthian, but Taylor staggered backward enough for Harry to run by him unimpeded.

Lewiston was so focused on his object of seeing Olivia that he'd hardly registered the full meaning of what Taylor had told him. He soon grasped it, however. The door to

Olivia's dressing room hung open. She wasn't alone. Hartland stood before her, a look of dismayed shock on his face. Harry's heart sank. Would Hartland be so cruel as to cry off that very evening? If he did, Olivia would need comfort. Harry knew he should retire discreetly and not impose himself on what was clearly a private conversation, but something made him stay near enough to hear Olivia call out if she needed anything. As to what he would do to his friend if he abandoned her in that way—it didn't bear thinking about.

OLIVIA EXPECTED HARTLAND TO COME AND FIND HER. SHE expected that he would tell her he had to withdraw his suit because of what she did, and then she would be able to tell her mother that she couldn't marry the duke—not because she was being contrary, but because he didn't want her.

What she didn't expect was what actually happened.

"Miss Fontenoy, I can only say how sorry I am that I behaved toward you as I did. You must know, it meant nothing. A mere trifle. If we had been betrothed I would never have done it."

He sounded sincere. Certainly he was sorry. His apology took some of the wind out of her sails. She had been intending to ring a peal over him and then shake hands and part. But she knew that she was in some degree at fault for keeping him waiting. For not being honest with him from the start. For not having the courage to brave her mother's tears and tantrums and refuse him outright. "Whatever you say, Duke, you may imagine that it was hardly trifling to me. However, you now have the perfect excuse to withdraw your suit and no one will censure you for it."

He looked down at the floor and shook his head. "I can't."

What was he saying? "Of course you can. You should

marry Princess Adelheid. She would make a much better duchess than I would. And I daresay her fortune is as ample as mine."

He gave a short bark of a laugh. "That's as may be. But I am not such a blackguard as that. If I do not marry you, you will be an outcast in society. No one will receive you and no other acceptable suitor will come forward, no matter your handsome fortune. Perhaps in a few years, someone on the fringes of society will offer for you. But you deserve better."

Olivia's heart started to pound. What was he saying? "I daresay I deserve worse. But what can that be to you?" She turned away from him and walked to the dressing table, picked up the hairbrush, and idly pulled some strands of her brown hair out from between its bristles.

"You don't see what you've done. Foolish, naïve girl. For all your remarkable bravery and intelligence, you've done the one thing that guarantees we will be bound together for life. You've made it impossible for me to cry off. I am not a man who would abandon you to such a fate. I won't do it for your sake—and for my own."

He stood behind her. When she lifted her eyes to the mirror, she saw his handsome face creased in sorrow looking at her in reflection. He put one strong hand on her shoulder and gave it a brotherly squeeze.

"What do you mean, for your own sake?"

"I would not consider myself a gentleman. Nor would any of the people I care about."

"You would rather marry me than set yourself free?" She turned around and faced him. "But you don't love me! And I don't love you! It would be a terrible mistake." All Olivia could think of was Harry's kind eyes, his warm embrace, his kiss. Had her actions rendered it impossible for her ever to be his? Tears of frustration welled in her eyes and spilled down her cheeks. Hartland reached into his pocket for a handkerchief and dabbed them away. His action only reminded her of Harry's earlier that day, and she wept all the harder. Hartland drew her to him and she leaned on his broad chest, allowing her tears to soak into his evening coat.

"It won't be so very terrible, Miss Fontenoy," Hartland said in a low murmur. "I'm hardly a monster. We'll find a way to be happy."

It was the saddest thing Olivia had ever heard. All at once she could see it. It had been all her fault. She dared to step beyond her sphere and set a series of events in motion that ended in this terrible impasse. It was no use crying about it. She must think. Surely there was a way out for both of them. "I need some time to consider this," she said, barely above a whisper. "Kindly leave me, Duke."

"You should probably call me Philip," he said with a ghost of a smile. "And I shall be so bold as to call you Olivia. We'll have to get used to each other, you know."

She shook her head. "No. I mean you may call me Olivia, but I won't marry you. I will find a way out of this."

"How will you do that?" he said a note of amusement in his voice. "I believe you are capable of a great deal, but one outrageous girl can't take on the entire *ton* and come out unscathed." He put his index finger under her chin and tilted her head up so that she had to look him in the eye.

"Why not? I've already done what no one else could have," she said, a defiant light in her eyes.

"So you have." Before she had a chance to turn away, Hartland bent down to her and kissed her lips lightly. "You are indeed extraordinary. But you may catch cold at this. Good night, Olivia. I'll call on you tomorrow."

HARRY COULDN'T HEAR ALL OF THEIR CONVERSATION FROM where he stood, but he could see what happened between them. He saw Hartland's face, all contrition and kindness. Olivia faced away from him most of the time until she turned, weeping, and Hartland put his arms around her.

And then, they kissed.

After that, Hartland left, and Olivia sank into the chair.

*She loves him*, he thought. He'd been mistaken in her. What he and she shared—was it just a love of music, and her own kindness? Did she think of him as a brother, as Mariana had? How could he be so mistaken a second time! But their kiss. That had meant something, he was sure. He'd never kissed Mariana. That had been a kind of idol worship, not actual love. He loved Olivia, of that he was certain. Whatever her true feelings, he couldn't allow her to suffer for her actions that evening. He would be her friend, if nothing else was possible.

Squaring his shoulders, he tapped a knuckle on the open dressing room door. "Olivia?"

Olivia at once stood, pasted a falsely cheerful smile on her face, and said with trembling lips, "Harry! As you see, I am now a hopeless, fallen woman. You needn't have risked your reputation by coming to see me."

He wanted so desperately to rush forward and take her in his arms, but he assumed she wouldn't welcome that. "You must know I don't care a jot about that."

"But you tried to stop me."

"For your sake, not mine." He stepped forward and put one hand out, but Olivia shrank back.

"Don't be nice to me. I couldn't bear it. I know what I've done. I've ruined everything for everyone. I presume my mother has gone home."

He nodded. "I think you must wish to be there too. If you will permit me I shall escort you back to Mount Street."

She cast him a grateful look and gathered up her cloak

and reticule. Lewiston spotted the discarded mask on the dressing table and picked it up. "Don't you want this?"

She took it from him and studied it, her eyes wistful. "No. I don't need it anymore." She laid it gently on the dressing table and then turned in a circle, looking all around as if trying to impress what she saw on her memory. "Shall we go?"

He put out his arm to her. She was about to lay her hand on top of it, but Harry grasped it and tucked it firmly into his elbow instead. He wanted to ask her so many questions. He wanted to know how things stood between her and Hartland.

He wanted to know, but dreaded finding out. He decided to let her tell him in her own time, if she wished to.

That's what friends did for one another.

# CHAPTER 31

*A*fter what passed with Olivia at the theatre, Hartland was in no mind to go home. *Foolish girl!* He thought. *Didn't she see what a hash she'd made of it?* He had held it all together and been as kind as he could to her, even bestowing an affectionate kiss on her, but a part of him wanted to scream with frustration. Why had she done it? Why hadn't she simply refused him before when it was clear she didn't want to marry him? And now, there was nothing either of them could do.

Every instinct for indulging his most reckless behavior screamed for attention in his mind. *Let me lose a fortune—or perhaps win one,* he thought. Except he had no fortune to lose, and nothing of value to stake. He didn't even have his large diamond pin to toss onto a piquet table, or risk at faro. He'd given it to her the other night. Well, if they were to marry, it mattered little.

He hurried out of the theatre, passing by the hackney stand and turning his steps toward Piccadilly. The only place he could think to go was Watier's. They might let him play on tick. If not, he would drink until he reached a state of oblivion. How could a slip of a girl with little beauty and no address manage to set everything so completely on its ear!

Although he knew they would have to marry, the sting of her deception went deep. It briefly occurred to him that, had it been the princess behind that mask, they would have laughed together about it, appreciated the absurdity of the situation and counted it a very good adventure to look back on when they were older.

If it had been the princess.

But it had not been she. And now, it never could be.

Brows drawn together in a fierce scowl, Hartland knocked and was admitted to the exclusive club. He tossed his cloak and hat to the porter and climbed the stairs to the main saloon to see who was there.

Even before he entered the wood-paneled enclave, the buzz of voices and snatches of conversation told him that many of those present had witnessed Olivia's earlier unmasking. They all knew of his determined pursuit of the heiress and would doubtless assail him with questions he did not want to answer. The only thing he could do was treat it as a good joke and assure them all that nothing had changed.

Lord Alvanley was first to challenge him about it. "So, your intended has quite a bit of nerve! I daresay you were as shocked as the rest of us."

"Not in the least," Hartland said, signaling to a waiter for a glass of brandy. "I knew all about it."

"And you permitted it?" The horrified look on Alvanley's face spoke volumes.

Hartland shrugged. "Why not? It was a harmless desire on her part, and she certainly won't be able to repeat it after we're married. That I assured her."

A few gentlemen nearby chuckled.

But Alvanley wasn't ready to let the matter drop. "So it's

settled is it? I don't see why the chit had to reveal herself, though."

"You know heiresses," Hartland said. "Always trying to set up as eccentric. She counts on the notoriety to bring the *ton* flocking to her parties, to shrug off some of the mushroom taint on her mother's side. How about a hand or two of piquet, Alvanley?"

"Ah, I was just on my way out. There's a Macao table in the small saloon, if you're looking for some spirited play."

Hartland suspected that Alvanley fabricated an excuse not to sit at cards with him, knowing that rather than a substantial rouleau, all Hartland could bring to the table at that moment were vowels. Besides, the duke was a skillful enough gamester to believe that his ill temper would affect his judgment, so he contented himself with one of Watier's excellent suppers, washed down with a quantity of superb burgundy.

Two hours later, more than a little foxed, Hartland rose and made his jagged way to the door.

"Shall I call your carriage, Your Grace?" the porter said.

Hartland waved him away and stepped out, missing one of the stairs and nearly falling on his face. *Steady, man!* he thought, exerting himself to clear his head. The walk to Grosvenor Square was not long. If he could just keep to the flagway he would arrive without mishap. The new gas lighting and the presence of the Watch made what was once a hazardous undertaking quite tame.

The cool evening air, which at first made his head spin, gradually had a salutary effect on him as he walked all around Mayfair, taking the longest route possible back to Grosvenor Square. He didn't want to think about what was ahead. He would have to go to Mount Street in the morning and ensure that the betrothal was fixed. He would have to put Princess Adelheid out of his mind by then. As it was, every time he tried to focus on Olivia and the future, the blue-green eyes and flaxen hair of the beautiful princess floated into his mind, obliterating the reality he would have to face.

About an hour later, Hartland reached the side of the square on which numbers twelve and sixteen were situated. He'd chosen—as had become his habit—to walk the long way around so that he would pass the house where Princess Adelheid lived and was surprised to see that a glow of candlelight leaked out around the window shutters on the first floor. She was not only still awake, but clearly not yet retired for the night.

He had an impulse to climb the steps and knock on the door, for what purpose exactly he couldn't say. It would definitely be unseemly to call on her at that hour, even though she told him he'd be welcome at any time. People said that, but only meant *at any acceptable time according to the rules of propriety*. Still, Hartland's curiosity took hold of him and he slowed his steps, looking for a place to discreetly linger for a time and see if anyone left the house. Ten to one the princess was simply accustomed to staying up late, perhaps to read or write letters. But she could just as easily do so in the comfort of her bedchamber rather than in one of the formal first-floor saloons. If she had had a dinner party followed by cards and tea, surely guests would have left by now, or would very soon do so. The thing was, Princess Adelheid had told him that she had no plans to entertain as yet.

While he pondered these questions, the front door opened to reveal a small figure in a white night shirt. Otto. The boy looked around, then reached up to the handle to pull the door closed behind him. A moment later he skipped down the steps and dashed across to the gated park in the center of the square.

After a few futile attempts to climb the high iron fence, he simply gripped the railings and pressed his face between them, as if he wanted to squeeze through to the dark trees and shrubs beyond.

It wasn't safe for a child so young to be out alone at that time of night. Without hesitating, Hartland crossed the street and approached the boy, saying in a low voice as soon as he was near enough, "It's Otto, isn't it?"

The boy started and stepped back quickly, stumbling on an uneven flagstone. Hartland dashed forward and caught him.

At first the boy struggled against him. "Steady on little one! I'm your friend, remember? I helped you down from the tree."

Otto's frightened eyes gazed uncomprehending into Hartland's. *Of course,* Hartland thought. He doesn't speak much English. *And I know little to no German.* After a moment, though, Otto said, *"Freund,"* and then as if struggling for a word said, "M-my friend."

"That's right! It's late for you to be out. Let me take you home." He set Otto on his feet and held out his hand. The boy took it, a dark little mitt disappearing in Hartland's elegant yet muscular fist. The difficulty, Hartland thought, would be not to rouse the whole house to get Otto back inside where he belonged.

But he was saved the trouble when the door of number twelve opened to reveal the princess, clad in a rich silver brocade dressing gown, a candle held high. "Otto!" she said in a hoarse whisper. "Where are you, *böser Junge!*"

Hartland caught his breath. The yearning, the undisguised concern in her voice, spoke of hidden depths, of secrets and mysteries bound up, Hartland was sure, in the history of a little boy who appeared to have no blood ties to her.

Hartland tugged at Otto's hand but the boy resisted, hiding himself behind the duke's much larger body. "No, no, you must go home," he whispered. He must return to the princess. Hartland understood that only the sight of Otto safe and well would erase the worry from her brow, an expression visible even at that distance. At that moment, he wanted nothing more than to be the instrument of soothing her anxiety. He nudged Otto in the direction of the house and said, "Go!"

Although Otto dragged his feet, to Hartland's surprise the boy obeyed him. As soon as he crossed over to where the glow of a street lamp revealed him, Princess Adelheid's brow cleared and she ran down the steps to meet him, taking hold of his hand and leading him back to the house. She spoke quietly to Otto, but didn't sound angry. The two of them disappeared through the door, the glow from inside the house was extinguished, and quiet and dark enveloped the square again.

Hartland stood there for a while before recollecting what he was doing and continuing to his own house. As usual, by the time he had set foot on the first of the front steps, Maberley had opened the door, branch of candles held high, and bowed him in.

"Brandy, Maberley," the duke said, and climbed the stairs to his bedchamber.

THE HOUSE ON MOUNT STREET WAS EERILY QUIET WHEN Olivia rose the next morning. She thought it might have been early, but the clock on the mantelpiece in her bedchamber told her it was after ten. Lewiston saw her to the door before ten the evening before, and she had gone immediately to bed, having been told that Lady Ambrose had already retired to her bedchamber requesting not to be disturbed.

"Morning, Miss," Hetty said with her usual curtsy when

she emerged from the dressing room, but she didn't look at Olivia.

"What's wrong, Hetty?" Olivia asked.

"Nothing. That is, nothing really. Only—" The girl couldn't continue. She sniffed, and soon it was obvious that her voice was choked with tears. "W-why, w-why'd you d-d-do it, Miss? Yer ruined for sure and all. You'll never make a match."

Although doubtless Hetty had been looking forward to being a lady's maid to a duchess, Olivia knew that her distress arose from genuine concern for her mistress's welfare as well as the credit of the family she served. She walked over to her and placed a consoling hand on her shoulder. "It's not as bad as that," she said, substituting one of her own linen handkerchiefs for the sodden cambric square Hetty had knotted in her hands. "You'll see. All will be well."

But would it? Olivia truly had no way of knowing. And what was "well," after all? Perhaps what she did that day would determine the answer.

"Now, Hetty, dry your eyes. I need you. I have a lot to do today. I may as well dress for walking, I think so at least, although I may not go until later."

"You're never going out, Miss!" She sniffed and wiped her eyes.

"Of course I'm going out. I shall have to eventually, and I refuse to hide myself away. But I have a few things to do at home first." Although hiding somewhere had been Olivia's instinct the night before, to flee to the country—or better still, go abroad, because despite everything Hartland had said, she refused to believe that marrying him was her only option—her long sleep had restored not just her body but her spirit. She had the sensation of having taken a leap from a great height, anticipating complete destruction at its end only to discover that the ground she landed on was soft, that it cradled her in a safe, secure place from which to launch the rest of her life. It was an illusion, but she clung to it nonetheless.

Now that everyone knew at least one part of her masquerade, Olivia felt oddly less isolated. Whatever her friends thought about what she had done, it was out in the open. No more sneaking around to Lady Mariana's house, or pretending carriages were going somewhere they weren't. She would have to explain it all to her mother eventually. Not right away, though. More important was ensuring that she would not have to marry the duke. Olivia had thought that the benefit and its immediate aftermath would easily extricate her from Hartland's pursuit. But he had made very cogent arguments about why it actually had the opposite result. And she was utterly dismayed.

Lewiston's behavior, too, had been difficult to understand. Instead of the scolding she expected from him for going against his advice, for not heeding his warning, he was all tender solicitude. He escorted her home with gentle consideration. He did not question her, or harangue. He said nothing at all about it, in fact. They might have been going home from any *ton* party, or a concert, where nothing out of the ordinary had taken place.

The only unusual thing about that short trip was that the two of them were alone in a closed carriage. An unmarried woman and a single gentleman. He could have taken advantage of the situation, especially since her actions that night had branded her fast and loose in the eyes of society. But Lewiston behaved with the utmost propriety, keeping a respectful distance as the carriage jolted over the cobbles from the Haymarket to Mount Street.

In fact, Olivia wished Harry *had* presumed to take a little liberty with her. After what passed between them earlier that same day, she craved the sensation of Harry's sweet, melting kiss, a kiss that awakened feelings in her she hadn't known existed.

So different from the sorrowful peck Hartland had given her. That kiss was full of resignation. It was a wistful reminder of what they would both be giving up. Two such different kisses in one day. Somehow, that felt more momentous than her unmasking. As if she had revealed more of herself in those private moments than she had in front of the two-thousand people in the theatre.

Such a day. One she would never forget.

Olivia's head already ached trying to figure out what to do. There was only one thing for it: go up to the schoolroom and lose herself in music. Music had its own rules, rules that led to harmony and beauty, not strife and discord. It had been her escape as long as she could remember.

As she climbed slowly up to the third floor, she felt the weight of expectations lessen the higher she rose. For the first time in days, her shoulders relaxed and a deep sense of calm embraced her. The schoolroom was her old friend, her sanctuary.

She sat down at the pianoforte and idly struck a C. The score of the Mozart violin and piano sonata she and Lewiston had struggled through on that carefree day—was it only a week ago?—still sat open on the desk. She had been a different person then.

A gentle scratch on the schoolroom door interrupted her reverie.

"Come!" she said, and stood, expecting perhaps that Hetty had arrived to summon her to her mother's room.

To her surprise, Signore Tetrazzini crept in, closing the door softly behind him. "Signore!" she said. "Why are you here?" She had made no arrangement with him to come to her that day. They'd tacitly agreed that the benefit would serve as her swan song, her final appearance on stage, so she had little to say to him beyond thanking him for helping her in her absurd charade.

Instead of answering her, he walked into the middle of the low-ceilinged room still in his white drab greatcoat, his high-crowned beaver hat in his hand, and bowed low to her. Had Ebbings not taken his coat and hat when he let him in?

"I came from ze back way," Tetrazzini said softly, as though he expected someone to be listening in. "*La cameriera di cucina,* you see, she let me in."

"I see," Olivia said, although she really didn't.

He folded his hands together and clasped them to his breast, closing his eyes as if recalling to mind some beautiful image. "*Signorina* Fontenoy, you are *il brindisi della città!*"

Did he come merely to congratulate her? Just to tell her that strangers all over London were toasting her success? Olivia felt she'd already gone beyond that. Whatever her triumph last night, it was over. Time to face what was ahead, not bask in fleeting glories. "Thank you, Signore. But as you know, a very short-lived one."

Tetrazzini tapped the end of his nose with his finger and cocked one fine eyebrow. "*Sì,* it may be as you say. Or *forsè no.* I come from Signore Taylor. The benefit—" He reached into the capacious interior of his coat and withdrew a folded newspaper, which he handed to her with a flourish. He'd circled a notice.

Olivia took it from him and read with a mixture of pride and chagrin. The critic praised the two sopranos effusively and said that, upon learning that *l'Incognita* was the daughter of Viscount Ambrose, they understood the necessity of disguise, since it was highly improper for a well-born maiden to appear on stage with players whose experience of the world rendered them unfit company.

Olivia winced. Lady Ambrose would be mortified to see her daughter's name in the newspaper anywhere other than the social notices. No doubt everyone they knew will have read it before the end of the day.

The critic went on to say how tragic it was that, for this reason, patrons of the King's Theatre would no longer have the privilege of hearing Miss Olivia Fontenoy, and idly speculated about how extraordinary it would be to have both Miss Fontenoy and Madame Catalani appear together in the same opera. *Something that would only occur if Madame Catalani could be persuaded to overcome any feelings of jealousy occasioned by being compared to a younger, stronger voice in the person of a fresh-faced beauty.*

"Hardly!" Olivia cried, and tossed the paper onto the work table. "What nonsense." She couldn't decide which was more preposterous: the idea that her voice was stronger than Catalani's or that she could ever be described as a fresh-faced beauty.

"No! Ees not nonsense, Signorina Fontenoy. Taylor say he will pay you *doppio* if you sing another *concerto*, with Madama Catalani."

Olivia said, "Are you mad? *Pazzo?* I don't care how much he wants to pay me, I cannot ever do it again." She whirled away from him, surprised by the sudden tears that started to her eyes. "Besides, he hasn't paid me anything yet."

She was aware of Tetrazzini walking over to the table and placing something on it next to the newspaper. "*Ecco, Signorina.*"

Her curiosity piqued, Olivia turned around and saw, to her amazement, a roll of bills on the table. A very large roll. And then Tetrazzini reached into his pockets and began to take out other similar rolls. Ten of them in all.

"*Cinque mille,*" Tetrazzini said, barely above a whisper.

Taylor must stand to make a great deal of money if the proposed concert comes to pass, Olivia thought, if he willingly parted with so much at one time. For a moment—just a moment—she was tempted.

But the time for such antics had passed. "Nonetheless, I cannot. You must understand. I have not even spoken to my mother, and what my father will say when word reaches him in Hampshire ... and there is something I must yet do. Today. Before I lose heart." She reached out her hand to Tetrazzini, who took it and raised it to his lips. "Thank you, Signore, for making what has been the most wonderful experience of my life a reality."

The Italian's face fell, and he bowed once again before letting himself out the door of the schoolroom.

Olivia dropped the rolls of banknotes into a drawer in the schoolroom desk. Although a paltry sum compared to the fortune that would pass into her husband's hands when she married, and a modest amount compared to the allowance she had at her disposal for whatever amusements took her fancy, she had never seen so much actual money in her life. What would it buy? It wasn't enough to purchase her freedom from all expectations. Perhaps she could at least pay for her own trip abroad, if her parents disinherited her. There must be some place in Europe it was safe to go. Or perhaps she could find some worthy cause to bestow it on. Because a moment's thought made her recollect that she could not be disinherited, no matter how badly she behaved. Her fortune had been settled on her by her grandfather.

It was noon by that time, and much as Olivia dreaded what she must do next, putting it off would not make it any easier. She must face her mother. She must try to explain to her why she had taken such a rash step. Why, when she might have remained the mysterious masked soprano, she had agreed to reveal her identity to everyone who mattered in London society.

Without further delay Olivia left the schoolroom and went to her mother's apartments.

# CHAPTER 32

*S*till groggy from his brandy-fueled night and stinging embarrassment, Hartland was ready to fling a pillow at Hinson when he entered his room and drew back the bed curtains.

"What do you mean by waking me at this ungodly hour!" he said, his voice a growl of displeasure.

"Forgive me, Sir, but Jacko is below requesting your immediate attention."

"I'm not going out this morning. Send him away."

"He said it was most urgent. I've taken the liberty of laying out your buckskins and top boots. I believe we can have you ready to accompany Jacko to the stables in a very few minutes."

Hartland sat up and rubbed his face vigorously. "To the stables? Whatever for?"

"He says there is something you must see, something he had no idea how to deal with on his own."

Thinking perhaps one of his horses had injured itself in a loose box or somehow developed colic, he slid out from between the sheets and suffered himself to be dressed.

"Here you are, Your Grace," said Hinson, handing him a glass full of an evil-looking cordial.

Hartland knew better than to doubt the wisdom of consuming one of Hinson's remedies for a thick head, so he tossed it down in one gulp, grimaced, and shook out his shoulders. Although for the moment it nauseated him, experience told him that within an hour he would be feeling considerably better. "All right, Hinson. Is Jacko in the hall?"

"Yes, Your Grace."

Soon Hartland found himself facing a very distressed groom, who passed his cap through his fingers and shifted from foot to foot. "What is it? What requires my immediate attention so early?"

"You better come see fer yerself, Yer Grace," he said, ducking his head in the semblance of a bow.

It was highly unusual for his groom to leave the stables except when accompanying him out in one of his carriages or bringing around one of the handsome cover hacks Hartland kept in London, so he nodded to Jacko to lead him out the side way to the stable yard.

"'E was there this mornin'. I woulda sent him away but for he was so beat up."

The powerful smell of horse piss, hay, and leather greeted Hartland as he stepped into the building that housed his blood cattle. Two stable boys with rakes in their hands hovered nervously, watching him with sullen expressions. Nostrils twitching, he followed Jacko to a box at the end of the row, one he knew to be unoccupied at present. Jacko stood aside and gestured into it.

"Lord!" Hartland exclaimed, then strode in and knelt down next to the pathetic figure of Otto huddled in the corner. He was shivering, one of his eyes was swollen nearly closed, and his nose had only recently stopped bleeding. He shrank away from the duke. "Easy! You know me. I'm a friend. Remember? You knew it last night. I won't hurt you. Let me have a look at you."

Hartland put out his hand and coaxed Otto to stand.

"No broken bones, I think. What happened? A horse kick you?" His lips twitched into a smile.

Otto shook his head and looked down.

"A mill then. How'd it come about?"

Otto lifted his eyes to Jacko who stood behind the duke, frowning.

"I've got this in hand, Jacko. You can go about your business."

"Yes, Yer Grace," he said, and then stalked off and yelled at the stable boys to get busy cleaning out the stalls.

When one of them said, "Yes sir," in a sullen voice, Otto's one good eye opened wide with fright.

"Oh. I see. Did you get into a fight with my lads?" The stable boys were each twice Otto's size. Hartland clenched his teeth in anger. A cowardly, cruel thing to do if that was indeed what had happened.

"*B-bitte*, Duke," Otto said, rather thickly. "I want to go home. *Zu Hause*," he said, as if he wanted to make sure Hartland understood.

"I'll take you. But first, we'd better clean you up a bit. Come with me." He reached his hand out to the boy, who stood trembling and uncertain. "No one will touch you while you're with me," Hartland said, and at last Otto put his hand into his.

As they walked by the guilty-faced stable boys, Hartland snapped at them, "I'll deal with you later. You'll be lucky not to be on the street by evening!"

Just before they left the stable, one of the boys said in a low voice, "Dirty blue skin."

Hartland stopped dead and wheeled around. "Andrew, isn't it?" He took two long strides in the boy's direction. To his credit, the boy held his ground. "Do you think it's manly to attack a child half your size? And if I ever hear you, or anyone I employ, address Master Otto in that way again, you will be out so fast you'll wonder what hit you. Now beg Master Otto's pardon."

Andrew scowled from under his brows and muttered "Sorry."

"I'm not the injured one! Tell him." He jerked his head toward where Otto stood shivering. "And tell him why you're sorry."

"Sorry I hit you," the stable boy said with a slight deferential nod in Otto's direction. Then, after a moment, he turned back to Hartland and said, "But he started it! He hit first!"

Hartland stared down at the stable boy for an uncomfortable thirty seconds, then wheeled around and took Otto out of the stable and into the house.

ONCE THE DUKE AND OTTO WERE ENSCONCED IN THE LIBRARY, Hinson tended to the boy's scrapes and put salve on his swollen eye. Mrs. Trantor, the housekeeper, brought up a tray loaded with sweets and lemonade. Otto waited until they were offered to him, took one, and said, "Sank you," before biting into it gingerly, carefully avoiding his bruised lip.

"Would you like to tell me what happened? I shall have to account for this to your guardian, you know. How did you come to be in my stable?"

Shamefaced, Otto looked away. "I want to see your chestnut."

"And?"

"I bring him *ein Apfel*."

"An *apple*," said Hartland, pronouncing the word

distinctly. "Challenger did not give you a black eye. So how did it start?"

"That *Kind!* He call me dirty black insect! Said I was *wiedernaturlich.*"

Hartland sighed. He could only imagine the word meant *unnatural.* Otto couldn't help standing out against a population that was mostly fair skinned. Those who were not mostly had dark eyes to go with their skin color. "Well, it's not true." He couldn't think what else to say. He feared that Otto would have a great many more such encounters once he was out in the world in whatever employment he was suited for. "You look a bit better now. I think I should return you to the princess."

He wouldn't, however, call on Princess Adelheid without first changing into respectable morning dress, so he left Otto to the enjoyment of the sweets and retired to his dressing room.

While he was tying on his neck cloth, he couldn't help wondering at himself. Why did he intervene with the boy? Why, in fact, did Jacko feel constrained to ask him? No doubt he knew precisely who Otto was—the network of servants being one of the most efficient ways to spread news of any kind. So why didn't the groom simply take Otto to the princess's house himself?

It occurred to Hartland that his groom—and probably everyone else in the household—had some idea of how he regarded Adelheid. They knew him well enough to predict his interest in so beautiful and captivating a lady. They also no doubt had already heard about the dramatic revelation at the King's Theatre the night before. Perhaps in his ham-fisted way Jacko was promoting a new match for his master, who he must know was in dire financial straits. He could hardly blame him for being anxious. If the house of Hartland fell, it would take with it an army of servants all around

England who would find themselves at least temporarily bereft of employment.

Still, that did not really answer why the groom had assumed that a child whose presence in another household was cloaked in mystery could be of any interest to a duke.

This forced Hartland to return to his own motives. He could have refused, could have told Jacko to clean him up and take him home. But he didn't. There was something about Otto, something more than his unusual, arresting looks. Even at just seven years old, Otto conducted himself with innate dignity, as if conscious that his worth was in no way represented by his appearance of lowliness. Besides, he mattered in some deep, undisclosed way to the princess. And if the child was important to her, Hartland realized with a start, he would have to be important to him, regardless of what the future held for either of them.

Although he was glad to have an excuse to visit Princess Adelheid, he had some misgivings. Did she know what had happened the night before at the King's Theatre? If she didn't, as soon as she read the morning papers she would. A part of him hoped he had been mistaken in her response to him on the occasions when they'd met. It was one thing for him to be—he almost thought *heartbroken*, but amended the word in his mind to *disappointed*. If the princess had developed any feelings for him he couldn't bear the thought that she might be hurt by his marriage to Olivia. What would he say to her now? And why was this situation any different from what it was at any time after he offered for the heiress? He had always been bound in honor. Perhaps he'd always been counting on a refusal from the heiress. That was no longer possible.

Otto walked next to Hartland in silence, chin high, shoulders back. Grandison opened the door after a single knock, and the two of them entered a scene of chaos. From the top of the house came voices calling, "Otto! Otto where are you? Naughty boy! Come out from your hiding place." A quick glance into the dining room off the grand hall revealed a maid looking behind and under furniture, twitching curtains aside, and appearing generally very harassed.

"Your Grace," Grandison said. "I'm certain Her Highness will be glad to see you—and you, Master Otto!" The dour butler's lips actually formed themselves into a small smile, while his brow creased in concern.

He'd turned to go up the stairs to find the princess, but she was already running down them, saying, "He's here! Where is he?"

"Safe, Princess," Hartland said. "Albeit a trifle the worse for wear."

She dashed forward, her eyes alight with relief and joy. It was worth everything to see her like that. And then she caught sight of Otto's bruised face and gave a little shriek.

"He's not badly hurt. Nothing a compress and a little rest won't fix," Hartland said. He glanced down in time to see Otto wipe a surreptitious tear off his cheek.

"I see I must thank you—again! I hope you will wait for me in the drawing room while I get this young hellion out of his dirt and give him into the hands of his—of Frankel."

The princess took hold of Otto's hand and drew him up the stairs, taking quick, concerned looks down at him as she went.

At the second landing, a man Hartland knew as the steward who had come with the princess from Austria took Otto from her to lead him up the rest of the way.

A steward taking interest in a little boy? It all seemed very strange.

It wasn't long before he and Princess Adelheid were once more seated in her formal drawing room, a room that seemed so unsuited to the kind of person she was. It had no trinkets, few paintings, and the furniture was heavy and somber. In contrast, her eyes bore a light from within and her graceful bearing made her surroundings fade into the background.

"Madeira, Grandison," she said to the butler and then gestured to the settee. "Now, tell me everything, Duke."

ONCE HARTLAND HAD RELATED TO HER WHAT HAD LED HIM TO discover Otto in his stables, and that the boy had come to cuffs with Hartland's two stable hands, Adelheid shook her head. "I don't know how I can stop him from wandering off. He was used to doing so in the country, you see, and to being under little supervision."

She was about to say more to the duke, to pour out her concerns and frustrations over her out-of-place little boy, but stopped. "I think, Duke, that you have had troubles enough just lately and the last thing you need is to bother over an errant little boy."

Hartland cast her a rueful glance. "So you've heard. Were you—"

"Yes, I was there."

Hartland nodded. "I expect you also know I've offered for her."

She had not known it for certain, but his actions toward herself—or rather, his reticence with regard to her—led her to expect as much. "Has she accepted?"

He ran his hand distractedly through his wavy dark hair. "No. But as I told her last night, we must marry. Her actions have made it imperative."

What was this? "But I would think such a provocation would mean the opposite!" These English proprieties were absurd. It made no sense. "Surely for her to act in that way would make it possible for you to withdraw your suit without censure." Adelheid saw his consternation and knew at least in part where it likely came from. Of course, he didn't know how much she knew.

"It is… complicated. But no matter. If I do not marry her, she will be ruined. Our marriage is the only way to protect her position in society. I would never subject her to the ignominy of being an outcast and will not cry off. Of course, she hasn't accepted that fact yet."

Adelheid hadn't expected this. Any of it. Something as unyielding as stone lodged in her throat, making it hard for her to speak. After a deep breath she said, "Why not? Why will she not agree to become your duchess?"

He met her eyes. "She does not love me. And—" He stopped and looked away. "I blame myself."

"How can that be? Her actions were her own."

"I believe that Miss Fontenoy would have felt no need to unmask in public had I not behaved in a way that … well, it matters not. I am a selfish creature, is all. I don't think I realized just how selfish until now."

Adelheid was silent. So, the duke was determined to marry Miss Fontenoy. Yet he sat here with her, baring his soul. It was as intimate a moment as she had ever shared with another person since Danton. "And yet, you saw fit to rescue a truant little boy, to patch him up and see he came to no further harm, with no thought as to how it might reflect on you." She met his eyes, and in them read confusion, self-deprecation, sorrow, yearning, and something else. Something she knew in her heart to be love. He loved her! How ironic that he'd been backed into a corner by his sense of honor, his fundamentally moral character. This was no callous rake, not at heart. If he had no concern for anyone but himself he would have withdrawn his offer for Miss Fontenoy and left her to her fate. And would not have interested himself in Otto's welfare to such a degree.

She was heartsick. This changed everything. The blatantly mercenary character of her own plans shamed her. The prince had manipulated her, made her into someone she never wanted to be. The time allotted for her to achieve this match would end in a couple of days in any case. She had failed, but did she really try to succeed?

How would it be if she confessed everything to Hartland now, when the charade was nearly over? She was tempted—oh, so tempted!—to open her heart to him. But that could achieve nothing now.

Hartland glanced at the mantel clock.

"I am keeping you from your business. You have been so generous with your time and thoughtful in your actions. Is there no way I can repay you for all you have done for—Otto?" She almost said, *my son*. She wanted to repay him with kisses, with caresses. She wanted so much to run her own fingers through his hair and let him do the same to her.

Hartland stood, and in two strides, reached her and sat next to her on the sofa, angling his body toward hers and reaching for her hands. "There is one thing. I only dare ask it of you because I think you understand me." He stopped, searching her eyes, as if uncertain what to say. "You must talk to Miss Fontenoy. Make her see that her only choice is to marry me. She believes I am simply a fortune hunter, and I suppose I am. She was never ambitious for a title, but now only my consequence can save her from complete ruin. I would not, I would never, ask this of you if I could think of any other way. Believe me. I would, if I could …"

His eyes burned into hers and Adelheid wanted to sink into the floor. He was asking her to do something that ran directly counter to her own happiness. He wanted her to ruin her chances not just of securing her late husband's fortune, but of having a life worth living at all.

She sat up straighter and eased her hands out of his. "I did not expect you to say this to me. I thought—well, it matters not what I thought. I don't know what makes you think Miss Fontenoy would pay any heed to me." The look on his face, the play of conflicting emotions and deep sadness, made her want to take him by the lapels of his coat and shake him, tell him that he would be whistling happiness down the wind on a point of honor. But she could not.

He clasped his hands in his lap, wringing them together until his knuckles whitened. "I don't know. But I could think of no one else to turn to. You have lived in the world, you know what it is like for a woman."

"I know, too, how it feels to be in a marriage where there is no love."

Hartland stood again and walked to one of the long windows. "Respect can ensure contentment. I respect her. It would have to be enough. She is too young to understand what her future would hold if we did not marry."

"Does she know what the future would hold if you did?"

He turned and locked eyes with her.

*I have lost him,* Adelheid thought. She was in a corner. He deserved her help for his kindness to Otto. She moistened her lips and forced a serene smile. "I will do what I can for you."

He returned to where she sat and held out his hand. She took it and he drew her to her feet. "I wish ..." he said, but did not continue.

"We both wish," Adelheid said in a barely audible whisper.

Somehow, they had drawn still closer together and Adelheid could see the complex tones that made up the deep ocean blue of his eyes. Something lit them in their centers, an expression Adelheid knew. Her breathing shallowed, her pulse fluttered. *This won't do,* she thought, and looked down.

"You are a remarkable woman, Adelheid," Hartland whispered. He broke himself away with a visible effort and made a low, graceful bow.

She said, "I will find a way to let you know what happens with Miss Fontenoy."

IT DOESN'T HAVE TO BE THIS WAY. ADELHEID REMEMBERED Nicholas's words to her when they first arrived in Grosvenor Square.

All at once she realized that, in fact, it hadn't then, and it didn't now. The fog in her brain cleared. She knew what she must do. The game was at an end. After all, she would not want a man to take her without knowing all the facts, or who had no room in his heart for Otto. She would not want a man who would feel cheated when the full extent of the deception was revealed. If she and Hartland were meant to be together, it would never be on those deceitful terms. He must know all, whatever the consequences.

The prince had forced her to use Otto as a pawn in a game of his design, rightly guessing that she would play it after his death in order to keep his fortune. She kept telling herself it was all for Otto, but was it? In any case, that game had almost reached its end. Only one more hand must be played out to its conclusion. And for that, she needed Miss Fontenoy.

Knowing all she knew about the heiress now, Adelheid's respect for this surprising girl deepened. Whatever happened, she would do her best to help Miss Fontenoy weather the inevitable censure that her insane, remarkable, foolhardy, courageous gesture would cause as she went on with her life, whether she married Hartland or Lewiston—or no one.

First, she would start as she meant to go on and bring Otto along with her for this conversation with the heiress.

She had little to lose at this point and it was time to make her son's presence felt to others aside from the duke and Lord Brattle. He would soon enough be known for exactly what and who he was and the last thing Adelheid wanted was for the world to believe she was somehow ashamed of him and therefore kept him hidden away.

The only shame she had ever truly felt was for marrying a man she knew in her heart did not love her.

# CHAPTER 33

*O*livia's encounter with her mother couldn't have gone any worse.

When the viscountess's taciturn abigail opened the door to her, she gave Olivia an insolent glance and sniffed before leaving the room. Lady Ambrose lay prostrate on the damask-upholstered sofa in her bedroom, swathed in her lace dressing gown, vinaigrette clutched in her hand. She looked older than her forty years and her eyes were red rimmed from a night spent weeping on and off. Olivia could still hear her wails of, "How could you do this to me? You'll never recover. You'll never be received. I shall be an outcast. The duke will withdraw his suit and our whole family will be in disgrace. Not to mention your presentation! The queen will never allow you in her drawing room."

When Olivia told her that the duke had no intention of withdrawing his suit, that she had no desire to marry him, and that she had no desire to be presented, Lady Ambrose jumped up in a sudden spurt of energy and took hold of her daughter's shoulders in a convulsive grip. "You must marry Hartland right away! And you must be presented!"

Olivia, fearing such a response, assumed that when she explained the duke's duplicity fully, her mother would see that marriage with him would be insupportable. She knew it would never be enough to simply tell her that they were not in love. That in fact, each of them was desperately in love with someone else.

Her tactic failed.

"What did you expect? You put yourself in the position of a trollop. You exposed yourself to such abuses. It was your own fault. Men will be men. You surely don't expect your husband to forgo all other pleasures when you are married!"

Olivia was too shocked to respond. Although she knew such behavior was commonplace, she never thought about what it would be like to be so treated by the man she married. Indeed, she fully expected that her husband would be faithful to her. She must have been deluding herself.

The interview ended in tears on both sides. Needing time to calm herself, Olivia decided to go for a walk in the park. It was too early for the fashionable promenade, so she had reasonable hope of not meeting anyone she knew. Besides, the sky threatened rain, and nothing so pedestrian as an umbrella would make a fashionable lady believe it was safe to venture out in such weather.

Olivia supposed she ought to be scrupulous in her adherence to propriety if she hoped to persuade the *ton* that she hadn't permanently besmirched herself by performing in public. But is that what she wanted? In fact, achieving the opposite outcome—having her outrageous behavior rid Hartland of his foolish need to fall on his sword because of some chivalrous belief that only he could rescue her from ruin—would in many ways be a preferable result. It made so little sense. Why did Harry, too, believe that she had no choice but to marry Hartland if he didn't withdraw his suit?

Why would the duke be the only person who could confer respectability on her?

Harry had it wrong, she was certain. He was worth every bit as much as the duke, if not more.

With these thoughts tormenting her, Olivia decided that there was no point in dragging Hetty out for a walk she did not want, and so put on her hat and gloves and, to Ebbings's utter horror, strode out to the street entirely unaccompanied.

Barely attending to anything around her, unaware that the boy who swept the crossing for her stood holding his hand out for a penny in vain, or that she attracted a few impudent stares from tradesmen making deliveries, Olivia soon found herself in the middle of the very stand of chestnut trees in which she'd vented her frustration when she first came to London, before her debut. In late February, only the suggestion of buds covered the branches. Now, the trees were veiled in bright spring green, although it was early for the fragrant cones of white flowers that would adorn their graceful branches in May. In the middle of this urban grove some thoughtful park designer had placed a stone bench. Olivia sat on it and stared straight ahead, picking at the ribbon that held her reticule closed and chewing her lower lip.

"Ah! Mademoiselle Fontenoy! How fortunate."

Startled, having been too absorbed in her own thoughts to notice anyone around her, Olivia turned to look in the direction from which the slightly accented, mellifluous voice had come.

She was unsurprised to recognize the elegant Princess Adelheid, but startled to see a little negro boy in spotless nankeens walking with her, hand-in-hand. Olivia stood as she approached. The two ladies curtsied to each other.

"I see you have escaped without a chaperone." The princess sounded amused rather than censorious.

"I hardly think such things matter for me anymore," Olivia said, unable to keep the sarcastic edge out of her voice.

"You speak of your performance last night. I saw it. You were splendid, truly. And so brave. Why did you do it?"

Why, indeed. "It's such a very long story. I would not presume to bore you with it."

"My dear Miss Fontenoy! I would think that a story leading to such a dramatic conclusion could certainly never be boring."

This made Olivia smile. "Boring is perhaps the wrong word. But I shall not sing again. I am nothing but an amateur with a bit of a voice."

"Now, this is not true. I know of what I speak. I think your secrets are deeper than simply your shocking appearance on the stage of the King's Theatre."

The boy edged himself a little behind the princess and eyed Olivia with frank curiosity.

Princess Adelheid, seeing the direction of Olivia's gaze said, "I, too, have placed myself outside the bounds of what is acceptable. That is in part why I have come to London, I thought to seek my fortune. But now, I think it is just to seek my heart."

"But…" Olivia was confused. The princess was wealthy! She'd taken one of the most expensive residences in Mayfair for the season, she rode a magnificent mare that must have cost well over three-hundred guineas, and she had attended the rout party wearing a fortune's worth of pearls.

Adelheid stepped up to Olivia and took her arm. "I must make a confession. I went to your house in Mount Street for the purpose of talking to you. They told me you had gone out for a walk. Something made me think you would choose the serenity of the park, and so I—we—came in search of you. Will you accompany us for a while? We may thus chaperone each other and I can speak to you in private. I know you must have questions." She glanced at Otto and smiled. "Besides, we have not had our opportunity to become better acquainted. You invited me to your ball, and we spoke at Lady Ferndale's party. Surely that is excuse enough to begin a friendship."

What on earth could the princess have to say to her? And who was this child? How could a little dark-skinned boy have anything to do with a princess? And why would that have any bearing her own situation? Besides, it would be a diversion to talk of something else and no harm could come of it that she could see. "As you wish," she said.

For a time they said nothing, only nodding to the one or two acquaintances they passed as they wandered along the footpaths in the park. One older lady stared at them and turned away. The cut direct. *Already*, Olivia thought. Or perhaps the cut had been directed at the princess and her exotic companion.

After that incident and with no preamble the princess said, "His Grace the Duke of Hartland called on me this morning."

A fierce, hot blush flooded into Olivia's cheeks. "How kind of him," she said, her tone belying her words.

The princess's laugh was as huskily musical as her speaking voice. "Ah, the English humor. I understand you are in a quandary. It may surprise you to know that I think we can help each other. In our own ways we desire the same things—if our methods of achieving them are not quite the same."

"I don't think I'm in a position to help anyone," Olivia said. "I have destroyed my own future in the most public manner and at the same time ruined my one chance of happiness."

"Yet when you come of age you will have a handsome fortune. Enough to allow you whatever life you desire. What is it, such a life, the one you desire?" the princess asked.

No one, as far as Olivia could remember, had ever asked her that question. Not even Signore Tetrazzini. Everyone assumed she wished for the same thing as every young lady of breeding: a good match and an establishment of her own. Certainly it was what her mother wanted for her. But truly, what *did* she want?

She found it much easier to say what she didn't want. She didn't want to be brought out and dangled as a prize in the marriage mart. She didn't want to marry Hartland. She had no desire for a lofty title. Failing the desire for a life of consequence and fashion, did she want to continue singing on stage? Part of her most certainly did. But at what cost? "I can hardly say," Olivia finally answered. Could she not? Perhaps she simply didn't want to.

In point of fact, she knew in her heart that what she truly wanted would be impossible. She wanted to continue singing on stage *and* to marry the man she loved. Two things that canceled each other out.

No one knew that not only did she not want to marry Hartland but that her heart was well and truly lost to Harry. She'd only recently admitted it to herself. She wanted to confide in someone, to pour out her overflowing feelings. She certainly couldn't tell her mama, or even Lady Mariana. They were too close, too involved. But what of the princess? Perhaps she could confide in her. Princess Adelheid stood just enough outside Olivia's world to feel like a safe repository for such a confidence. What harm could it do at this point? The princess had already seen the worst of her.

With a deep breath of resolution, Olivia turned to the

princess. "May I trust you with something I have told no one else?" She glanced around to see if they were far enough away from any other people so they wouldn't be overheard.

The princess lifted her fine, straight brows and looked directly into Olivia's eyes. "You do not know me. But you may be certain that I would never betray anyone who told me something she wished to keep private. You only have my word, of course, and perhaps that is not worth anything. But I wish you will believe me."

Quite illogically, Olivia realized that she did believe the princess. Or at least, she chose to do so. "What I wish to tell you is that I have no intention of marrying the duke. He behaved scandalously toward me."

"I know."

She knew? How? "Then you understand that because of it, I cannot marry him."

A light of amusement leapt into the princess's eyes and Olivia suddenly felt the difference in their ages. This woman, she thought, would have known how to handle Hartland in that situation. Perhaps it wouldn't have mattered to her. She might have found it amusing. Beguiling.

The princess squeezed Olivia's arm. "You do not care for the handsome Lord Hartland? But is he not the marriage prize? Surely worth overlooking his so-called scandalous actions."

"It's impossible. It's not just what he did. It's …" Olivia took a deep breath. "We do not love each other. In point of fact, I am in love with someone else."

The princess said nothing as they strolled along, only looking off into the distance as though peering into another world. After a minute or two, she said, "You are in love with Lord Lewiston."

Olivia stopped in her tracks. The princess walked a pace or two on, then turned.

"How did you …" Olivia said.

She cocked her head a little on the side and smiled kindly. "Only a blind person could fail to see it, especially if she'd watched you waltzing together."

Olivia's face flushed hot. She put her hands to her cheeks. "Then …" Before she could prevent them, tears overflowed from her eyes. She dug into her reticule for a handkerchief and tried to wipe them away as quickly as they formed.

"It is quite clear that he is just as much in love with you." Adelheid pulled Olivia on to continue walking. "This should not be a reason to weep!"

"You don't understand! He-he too thinks I have to m-marry H-Hartland."

The princess huffed out a long sigh and shook her head. "These gentlemen and their honor. But I think there may be a way to change their minds."

"The problem," Olivia said, gaining a degree of control over herself, "is that the duke needs my fortune as well."

"Yes, that is a difficulty. But not a reason for him to—what is the expression? Stab himself?"

Olivia gave a watery chuckle. "Fall on his sword."

"He risked all on one roll of the dice and now believes he must take his luck. I think the duke is a gamester in his heart," the princess said. "This is one reason why I have so great an interest in him myself. I, too, am such a one to embrace a risk. Else I would not be here. I would have stayed in Hungary in the gate house of the chateau, to live like a disgraced widow with my son, out of sight."

"You have a son?" Olivia wondered if everyone in the *ton* knew this.

The princess did not answer, simply smiled. "I, too, must marry. What would you think if I married your duke?" A far-off look had come into the princess's eyes.

"Do *you* have a fortune?" The impertinent question

sprang from Olivia's mouth before she could recover from her astonishment.

"Not yet!" the princess said. They reached the Stanhope Gate. "Will you come and take tea with me? I can explain all to you, and together we can figure out how we might help each other achieve the endings we desire."

# CHAPTER 34

*A*lthough the dowager duchess still kept to her room, she stayed abreast of all the goings on in the *ton* by reading the *Gazette* and the *Post* every day and corresponded regularly with her many friends. Thus it was that she had heard about the extraordinary events of the previous evening —at least, the ones that had occurred in public.

Hartland arrived in his mother's sitting room after her summons to see her pacing up and down in front of the hearth.

"Mama, you've heard—"

"Yes. Had you any idea?"

He shook his head. "I was as shocked as everyone else." Although no one but he had as much reason to be. Would the duchess tell him to cry off?

"She's placed herself *hors du ton*. Unless, that is, she makes a good marriage." She stopped pacing and looked her son full in the face. "Not to do so would spell ruin for her, which is something I'm certain you would not want the lady you'd offered for to suffer, whatever your true feelings."

After a stunned moment, Hartland realized that his mother wasn't telling him he should withdraw his offer but agreeing with his own assessment, encouraging him to go through with it. She also guessed that his heart was not engaged in his pursuit of Miss Fontenoy. But that was not difficult to see.

The duchess put her hand out and pulled Hartland down to sit next to her on the small sofa. "This change in Miss Fontenoy's circumstances would certainly give you a reason to end your courtship, and no one would blame you for it. Do you want to cry off? Or are you—as I hope—too chivalrous to abandon her to her fate? The *ton* can be more vicious than a mad tiger."

"There is no need to tell me that, Mama. I have already made it clear to Miss Fontenoy that not only will I not cry off, but that marrying me is the only course of action that will save her from becoming a social pariah. She is very young, you see, and I'm not sure she fully realizes the consequences of her actions."

The duchess appeared not to have heard what her son said. "I can't help wondering, why did she do it? Surely she could have simply disappeared, allowed the mystery of the masked soprano to live in everyone's memory and hoarded the experience to herself to dream over later in life. By all accounts her voice is remarkable. That she would want the experience, the thrill of singing a great role, I perfectly understand. What I don't understand is why she felt compelled to reveal her identity so publicly."

What could he tell her? He did not want to admit his own role in provoking her to take that unwise step. Honesty was all well and good, but his mother needn't know just how much of a selfish rake he was and how badly he'd behaved. "I don't know."

The duchess fiddled with a bit of lace at her cuff, frowning down at it as if she'd noticed a tear. Without looking up she said, "She doesn't want to marry you, does she."

"No," he said, watching her delicate fingers trace the pattern of the lace.

"She doesn't want to marry the catch of the season, the nobleman all of the unmarried ladies of the *ton* have sighed over for ten years. That seems odd for a girl possessed of little beauty and apparently less address. She must have a very good reason." At this she lifted her eyes to his.

"I hope I can persuade her to change her mind," Hartland said. "We need each other, you see."

"Yes, I know. I guessed that your father left us worse off than anyone has told me. Although many would think that enough of a reason to marry with or without affection, I do not share that sentiment."

"But you don't know all! We are quite done up, unless I can bring us about by the end of this season."

She took his hand. "Do you think I couldn't survive in the dower house with only a few servants? Or not survive without being dressed in the kick of fashion every season? I'm not so shallow as that."

He shook his head. "I don't think you could bear it. Think how you've lived your whole life." And how he had lived. He couldn't help thinking ruefully back to his wild extravagances. Why had he indulged himself so? Had it really made him happy?

"But this is *your* life we're discussing. Of course, I can't tell you what to do. I want you to be kind, but I also want you to be happy. By all means marry Miss Fontenoy. It's the right thing to do, if she'll have you. But don't do it for the sake of her fortune. Because if you find your marriage does not satisfy you, you would have traded one bad circumstance for another."

He knew it. If he'd had any doubt about that fact, his conversation with Princess Adelheid earlier made it abundantly clear that he would never be content—no matter how much he liked and respected Miss Fontenoy—to be leg shackled to her. He had gone through life able to captivate whatever female he'd set his heart on, to enjoy a passionate affair or a light flirtation, and then pass on to the next adventure with an unscathed heart. But no more. This was the first time he had truly fallen in love with someone. The irony was that she could never be his.

The duchess was silent for a while. After taking a deep breath, she looked into her son's eyes and said, "Mrs. Trantor tells me we had a little visitor this morning."

Of course she would hear about that. "Yes, young Otto, Princess Adelheid's ward. He got himself into a scrape in the stables."

"I wonder you didn't simply let Jacko take him back to number twelve. Although I hear he is quite an engaging boy."

Hartland couldn't help wishing he could tell his mother about the princess. She would like her, he was certain. "I felt responsible. He came to see Challenger. Apparently the princess's groom had told him about the horse. He's a bit horse mad."

"Why did the stable boys set upon him?"

Did she not know what he looked like? Perhaps the housekeeper hadn't said. "He's different. Half Negro, with startling light eyes. I expect perhaps they thought he was bewitched."

The duchess was too well bred to betray any shock, except in not speaking for several moments. "How comes it that the princess is his guardian?"

"He is the natural son of a dear friend of hers, apparently."

"So by caring for him and being the one to take him back to her, you are making yourself agreeable to her. Take care, my son. I doubt very much a princess is to be trifled with, however beautiful."

He forced himself to laugh. "You forget, Mother, that I intend to marry Miss Fontenoy."

*And trifling with the princess could not be further from my mind.*

"If she'll have you. Although I imagine Lady Ambrose will bring pressure to bear."

Or perhaps Princess Adelheid will be able to talk some sense into the girl, he wanted to say, but refrained.

When he thought of what he'd asked the princess to do for him that morning he could scream with frustration. What a deuced stupid world they lived in!

And what a deuced stupid fellow he had been. But what could he expect? He'd brought it on himself, after all. And now he must live with the consequences.

ADELHEID KNEW SHE WAS TAKING A RISK BY THROWING HERSELF on the mercy of this ingenuous heiress. Although she didn't think the girl would expose her, she had no way of knowing for certain that she had judged her correctly.

They sat silent in the small drawing room in the house in Grosvenor Square, at first only the tinkling of spoons and tea cups breaking the stillness. *We are strangers,* Adelheid thought, and yet they were bound in a strange dance of fate. It was up to her, she knew, to initiate the discussion.

"I was a diva, you know. A mezzo."

Miss Fontenoy looked up at her over the rim of her

teacup, her eyes glowing almost green in the sliver of sunlight that shone through one of the windows. Green, and vaguely catlike. "I thought so. At least, I thought you would be a mezzo if you were a singer. But I have never heard your name."

"I performed only in houses on the Continent. I was Adelheid Braun. And that is where I met the prince, my late husband. He courted me with such fine words and gifts and promises. That was nine years ago. He asked me to marry him and I thought, yes, I would like to be a princess and live in a grand chateau." Adelheid smiled bitterly at the memory. "I was such a fool. He didn't love me. He simply wanted to own me."

A thoughtful look passed over Miss Fontenoy's face, but she kept her gaze steady.

"He was a cruel man. When I couldn't give him an heir he tormented me. He abused me, beat me. He would publicly humiliate me, call me a whore, tell the whole world that he had made a terrible mistake. It was during that time that I met Danton."

"Danton?"

"The only man I have ever truly loved, until now. The prince brought him over from Jamaica, a curiosity, he thought. A Black man with manners and education. Danton was beautiful. He had such deep, sad eyes. And he *saw* me. He saw my suffering. We fell in love. The prince discovered us in each other's arms and sent him away. But he was too late."

Adelheid watched the emotions play over Olivia's face as she told more and more of her tale. Her pregnancy and childbirth when she bore Danton's son instead of the heir the prince wanted so desperately.

"You're wondering, perhaps, what my sad story has to do with the duke and you. You see, by the terms of the prince's will I must marry a nobleman within the next few days, and this nobleman must be willing to adopt my son as his heir. If I fail to do this, I will be left with nothing."

"But," Olivia said, "do you truly need the prince's fortune? Could you not simply return to the stage? "

"I could, were it not for Otto."

"Is that your son? Where is he?" Olivia asked.

"You've seen him."

"I have?"

"Today. He walked with us through the park."

Miss Fontenoy's eyes opened wide. "Your ward?"

"I had to distance us from each other a little. But that will end very soon. I will acknowledge him as my son either when I become betrothed, or ..." she paused to choose her words carefully. "Or when I do not. I find I have no wish to hide the fact that I am his mother."

After a brief interval of silence, Miss Fontenoy said, "You said you had never been in love with anyone besides Danton until now. Who is it that you now love?"

The answer was so clear, so obvious. Adelheid conjured up an image in her mind of the duke's tall, handsome figure. She could imagine his fathomless blue eyes, the strain of his muscles as he clambered up over the gate into the square, the way he saw her into her house, so solicitous and protective. How he looked at her at the end of their interview the day before, his vulnerable, confused eyes. How he'd held Otto's hand when he returned him to her. And she suspected he must have guessed something about Otto. But she knew in her heart it went deeper than that. "I have fallen in love with the Duke of Hartland." Exactly what she hadn't wanted to happen.

"To be honest, I thought as much. You see, I watched you too—in his arms, waltzing, at the rout party." Olivia shook her head and smiled. "It's Figaro. Only you're the Countess and I'm Susanna. And I even have the incriminating jewel."

She was exactly right. The circumstances were tragically absurd. "Ah," Adelheid said. If the stakes were not quite so high, she might find the whole situation comical. "You do not have the trinket you mention, as it happens."

"No, not in my possession right now, but hidden away in the theatre."

"I am afraid that is not so." Adelheid rose and went to the desk by the window, unlocked a drawer, and brought out a small wooden box. She gave it to Miss Fontenoy. "Open it."

Olivia did so and lifted the valuable diamond pin out of the nest of silver paper, holding it up to catch the afternoon light streaming through the south-facing window. "I don't understand." Her brows drew together in a puzzled frown.

"Félicité is an old friend of mine. And she knows *toute mon histoire*. She brought this pin to me in part because she knew that it would be stolen if she left it at the theatre."

Miss Fontenoy's mouth opened in shock. "So you know what Hartland ..."

"Yes."

"And you still love him? Despite his duplicitous actions?" In her agitation Olivia jumped to her feet and walked to the window. "What was the other reason Félicité brought you the pin?"

"She knew why I came to London and thought she could help me. But I would not try to win the duke in that manner."

Miss Fontenoy whirled around. "So even at my ball and the rout party. If only I'd known. But in a way, I think I did. I saw you with the duke then, as I said, and I thought you belonged together."

"If only we could have said such things to each other! But that is not the way it is done, Miss Fontenoy. Or perhaps I may call you Olivia?"

Olivia nodded.

She patted the space next to her on the sofa and Olivia

took it. "You do not love the duke. You love Lord Lewiston. I love the duke and he loves me, but to forsake you would be against his code of honor."

"What can we do?" Olivia said. "I see no way out. My mother insists I accept Hartland's suit as the only way to avoid complete disgrace not just for me, but for my family. And both Hartland and Lord Lewiston think the same. I am not of age. I have no power."

Adelheid smiled. "You are a woman. You have a great deal more power than you know."

BY THE END OF HER TWO-HOUR VISIT, OLIVIA FELT AS IF HER eyes had been opened and the realities of life spread before her as on a massive carpet. She could not imagine the princess's suffering, how she had come through it all still looking serenely lovely, only, perhaps, the slightest lines at the corners of her beautiful eyes to betray her tribulations. So many things she had no idea about, forces in the world, evils she'd been shielded from all her life.

She not only respected Adelheid—for they had agreed that she should drop the "Your Highness" and "Princess"— but she was in a fair way to loving her as a dear friend.

They had decided on a strategy so bold it made Olivia shiver. No half measures would suffice. She had to play her part and she wasn't entirely certain she would be able to. First, she must bring Lady Mariana into the scheme. Without her help, it would be impossible.

Once again, Olivia thought, she must find strength in the way she found it when she stepped onto the stage and sang. She would not be able to hide behind the music, although neither had she been able to do so at the rout party, and she got through that in one way or another.

Only this time, her way couldn't be to imagine herself the

Countess. Adelheid was too fixed in that guise for Olivia now. Perhaps, she thought, she should write her own story. Perhaps she need only be Olivia, a character in an opera yet to be written.

This made her smile, and she lifted her chin as she turned her steps toward South Audley Street and Lady Mariana.

# CHAPTER 35

*K*nowing that the very next day she would be
revealing things about herself to people who
had the power to destroy her should they wish it, Adelheid
decided it was time to tell Otto that she was not simply his
guardian—she was his mother. He had not been ready for the
revelation when she first removed him from his foster
mother, but now, she believed he would be.

The question was where to do so. Should it be in the
park, in a neutral setting? Or in the comfort of the nursery?

In the end, the decision was made for her. Just after she
finished her solitary dinner a furor arose that made itself
heard from the third floor to the dining room on the ground
floor. Adelheid recognized Otto's shouts and protestations,
leapt to her feet and raced up four flights of stairs to see what
was happening.

She found Otto clinging to a tiny kitten and Frankel
remonstrating with him to give it up so she could drown it.
Tears streaked Otto's cheeks and his full lips turned down at
the corners.

"*Nein*! No! He's mine!"

"I tell you, the poor thing won't live! He's too small and it would be kinder to destroy it."

Adelheid swiftly intervened, shooting an anguished glance at Frankel. "Thank you, Frankel, you have done your duty. If you would kindly leave us."

The nursemaid tsk'ed and stormed out of the room, slamming the door behind her.

She would recover. She was only trying to do what she thought right, but Adelheid had come to understand that Otto had a tender heart and an affinity for all living creatures—especially, perhaps, those who were most vulnerable. It fit with his personality and his heritage.

She approached Otto. He turned away from her at first, saying "No!"

"I won't take him away. Let me see him." The setting sun cast a rosy glow through the small windows, burnishing Otto's warm brown skin. *How beautiful he is,* she thought. *So like Danton.*

Otto's breath shuddered in helpless sobs. The tiny kitten—a fluffy black one—mewed at him and stretched a scrawny paw up to cling to his nightshirt.

"Where did you find him?" Adelheid asked, kneeling down next to Otto.

"I-I f-found him in the stable," he said, through his hiccups. "H-he was lost."

Otto's English had improved so much just in these weeks. He was as smart as his father. "You know his mama might be looking for him. Likely he has brothers and sisters somewhere."

"He has no mama, *weder Brüder, noch Schwestern*—b-brothers or sisters—like me." A fresh flow of tears accompanied this observation.

Otto's words seared Adelheid's heart, burning into that place that had been empty from the moment the doctor took her newborn from her arms. Remembering that horrible time would not help her now. She steeled herself and said, "That's not true. What if I told you that you do have a mother. A mother who loves you very much."

He raised his tear-streaked face to Adelheid, a pinched crease between his eyebrows.

"I'm telling you the truth. What is more, she is with you right now."

One errant tear fell on the kitten's head and it looked up. "*Wo?*" Otto said.

"It is I. I am your mother."

Adelheid watched Otto's expression move through bewilderment to disbelief to wonder. Would he believe her? What could she say? How to explain? "I was forced to give you up just after you were born, and I couldn't come to find you until after... Well, until after the bad man who took you from me died."

And until she discovered that he was still alive, but she would reveal that to him when he was older. "I should have said something to you before now. But there are things, things you don't understand, that made it important for others not to know."

"My black skin," Otto said in a small voice.

Adelheid put her arms around him and, taking care not to crush the kitten, cried, "No! No! I loved your papa very much and he was blacker than you are by far. I have so wanted to tell everyone that you are my precious little boy. I have wanted to do that more than anything.."

With a slightly feral, suspicious look in his eyes, Otto said, "I don't look like you."

"Is that what you think? Well, you're wrong. You look like your father, and you look like me," Adelheid said, stood, and steered him toward the small mirror on the wall near the table. "Look at your eyes, and at mine."

He looked back and forth between his own reflection and hers. Recognition gradually dawned as he saw that their eyes were nearly identical in color and shape, down to the dark lashes that surrounded them.

Adelheid wished she could see inside Otto's mind and glimpse what he thought about this new information. So much to comprehend after so many changes in such a short time. Better for him to know the truth now, though. She would no longer have to pretend that he was simply the child of a beloved friend. His blood was noble, even if no one in the *ton* would recognize it as such. Danton had been a descendant of African kings.

Otto looked down at the kitten, which had curled into a ball and fallen asleep in his hands. "Can you be his mama too?" he asked.

Adelheid laughed. "If you wish it! Now, what will you call your kitten? Let's ring for a maid to bring him some milk. He looks old enough to lap, so I think he'll survive. But you must take very great care of him. Just as I am taking very great care of you." She couldn't help wondering how her servants would greet the news that the troublesome child with inconveniently brown skin was her son. She supposed some of them might have guessed by that time. Would any of them give their notice? So be it if they did.

Otto's tears stopped, leaving only salty trails down his face. He smiled, dimpling his cheeks. "Thank you P- ..." He paused. "*M-Mutter.*"

It was all Adelheid could do not to dissolve in tears herself, so long had she yearned to have her son call her *mother*. "Of course, my child," she said, her voice breaking a little at the end. She cleared her throat and said, "Now, let's see about that milk, and then get both of you to bed."

. . .

ONCE SHE'D SETTLED OTTO ADELHEID WENT DOWNSTAIRS TO the drawing room, her imagination still full of that magical word: mother.

"Shall I bring the tea tray, Your Highness?" Grandison asked, entering the drawing room soon after her.

She looked up at him a little vacantly. He was well trained not to reveal any emotions, but she caught a concerned light in his eyes before he blinked it away. "Yes, tea would be lovely."

A moment later, someone knocked softly on the door of the room.

"Come!" Adelheid said.

It was Nicholas. After bowing to her, he held out a card. "This arrived earlier. I took the liberty of seeing what it was and wanted to give it to you. And we should talk a little, I think, Your Highness."

Adelheid took it from him and stared at it, unseeing. When she finally made her eyes focus on it she saw that it simply bore the name *Phineas Bunford, Esquire*, with a direction in Lincoln's Inn Fields.

"What is this?" she asked. "Who is this gentleman?"

"He is an attorney."

"An attorney? Why should an attorney be contacting me?"

Nicholas did not answer her immediately. Instead he said, "Are you still determined to fulfill the terms of the codicil to the prince's will?"

Adelheid stared at him. "Yes. No. I don't know, to be honest. I'm almost out of time anyway. And everything has become a bit cloudy in my mind. I'm not myself."

"It's no wonder. You have been much in the duke's company of late. You have not told him anything?"

She shook her head. "No. I daresay he would run away if I did anyway. But the time for secrets will soon be over."

Nicholas appeared, if anything, downcast when she said

she hadn't spoken of the will to Hartland. But in a gentle voice, he said, "Secrets poison happiness, I think, Your Highness."

Adelheid smiled weakly. It had been exhausting, the pretense, the worry. Sitting up straighter and lifting her chin, she chided herself. She must not succumb to self-pity. Matters were far from settled. "This attorney. What does he want?" she asked, and imagined some further complication that would render her position in London untenable, although surely any such thing would have come through Mitterling rather than an English lawyer.

"I cannot say," Nicholas said. "With your permission, I should like to pursue Mr. Bunford's inquiry."

"Would you? I'd be so grateful."

After several weeks in his company, seeing him every day, knowing that it was almost entirely due to him that the house ran smoothly, Adelheid still felt she didn't really know Nicholas. Far from acting like the spy sent to ensure her good behavior according to the terms of the will, the steward had been a quiet support to her ever since the death of the prince. This support was so discreet that she sometimes worried he did not know how much she valued him, and believed that she was ignorant of all he did. "You've been so kind to Otto. I haven't thanked you for that," she said.

"I'm fond of the boy," he said.

"I've told him, you know."

"Who? The duke?" Nicholas appeared confused.

"No, not him, not that," Adelheid said with an apologetic smile. "I haven't transgressed the terms of the will. Yet. I mean Otto. I've told him that I'm his mother."

After a brief silence, Nicholas said, "I'm very glad, Your Highness. It was time. But will he keep that knowledge to himself?"

Adelheid gave a sad little laugh. "Probably not. But I

couldn't stand it any longer, and, besides, after tomorrow night everyone will know. At least, everyone who matters."

She paused as Grandison entered with the tea tray and set it down on the table between the two settees. He'd brought two cups, Adelheid noted. She said, "Thank you Grandison."

After the butler left them alone again, Adelheid motioned Nicholas to sit. "It's such a strange world, don't you think? Why should you and I not drink tea together, just because I married a man of title and fortune and you—I don't know where you came from before you were in the prince's employ."

"I was in the ring. A lightweight. My father was a respectable man who wanted me to go to Oxford. But the money wasn't there."

"So," Adelheid said, "both of us had to earn our living. That makes us alike, don't you think?" It also explained the steward's classical education. She poured out tea and handed him a cup before taking one for herself. "What will you do if I fail to meet the terms of the will? I could not afford to continue your salary. I would give you an excellent character, however." The thought that their small family of sorts would have to break up had not occurred to Adelheid before, another reason to ensure her plan succeeded. But if it didn't, Nicholas was educated and able and would no doubt easily find another position.

"I prefer not to contemplate that eventuality, Princess Adelheid," he said, and then drank his cup of tea down in three gulps. "I beg your pardon, but I must leave you now."

"Of course. Thank you."

"Thank me? For what?"

She shrugged. "For all of it. For what you've done and for everything you will do before our little drama has been played out."

He stood and bowed to her, then took his leave.

# CHAPTER 36

ortunately, Mariana was at home that morning. Olivia dreaded seeing her, knowing that she hadn't wanted her to sing in the benefit and perhaps would be cross that her advice had gone unheeded. That couldn't be helped now.

After they greeted one another, Olivia said, "Forgive me? And allow me to tell you the whole story, all the reasons why I behaved as I did."

She then explained the details of Hartland's role in the affair, how she had seen him at his most rakish and wanted to teach him a lesson. She expected Mariana to be shocked.

But instead, Mariana burst out laughing and continued until tears came into her eyes. "Oh my dear, I wish I could have seen his face! I really am so sorry you had to find out about him in that upsetting way. You must admit, though, it is all quite hilarious."

Mariana's peals of helpless laughter first made Olivia smile. In another moment the full absurdity of the scene at the theatre struck her. "I thought he would collapse when I looked out at the audience!" Olivia said, now laughing every bit as hard as Mariana was.

"It's like a bad melodrama, or a frivolous libretto by an obscure poet," Mariana gasped, making a supreme effort to stop laughing. "And we're the actors who have to keep saying the ridiculous lines."

This observation doubled Olivia up in renewed squeals of laughter.

Once Mariana regained control of herself, she said, "To be serious, though, Hartland is right, you know, about marrying him. And it makes me think well of him that he won't cry off."

The thought quickly sobered Olivia up. "I don't think he is right. I won't marry him."

"Then what do you propose to do? You may not want to marry him, but you say your Mama still insists you do." She patted her damp eyelashes with her lace-edged handkerchief.

"The princess and I believe there's a way to work everything out to the satisfaction of all. But we need your help."

"The princess? What has she to do with all this?"

Olivia realized she had assumed that Mariana would make the connection simply because it existed. "Let me explain," she said, and quickly filled Mariana in on the shocking facts concerning the prince's will and little Otto, wondering how she would react.

Mariana appeared thoughtful, but not at all perturbed. "Extraordinary. I have enjoyed coming to know that lady. I thought she was out of the common way. She must have immense courage to have grasped the chance that she might be able to secure her son's future."

"She may yet achieve her object. But she has only a few more days before the term specified in the will elapses," Olivia said. "That's why we need your help."

"My help? I don't see what I could possibly do. Besides, I wouldn't want to reveal my complicity in your operatic career to your Mama. She would never forgive me. If Jeremy were to find out the whole he'd think I was an unregenerate hoyden, that I had gone back to my rebellious ways. And now that I'm a respectable wife of a prominent politician, that wouldn't do."

"You need not reveal any of your part in my affairs to anyone. I certainly will not."

"What then? How do you want me to help you?"

Olivia drew herself up. "Have a dinner party. Tomorrow."

It was a good minute before Mariana spoke. "A party? Whatever for? I don't know. It's a bit sudden! Who would attend on such short notice?"

Olivia pulled a slip of paper out of her reticule and handed it to Mariana. "These people. I would like you to invite them and none others."

Mariana scanned the list. "The dowager duchess? She is still in seclusion, I believe. I don't even know if she's receiving visitors yet. Lord Lewiston as well? And who is Otto? Ah! Yes, you told me. But a child at a dinner party?"

The blood rose into Olivia's cheeks and she thanked her stars that she wasn't one of those fair damsels who turned scarlet all over when embarrassed. "Will you trust me in this? I think it will only work if every one of these individuals can be here at precisely the times I specify."

Mariana sighed. "This is all most peculiar. I don't know why I feel compelled to help you. Although that is not entirely truthful. Not only do I see in you someone akin to me in many ways, but I confess, I wondered what I would do for excitement now that your identity is known and you won't be returning to the stage." Lady Mariana smiled warmly and held out her hand to Olivia, who took it and pressed it between both of hers.

"I am presuming on your kind nature as I have done too many times in these weeks," Olivia said, "but truly, if our plan works, you will be helping to make so many people happy."

Mariana brushed a wayward strand of hair out of Olivia's face and tucked it behind her ear. "Now, how shall I word these extraordinary invitations?"

~

OLIVIA HARDLY DARED THINK ABOUT WHAT SHE AND THE princess had agreed to do. If all went as they hoped, the Duke of Hartland would ultimately marry Princess Adelheid Kinsky and she, The Honorable Olivia Fontenoy, would marry the Marquess of Lewiston—if he truly wanted her. He hadn't actually offered for her, but how could she mistake his intention? That one kiss—it meant something. Just thinking of it sent a shock of desire all the way through her body and made her lightly touch her lips and smile.

But it had happened *after* he knew she appeared in the opera and planned to reveal her identity, so perhaps he simply thought she was fast.

No. Harry was not like Hartland. She couldn't imagine the marquess behaving in the way the duke had, chasing after a lightskirt backstage.

As she walked the short distance from Mariana's house to Mount Street, the question Adelheid asked her the day before swirled in the hidden places in Olivia's mind. *What is it you want?* It had pulled her up short. People, parents, didn't ask girls such questions. It didn't matter what they wanted. Their lives followed a single trajectory, toward marriage and family. It was their destiny, and many wanted nothing more. But what happened to those who did? The only other option for a gently bred female who failed to marry was to become the maiden aunt beloved of nieces and nephews or to retire into crotchety eccentricity.

Something Adelheid said made Olivia think she believed there could be a third way. Perhaps not in avoiding marriage, but in making an alliance on a more solid footing, a marriage of equals, and not just in the realm of rank and fortune.

What *did* she want? She had told Adelheid that she wanted to marry Harry. And it was nothing less than the truth. Would that be enough? If she were not the daughter of a viscount, would she pursue a career as a soprano? To be honest with herself, now that she'd experienced the thrilling, terrifying, sordid world of the stage, life as a professional opera singer had lost some of its appeal. The moments spent singing gave her joy beyond any she had ever experienced. But she could not imagine herself fending off importunate Lotharios seeking her favors after every performance. One such experience was quite enough—although no doubt she would learn how to handle herself better in such situations.

Yet if she trod the path that everyone expected of her, she would have to put all of it behind her to become a society hostess and mother. Such would be her fate if she married anyone, even Harry.

One thing she would never do, despite the fact that her secret was out, was sing at a party, not even her own. She had vowed as much in February. Her voice was far too big anyway. Regardless of what Mariana had said, having tasted the exhilaration of a grand stage, the paltry setting of a genteel drawing room simply wouldn't satisfy her.

Olivia's throat tightened as if her vocal cords wanted to protest against being relegated to inactivity, gathering metaphorical dust, nothing more than relics of past triumphs.

At that moment, Ebbings opened the door for her, looking at her with a mixture of disapproval and pity.

"Is Lady Ambrose in?" Olivia asked.

"She has not yet left her chamber," Ebbings answered in his smooth, expressionless voice.

Olivia didn't bother to remove her pelisse, untying her hat and peeling off her gloves as she mounted the stairs. She had Lady Mariana's invitation card in her reticule and hoped it might soothe her mother's agitated spirits to know that they were still being invited somewhere.

She knocked softly on the door of her mother's apartments and a feeble voice said, "Come."

The blinds were drawn, and the viscountess lay on the sofa near the hearth. "It's you," she said. "I'm glad, because I've instructed Hetty to start packing your trunks to go back to the priory tomorrow. I've come to the conclusion that you must get away from London for a time. I shall invite Hartland to visit and you will accept his proposal."

Leave London? Now? "But Mama! I have an invitation for us, to a dinner at Lady Mariana's house tomorrow evening. We can't go now!"

"I shall send our regrets. She must understand."

This was a disaster. It would ruin everything! "I think," she said, tossing ideas around in her mind and hoping to alight on one that would persuade her mother to postpone this departure for at least a day or two, "that to flee from London now would be more damaging to my reputation than staying and behaving as though nothing very terrible had happened."

"That's absurd. Only distance will eventually silence all the wagging tongues. You've acted shockingly. You've ignored all the rules of polite society. I don't know why you did it. Did you not think of what would happen to all of us? I'm frankly astonished that, having reflected soberly overnight, the duke hasn't come to withdraw his suit."

"He won't." Olivia sat in the low chair by the fireplace and tossed her hat and gloves onto the floor. "He believes it's his duty to marry me, even though he doesn't love me."

"So it is! Nonetheless, we shall go to Hampshire tomorrow. I can't bear the thought of showing my face to any of my friends."

"I, however, have no intention of leaving," Olivia said. "And for my sake, you will bear London for at least one more day." She stood and looked down at her mother. "We *must* go to Lady Mariana's dinner tomorrow night."

Lady Ambrose stared at her daughter open-mouthed for a moment, then said "How dare you tell me what I must do! Lost to all propriety, you are. Tainted. Soiled. If you don't do as I say I shall cut off your allowance. Well, perhaps not that. But I shall think of something. I have a headache. Leave me. I can't talk about it any longer."

Olivia turned on her heels and left the room, her low spirits suddenly agitated, as if knowing her mother's intentions had awakened her to her surroundings. All at once she noticed the signs of feverish preparations for imminent departure. Trunks had been hauled out of the attics. A housemaid went by with a roll of silver paper in her arms for packing. Two footmen with armloads of Holland covers descended the stairs to the first floor.

Her mother was serious. Olivia thought perhaps she simply said it to be dramatic, that she was a little hysterical. But it appeared not.

She entered her room to find Hetty already placing gowns in trunks.

"What are you doing?" Olivia said.

Startled, Hetty paused with a muslin day dress draped across her arms and dipped a shallow curtsy. "Lady Ambrose said—"

"It does not matter what she said. I will not go away tomorrow." It had taken no more than a minute for Olivia to make her decision. "Instead, I shall go tonight, but I only need a valise. Please pack that for me, with a walking dress and an evening gown and whatever I need for the night. I suppose I should have a bandbox as well, for a hat and headdress, and my topazes."

Hetty's eyes opened wide. "Where will you go? Shall you take me with you?"

"No. I can't. You must stay here. I'm sorry and there's no time to explain."

The look of real chagrin on Hetty's face nearly broke Olivia's resolve. But if she wanted to sneak away without attracting any notice she could hardly take her abigail. "I shall return, I promise. I just don't know when," she said.

Hetty curtsied, eyes focused on her feet, and said, "Yes, Miss Olivia."

Olivia approached Hetty and said, "I beg you to tell no one that I have gone." She placed her hand on Hetty's shoulder, and gave it a squeeze. "You've been loyal to me and I know it's been hard. I am grateful."

No more than thirty minutes later, Olivia stepped out of the servants' door at the back of the mansion carrying her own bandbox and valise and walked to the nearest hackney stand. "Grosvenor Square," she said to the jarvey.

With those words, she took an irrevocable step. One that was even more daring in its way than unmasking herself on stage. Every muscle in her body tensed and her skin tingled with excitement.

Adelheid would take her in. And no one would look for her there because they could not know of the friendship newly formed between them. It was the only way she could think of to ensure that her mother would attend Lady Mariana's dinner the next night. And that was absolutely imperative.

Lady Ambrose must be there to see her daughter take charge of her own life.

∽

THE LAST THING ADELHEID EXPECTED WAS A VISITOR THAT evening. Her conversation with Otto had exhausted her. She wasn't certain she'd told him very well, that he really believed her. But it was a beginning at least.

She was going over and over the scenes from earlier in the day when Grandison announced Olivia. He'd barely uttered the last syllable of her name before the girl ran into the drawing room carrying a bandbox.

"Olivia! What is it?" Adelheid turned to the butler, who stood expectantly behind Miss Fontenoy. "Grandison, have the best guest bedchamber prepared and take Miss Fontenoy's things up."

"Yes, Your Highness," he said, bowed, and took hold of the ribbon holding Olivia's band box together. She was so distracted she didn't let it go and he had to clear his throat before she looked in his direction and relinquished it.

Once he closed the door behind him, Olivia said, "Oh Adelheid! Everything might be ruined! It will never work!" She clutched her hands together and walked back and forth in quick strides in front of the hearth.

"First, *sei ruhe*, calm yourself. You're obviously going to remain here tonight." Adelheid rose and started unbuttoning Olivia's pelisse while Olivia yanked off her gloves and untied the ribbons of her poke bonnet.

After laying the discarded garments on a chair, Adelheid said, "That's better. Now sit down and tell me what happened." She took Olivia's hands and propelled her to the sofa, gently pulling her down to sit next to her. Never had Adelheid been so aware of how young the heiress was. In that moment, she seemed almost as much a child as Otto. "Does Lady Ambrose know you are here?" She guessed, on the evidence of almost no luggage, that Olivia had fled from her home.

"No! She doesn't. If I'd stayed there she would have made me go to the country tomorrow. She's already having all my gowns packed in trunks and getting ready to shut up Fontenoy House!" Olivia's eyes darted around as if looking for a solid anchor somewhere, or the answer to a question she hadn't yet asked.

"Ah, I see," said Adelheid. "Coming here will put you out of her reach. But not forever! The solution to that problem must be faced at tomorrow's dinner. Will she still come?"

Olivia bit her lower lip. "I think I can make her. I'll send a note telling her I am safe, and that she will find me at Lady Mariana's when she arrives at the time on the card, half-past seven."

"Are you certain she won't just send someone to get you and spirit you away?"

Olivia shook her head. "She wouldn't do that. She'd want to keep it from the servants and from anyone else. I believe she'll come. I'll tell her that if nothing changes by the end of the evening, I will go home with her and accompany her to Hampshire the day after."

Adelheid laid her hand on Olivia's cheek. "My dear, I believe all will be resolved tomorrow. You will not have to flee London. I feel in my heart that our plan will succeed."

The two friends talked for a time and later supped together. Adelheid sent Olivia up to bed early, instructing her own abigail to help her with whatever she needed.

As Adelheid walked to her bedroom down the corridor from Olivia's, she asked herself where her confidence came from. She had no idea if the next day would result in the resolution they both desired. In fact, all could easily go horribly wrong. But would either of them be any worse off? It seemed the only thing to do, for her as well as Olivia.

So much was at stake. At least she'd gotten over the hurdle of telling Otto the full truth. What came next would be easy compared to that.

NEVER BEFORE HAD HARRY BEEN IN SUCH CONFLICT WITH himself. As he sat over tea in the dining parlor of his set at the Albany, every fiber of his being wanted to reach out and comfort Olivia, to tell her that all would be well and that he loved her to distraction.

But she would soon be betrothed to Hartland. It was the only way, despite what Olivia insisted she would do. Only the rank of duchess would protect her from censure, ensure her a respectable life. He tried to banish the thought that she might be equally protected as a marchioness. What good did it do to think it? Who would ever prefer reserved, retiring Lewiston to the dashing, daring, charming Duke of Hartland? It wasn't as if he, Harry, had a handsome fortune to go along with his rank. And he'd seen them kiss.

Yes, to save Olivia, he must relinquish all hope of marrying her. It was the only way.

*This is madness!* Lewiston thought, and was about to dress for dinner when his man came in with a card on a silver tray.

A dinner. At Lady Mariana's. Tomorrow night. How very odd. Not only that, but the invitation requested that he arrive at precisely a quarter past seven. Why? he wondered. It was too early for town hours. But the invitation was specific. And it was from Mariana. Even in his disappointment he liked her too well to ignore such a summons, for summons it did appear to be.

He had thought at its outset that this season things would

be different. They were, very. Just not in the way he'd hoped. Perhaps he was destined not to marry at all.

Perhaps when his sisters came out he would meet someone he would like well enough to wed and who would tolerate him.

That lady would have to love music, however, and he had a sinking feeling she might not exist.

HARTLAND WAS SURPRISED WHEN HIS MOTHER SUMMONED HIM to her room after breakfast the next day. He thought they'd said everything to the purpose the night before. But clearly she had something further to tell him.

She was still in her black lace dressing gown and cap seated in a chair by the fireplace.

After he greeted her she handed him an elegant pasteboard card with gilt edges. A flowing scrawl that Hartland recognized as belonging to Lady Mariana Thorne requested the duchess and her son to come to a small dinner party that evening. They were to arrive at precisely a quarter to seven. She said it had something to do with a planned entertainment.

"You know I don't go out yet, but of course you must go, if you wish," the duchess said.

Hartland examined the card. It was an odd invitation, to be sure. Lady Mariana entertained frequently, but rarely did she have dinner parties. Her dining room was too small to accommodate many guests. He thought it must be something particular for her to request the presence of both him and his mother. "Won't you consider going with me?" he asked. "You've been in seclusion for months. It would do you good to get out."

"I don't know. I'm still in my blacks."

"I expect she realizes that and will respect you for attending so attired. It would please me to escort you to a private dinner. You like Lady Mariana."

After a few minutes the duchess sighed and said, "Very well. To please you. But I won't stay late."

"I shall take you home whenever you are ready," Hartland said, and kissed his mother's cheek.

# CHAPTER 37

Olivia was to be the first to arrive at the house on South Audley Street. Adelheid would be the third, once Hartland and his mother were already there. One of Adelheid's footmen summoned a hack for Olivia. After checking to make sure no one saw her, she climbed in and directed the driver.

Fulton opened the door and led her up to the drawing room, where Lady Mariana stood instructing a footman to place a selection of spangled loo masks on a central table. She came forward to greet Olivia and said, "You look lovely, my dear."

Olivia wore an evening dress that had just been delivered from Madame Pauline's a few days earlier, an ivory silk gown fastened with tiers of lace on the short sleeves and green satin ribbon trim. The décolletage was edged in scalloped lace and Adelheid's abigail had woven matching ribbons through her curls. Her only other ornaments were her topaz and emerald necklace and emerald earbobs. The colors picked up the green tints in her hazel eyes and set off her complexion to advantage. Not for Olivia the pale blues and pinks so popular at the time. They made her look sallow.

"Is all prepared? I'm very nervous. What if no one acts as we hope?" Olivia took the glass of sherry Mariana gave her and put it to her lips, thought better of it, and placed it back on the silver tray. "I need my wits about me. Is Mr. Thorne at the House?" She tried to think of some ordinary topic of conversation to distract her from the sensation that her heart was tumbling wildly in her chest, as if she had leapt off a mountain and was hurtling inexorably toward the hard, unyielding earth.

"Yes, at a late sitting. I've told him a little of what will transpire this evening in case he comes home while we're still in the middle of everything."

Olivia nodded but hardly heard her. This one evening would determine the direction of her entire life. The next couple of hours would be the most important she had ever spent, even beyond those on stage at the King's Theatre. "I suppose it's time for me to go to your dressing room."

She turned to leave, but Mariana stopped her, handing her one of the masks. "You'll need this when I send for you," she said.

A footman escorted Olivia upstairs to the dressing room attached to Mariana's bedroom. They chose this room because it was directly above the drawing room and, by leaving the door open a crack, she would be able to make out some of the voices and hear the guests arrive.

Olivia had been over and over the plan, had rehearsed her lines the night before until she could keep her eyes open no longer. She hoped Mariana had taken the time to commit hers to memory as well. Only she, Adelheid, and Mariana knew of the intricate ballet they'd created to unravel the complicated knots of misunderstanding, mistrust, and misplaced scruples.

It wasn't long before another knock sounded on the front door. Olivia closed her eyes, hoping that it would be Hartland and the duchess, who had been asked to arrive at that time.

"Lady Mariana, I believe you know my mother, the Duchess of Hartland." The duke's rich voice carried up the stairs.

Olivia let her breath out and put her hands together in a gesture of prayer. *Please, Mariana, please make everyone understand.*

HARTLAND WAS SURPRISED THAT NO ONE BESIDES LADY Mariana was there to greet them.

Mariana curtsied and said, "Thank you for gracing our gathering with your presence, Duchess. I know you are still in mourning. But this will be a small party, almost all people you already know, and others whose acquaintance you will most particularly wish to make."

The duchess declined a glass of ratafia. Mariana led her to a chair by the fire. "I believe you are in daily expectation that your son the duke will be most suitably betrothed," Mariana said.

The older lady looked up at Mariana and raised one eyebrow. Hartland cleared his throat. What was Mariana doing? Nothing was settled. In fact, the last time he'd spoken to her, Miss Fontenoy had flatly refused him. He was by no means certain he could persuade her that marriage to him was truly her only option.

"You have not yet made the acquaintance of the fortunate lady, I understand," Mariana said, directing a quelling look at Hartland.

Why had she not uttered Miss Fontenoy's name?

A moment later another knock at the front door announced the arrival of more guests. A low murmur of greetings was all Hartland could hear.

Mariana walked over to a table and picked up two loo masks, handing one to the duke and one to his mother. "I am afraid I could not resist the temptation to make of this evening a bit of a game. If you would kindly use these masks. I promise there is nothing improper. I just wanted to indulge in a little innocent intrigue."

Hartland had, quite frankly, had enough of masks to last a lifetime. He exchanged a glance with the duchess, who then dutifully did as Mariana bid her. What was this notoriously mercurial woman planning? Whatever it was, he had little to lose now. He sighed as he lifted his mask on its slender wand and held it up so he could see through the eyeholes.

A moment later, Mariana went out to the head of the stairs carrying two more masks. She exchanged no words with the guests who had just arrived, but the mystery of their identity was soon solved—for Hartland at least—when a tall, stately figure with blond hair swept up into an elegant coiffure, one long curl draped over her shoulder, glided into the room. At that moment, he was glad of the mask. The effect of the princess's arrival on his mind and heart would have been easy for his mother to read. Behind the safety of the flimsy paper, he could look his fill at the lady who had most recently disturbed his peace but who now was as unattainable as the moon.

When a small child dressed in fine knee breeches and stockings and a velvet coat emerged from behind Adelheid, Hartland smiled behind his mask. He wondered how long young Otto's clothes would remain so pristine. He looked toward the duchess. She sat bolt upright in her chair, immobile, the mask so still its stem looked like an extension of her slender hand.

The princess made a deep curtsy to the duchess and motioned Otto to bow. "I am pleased to make your acquaintance, Duchess."

The duchess put out her hand to Adelheid. "You must be the lady who has captured my son's heart."

Hartland was about to correct his mother's misapprehension when Mariana stepped in quickly and said, "I believe so."

"You believe so?" The duchess turned to her son. "You didn't tell me she was so beautiful. I can see even through the mask, although I wish we could put these things down!"

Mariana hastened forward and touched the duchess's hand. "Soon, Your Grace."

"I don't think I understand why there is a child here. Is he your page? Such an odd affectation for a lady in her first season."

Hartland's heart was pounding. Standing before him was a woman who was the very embodiment of everything he ever wished for. But her small shadow, young Otto, complicated everything. The princess must have a reason for bringing him to that party. She could easily have left him at home with the nurse. It flashed through Hartland's mind that, after Otto's recent adventures Princess Adelheid might have decided it was simply safer to keep the boy at her side— a thought that made him smile.

As if he had read the duke's mind, Otto walked out from behind his mother and approached Hartland, making him a bow and then tentatively reaching for his hand. Hartland grasped the warm little mitt and gazed briefly down into the extraordinary eyes glittering up at him through the holes in the mask.

Another knock sounded and Mariana once more picked up two loo masks and left the room.

"Philip, what is to do here?" the duchess asked, letting the hand holding her mask fall and looking back and forth between Hartland and the lady whose eyes he could not tear his own away from. "Are you or are you not Miss Fontenoy?" she asked.

Hartland found he couldn't speak. He wanted to tell his mother everything. If not for the masks, she would have guessed instantly. But what would that serve? He would have to go through with his betrothal to Miss Fontenoy. They would have a loveless, yet possibly an affectionate marriage. That must be enough. It would have to be enough.

Perhaps his inner turmoil communicated itself to Otto, who inched closer to him and clung more tightly to his hand.

ADELHEID WASN'T READY TO REVEAL HER IDENTITY TO THE duchess yet, so she simply nodded in her direction in answer to her question. She was saved the trouble of figuring out what to say when Mariana reentered the room with Lord Lewiston and Signore Tetrazzini in her wake.

After Lewiston greeted the duchess, Mariana introduced Tetrazzini to her. "*Eccelenza,*" he said, bowing extravagantly. He turned to await a similar introduction to Adelheid, but when he saw her he stiffened.

Adelheid moved away from Hartland to stand near Lewiston. She didn't know him, having only seen him from afar at the ball and the rout party. Now that she stood closer to him, she could see more clearly what sort of man he was and understood immediately why Olivia loved him. His expressive eyes indicated that he was alive to the currents of emotion already swirling through the formal room. Lewiston was the kind of man who would love with consideration, with depth, with his whole heart and soul.

This, perhaps, accounted for the fact that he did not seem

entirely composed as he walked over to Hartland and gave him a stiff bow. Otto looked up at the duke and then transferred his attention to Lewiston. The two men hardly noticed the boy. If Lewiston saw that Otto's small brown hand was engulfed in the duke's strong grip he gave no indication of it.

*It's time, Frankel!* Adelheid thought. *Where is she?* Otto would have a part to play, but she wanted him out of the way for a while.

Meanwhile, Tetrazzini wandered closer to her. The trouble with the masks was that it was hard to signal danger to Mariana with a look.

Somehow she got the message and hurried over to say to Tetrazzini, "And of course, you know the opera singer."

It wasn't a lie, Adelheid thought, a surreptitious smile lighting her face behind her mask. Tetrazzini recognized her most certainly. Would he stay silent? She'd seen him last at La Fenice. The singing teacher had been in London ever since she married the prince, and doing very well for himself, as she understood. She put out her hand to him. He took it and bowed over it. When he unbent he opened his mouth to say something. Adelheid met his eyes and winked at him when no one was looking. Through the holes in the mask those piercing dark Italian eyes narrowed suspiciously. Nonetheless, he took the hint and closed his mouth.

Adelheid then returned to where Lewiston and Hartland stood as rigid as if they had put down roots through the floor. She reached out and wrested Otto's hand from the duke's. Hartland looked down as she did so and their fingers touched, sending heat all through her. *No,* she thought. Perhaps when all this was over they could find somewhere to talk. She needed to finish the conversation they had started the day before.

Instead, she turned to Lewiston. "Lord Lewiston," she

said, and curtsied lower than her degree required. She was certain that the marquess had also not failed to recognize her, but she believed the duchess still hadn't guessed her identity. Lewiston nodded to her, picking up her unspoken hint, and then his eyes shifted back to Hartland.

It was so odd! Almost all of them knew each other—certainly no one was fooled by the superficial masks, but it seemed as if these flimsy bits of decorated paper cast a spell over them and robbed them of their ability to act like sentient beings.

Otto yanked Adelheid's hand to get her attention. He was near to bursting, so impatient was he becoming with his enforced silence. Adelheid had explained to him that he wasn't to utter a word to the guests and to keep his mask up in front of his face. She told him he wouldn't have to stay quiet for very long because Frankel would come to take him away after a short time. To him, it was a game, and he was beginning to tire of it. To Adelheid, nothing could have been more serious.

"We shall have our own little unmasking once everyone is assembled. I'm waiting for two more guests." The note of humor in Mariana's voice cut the tension that had started to mount in the room, particularly between Lewiston and Hartland.

Adelheid kept her eyes on the marquess and the duke. It was easy to see that Lewiston was fighting to contain himself almost as much as Otto was. If what Olivia had told her was indeed true, he must surely be in an emotional stew. He clenched and unclenched the fist that wasn't holding the loo mask, his jaw so rigid Adelheid suspected he was grinding his teeth.

Mariana moved closer to Adelheid and whispered, "What if she doesn't come? She has to be here."

Olivia had told Mariana she worried that her mother

would stubbornly stay at home despite the message she sent her, a message that hinted that if she didn't come to the dinner, Hartland would cry off.

Uncomfortable silence reigned for a few more moments, until a peremptory knock on the front door made everyone flinch and Mariana once again left to greet the next guest, loo mask in hand.

Adelheid moved slowly back toward Hartland until she was standing near enough to hear his slow breathing, to smell his hair pomade and shoe polish. It was the way a gentleman smelled. Her movement forced Lewiston to step courteously away, breaking the tension between him and the duke. The effect of Adelheid's sudden proximity to Hartland heightened her awareness of his body, his strength. She yearned to lose herself in his arms. But she mustn't think such thoughts. Not now. Not yet.

Quick steps mounted the stairs and the small, plump figure of Lady Ambrose burst into the room, her loo mask only held in the general direction of her face. "I don't know what everyone is doing here, if this is some kind of pleasantry. A game, Lady Mariana called it," she said. Then she noticed the duchess seated by the fire and curtsied deeply as Mariana made the introduction.

Her polite greeting accomplished, she said "Where is my daughter?" The viscountess turned in a slow circle, examining each person in the room, letting her eyes rest longest on Adelheid. Not seeing Olivia, said, "She is not here."

Her words acted like a stone dropped in the middle of a still pool, and everyone started talking.

"What are you doing here?" Hartland asked Lewiston.

"I might ask you the same."

Sensing imminent trouble, Adelheid said, "You will both soon enough know the reason for this gathering."

"I really would prefer to see everyone's face. It is most unsettling," the duchess said.

"*È pazzo!*" exclaimed Tetrazzini, "*Ees* clear who we are, so I no understand the masks." To prove his point, he removed his and waved it around.

Lady Ambrose eyed him with disdain. "I blame it all on you, Signore!"

"All what?" the duchess said.

This signaled to Otto that he could also lower his mask and he joyfully did so, releasing his mother's hand and snaking through all the guests, a somewhat fiendish smile lighting his face. As he passed close to Hartland again, the duke reached out one strong hand and gripped his shoulder. "You are in a drawing room. Use your manners young cub! Or I will dunk you in a horse pond."

At the sound of this command, Adelheid turned away from the duchess, ready to spirit Otto out of the way, with or without Frankel. But to her surprise, her son stood erect and docile next to Hartland, still smiling.

No one had noticed Mariana leaving the room to meet another guest and give her a loo mask.

THE MUFFLED SOUNDS OF INTERMITTENT REMARKS FILTERED UP to Olivia. Mariana promised she would send for her as soon as everyone was assembled, which seemed to be taking a very long time. Then, she heard the unmistakable hectic rhythm of her mother's footsteps on the stairs. Soon after, conversation erupted in the drawing room. *It must be time!* Olivia thought, checking herself in the mirror on the dresser.

She was pale and her lips trembled. Could she really do this?

A moment later, Mariana walked into the dressing room,

followed by Félicité, whose arrival no one noticed in the chaos that followed Lady Ambrose's entrance.

"Are you quite ready?" Mariana asked.

Félicité tutted. "You must permit me, Mademoiselle Fontenoy. Just a little rouge." She reached into her reticule but Olivia caught hold of her wrist.

"No. I must be as I am."

"I have the pin," Mariana said, and gave it to Félicité. "You know what to do."

"*Ouai*. But I still say, *tu es folle.*"

Her comment gave no opportunity for answer. The three of them left the dressing room and walked quietly down the stairs—first Mariana, then Félicité, then Olivia.

The footman opened the drawing room door and a cacophony of voices crescendoed into the stairwell.

"Explain to me exactly who you are."

"You would not be so cruel!"

"Of course not!"

"*Ma non so che passa!*"

Mariana cleared her throat and all seven guests turned to look at her, only Adelheid still holding her loo mask in front of her face. "Before we go down to dinner, this lady has something to say to you all." She and Félicité stepped into the room and flanked the door, which now framed Olivia, standing tall and calm, holding her mask up and surveying everyone in the room.

No one spoke for a moment, then Lady Ambrose said, "How dare you! What were you thinking to run off like that?"

Mariana held up her hand, "If you would allow Miss Fontenoy to speak, Lady Ambrose."

The viscountess shrank back, her eyes glittering with rage.

Olivia took two steps forward. "You are all here because of me. You are here because I chose to disguise myself so that

I could sing at the King's Theatre, a dream I have had ever since I knew I had a voice."

"*Che belissima voce!*" Tetrazzini whispered.

"You ..." She looked directly at her mother. "You see in me only the means to an end. I am sorry, truly, that I have found a way to interfere with your plans to elevate our family's rank in society."

At that, Hartland took a step forward. "Miss Fontenoy, you know we must marry—"

"Don't speak!" Olivia said. "I have not finished. I know my actions have transgressed propriety in the most public way. But I am not sorry. On that stage I felt more truly myself than I ever have in a ballroom or a drawing room. It is places like this ..." she swept her arm around to indicate the room, "where everyone sees me as an heiress that I must put on an act as an eager come-out, as someone willing to play the mercenary courtship game that is required of every young lady in the *ton*. That person, that member of the *haut ton*, is not me. I may as well have been masked through the entire season for all I have revealed of my true character."

Olivia, keeping her mask steadily in front of her face, walked forward to where the duchess sat, and curtsied deeply. "From what little your son has told me, I believe you are very fond of him. Surely you would not want to see him unhappy? I think that, if he married me, he would be."

The duchess kept her keen eyes focused on Olivia.

"Yet perhaps you believe that if he withdraws his suit from me, he will be behaving in an ungentlemanlike manner —even though I have given him every reason to do so. In fact, I had that purpose in mind when I unmasked myself at the benefit."

At this, Lady Ambrose gasped. "You don't know what you are saying!"

Olivia took hold of her mother's hand. "Yes, I do know.

And I told you so already." She turned to face Hartland directly. "As I did you. But I want to tell you now, again, in front of everyone, that I do not accept your offer of marriage."

Hartland took a step toward her and reached out his hand. "If it's because of the way I behaved, I know I was at fault, that you wouldn't have unmasked yourself without that provocation and so none of this would have happened were it not for my thoughtless actions."

Olivia couldn't help softening a bit at this. He hadn't actually apologized to her at the theatre, for all his noble words. "I believe you never meant to hurt me, Duke. You behaved toward Miss Fontenoy with courtesy and kindness. A different lady would have found you impossible to resist. Honesty compels me to say that no matter how you acted toward me, I would have ended up making this decision."

Lady Ambrose staggered. Seeing this, Lewiston ran to her and guided her to a chair. "Someone get some smelling salts!"

The duchess stood and walked slowly to face Olivia. "You refuse the dignities of a duchess?"

"I care nothing for such things. I never have. My dear friend, Princess Adelheid, asked me only yesterday what I wanted from my life, something no one has ever asked of me —not my mother, not Lord Hartland, nor even Lord Lewiston has thought to inquire about my own wishes." She reached out her hand toward Adelheid who came forward and lowered her mask. "We are alike. We are both opera singers. Only Adelheid left the world of the stage to rise into the nobility, and I left the nobility to descend to the level of the stage."

"We are ruined," Lady Ambrose murmured in a stifled voice.

Olivia's heart was thumping. She needed to continue, but she felt as if she could not draw breath. What she said next mattered more than anything she'd said to that point. "We need not be." Olivia gentled her voice and knelt down beside her mother, placing her almost at Harry's feet. She laid her loo mask down on the floor and lifted her eyes to meet Harry's.

"Harry, you, of all people, must know that music flows in my veins, and that to take it away would kill me as surely as draining all the blood from my body." She reached up her hand and he took it, gently trying to pull her up to her feet, but she resisted and instead drew him down to kneel next to her. At first he looked confused and blushed. Then she smiled at him. "What I want is to marry someone who feels just the same as I do, who understands that important part of me, and who might—possibly—enable me to continue performing in some way."

"Impossible!" Lady Ambrose said, her voice sharp.

But Lewiston said, "No, it's not impossible. At least, the marrying part. I know this looks very undignified, but Lady Ambrose, since Lord Ambrose is not here, and since your daughter has refused the duke's proposal, I am asking your permission to pay my addresses to Olivia."

Before she could answer him Olivia said, "There is no need, Harry. I am already yours in every way that truly matters."

He stood, still holding her hand, and Olivia allowed herself to be pulled up and into his embrace.

The world fell away. It did not matter that eight people were watching them, doubtless some of them disapproving. They could look all they wanted—but only one person truly saw her. And that person held her in a fierce embrace, an embrace she had wanted since the moment they first met.

·  ·  ·

HARTLAND DIDN'T KNOW WHETHER TO BE GRATEFUL, TO FEEL ashamed, or to laugh. Of course Harry should marry Olivia.

While everyone was riveted to the drama the couple was enacting, Félicité had made her way to where he stood. "You recall me, per'aps, M'Lord?"

*Christ!* he thought. Could he never escape from that humiliating circumstance? "The seamstress. Yes."

"I am also a *chère amie* of the princess and she said I should find a way to put this back into your 'ands." She reached into her reticule and drew out something wrapped in a lady's handkerchief.

"What is it?"

"Oh, *je pense que vous sauriez.*"

He did not unwrap the object, but felt it, and in an instant knew precisely what it was. When he looked up, he found that Adelheid was standing in front of him, one eyebrow raised and a smile lurking in the corners of her mouth. "Your friend has—what do you English say—cut you out?"

"Thank heavens for that!" he said, taking her hand and pressing a tender kiss on her fingers. "Might I call on you tomorrow, Adelheid?"

"If you still wish to after this evening, of course."

What on earth did she mean? "Why would I not?"

She made no answer, instead turning away to the assembled guests who were all clustered around Harry and Olivia, smiling and felicitating. "If I may be so bold as to wrest your attention from so happy a scene!"

One by one, the others looked in her direction, all traces of confusion and anxiety now gone from their faces. Even Lady Ambrose had color in her cheeks and a reluctant smile on her face.

"I must tell you a story," Adelheid began.

Just then, Frankel arrived. The nursemaid's presence gave Adelheid an opportunity to pause and gather her thoughts.

The nurse came to Otto and took his hand, pulling him away from Hartland's side.

"*Komm, Kind,*" she murmured. "We will have supper here."

Otto gave a wide-mouthed yawn and a quiet chuckle skittered among the guests. Adelheid waited until the door closed behind them before speaking again.

"My story is long. I suggest you all be seated," she said.

And then, summoning all her courage, she told the entire group about everything that had happened to her since she left the operatic stage and married a prince—a group that comprised her new friend Olivia, standing close to her betrothed; Olivia's mother, wearing a look of relief; Lord Lewiston, who now smiled beatifically; her old friends Tetrazzini and Félicité, clearly waiting for an opportunity to gossip about their worlds; the remarkable Lady Mariana Thorne, standing like a good angel spreading her wings over the people she cared about; and the Duchess of Hartland and her son, who held all her hopes for the future in their hands.

WHEN SHE FINISHED HER NARRATIVE, EVERYONE SAT IN stunned silence.

"The boy. He's your son?" It was the duchess.

Adelheid nodded.

"What do you intend to do?"

"I can tell you what I *had* intended to do, Duchess. When I first came to London, it was with the sole purpose of beguiling your son, of making him fall in love with me and, with the dazzling fortune I would dangle in front of him, persuade him to offer for me and to adopt my son. I intended to leave the final condition of the will shrouded in mystery, only revealing it when it was too late for him to back out.

"The fact that he offered for Olivia did not deter me, because I could see how it was. They did not love each other.

It became completely clear to me the night of Lady Ferndale's rout party that Miss Fontenoy and Lord Lewiston were destined for each other. So I felt my way was clear.

"But in a very little time, I found I could not do as I planned. I began to care too much for Hartland's happiness to trick him like that. And there was Otto…"

At this, tears filled her eyes. She tried hard to blink them back but a few escaped her quick handkerchief and rolled down her cheeks.

"I don't know what I shall do now. Otto and I will find a way to survive. Perhaps you, Signore Tetrazzini, can help establish me as a singing teacher in London, where my shameful story is not generally known."

At this, Hartland rose quickly and in two strides reached Adelheid's side. He took both her hands, clasping them palm to palm in a strong grip. "You shall not do so. You shall marry me and, if it is not too disagreeable to you, resign your princess crown to adopt instead the coronet of a duchess." He opened her sealed palms and pressed kisses on them one at a time.

Adelheid could hardly breathe. "Philip, do you understand what this means?" She looked past him at his mother. "Duchess, you know I would not permit him to throw the family name away like this if you have any objection at all."

The duchess rose. She started to speak but was interrupted by the abrupt arrival of another guest who had pushed past Walton and entered the room unannounced.

"Nicholas!" Adelheid said. "What are you doing here?"

He bowed to the assembled company who gaped at him in varying expressions of confusion. "Forgive my interruption, but I have something important to say to the princess, and it cannot wait a moment longer."

Adelheid gripped Hartland's hands. She had no idea what Nicholas was going to say, and feared that—having been a close confidant of the prince for most of his life—he would say that in any case, even marrying as stipulated in the prince's will would not secure her the inheritance. So be it. She'd already reconciled herself to a different life.

"Please speak, Nicholas." Adelheid fought to keep her voice steady.

"I could not help overhearing from outside in the hall—your butler did quite right trying to keep me from entering, Lady Mariana, so do not blame him for this breach of etiquette—I could hear, Your Highness, that you have confessed all not only to the duke but to everyone who could have any concern in the affair."

He looked to Adelheid for confirmation, and she gave a slow nod.

He reached into his coat and pulled out a document. "I took the liberty of consulting an attorney, as you may have guessed, a Mr. Phineas Bunford, Esquire, about the peculiar terms of the prince's will. This attorney gave me to understand that the will was perfectly legal so long as it was properly witnessed, that the codicil could indeed be enforced."

The silence rang in Adelheid's ears. What was the man doing? Why did he have to come just to tell everyone what they already knew?

"I also have a copy of Prince Alexander's will." He drew another document from his coat pocket, a document tied with a scarlet cord. He unpicked the knot on the cord and opened it. "I was that witness."

*Why? Why? Why did Nicholas come to England with them?* Adelheid thought, her mind awhirl. *Why take such care and interest in Otto if his intention was all along to disrupt her plans?*

"But the witness's signature is not mine. I did not want to put my name to such an infamous document so I penned a false one. I scribbled it so that it could hardly be deciphered. The prince was close to death and didn't notice. In any event,

Attorney Bunford is persuaded that this fact renders the codicil null and void."

Everyone gasped. Adelheid's breath was trapped in her lungs. When she could finally speak, she said, "But you were loyal to the prince! You always did as he asked. If your actions did not reflect your true feelings, why did you not help me before that time?"

"I did not know until the drafting of the codicil that Otto still lived. I'm not sure what I would have done had the prince survived, but in these past weeks I have come to know myself better as well."

"Why did you say nothing to me at the time, that the signature wasn't yours?" Why did he stand by while she put herself through so much trouble and now pain?

"I am sorry, Your Highness. I didn't know for certain that what I did would have such an effect. Not until I consulted the attorney in London. I also hoped that you wouldn't show yourself to be little better than the prince, that you wouldn't seek to gain your inheritance and secure Otto's future at the expense of your own and another's happiness. I see that you have chosen not to do so and I reveal this to you now with true joy."

He held out the two documents to her. She walked forward and took them, still in a daze.

"So does this mean the duke can marry you without adopting Otto, and you'll still inherit everything?" Olivia said.

Suddenly, Adelheid blushed. How foolish, she thought. Before she had a moment to consider, she found herself engulfed in Hartland's strong embrace. She dropped the documents and threaded her arms around his neck, lifting her chin to meet his kiss. They only broke apart when everyone in the room began to clap and cheer.

Adelheid felt the tears on her cheeks and tried to wipe

them away with her hands, but Hartland stopped her and kissed them away. "Will you marry me? And will you permit me to stand in the role of father to that rascal you call Otto?"

She laughed, and said, "Yes! Yes! But you don't have to, you know."

"I want to. I can imagine liking nothing better than teaching him how to behave and ride and handle the ribbons like a gentleman. Except, perhaps, being able to wake up every morning with you."

A chorus of voices began to speak in accents of delight and excitement until Lady Mariana clapped her hands and said, "My lords, ladies, and gentlemen, *È finito—la commedia!* And Fulton tells me dinner is served."

Everyone laughed, and they all wandered out, chatting merrily and congratulating both happy couples as they went down the stairs to the dining room.

AFTER DINNER THAT EVENING, ADELHEID, OTTO, FRANKEL, and Nicholas went back to number twelve Grosvenor Square in one carriage, while Hartland escorted his mother in his carriage to Hartland House in the same square and saw her into the hands of her abigail.

"Do you wish me happy, truly, Mama?" he said.

She laid her hand on his cheek and said, "Yes. I believe this is the match you were meant to have, in spite of all your efforts to the contrary. I think Adelheid will make you happy and although I don't know her well enough yet to say, I believe you will also make her happy."

Hartland kissed his mother's cheek. "I want to marry her tomorrow."

"The *ton* would never forgive you!" the duchess said, a saucy gleam in her eye.

"Do you really expect me to wait?" Hartland said, smiling.

"No. Good night, Philip."

It was not late and Hartland was too restless to retire yet. So he put his evening cloak on once again and let himself out the front door of the house intending just to wander around until he was tired enough to sleep.

Of course, his steps took him in the direction of number twelve.

He was halfway there when the door of that house opened and a willowy figure in a black evening cloak, her fair hair covered with its hood, walked down the steps, turned toward number sixteen, and smiled.

They met halfway to her door.

"Good evening," Hartland said as he took Adelheid into his arms.

"Good evening," she replied, even as her lips responded to his kiss, opening to him as if she was already completely at home in the circle of his embrace. She surrendered to him, accepted the urgent probing of his tongue, returning the passion she could feel coursing through his body.

When they broke apart, she felt as if her limbs had turned to liquid. "We can't stay out here," she whispered into his ear.

He groaned with desire. "I want you. I have wanted you ever since I first saw you."

"Then have me," Adelheid whispered, taking his hand and leading him back to her house. He desired her, she did not doubt it. But did he love her? With men, that was always hard to know.

He put his arm around her waist and said, "Are you certain?"

Adelheid looked up at him with such pure longing in her eyes that she answered his question without a word passing her lips.

Together they entered the house and climbed the stairs to

her bedchamber. She opened the door and drew Philip in, closing and locking it behind him.

"The servants?" he said as he kissed her temple and the corner of her eye, then ran his tongue down her nose until he met her open mouth again.

"I don't care," Adelheid breathed as she tugged at his neck cloth and unbuttoned his evening vest.

Philip tore off his coat and pulled his shirt over his head. Adelheid kissed his naked chest.

"I have not lain with a man since before Otto was born," Adelheid said, her pulse racing as Philip led her to the bed, threw the covers back, lifted her off her feet and set her gently on the white sheets.

He stretched himself out along her side, pressing into her.

"Wait, just a moment," Adelheid said.

"What is it?" Philip asked, trailing his fingers down her arm and watching the gooseflesh follow them.

"I just wanted you to know that I love you, all of you, everything you are," Adelheid said, punctuating her words with another kiss . "I was lost almost as soon as I met you. You are not my first love, but you will be my last."

"And I love you," Philip said slowly, with wonder in his voice. "I know now that I have never loved anyone before."

Adelheid smiled as they continued their embraces, each of them basking in the fulfillment of all they had imagined in their dance around each other over the past weeks. She wanted to tell him that although she believed him in that moment, she also knew who he was. It was part of what she loved about him, his extremes of passion, his love of risk. She would do her best to be all he needed or wanted, but she would enter this marriage with her eyes fully open, and a lifetime of sadness and suffering behind her.

What she knew for certain, what she'd known the moment Philip helped Otto out of that tree, was that here was a man with a truly kind heart, a kind heart he took pains to hide. A man who would never be cruel to her and who would learn to love her boy.

Danton would be happy for me, Adelheid thought. He and Philip would have liked each other.

IT WAS POSSIBLE THAT ALL THE SERVANTS KNEW THE NEXT DAY that the Duke of Hartland had not, in fact, arrived for breakfast in his evening clothes. But none of them said a word about it, only smiling at the glow in their mistress's face.

# CHAPTER 38

$\mathcal{B}$oth betrothals were announced in the *Morning Post* and the *Gazette* in the following days, to the surprise of everyone in the *haut ton*.

Adelheid and Philip had a private wedding by special license that same week, deciding to forgo the pomp and ceremony and indulge their need to be together as soon as possible. As a widow, Adelheid was not expected to have a grand wedding, and Hartland was still in mourning, so the *ton* forgave them for their haste. The information that the new duchess's Negro ward was in fact her son and that the duke would be adopting him and raising him in high style was received by the *ton* with some misgivings. But rank will be rank, and the idiosyncracies of a duke and duchess must be tolerated.

Adelheid and Philip spent their honeymoon at Hartmoor Hall, where Otto met his new pony and his new tutor and got up to as much mischief as he could. The dowager moved into the dower house, despite Adelheid's sincere desire for her to stay in the Hall. But she visited with them almost every day, and soon doted on her adopted grandson, spoiling him and cosseting him to Adelheid's delight and vexation.

LADY AMBROSE AND OLIVIA CAME TO AN UNDERSTANDING, and the viscountess forgave her daughter for putting her nerves through such an unpleasant trial. She was only a fraction less satisfied with a marchioness for a daughter than she would have been with a duchess. And she was kindhearted mother enough to rejoice in her daughter's true happiness— even if she would never understand how a shared love of music could be the glue that would bind Olivia and Harry to each other for a lifetime.

Every day before they were married, Lewiston came to the Mount Street house. Lady Ambrose gave up ensuring that someone chaperoned them in the music room, where they went to play duets for piano and violin for hours at a time.

Olivia did not sing, however.

"Are you still determined never to sing in a drawing room?" Harry asked, as they stood shoulder to shoulder sifting through all of Olivia's sheet music, looking for something to play.

Olivia turned to him, searching his eyes. "How could I? Now it would be an affront to my mother, reminding everyone in the *ton* of my disgrace."

"Yet I know you long to sing. And sing on a stage, at that."

"You know I can never do that again." Her voice was quiet but firm.

"Why?" Harry asked. "Why can you not? In a private theatre, perhaps."

"I don't know anyone who has such a thing," Olivia said with a chuckle.

Harry stored this thought away to consider another day, and kissed Olivia before they sat down to play a Haydn sonata.

OLIVIA AND HARRY BECAME MAN AND WIFE IN A PACKED ST. Clement Danes in early June, attended by Harry's sisters as bridesmaids and Hartland as groomsman. The bridal couple spent a tentative but satisfying wedding night together in Mount Street then embarked on a honeymoon to see all the opera houses in Europe before returning to set up house in the elegant abode purchased as a wedding present for them by Lady Ambrose.

The house was not quite as grand as the Mount Street mansion, but still enormous by anyone's standards. A former owner had added a large ballroom on the third floor, extending to the back and consequently enlarging the two floors beneath it.

Olivia shook her head when Harry told her about it. "I can't imagine we'll give many balls. It seems a waste."

"Let's just take a look at it and we'll see what can be done," he said, punctuating his sentence with a kiss on the tip of her nose.

The staff had all been newly hired, so greeting them at the end of their bride trip took a deal of time. As soon as that ritual had been completed, Harry said, "Come with me."

Most couples in the glow of their honeymoon would have discreetly retired to one or the other's bedchamber, ostensibly for a private chat. But Harry led Olivia up past the second floor to the third.

"Ah, you're going to show me the famous ballroom!" Olivia said with a sparkling smile.

Harry just smiled and threw open the doors.

Olivia gasped. There before her was not a ballroom, but a small theatre, with a pit and one tier of boxes, a raked stage large enough to hold a small cast of singers, and dressing rooms and workshops behind. She walked slowly into the high-ceilinged room, touching the gleaming walnut benches, running her hands over the velvet railings of the boxes, and finally climbing the three steps up to the stage.

She looked out over the small theatre. Harry had sat down in the middle of the pit and smiled up at her with such tenderness she could hardly bear it.

Olivia spread her arms wide, took in a deep breath, and sang a glorious high C—something she hadn't done since that cold February day in Hyde Park.

That one note held all her hopes for the future. She wouldn't have to be a society hostess after all. She would stage operas right here in her own theatre, and perhaps when the *ton* became accustomed to seeing her standing on this more genteel stage, she would be able to step onto the boards at the King's Theatre again, even if only for a benefit concert.

Unlike the high C Harry had heard in Hyde Park, which had been born of frustration, the one she sang that day came directly from her overflowing heart.

Who but Harry would have known to create this space for her? Life was wonderful indeed.

"So, Harry, what shall we have first? I've a fancy to sing Eurydice. Or perhaps something by Paisiello. No, I think Mozart to start with, don't you? *La clemenza di Tito*, or perhaps…"

"Whatever you want!" Harry said, laughing. "As long as you don't wear a mask."

# MOZART PLAYLIST

If you would like to hear wonderful performances of the music mentioned in this book, check out my YouTube playlist here:

https://www.youtube.com/watch?v=BTWBieDvZb8&list=PLij84-Uja52B6fPwvKIglOarU0hu50ivw

## ALSO BY SUSANNE DUNLAP

Stay informed about forthcoming books and get free content, including a free novella at Susanne-dunlap.com

Or scan this QR code:

# AUTHOR'S NOTE

It probably behooves me to confess to my readers right now that I have a PhD in music history from Yale and that my concentration was in 18th-century opera. Knowing that, you can easily imagine that I absolutely loved doing the research for and writing this story.

Italian opera was very popular in London at the time, with rabid partisans ranging themselves on the sides of different singers—among them Angelica Catalani, who was a frequent performer at the King's Theatre. In fact, she performed in *The Marriage of Figaro* in March of 1813—the very period of this novel. Although I knew that the opera was being offered during that spring season and that Catalani was one of the divas, I did not know until after I was well into writing this book that the opera and Catalani's presence coincided with the exact dates in which I'd chosen to set my story—one of those magical serendipities that sometimes occurs. The difference was that Catalani sang the role of Susanna, the real starring role of the opera, not the Countess.

As far as I know, there was no masked soprano who took her place in any performances. Mr. Taylor was indeed the beleaguered theatre manager though, and he had serious money troubles. I shifted the exact timing of those troubles—as well as the dates of the theatre renovations—to suit my story.

Anyone who knows Mozart's delightful comic opera might wonder why I didn't have Olivia step in to take the bigger role, the one Catalani actually performed. It was a stretch to begin with that an 18-year-old novice could perform at all in a complete opera after only minimal rehearsals, and Susanna is on stage and singing for almost all of the four acts. It seemed marginally more believable to me that she could manage the role of Countess Almaviva.

And besides, she would get to sing *"Dove sono I bei momenti,"* 'Where have all the beautiful moments gone," one of Mozart's most gorgeous and poignant arias.

The theatre itself was different in its interior than theatres today. There was no curtain, some spectators sat in boxes on the stage itself—although by 1813 there were no longer other seats on the stage—and the entire space of the theatre was illuminated throughout. No dimming of house lights, largely because the audience itself was part of the spectacle opera goers expected to see. And yes, people really did talk during the recitatives.

In addition, complete operas were the exception rather than the rule. Evenings often included ballets and farces as well as operatic performances. But *The Marriage of Figaro* was performed in its entirety and without additional pieces.

I could not discover with certainty whether the stage of the King's Theatre was raked in 1813. However, that was the norm at the time because the seats in the pit—what is now called the parterre or the stalls—were all on one level. Tilting the stage made it easier for spectators to see all the action. And that, of course, is where the convention of referring to "upstage" and "downstage" originally came from.

The story itself is entirely a work of fiction. I will also confess that almost from the beginning I had decided to have my climactic scene echo the final ensemble in *The Marriage of Figaro*, with all eleven cast members singing at the same time, tying up the loose ends and moralizing on the tale.

I sincerely hope you enjoyed getting to know Olivia, Adelheid, Hartland, and Lewiston, and will follow along when some of them appear in the next book in this series of Double-Dilemma Romances! Sign up with the QR code below to join my newsletter!

# ACKNOWLEDGMENTS

Once again, I must thank my patient and capable book coach, Julie Artz, for pushing me to make this novel the best it could be.

I would also like to thank my beta readers, fabulous author Melissa Addey (I highly recommend you check out her books), Amy Goldmacher, and Cate Townsend. Early reader feedback is vital, and I so appreciate you plowing through typos and other manuscript irregularities!

Thank you again to ace proofreader, Susan Babcock, whose eagle eye has saved me from a multitude, of, unnecessary, commas.

And a special thank you to my friends and neighbors Caroline, Jen, and Kerry who have cheered me along so generously. Love you guys!